THEREIN LIES THE PEARL

CATHERINE

HUGHES

HISTORIUM PRESS

THEREIN LIES
THE PEARL

HARDCOVER ISBN: 978-1-964700-67-0
PAPERBACK ISBN: 978-1-964700-68-7
EBOOK ISBN: 978-1-964700-69-4

HISTORIUM PRESS
Printed in the U.S.A.

CONTENTS

STORM AND STONE
THE NORTH SEA - 1068

Nothing. It was all for nothing.

The boat tilted sideways. Celia bit her bottom lip as she fought against the pull, her hands clinging to the mast, fingernails leaving wedges in the wood. Unable to see clearly, she could neither discern nor anticipate, only react. At the mercy of the elements she was.

For hours, rain had poured down on the defenseless vessel, and now an even greater threat arose when the storm intensified. Oarsmen fought against futility, heeding the master's command.

"Bring her back out to sea. We will not make it to shore!"

Celia barely listened. Lost in her own thoughts, she refused to let go of the mast. Her breath quickened as the boat rose up on the crest of the next wave. Fast and shallow were the gulps she took as the vessel climbed higher and higher. On this night as black as doom, she could sense the moment they would begin to plummet. When the upper half of her body tilted slightly forward, the precise time had come. Recognition coincided with immediacy as the ship dropped rapidly into the trough. Unfastened items rushed past her, crashing up against the railing. A howl cut through the wind and rain. *An ill-fated passenger*, she supposed. Soon she too would be another. For the time being, however, she held fast.

Earlier that day there had been scant warning that severe weather was coming, and judging from the frenzy of the men, they had underestimated its wrath. No longer mere nuisance, the storm struck them full force. The creaking and groaning of the boards signaled their buckling. The boat had taken on too much water despite the efforts of the passengers who—only a short time ago—had been schooled in the art of bailing. Celia heard the low rumble first, then the thunderous trumpeting of seawater as the wooden hull caved in to the mounting pressure.

She was frozen in place, her rage keeping pace with the ever-increasing water level on board the boat. *I never asked for this.* Her words alluded to something beyond the current tempest. *I have done what I have done. I accepted it then and I accept it now. Oh, what does it matter? I could not protect her. The end is still the same. I accomplished nothing and lost everything.* Driven by the wind, her hair lashed across her face like the whip of an overzealous executioner. In defiance, she shook aside the strands and stared directly into the gale, ready to face her final moments.

Just then, someone grabbed her wrist, attempting to pry it from the post. She imagined it to be one of the worthless mariners who had put her into this predicament in the first place. "Get your hands off me, you louse. Leave me to my own ways!" Her eyes flashed as she narrowed her lips to spit upon the man trying to save her life, a life she had already bequeathed to the waters below.

But instead of the weather-beaten face of a sailor, Celia saw the flawless complexion of a young girl, her countenance the single glimmer of light amidst the darkness. The girl's eyes, green and luminous, reflected a beam of yellow at the center so radiant and so strong that it silenced the rain and wind and tumult. A thin line split the space between her eyebrows, a perceptible trench that marked her refusal to be ignored.

The girl tilted her head for a brief moment, and then her face softened as she heard the sound of the sea crashing upon the shore. Comforted by the idea that they were close to land, the spectral maiden tightened her grip on Celia's wrist. With urgency, she whispered the single word, "Come."

As much as Celia yearned to surrender her miserable existence to the depths of the sea, she—for some unknown reason—obeyed.

PART ONE

THE RIVER RUNS CLEAR

Winter 1056 – Spring 1057

CELIA

WITH DEATH COMES LIFE

CAEN, NORMANDY – WINTER 1056

Beside a flowing river, two children lay on their stomachs propped up on elbows. Both were deeply engrossed in the pebble fortress they were constructing. Unlike recent days which were marked by heavy rainfall and high winds, that afternoon embraced the two in a circle of warmth. A fresh sun asserted its dominance, breaking through the mass of wintry clouds until only small wisps remained. The girl, moving her head from one side to the other, looked critically at the new structure they had been building.

Clicking her tongue, she announced, "This won't do." She searched her mind for a solution. Unable to find one, she turned abruptly and cast her frustration upon the boy beside her.

"Go, get more rocks," she demanded, her blue eyes menacingly cold. "This won't do." At his hesitation, she shouted again, "Go!" and pointed emphatically at the meadow behind them.

Jolted from his reverie, the boy looked at his sister in disbelief. Normally, his upturned nose and dimpled chin gave him a look of perpetual contentment, but now it showed only bewilderment. "But why, Celia?" he pleaded.

"Why? Because I said so," she countered. "Because it is ugly and unfinished and unsightly. And, it is *my* fortress, and you are *my* servant, remember? And if you do not follow my orders, I will throw

"

you out of my kingdom forever, so go and get more stones and bring them back here, or I am exiling you for the rest of the day." She stared unflinchingly at her brother until he stood up and plodded away, down the path toward the river bank.

The cows had been milked, the animals turned out, and breakfast eaten by the time the two had wandered from their cottage to this outdoor playground, anything to get away from the harrowing sounds coming from their mother's bed. Despite the distance from the farm to this site, another sharp scream sliced through the air, singeing Celia's ears like tongues of fire. The fingers on her extended hand trembled at the sound, and she dropped the pebble she had been affixing to the tower. It was not fear that made her quiver. It was disgust. *I will not let anyone do that to me*, she vowed silently. *This is what all those stolen kisses amount to. Suffering and pain.* Firmly placing the stone atop the tower and hovering her hand over the spot a few moments longer as if to charm its balance, she resumed thinking and vowed to herself that she would never marry.

Farther downstream, Phillipe shook out his red, chapped hands and wiped them on his cloak, incredibly pleased with his efforts. In front of him was a pile of rocks he had taken from the river, all different shapes and sizes. Placing a finger on the dimple in his chin, he considered how he would carry this heap back to their garrison. After a brief pause, he tugged at his jacket with one hand, scooped up the stones with the other and loaded them into the pouch he had created.

When his mother's screams reached his ears, he began to work more feverishly, eager to get back to Celia who, despite her constant impatience with him, was still a comforting presence. In his haste, he dropped a few stones out the sides of his sack as he trotted quickly toward her. By the time he had reached their play area, nearly half of his hoard had fallen by the wayside. The remaining treasure he dumped upon the ground in front of their castle with a triumphant flourish, but instead of receiving recognition for a job well done, Philippe watched Celia get up and march back toward home without taking the slightest glance at the fruits of his labor.

Craving the closeness and security his sister offered, he attached himself to her side nonetheless as she stomped her way back toward the cottage. With cold detachment, she said, "I must go check on Mama." Philippe struggled to keep pace with her steps but, he reasoned, moving quickly was a much better option than being left behind to hear that mournful wailing all alone.

*   *   *   *   *

At Celia's touch, the wooden door creaked with age as she and her brother moved from the bright landscape into the shadowy interior of their home, a simple one-room structure made of straw, sticks, and mud. Her eyes were blinded by the stark contrast, the only illumination coming from the smoldering embers in the hearth. Her lungs soon became clogged with the thickness of the air that reeked of mucus and sweat. The metallic taste of blood rested heavily on her tongue. Now that distance was erased, her mother's cries for help were more immediate and pronounced. Her moaning poured forth in an unending stream that flowed unchecked from the straw pallet upon which she lay. The woman, her legs bent at the knee in two matching triangles, grimaced in anguish. Celia stood before the bed motionless, absorbing the wretchedness of the scene before her. An immovable barrier had formed in her throat, as if she had ingested the pebbles from the riverbank and could not dislodge them. After a third attempt at swallowing, she broke through the blockade and managed to squeeze out a whisper.

"Mama?"

Dropping to her knees before the bed, she clasped her hands together. "What can I do? How can I help?" Wishing to appear stronger than she truly was, Celia fought hard to keep her voice from quaking. To her right was their neighbor, Ada Renouf, seated upon a stool and patting the forehead and cheeks of her patient with a soiled rag. Celia sucked in her bottom lip, clamped down on it with her teeth, and waited.

The young girl was no stranger to the events unfolding before her. She had witnessed her mother in this same situation at least four times already in her brief life. Too young the first time to understand that this was the lot of women, Celia thought her mother had been trampled by one of her father's wild horses when she had come upon the twisted body on the ground. She and Mama had been in the apple orchard together, harvesting the ripened fruit, when Celia was sent back home to secure another basket. For many months, she blamed her seven-year-old self for being distracted by an orange-yellow butterfly which then delayed the retrieval of the basket and her return.

By the time she had made her way back to the orchard, she found her mother on the path, cinched into a tight ball and howling in pain. Red ooze drifted slowly down from beneath her skirts to mingle with the apples strewn about the ground. Celia assumed that her mother must have been run down by Papa's latest "project," an untamed black stallion that had the spirit of the devil in him. But no animal was nearby, nor had there been. And in the absence of such evidence, Celia began to question her own concocted theory. After summoning Ada Renouf at her mother's request, Celia then kept herself away— both physically and mentally—so that she could continue to bury the truth about her mother's affliction.

Her imagination helped her cling tenuously to this theory until her mother's belly swelled once again, and the arrival of little Philippe played out nearly the same. The delicate thread that had linked her mother's suffering to some outside force or random accident was thus severed, and Celia could no longer pretend, especially when two subsequent pregnancies left her to watch her Mama teeter between this world and the next. And with each episode, Celia felt her own heart being trampled all over again. The agony, the blood, the misery. To be forced to the brink of death in order to bring forth life? God surely had a twisted way of administering justice. *Adam's punishment paled in comparison to Eve's,* Celia reasoned, reinforcing more intensely how this would never be her fate.

The young girl recalled all of this as she squeezed together her interlocked fingers and stared at her mother's contorted body on the bed.

"Your Mama cannot speak right now, so you must do as I say," Ada said firmly. "Go, bring me more rags and some wine, and Philippe, run to your Papa and tell him he must come home. Tell him it is urgent and that I have sent you." While she continued to wipe away the beads of sweat from their mother's face and neck, Ada nodded to both Celia and her brother to make haste.

But Celia needed little convincing. She had no intention of remaining in this room of torment. She grabbed the few spare cloths from underneath her own bed, seized the tankard by the door, filled a cup with wine, and delivered both the rags and the drink to the midwife. Snatching Philippe's hand forcefully, she declared, "I will accompany Philippe just to make sure he finds Papa, and we will bring him back quickly."

Practically lifting the boy across the threshold, Celia escaped before there could be any further exchange.

*   *   *   *   *

Celia and Philippe sprinted over the rolling hills and soggy grasslands as they made their way toward the castle in Caen which, though still under construction, was the place of their father's employment. Despite the sun that shone from above, the saturated ground from the recent rains and the overflow of the small rivers branching off from the Orne itself slowed their progress. It was not long before Philippe, shaking his arm free of Celia's grasp, stopped completely.

He ignored the sensation of his feet sinking slowly into the mud. "Stop dragging me, Celia. I know the way, and I would run much faster if you were not pulling my arm so hard!" He rubbed his forearm to wipe away the indentations left behind from her grip. "Besides, this was my job anyway, not yours. You should have stayed to help Ada Renouf with Mama, but you would not . . . or could not . . . so now you are taking over what is mine, like you always do!"

"Oh, stop your whining, you cackling hen," she looked at him in exasperation. "It is easier for me not to have to drag you along like some mule pulling a plow. But just know that if you cannot keep up with me, then I was right to 'take over' what was yours because your delay could cost Mama her life." Squinting her eyes and scrunching together her lips, she fixed him with a sharp nod and sped off. *There. Let him feel the pangs of guilt,* she thought. Philippe's little legs churned and spun, but he could not keep pace with Celia, and as her image moved farther and farther from reach, he felt his courage slipping from him in the same manner that his feet slithered and faltered beneath him.

Celia arrived at the stables first and went about the business of searching for her father. He had only been working there for a few months; it had all come about so fast. The master groom, Jacques, had sought her father's counsel with regard to an ailing mare, and Papa had come and restored the animal to good health. When Duke William discovered that his favorite mount had eluded death, he wanted to meet the man responsible for such a miracle. And so, Celia's father found himself hired as one of Duke's stablehands, working under the supervision of the kind but aged Jacques

Devereaux, who now limped his way out from the stalls and directly into Celia's path.

Catching herself just in time to avoid a collision, Celia thrust her hands before her, softly grazing the old man's back as she came to an abrupt halt.

"Whoa, what have we here?" asked Jacques, a broad smile breaking across his deeply-lined face, his blue eyes twinkling with amusement.

"Oh, sir, I am so very sorry that I nearly ran you down," she explained, "but I must speak with my father immediately. Would you know where I might find him?"

Shaking his head and still grinning, Jacques was amused by Celia's seriousness. "Well, it certainly must be quite important for that kind of arrival, I suppose. He is out exercising one of our finest steeds, testing its stamina and strength," he explained. "He has been gone all morning, so he should be on his way back soon. Is there anything I might help you with in the meantime, my girl?" Jacques hung the tack up on the wall beside the stable door and lumbered over to the nearby stool, sat down, and motioned to Celia to join him.

She inhaled the earthy smell of the barn and the distinct aroma of the horses, a scent she had always associated with her father, for to her, they were one and the same. Being there was like being in his presence, and she let out a deep sigh before answering. "I am afraid not, sir, this is something only my father can address."

She rested her eyes on the man's twisted foot, recently broken after a nasty spill. It had not mended properly as his ankle stuck out at a weird angle, and his foot pointed inward toward the other leg rather than straight in front. Celia wondered if he could see the brokenness of her own heart which, though invisible, was so much more debilitating.

"I see," he said softly, placing one calloused hand upon the other in his lap. "Might it have something to do with the new babe that is coming?"

Before she could answer, a voice boomed from behind them.

"Is he suitable? What is the news?"

Celia heeded the sound and turned to see a robust man standing before her. His hair was black and well-shorn, there was no mistaking the Viking blood in him. Invincible in size and vigorous in health, he filled the room with his presence. Her mouth went dry as she curtsied before him, her mind swirling with stories she had heard last spring when she had eavesdropped on her parents' conversation. About her father's hesitation to work for a man who had cut off the hands and feet of the people of Alençon over an insult. And her mother's reassurance that Artur would never be out of favor, so long as he tended well to the man's horses. If indeed, the Duke had ridden from Valognes to Falaise in a single day, then there would be plenty to keep Artur busy and far from trouble, her mother had said.

Celia considered all of this as she remained deep in her curtsy. This then was William the Bastard—she canceled that expression as soon as it arose for fear that this imposing figure was capable of reading her thoughts.

Scrambling up from his seated position, Jacques bowed before his master in deference. "My Lord, Artur has not yet returned, but that is a very good sign, yes? An indication that the stallion is indeed durable and strong." Clearing his throat, he continued. "And may I introduce Artur's daughter, Celia, who has come here to find him regarding a matter of urgent business."

"Stand up, girl," commanded the Duke. "How many years have you?"

She dropped her eyes to the ground afraid to show disrespect. But why was this man asking her such silly questions when she needed to find her father before time ran out? And time was assuredly running out. She answered simply. "Sixteen, my Lord."

Again silence ensued as William examined the girl with greater attention. Her long, black hair, fastened with a single piece of ribbon, fell like strands of silk down to her waist. The flush upon her cheek was a soft shade of rose, a mild hint of the passion hidden beneath her full red lips. Most enchanting were her eyes, rich blue globes curtained by thick lashes. William found himself bending slightly and tilting his head to peer at her more closely. "Well, perhaps I should speak with the Duchess to see if there is some help needed here at the castle. Perhaps we are in need of another scullery maid. Then you would be able to locate your father more readily I daresay."

The Duke smiled, waiting for Celia to acknowledge his generosity, when a mud-spattered boy interrupted his musings. Darting right past the Duke, the child called out. "Celia! You are... still here. You have not left yet ... with father ..." He wiped his nose and strove to catch his breath. "See ... I was not that much ... slower than you ... was I?" But when his sister made no attempt to answer him, and he saw how reserved she was—instead of her usually combative self—he questioned the cause of her sudden meekness.

Philippe turned slowly to take in the identity of the man he had jostled and knew immediately that he had committed a grievous error. Taking a cue from his sister's demeanor, he went down upon one knee and bowed his head in apology. "I am very sorry, sir, for rushing past you like that. But you see, I have run a long way to catch up with my sister, and when I saw her standing here, I saw only her and nothing else. Forgive me, sir, for being so clumsy, but I have an important errand to fulfill. Do you know where we can find our father, Artur Campion?"

Philippe cringed when he saw the large feet of the man stepping closer to him and winced in expectation of a blow. But rather than delivering a punch or a slap, the man tousled his hair and encircled him with a ring of laughter. "That is quite all right, young man. I am not one who flinches from confrontation of any sort whether it be a minor skirmish or full-scale war. But if you can run with such alacrity, I wonder if you could ride with such speed as well? I am in need of swift couriers who can deliver my messages with efficiency. Perhaps someday, you can be a member of my cavalry."

He grinned when the boy's eyes lighted with excitement, but then, as quickly as the sun disappears behind a sudden summer storm cloud, the Duke turned to the head groom and thundered, "Jacques, come. Let us inspect the mounts I am here to see."

As the two men departed into the recesses of the stable, Philippe, still kneeling, stole a glimpse at them from over his shoulder. Just as his lips started to form the question "Was that—?" Celia had already bounded right past him, leaving him to struggle to his feet and call out to her, "Wait for me!"

*   *   *   *   *

A figure on horseback emerged just beyond the bare trees that lined the outskirts of the estate. The horse was in full gallop, all four legs suspended in mid-air, until they touched ground and bounded back up again. Rider and horse melded into one, as if there were no distinction between man and beast. Philippe recognized his father immediately. Before his sister could assert herself, he ran to claim him first, waving his arms and shouting, "Papa! Papa!"

It took great effort on the rider's part to pull hard enough on the reins to slow the majestic creature, and the animal twisted his head to the side in refusal. Eventually, the horse acquiesced, going from gallop to trot to walk until it finally came to a complete stop as the yelling child drew near.

"Papa! Papa! I am going to be part of Duke William's cavalry! I am going to be one of his messengers. He just told me so. Maybe he will take me into battle with him, Papa!" Philippe's words tumbled together in a mixture of excitement and pride. "I am going to be speedy and ride horses just like this one someday. Maybe tomorrow I can practice on him? Yes?" The boy moved to the side of the animal, placing his hand on its neck which was lathered in sweat. "Someday I will have him run even faster than he has run today, Papa. You will see!" He continued to pat the horse's body, sweeping toward the ground the layer of moisture that covered its hide.

"My son!" Artur exclaimed as he swung one leg up and over to dismount. "You have come to visit me this day, have you? And how did you learn such amazing things about your future, eh?"

Artur kept the reins in one hand and held his son's hand in the other as they made their way down the hill toward the stables. Philippe already measured up to the belt on his father's tunic, for Artur, though commanding in his trade and his breadth of knowledge, was small in stature. His hands, however, were completely out of proportion with his height. Thick and knotty and much too large, they dangled heavily at the end of his slender arms. But those hands were his finest tools, for they had the strength to pull a breech foal from its birthing cavity as well as the tenderness to calm a distempered mare with salve upon an ulcerated sore.

As Artur see-sawed his arm with his son's, he wondered why the boy had even mentioned the Duke. "And where did you get such grand dreams of the future? Did you come here to find your Papa or did you come here today to petition Duke William for hire? Hmmm?"

Philippe's playful spirit evaporated as he let out a squeal in recognition of his forgetfulness, another glaring example of his failure to perform his duties. "Oh, Father. I forgot to—" but his words were cut off when Artur noticed a frantic Celia racing toward them.

"Both of my children come to visit me today? What a treasure!" Artur's voice lifted with feigned joy in front of Philippe, but his countenance revealed what he knew to be true—something was terribly wrong. There must be trouble at home involving Joseline and the babe.

Celia called out across the distance before reaching them. "Papa! You must ride home. Ada Renouf says it is urgent. She told us to come get you. Mama is not well." Celia broke down into hiccupping sobs after pronouncing those last four words.

Her mission now accomplished, she felt as if she could hand all of her sadness over to her father, and he, as he had done when she was a child, would make everything better. She felt confident this would be the case once again when he cushioned her face with the blanket of his hands, kissed her lightly on the top of her head, and mounted the horse to ride away. Like the stories he had told her over a flickering flame before sleep, there was always a valiant warrior ready to sally forth and set the world right again. Celia prayed silently that he would continue to be their hero.

*   *   *   *   *

The winter sun dipped early below the horizon, so it was already twilight when the children arrived back home. On their journey, the purplish-pink glow of the heavens should have been a comforting sight, but Celia and Philippe never bothered to look up. So cold and isolated were they in their own thoughts that all they could do was trudge on. Philippe was still filled with self-loathing for proving his sister right in her estimation of him, and Celia was tortured by wanting to believe in her father yet recognizing that no man—not even he—could turn back Death. The world was a harsh place. Life was bleak. Whether one lived fifty years or ten, butterfly-chasing moments float away when reality intrudes. Under the weight of such sorrow, they dragged themselves toward the cottage, mired by thoughts of mortality.

Artur, who had been home already for quite some time, lifted his head when he heard the door open, but in the darkness, he could not see the faces of his children as they walked in. He figured it would be the same for them as well, so he waited until they approached the bed before he revealed what had happened

Celia noticed that her mother's legs were now straightened flat onto the pallet and that there was a stillness in the room not present before. Ada Renouf was gone. Only her father kept vigil, and he sat there in quiet knowing. Grief flooded her insides, mounting from her stomach up to her throat. She yearned to hear Ada Renouf snapping orders at her, but the silence persisted. She was forced to accept no further errands needed to be done.

She looked pleadingly into her father's face, begging without words for a different outcome. He closed his eyes, clenched his lips, and shook his head. While she stood there stunned, Philippe covered his face with both hands and crumpled to the ground, disjointed sobs shaking his little shoulders up and down. Feeling unsteady when she started to take her first step forward, Celia shortened her stride and made her way very slowly to the other side of the bed across from where her father was sitting. She dropped to her knees on the earthen floor, and the straw prickled the skin on her legs. Ignoring the irritation, she stared at the woman who lay motionless on the bed.

Celia gazed in disbelief at the body, pondering the slim line that separated life and death. Just a short time ago, her mother pulsed with life, her hands washed the clothes by the river, her fingers kneaded the bread they had eaten, her arm interlocked with Celia's own as their voices sang together while waiting for supper to cook. Where did she go? The hands, the fingers, the arms—all were still there, but now they were lifeless and grey. Visible and present, yet powerless and unmoving. Where was Mama now? This was not her mother. This thing before her was but a shell, as empty as the ones she often found along the riverbank and tossed away for lack of treasure inside. Celia wanted that treasure back, the tinkling laughter that rang throughout the house, the comforting word that calmed a stormy night, the wise counsel that inspired and bred confidence. Celia would now have to endure the silence all alone.

The stillness in the room intensified the sound of weeping until a muffled gurgle punctuated the air. Celia looked over to her father whose head was bent in grief. Moving toward the direction of the sound, she stepped gingerly toward the head of the bed where a bundled cloth lay resting on the side of her mother's face, opposite from where Celia stood. Wanting to hope but daring not to, she leaned closer to the clump that lay covered and nestled in the crook of her mother's arms. As she extended a trembling hand ever so slowly toward the bundle, her fingers tingled with anticipation as they made contact with the woolen cloth.

Carefully pulling down the coverlet, she saw the delicate features of an image captured on an artist's canvas come to life. A tiny cough, then another, animated the fragile creature until its whole body rippled with life. Instinctively, Celia scooped up the parcel and placed it against her heart, hoping to infuse the babe with strength from her own body.

"Papa, Papa? It is a miracle! She has come back to us—she is alive, Papa, she is alive!"

Celia stopped blinking back the burning tears she had been holding inside and let them spill over in this triumph of joy over sorrow. Philippe rushed to Celia's side to peer into the blanket at the resurrected child, but her father did not move. Lost in his grief, he kept his head down resting upon his folded arms. His back rose and fell with sounds of mourning. Realizing that she could do nothing for him, she decided that she must do something for the babe who had returned to them from beyond.

Turning her attention toward this wonderful gift in her arms, Celia marveled at the reddened face of the small child who had entered the world amidst such sorrow. "I will call you . . . Vivienne."

THE STRUGGLE FOR SURVIVAL

CAEN, NORMANDY - EARLY SPRING 1057

Here, try this spot," he said, extending the small gardening tool he had been using to dig into the earth. His hand was weathered and freckled from the sun, his fingers thick and callused from manual labor. Yet when he grinned at Celia, his smile shaved years off his battered body. *She is not one to shy away from unpleasantness,* he thought, *that is why I feel comfortable around her.* Simon knew he was hard to look upon—ugly, perhaps, if one were to state the truth—but around Celia, he felt no need to hide his crooked teeth behind closed lips or shield his scarred cheek and jaw from her view. They were simply two friends fully immersed in the task at hand, relaxed with one another and excited with anticipation.

Celia adjusted the sling which housed the napping Vivienne a little further up her left shoulder, freeing her right hand to accept the tool and plunge it into the soil. Just beneath the surface coiled a host of segmented, slimy worms in a frenzy to burrow back into the darkness. "Oh, my! You were right, Simon!" Celia celebrated as she dipped her fingers into the earthen tunnel. With a few quick movements, she plucked out five and dropped them into the jar which contained others they had found earlier.

"That should be good then for now." Simon rose to his feet, reaching down for the willow basket that had been next to him. "You take the jar, and let us head down to the river."

Nestling the baby's head with her left hand, Celia got up and reached down with the other to grab the jar and followed his lead. She examined the width of his back and shoulders, the muscle pulsing beneath the fabric of his shirt. His physical presence should have dominated the landscape, but instead he was absorbed into it. He moved with a grace that made him seem as if he belonged. Her heart softened. "You know," she paused momentarily, "I am very grateful to you for your help, Simon. You do know that, yes?"

He nodded without speaking. Certainly, he was aware of her appreciation, but was it wrong of him to want more? More than just appreciation? He knew he would never reveal such longing to her. He could not risk scaring her away. Besides, she could never feel the same towards him. She was the brightest jewel he had ever beheld. So precious. So perfect. Her smile disarmed him. Her voice stirred his soul. He yearned to place his hands at the base of her head and run his fingers through the silky strands of her thick black hair. Most of all, he hungered to taste her lips, lips that tantalized him with the tingling freshness of ripe raspberries in early summer. But the passion surging through his body needed to be quelled. He set his mind on their walk to the river to stem the rising tide of his desire.

"Yes, of course," he responded to her, "but you must realize I do this as much for myself as for you, Celia. I cannot have you go hungry whilst I am away with William's army. They say King Henry and Martel are seeking vengeance over the Duke's successes in '54. It is only a matter of time before their troops invade this region. And how could I concentrate on the battle if all I am thinking about is the table you are setting for Philippe, Vivienne, and your father?" He lifted a drooping branch to allow for her to pass through on the trail he was carving between the trees.

"Well, you can put your mind to rest regarding Philippe at least, for I have only two other mouths to feed and soon perhaps only one."

They both stepped into the clearing where the gurgling rush of water rose to their ears. "Philippe has been boarding with Jacques at the stables now, ever since father has been unable to work."

"What is that you say?" Simon rubbed the stubble on his chin, his right index finger settling into the scarred crevice on his jaw. "I thought Philippe had been walking your father to and from work each day. How long has Artur been abed?" Realizing the extent of Celia's plight, Simon began to comprehend the gravity of his imminent departure.

She tried to make light of her own isolation. "About a fortnight now. Remember the evening you dropped off that bounty of scallops for us, but could not stay for supper because you had business to tend to? Well, that was the last night father ate any solid food, and it was the last time he rose from his mattress." She breathed deeply to mask the cracking of her voice. "The following morn I could not rouse him, so I sent Philippe in father's stead to do some of the chores that at least a young boy could complete, and then the next day, Jacques rode out to our house to check on things. At that point, Father was still eating spoonfuls of broth, but that stopped about three days ago." Celia kept her eyes cast downward, hiding their moistness from him. "When Jacques spoke to him, Father had no recollection of who the man was. Did not even sense that Jacques was in the room. Wide-eyed and silent he was, gazing up at the ceiling as if he could pierce it through and get a glimpse of heaven if he looked hard enough."

She stopped walking to look up at her companion. "Even though he lay on the pallet in the room, he left us some time ago. The day Mama crossed over." Searching for reassurance, she added softly, "Is it wrong of me to want him gone?" She asked the question in a detached way, staring deeply at him with no trace of melancholy or tears. "Because I do want him to go." Her blue eyes bore into him, silently begging him not to think her evil for having such thoughts.

He wanted to answer her with his touch. It took all of his will to restrain himself from wrapping his arms around her slender body and pulling her up against his chest. Once there, he would soothe her fears with his unshakeable belief in her goodness. But he could do no such thing. She would not welcome such intimacy—not from a coarse man like himself, so far beneath her in beauty and charm. He should just be grateful she tolerated him as a friend.

Simon inhaled, carefully considering his words. He knew too well the kind of wish she was making. A request with which he was all too familiar. He understood how you could want someone to be "gone," as she had said, because it was too painful to be around them, too painful knowing how you, yourself, had no place in their world. He could not tell her everything about his past, but he could share some of it so that she would know she was not alone.

Staring out at the river in the distance, he spoke softly. "It is not wrong to feel that way, Celia. Our circumstances are very different, but I once felt that way too." He waited a moment, wondering if he should stop there or if he should open up a chamber that had been slammed shut five years ago. He chose to lift the latch and venture in. "You know I had a wife once, yes?" He continued to look at a point far in the distance.

Celia nodded, her eyes focused on the captive creatures in the jar. He did not see her respond, but when he heard no objections, he went on. "Not all unions are like that of your parents, Celia. They had a very special bond. Each felt incomplete without the other. Your father wants to leave this realm so that he can be with Joseline in the next. My wife wanted to leave this world because she could not abide being with me in *this* one. Our marriage was a lie. And I knew it. So you see, I was very angry inside when I said that I wanted her 'gone,' which makes our two situations very, very different. When you say that about your father, you say it out of love for him. When I said it, I had only hatred."

Celia bit her bottom lip, nervous and uncomfortable from this unsolicited confession. She had no desire to delve any deeper into Simon's past. Everyone in the village had heard of Giselle's mysterious disappearance and the subsequent discovery of her pregnant corpse which washed ashore one stormy night. Celia knew of the rumors that circulated about Simon and the names people called him, but she did not care about any of that. Her immediate concern was for survival, and this man—villain or not—was a friend to her, a savior who had kept her going when all seemed impossible. And for the sake of that purring child who lay in the sling across her heart, Celia was willing to trust in him. For a time, the silence hung suspended between them, and when Simon broke the quiet by resuming the trail, Celia asked no further questions.

*   *   *   *   *

The heaviness of the moment had passed even though neither of them had spoken. Oppressive thoughts of impending death and the suspicion surrounding a past one were simply swept away like the current that sent the water cascading over the rocks. It was with a lighter step that Celia kept pace with Simon as they neared the edge of the stream, the place which would be the site of her fishing lesson.

The tide was low and the sand moist, the dampness seeping through the thin soles of Celia's shoes. Whether it was the sound of the rushing water or the tangy smell of salt that lifted upon the wind, Vivienne cast aside her slumber and began shifting with awareness in the sling. "Give me a moment, Simon." Celia stopped and put the jar down on the ground. She placed one hand under the child's body and used the other to lift off the sling from her shoulder. "I need to tend to her." As she spoke, she undid the knot and lay the fabric on the sand, some distance away from the lapping waves.

"My, my, she is a feisty spirit, that one!" His own laughter made him feel warm inside as he marveled at the child's legs and arms pulsing like a fish hauled onto land and fighting to return to its watery home.

"That she is, no doubt," Celia smiled with pride at the thriving creature beneath her touch. "Borne of tragedy she may have been, but there be no mark of sorrow on her. In a strange way, she saved more than herself the night Mama died. Did you not, my love?" Celia nuzzled her nose into her sister's belly, blowing gulps of air onto the sensitive pink flesh. Soon Vivienne's laughter matched the gurgling of the river.

Simon stood tall above them, distancing himself from such intimacy. He pressed down the ache in his heart when he thought of his own lost chance at being a father. He had wanted Giselle's child so much, with a sincerity he had not thought possible nor one that she believed. But he could not allow his spirit to sink down into those dark places. Not here, not now, not with the sunlight caressing the ground and the tinkle of laughter in the air. He banished the memory, wrapping himself instead in the folds of the girls' shared delight.

"Simon, will you sit with her while I rinse out this cloth in the water? Simon?" When he did not answer, she looked over her shoulder at him. "Are you all right?" Her blue eyes softened with compassion.

"Yes. Yes, of course. I was just thinking about maybe showing you how to use the long-line as well as the eel trap. This way you could catch even more fish than your family would need, and then you could barter the rest at market." He moved over toward the playful child and set himself upon the ground, leaning back on his elbow in the area next to her. Extending his thickened hand toward Vivienne's tiny one, he moved with a gentleness he usually reserved for the small animals he had befriended near his cottage. Since

Giselle's death, they—red squirrels, deer, rabbits—had been his primary diversion. They kept him company in the early morning hours on his walk from his home to the river, and they sat with him at dusk while he whittled away at his carving as the sun dipped behind the deepening greens of the forest. This little one too also seemed to enjoy being with him. She reached out and held fast to his index finger, grabbing it with her entire hand, trying to sample it in her mouth. "Ach, no! You will not be liking that now. Too fishy for your tastes." He laughed warmly and shook his head in wonder at the miracle of life before him.

Celia smiled to herself when she heard Simon's amusement, finding it remarkable that so small a creature could make the most serious of people carefree and winsome again. She counted herself among those somber personalities whose heaviness melted away in Vivienne's presence. Wringing out the wet cloth, she made her way back to the frolicking pair. "Adorable, is she not? I have some goat's milk in my pouch there. Could you get it for me?" From her pocket, Celia took out a fresh, dry cloth and swaddled it around Vivienne's bottom, and then lifted the child to her heart. After Simon handed her the cow horn with the leather attachment at the top for suckling, Celia placed it between the child's open lips and felt contentment wash over her when she gazed into the babe's trusting eyes.

Simon paused to witness the feeding, deeply moved by the profound serenity of it all. He, like most of his neighbors, was well aware of Celia's fiery temperament and sharp tongue, but few if any had been privileged enough to catch a glimpse of the tenderness he was now observing. He was pleased to be able to count himself among those privileged few. Careful not to let her know he was aware of her secret, Simon went quickly about the business of teaching her what he had promised to do.

Bringing the willow trap alongside them, he began the lesson. "Now, what you are going to do is place a heavy rock at each end of the trap—like so—to weigh it down so that the basket will rest on the bottom. You keep the rope attached here at the front, and you knot it around the stake in the ground. This way, you can use the rope later to pull up the trap." Celia nodded, keen to understand his directions.

"The trap works on a simple principle. After the eel swims through the mouth cone at the upstream end of the trap, it is lured in by the darkness and by the bait to travel further into this narrower cone. The narrower one has sharp edges, see? They bend to let the fish in, but they make it nearly impossible for the eel to find its way back out again." Simon reached for the jar and pulled out a few choice worms. "Now, put your bait deep into this narrow cone—even though I have caught eels sometimes with no bait at all just because they love searching dark holes so much—and then lower the basket into the water so that the opening is facing downstream." Physically performing each step in the process, Simon now removed his shoes, rolled up his pant legs, and stepped into the shallows, walking a few paces into the deeper water. He then released the trap and watched it sink beneath the surface until it hit the sandy floor. Holding the rope in one hand, he exited the water and headed back up the river bank.

"See this stake here? It is the perfect distance for anchoring, so you can either knot the rope onto it first and then walk out the trap, or do the opposite as I am doing right now." Having spent so much time with her father in the stables, Celia knew very well how to fasten all kinds of knots, so she took this opportunity to put aside Vivienne's bottle and raise the baby to her shoulder, gently patting her on the back in order to settle her stomach.

Simon clapped his hands together, signifying the lesson's end. "Now with all of those eels, a bundle of sweet herbs, and an onion or two, your stews will last you through the months I am gone."

Before she could properly thank him for his kindness and generosity, he began speaking on his next topic.

"Oh, and let me show you the long-line too while I am at it."

When he turned his back to walk toward his next demonstration, Celia wondered if it was only gratitude that she was feeling. She was never one to care for men who primped and primed themselves, those who spent more time on their appearance than she did herself, so Simon's ruggedness did not bother her one bit. In fact, she found it somewhat provocative to look upon a man whose scars, and not his wardrobe, betold more of his personal history and character than any fancy cloak or piece of jewelry ever could. The mark across Simon's cheek and jaw was a visual reminder of the blows he had suffered at the battle of Mortemer where, it was said, he rescued a pair of young sisters from King Henry's rogues. Rumor had it that he was outnumbered four-to-one, and despite being badly wounded in the process, he dispatched the first two with sword and dagger and the other two with his bare hands. Most importantly, the sisters retained their maidenhood.

Who needs a courtier's glib word or his delicate touch? Not her. Not when a person could have a champion by her side to ward off danger and reassure her that she was not alone. When daily existence is a perpetual struggle, which would any girl prefer? The empty rhymes of a talented poet or a method for putting food on the table? She knew what answer worked for her. She was undeniably drawn to his strength, his unflappable stoicism, his palpable manliness. Indeed, there was some degree of attraction that existed between them. On the few occasions when Celia and Simon drew near one another—to assist her father walking or in bringing him to table—she felt the spark of a small fire glowing deep within, a warmth that spread to the tips of her fingers when her hand grazed his. But like a pot of cold water poured to douse the hearth, the memory of her mother's final hours extinguished any desire Celia may have felt to fan that flame. Her mind shifted to the mound of dirt that marked her mother's grave, an image that proved enough for Celia to remember her vow.

With that decisive commitment renewed, she could listen again to Simon's voice telling of hooks and snoods, long-lining and low tide, all thoughts of intimacy vanquished and buried.

LOVE'S LAMENTATION
CAEN, NORMANDY - SUMMER 1057

Vivienne loved the sound of singing. Her mottled pink face, so often scrunched tightly in thought or frustration, would inexplicably relax once her ears lighted upon a melody. The lyrics were of no consequence. It was the sound itself that lifted the child from her earthly home to the one above. There she dwelt in the company of angels, lifting her head as if hearing once again the gentle whispers of God's grace. And so, despite the jostling of the sling and the pungent smell of fresh eels in the bucket, the child smiled serenely as they made their way home from the river to the garden beside their cottage.

It was late summer, and gone were those balmy evenings when the lingering sun painted the sky with pink and purple bands of color. The line between day and night was more stark now, the gentleness of transition vanished. Light departed, and the air chilled with an abruptness that hastened travelers to the warmth of their homes.

It had been weeks since Simon departed to serve in Duke William's army. Jacques too had left, taking young Philippe with him as a kind of assistant stable hand—not so much because of the boy's horsemanship but mainly because Jacques could not leave the child behind to witness his father's slow death. Aside from the resulting solitude, Celia knew that she had managed quite well, all things considered, and silently she gave herself permission to feel proud. In the garden, the strawberries and blackberries had been plucked and preserved. Cabbages were swelling atop the soil. Peas and beans continued to offer up their bounty for the table. Moving with a certainty that comes from confidence, Celia placed the pail on the ground and unfastened the carrier that held Vivienne, noticing the sweat stains that marked her clothing where her sister had lain. Offended by her own smell, she spoke aloud in her customary one-sided monologue.

"Bleck!" Celia crabbed after putting the child down and taking a sniff under her bodice. "Foul sister I am, yes? Well, we shall both have a good washing today once we get home. But first we must gather the vegetables for tonight's stew."

Her never-ending list of chores made Celia feel tired. She longed for bygone days when she could rest easy, letting adults worry about such things as what to eat and where to fish and how to stay warm. While she went about her work, she escaped into one of those treasured memories. It was late afternoon. She was sitting on the ground before the stable, a single stalk of hay in each hand. With the thin reeds, she reenacted the words of the song her Papa was singing while he was busy tending the horses. It was a sad tune, a tale of tragic love from the days of Charlemagne, but she felt none of its underlying sorrow. Aude's heartbreak was of no concern to the young Celia. It was the sound of her father's voice, not the content of the song, that captivated her. And that same magic now charmed little Vivienne, for as soon as Celia's voice danced upon the air, the babe's tiny fists unclenched, and she gazed up at her sister with enchantment.

Summoned to the front gates

She ran with full abandon

Yearning for the warm embrace

She would seek from her man then.

But soon she slowed and held fast

When she saw 'twas not he.

Was she bold enough to ask

What message could this be?

Before her stood the king

Travel-worn and heavy of heart

Off'ring his hand for her to cling

Dreaded news he must impart.

Celia sang as she gathered sprigs of rosemary and mint, her voice lilting on the breeze. Like fingertips gently stroking the skin, the music soothed Vivienne. A look of tranquility spread across the child's face, an expression of innocent rapture. Celia, unaware of the impact of her song, remained intent on her work without breaking the cadence of the music. She took out the small knife she carried with her and cut the stem of a firm cabbage.

"Your true love Roland, so proud and strong

An inspiration to every man

Battled fearlessly amidst the throng

From morn until the end.

But the enemy force was so vast

And Roland's troops counted so few

That the battle they could not outlast

And so I bring these words to you."

Vivienne swiveled her head to follow her sister's movements in the garden, her ears telling her eyes which direction to turn toward to stay connected with the melody. At this point, Celia was kneeling upon the dry soil, clods of dirt crumbling beneath her clothing as she edged her way between the measured rows of onions. Each stalk, its tip yellowed with ripening, lay flat upon the earth, seemingly caught in a lover's swoon. Celia pulled one set of dried ends and then another, careful not to bruise them with handling. She kept singing.

Charles then placed his hand on hers

Closing his eyes as if Roland did speak.

"Aude, my love, I am always yours,

But in this world, we never shall meet.

For I have been called by God above

It was He who said 'twas time.

I fought for life so we could love

But was told in heaven you'd be mine.

So what are days and months and years

When compared with eternity?

Love, brush aside those falling tears

And promise you will come to me."

Finished with her task, Celia placed the rosemary, mint, and cabbage into the bucket that held the eels. The onion stalks she tied together and threaded them through her sash, making certain that the bulbs were separated and unlikely to bump into one another. These two, which would air dry inside the cottage for a few days, would take the place of the pair she would use for the evening meal. As her harvesting came to a close, so too did the ballad.

Aude's eyes glistened with sorrow

And her hand began to quake

She knew she would never see the morrow

As her heart began to break.

She crumpled slowly to the ground

And soon she breathed her last.

There was no doubt where she was bound

Into his arms as he had asked.

The final verse faded into the approaching darkness. Celia stood still in the silence, thinking about the lovers from the song. She questioned the nature of such passion, a feeling so intense that it took Aude's breath—and indeed her life—away.

Once Celia stopped singing, Vivienne returned to earth, leaving behind the celestial experience of music. Her hands clenched into little fists once again, and her feet double-kicked at the vacant air. Celia noticed the child's agitation.

"Well, Vivienne, you can count me out. Trembling and swooning and heartbreak may seem romantic, but they are the mere stuff of fairy tale and legend. Funny how in those stories no one ever seems to worry about when to fetch more firewood or how the stew is going to be made. Come, my love, let us go make supper."

She did not bother reconfiguring the sling, but rather swept up the babe in her arms, balancing her on her hip. As Celia made her way home in the encroaching darkness, she tried to ignore the added weight of the loneliness she felt from having a sister unable to talk and a father who refused to. Only the pulsating movements of the child at her hip and the crunch of the fallen leaves beneath her footsteps answered the silence.

*   *   *   *   *

She put the barley into a pot of simmering water and left it over the hearth to soften. As Vivienne played quietly with her rag doll, Celia went about the business of chopping the vegetables on the small wooden table that was once the site of lively conversation. The phantom echo of her parents' laughter drifted further and further away until all she could hear was the faint cooing of the baby and the snap of the knife onto the wood. At such times, she felt so very alone.

Blaming the welling of her eyes on the onion she sliced, Celia willed herself to move beyond self-pity to glance at the child she had been given to raise. *There are people far worse off than you,* she reminded herself. *People who have no one to care for, no one to live for—and no one to cook for.* And with a heart made lighter by her own reprimand, she wiped aside the fallen tear and resumed her conversation with people who could not or would not respond.

"So, let me put these vegetables into the pot, and then we shall check on Papa, yes, my little angel? I will get a fresh cloth to wipe him down, and then I shall do the same for you and for me while dinner continues to cook."

As if on cue, Vivienne inserted the head of the rag doll into her mouth, slathering the fabric with a stream of drool that spilled from one corner of her tiny mouth. Celia's eyes danced with amusement when she saw her sister's reaction to the spoken word "dinner." "Well, I suppose Papa can wait then, eh? Someone needs to be fed right away I see," and without delaying any longer, Celia picked up the bottle she had filled with fresh goat milk and nestled Vivienne in the crook of her arm, returning once again to sit at the table.

The child sucked its meal with enthusiasm, her dimpled legs pumping joyfully. Celia then lifted her head to address the other occupant in the room. "We had quite the day, Papa. Vivienne saw her first deer this morning, and I was able to show her a quarry of nuts that a little gray squirrel was storing away for the winter. His cheeks were so round and chubby, were they not, Vivienne, when he dipped into his storehouse to have a nibble today? Tell Papa how you laughed at such a sight, and how you clapped your hands over the show he put on for us! Oh, and yes, we had great success with the willow trap once again, Father. We shall have fresh fish in our stew tonight thanks to Simon and the care he took to teach me well."

Celia spoke these words from her chair at the table, her father's bed within earshot just a few paces away. But she knew no sound was forthcoming. She had grown accustomed to the perpetual quiet that greeted her commentary and was unfazed when her words melted into the stillness. The child's eyes grew heavy as she blinked more and more frequently, holding them shut for longer and longer periods of time until they remained closed altogether. Celia studied the babe in her arms, grateful that her sister seemed oblivious to Celia's own heartache. Vivienne's lashes sealed the dreams that lay behind her eyes, and her rosy cheeks were flush with life despite the somber circumstances under which she lived. Celia smiled softly when she saw the nipple of the bottle dangling off to the side as if sleep seized her mid-swallow. To slumber without a care in the world, that was Celia's gift to her sister, and she was filled with pride that she had been able to keep things together for them all. How strange it was to think that, just a few months ago, she was petty enough to have thrown a tantrum and fallen to pieces if Philippe had but borrowed one of her carved horses without asking. She had certainly come a long way since then.

"It is been a hard road, no doubt," she said aloud, "but we are doing just fine, and that spoiled child I once was has grown up to become the head of this household." The words were barely out of her mouth when she gasped in horror at the thought that her father may have heard and understood what she said. Although he had not spoken for weeks, who was to say that he was unaware of what was happening around him? Celia hung her head in shame at having insulted him like that. Despite what she had said to Simon about wanting her father to "leave" this world, she still prayed daily for his recovery and wondered if it were possible that he knew what was happening around him. With a leaden sense of guilt crushing her heart, she placed the sleeping child down upon their shared pallet and turned to give her undivided attention to her father as reparation for her unkind words.

Before taking the few steps toward his bed, she poured some water from the jug onto a cloth and carried with her the undergarment she had laundered the day before. Because he had so few items of clothing, Celia was continually washing, drying, and replacing his braies for him since he was unable to get up of his own accord and use the chamberpot. "What a delightful afternoon we have had today, Papa. Vivienne is growing so fast; she is pulling herself up now and can sit tall and upright in my lap." Celia tried to ignore the stench of the soiled bed clothes by keeping the conversation going. "Perhaps tomorrow you would like her to sit with you? Would you find that pleasing?" She slowly lifted the blanket from the bottom of the pallet and began rolling it upward toward his chest so that she could clean his lower body.

"Tomorrow I shall bring over a chair and sit nearby to make sure she does not topple off to the side, that way you need not worry about having to move around so much yourself. I shall be there the whole time, so you can just relax and enjoy how alert she is and how much she loves being with her Papa!" Celia swallowed hard before reaching to lift up his thin legs. She had to elevate them in order to pull away the covering that was stained and damp with urine. In the early stages of his illness, she would have to raise one leg by itself and then the other, but now he had become so frail that the pair felt like two dried twigs that would snap if handled too roughly. She extended her arms toward his body. "You are going to love tonight's supper, you know. Can you smell it cooking? Maybe you will even have a taste this time, yes? Pa...?" Celia broke off mid-sentence at the touch of his body. She jumped back quickly. His legs were cold and rigid.

She stared down at her hands for a moment in disbelief, wondering if they had somehow deceived her, but after drawing closer to the top of the bed, confirmation came when she rested her cheek upon his. He was gone. Beneath the papery skin of his face was an iciness that seeped into her blood. "Papa?" She finished the word. She did not cry out. Her tears would come later. Overwhelming relief washed over her now, and she refused to scold herself for feeling so.

"Well."

Hesitating only long enough to ask herself what to do next, Celia quickly assessed the situation and took action. She finished cleaning him and then lifted his body onto a different blanket stretched out upon the floor. Placing her hands on the side of his chest and legs, she rolled his lifeless form, winding the shroud tightly around him, and then in deference, she gently placed a cloth upon his face. When morning came, she would go to Simon's house to borrow the cart to transport her father's body to the hill where he would once again lie next to his wife. In the meantime, there was nothing more she could do for him. She wiped her hands on the sides of her skirt, grabbed a bowl, and ladled some of the stew into it. He may now be at rest, but she had just added two more tasks onto her long list of chores for tomorrow. Celia did not mind though. As she brought the spoon to her lips, she realized that her father's wish had finally been granted and, in a peculiar way, so had her own.

*　　*　　*　　*　　*

She kept her mind on other things so that she did not become too consumed with the physical task she was performing. But no matter how many times she tried to distract herself by thinking about sewing or fishing or cooking, she could not liberate herself from her current labor. Her thoughts always returned to how awful it was to dig a grave.

A gravedigger suffered a double form of anguish. First, there was the spiritual upheaval and debilitating grief that ensued after having lost a loved one, and second, there was the physical misery of having to complete such an onerous task. In her case, she set aside her emotional connection to what she was doing and tried to simply perform the job while commanding her mind to wander into regions far from this location. After intense effort, she was now about an arm's length deep into the soil where, thankfully, the dirt had softened a bit and broke apart more easily than at first.

Just a few months ago, she had been at this same spot, only it was not her hand that grasped the handle but Simon's. At the time, her father had shown no sign of understanding what was required of him, so it was her friend Simon who had come to dig the resting place that would house her mother's body. Back then, Celia took no part in the digging. The hole stood empty and wide, fully completed by the time she, Papa, and Philippe had arrived with the cart trailing behind them. Only now with the sweat trickling down the back of her neck and along the column of her spine did she realize just how exhausting an endeavor it was. Her arms ached with strain and fatigue. Her lower back pinched and tensed each time she tossed the next batch of dirt over her shoulder. Even switching her grip and alternating sides did nothing to alleviate the pain.

An arm's length was not deep enough to keep the scavengers away. She needed to make certain that the hole went down far enough to be beyond the reach of hungry foragers. Some small measure of dignity had to be preserved, especially since there was no ceremony or funeral to commemorate her father's passing. He deserved that at least.

Pausing to wipe her brow with the back of her grimy hand, Celia's eyes rested on the cart she had pulled by herself to this newly sanctioned family cemetery. The wagon made her think of Simon and of how he was still helping her despite being miles and miles away. And after a deep intake of breath and an even longer exhalation, she pointed her shovel back toward the ground and continued to deepen the trench. She recalled the strangeness of his house. She knew it would be spartan. After all, he was a serious minded man whose time was spent dealing only in practicality and necessity. She had expected that. What was odd though was that there was no trace, no touch, no evidence that a woman had ever shared that space with him. No spindle, no comb, no brush, no clothing, no trinket, no craft, no indication at all that Giselle was once his wife. Perhaps Simon had gotten rid of all of her possessions so that no reminders of her were left behind to haunt him. Perhaps he had bartered them to find compensation for his loss. Whatever the manner with which he disposed of her belongings, it was clear he had chosen to wipe away Giselle's entire history.

As Celia pulled more and more earth from the ground, she tried to recall Simon's words when they had last spoken about her father's impending death and Giselle's prior passing. *What was it that he said? Something about her wanting to leave this world because she could not abide being in it with him there too. Well, if a woman felt that way about her husband, is it any wonder then that he would want to erase everything about her from his mind? And what better place to begin than by removing all things associated with her presence? If all the physical reminders disappear, then it is only a matter of time before the mental pictures fade as well. So did he do this out of grief because of her aversion to him, or did he do this out of rage because of her rejection of him? Was it sorrow or was it fury that drove him?*

Even though her task was far from done, Celia paused. Deep inside the rectangular pit she stood, cold and unmoving. *But why would a woman—one who was with child—set out upon a boat during a storm? Was she trying to escape to start a new life on her own, or had she been put there against her will for someone to end it...?*

Was his house empty because he was heartbroken over her death, or was it empty because he was guilty of causing it?

There are some questions that are better left unanswered, just as there are some secrets that are better left buried. The dead find release, but life remains a filthy business for the ones who are left behind. Celia readjusted her grip and plunged her spade once again into the dirt, deepening and widening the plot with each thrust.

MARGARET

THE SUMMONS

Little Edgar sat in the snow, scooping up the white powder to make lopsided mounds. Three asymmetrical hills were spaced out unevenly between his splayed legs as he continued to work on fashioning and molding the fourth. His hands were gloved and his movements lacked coordination, but he was content and in a far better place than he had been earlier when he had sniveled, cried, and screamed at being left out of the fun.

Edgar's older sister was propelling herself upon the ice with an iron-tipped pole in hand. Their tutor, Gerhard, followed close behind, shouting words of instruction and encouragement to Margaret as she struggled to maintain her balance and remain upright.

"Keep pushing backward. Do not bend your legs, hold them straight," the man directed. The snow had stopped falling, but crystals of frost rested upon his bushy gray eyebrows, thickening them with an additional layer of white. With his long, lanky frame, he seemed no wider than the tall reeds that encircled the small pond during the warmer months. Yet the elderly fellow seemed to recapture a spark of his lost youth as he performed the same movements, keeping a slower pace behind the young maiden whose blond plaits, thick as rope, rested upon her shoulders.

"I am flying!" Margaret rejoiced as she picked up more speed and glided in the direction of her uninterested brother who was busy with his fortress of sugar plum turrets. Not wanting to spark another tantrum, Margaret drifted past him in silence, only the scraping of the stick and the jagged clacking of the bone-skates upon the ice wafted upon the wintry air. Clouds of vapor rose from her mouth as she strained to create a smooth, lengthy glide. Once free of her brother's presence, Margaret exulted, "Yes! What fun, Master Gerhard!" With greater frequency, she pushed the tipped pole into the ice and thrust it backward between her legs, reveling in her ability to fly upon the glistening pond.

How long she had waited for this day! Years of listening to her teacher recount stories of those Nordic winters where he would skate for months on end, when a blanket of snow would wrap itself around the small village in Sweden he had called home. But the mild climate in Nadasd refused to cooperate with that vision as Decembers and Januarys passed by, year after year, with nothing more than a thin sheet of glass resting upon the water's surface, a layer so fragile it crinkled and broke under the passing weight of a mere snow bunting. But today was different from all those empty winters of the past. For nearly a week, the region had been under a freeze, and although the snowfall ended, the air continued to numb and chill, creating the solid surface upon which Margaret sailed. The sun sparkled and danced upon the frosted layer of the water, but her eyes were fixed solely on the spot in front of her where she would place the pole tip. This was why she did not see the broken twig resting near the bank and off to the side of her right foot.

But Gerhard saw it. "Margaret, take heed!" Just as she lifted her chin to look up toward him, she toppled toward the left, spun about, and landed with a thud. Gerhard pulled alongside, placing his hand beneath her arm to lift her again to a standing position. "Carry on." Obediently, she dusted off her skirt and took a deep swallow of mountain air. With a quick swipe of her hand beneath her nose, she accepted the pole from his extended hand and pushed off, her braids trailing behind her once again.

After the spill, Gerhard glanced quickly over his shoulder to take note of a change on the horizon. Visitors on horseback were making their way up the steep hill toward Reyka Castle. From so far a distance, he could not tell who they were, but he could see they were not from this region. Their approach bespoke a certain degree of urgency. Removing the skates from his own feet, Gerhard stepped off the pond and began walking in the direction of the men. He kept hold of his own iron-tipped stick, pausing to observe further. He counted five riders in all, the foremost mounted upon an animal whose body was draped in a blue blanket. The design featured a golden cross and five golden doves. Playtime was over. The day had finally come.

*   *   *   *   *

Margaret leaned carefully over her work, the edges of the feathered quill tickling the side of her cheek as she scratched the words onto the vellum. "*Let not ...*" She breathed in contentedly, the warmth of the fire caressing her face and infusing her body with heat. The wintry chill from the morning skating session had softened from crisp immediacy to treasured memory, a vision to be recalled at will when her spirits needed lifting. As her lips curled slightly upward in a knowing smile, she continued to form letters in a rhythmic flow; soon "*your heart*" was spelled out upon the page. She wrote with precision, adding a flourish around the "*h*" as she wondered what other incredible adventures life would have in store for her. Perhaps the men visiting with her father in the next room had some say in that. From the reaction of the servants in the castle, it was clear that their arrival was of great import. Margaret lifted her eyes to gaze up at the vaulted ceiling, bending her head sideways in thought. What impact would this visit have upon her own world, a world whose boundaries were normally confined to her father's estate?

Returning to her copywork, Margaret glanced at the next set of words from the gospel text and began forming the closing of the sentence, *"be troubled."* Her normally even-tempered tutor was troubled over these new events, but why? For this, she had no answer.

Gerhard had so often praised historical figures and brave pioneers who took risks and made daring discoveries. If new experiences resulted in future blessings and achievements, then why were his fingertips drumming nervously upon the table while his eyes were set and focused on some imaginary point far beyond the castle wall? Why did he continue to *tap, tap, tap* upon the wood and say nothing? And if change is supposed to bring with it the opportunity to grow in mind and spirit, then why did he retreat so far into his silence that Margaret's earlier questions about the travelers remained unanswered? These thoughts, hovering in the air, felt like a threatening cloud above her head. Her eyes sought his approval. Slowly, she inched the parchment closer to him, letting the apostle deliver her message: *"Let not your heart be troubled."* Halting his raised fingers mid-air, he read the inscription. The clacking on the table ceased. He stretched out his fingers and lay them lovingly upon her hand, nodding to her in tacit understanding.

They both jumped when the door opened abruptly. A servant motioned for Gerhard to come. "My lord requires you in his chamber. He asks that you hasten without delay."

With a quick squeeze of her hand, the old man pushed himself away from the table and unfolded himself to a standing position. Hearing the creak and pop of each knee he straightened, Margaret immediately rose from her chair to offer herself as a walking stick as he navigated his way toward the door.

"I will get along just fine, my girl. No need for that." Patting her head, he nodded toward the work she had been completing. "Keep copying that passage. Perhaps there shall be further messages contained within that we can discuss upon my return, yes?" Carefully extending his leg to take his first step, Gerhard wobbled just a bit while testing his old joints, but soon moved more steadily once balance and strength were confirmed. Margaret then resumed her seated position, listening to his footfall as he made his way across the room.

Glancing down at the biblical passage, she soon became distracted by the quiet. Her eyes left the page as she raised her head to look behind her. A strand of her yellow hair came loose and dangled in front of her eye; she exhaled quickly to blow it aside. The door had been left open. Gerhard and the servant had gone, but the door remained ajar. Could she pass up this invitation to find the answers to her earlier questions? But was she not told to stay? To keep working? While Edgar continued to nap on the pallet in the corner of the room, she looked over her shoulder again at the opportunity that lay before her. Torn between curiosity and obedience, she turned once more to the gospel page on the table. *"In my father's house are many mansions...I go to prepare a place for you."* Margaret was not entirely sure what the words meant, but she felt she they justified the decision she was about to make. This was her time to explore what "place" God had in mind—for her, for her family, and for her beloved teacher. Delicately laying down the pen upon the parchment, she tiptoed out of the room and toward the hall to discover exactly what adventures lay ahead for them all.

*   *   *   *   *

Her slippers muffled the sound of her steps as she crept closer to her father's chamber. Once there, she melted her body against the wall, feeling the edges of the cold stone against the back of her homespun dress. After a few breaths to calm herself, she slowly craned her neck to get a look into the room.

She saw her father seated at the head of the long table with Gerhard standing behind the chair at her father's right. Because Gerhard's back was to her, she could not guess what he was thinking. She could only see the knotting and twisting of his fingers which were tightly clasped behind his back. Drawing her head back up against the wall, she thought about what she had just observed. Clearly, he was concerned about something. She must wait patiently to hear what that *something* might be. Her hands trembled. Was it from cold or worry? An uneven rhythm deep within her chest pounded in her ears.

Extending her neck once more to peer into the room, she saw her father adorned in full regalia. His doublet of bright purple and gold captured glimmers of light that bounced and radiated off his person. Just like the times when he presided over major celebrations at the castle, Margaret marveled at the spellbinding aura that transformed her Papa into this magnificent being at the table. Pulling away again, she leaned back against the icy stone. Despite the chill, she felt snug and warm, filled with love for him. This imposing ruler who governed the region was the same man who pushed her on swings and tucked her in at night. Her cheeks bloomed pink with joy when she recalled how last spring in front of the entire assembly he dismounted and bent down upon one knee to accept the wild flowers she had gathered for him. He had just returned from battle, his tunic soiled and bloodied from combat. And yet beneath the weaponry and the gear, he remained her Papa. He belonged to her as much as he belonged to his people.

She listened.

"Well, what do you make of it?" Her father steepled his hands together, the tips of his first two fingers resting upon his chin.

"I wish I knew," Gerhard shrugged his shoulders. He walked around the long table, speaking as he paced slowly over to the other side. "Together we have been through so much, my lord. In truth, I had given up believing this day would ever come." He pulled out the chair closest to her father and sat down. Margaret could now see the doubt that blanketed Gerhard's face.

Her father smiled, recollecting the miles they had traveled and the challenges they had overcome. "You were our lifeline, you know, my brother's and mine. After father's death, it was you who shielded us from Viking blades thirsting for our Saxon blood. And though my memory of Sweden is vague at best, the safety we found being by your side was, and continues to be, a great comfort to me. And when the Danes cast their net of intrigue further north into Olaf's court, it was your strength that anchored us as we fled over the sea and down the river Neva until we settled here. Without you, friend, the cradle would have been my tomb."

"Those were dangerous times indeed. But there were good times too. Do you remember much of those days? When I filled your hours with lessons in so many things—woodworking, astronomy, Latin, swordsmanship. Days of discovery and wonder." Gerhard's eyes danced with brightness, his smile sending creased lines extending out from his eyes. "I am not sure who had more fun. You and Edmund, or myself?" He laughed softly.

"I do remember, my friend, I do." Edward smiled, "And I can tell you that my brother and I relished sword and buckler more than we ever did declensions, so perhaps we all found joy at some point but from different sources."

"You were both so young, so young and so innocent. I was blessed to have two boys whose minds were open, curious about the ways of the world." Gerhard's voice faltered. "It has been my life's honor to serve you," he paused, "I only wish your brother were still here with us to witness this unusual turn of events . . ."

"As do I."

Margaret saw her father push his chair away from the table. He stood tall and filled his chest with air. "And now? Why now?"

Gerhard looked up at him earnestly. "I do not know. First Cnut, then his son, then this man Edward, this childless king. Is it finally you they want?"

"Until today, I had resigned myself to fate. All thoughts of England faded away like the early morning mist off Lake Ulmen that vanishes with the onset of day."

Gerhard nodded in agreement."But there is change in the air. I feel it in these old bones. And change is neither good nor bad, in and of itself. What one makes of it determines whether it is to be welcomed or dreaded. I do believe you must proceed with caution around these men. They have not yet voiced their intentions, so let us remain vigilant."

Gerhard rose from his chair and reached out his hand to grasp Edward's shoulder. "Have Jozsef send for the guards to be at your disposal should their news be ..." he hesitated before finishing, "less than welcoming."

Reaching his arm across his body, Edward patted Gerhard's hand that still rested on his shoulder. "You are like the stinging nettle that covers and protects the plant, safeguarding me all these years, my friend. Your counsel is invaluable." He called out to the servant who had been standing at the other end of the room beyond Margaret's field of vision. "Joszef, summon the guards and have them present during supper."

Without hesitation, Jozsef marched vigorously toward the door, leaving Margaret no time to scurry away without being caught. Forced to hold her position, she squeezed her hands together in prayer, hoping that the servant would turn in the opposite direction from her hiding place. When he did just that, she let her breath tumble through vibrating lips in relief. After blessing herself with the sign of the cross, she tiptoed down the dimly lit hallway back to the nursery to continue her copywork, equipped now with the knowledge of "the place" that the Lord had prepared for them.

*   *   *   *   *

The three foreigners who sat across from Margaret at the table seemed a bit confused, sharing furtive glances amongst themselves. Behind them stood a servant with a towel draped over his shoulder just as there was another servant behind her father and mother, and a third behind Gerhard, Edgar, and herself. Not knowing what to do, the three men simply waited, allowing Margaret to study them more closely.

The one who sat closest to her father filled the chair with his girth, making the table before him appear as small and breakable as the tiny one Gerhard had carved for her dollhouse. His red hair was thick and unruly, tumbling down from his head in waves that defied taming. Wild and free flowing, it fell down to his shoulders giving the appearance that he was still on horseback, riding recklessly toward some unknown destination. A deep hue of red it was—no, she reconsidered—more like the rusty brown of the tree trunks after a rainstorm. That was also the color of the man's mustache that draped either side of his mouth, dangling far past his chin. She watched the two cords flutter and move with his breath as he sat impatiently wondering what to do.

Immediately next to him was another fellow, perhaps a relative she thought. The two shared the same pair of sharp beady eyes that receded deep into their sockets, thanks to the low-set brow that hooded them. But this man was much leaner than the first, and the wings and sides of his chair remained visible to Margaret despite his occupation of the seat. A third man seemed to carry the same degree of authority as the other two, mainly because of his similar style of clothing and his inclusion at the table. Not as imposing as the first nor as wiry as the second, this visitor seemed positively bored at the prospect of waiting, so he spent his time darting his eyes about the room, searching for some form of distraction.

In quick succession, starting with the servant behind her parents, then shifting to the next one by the visitors, and then her own, water was poured into a dish, and the towel was proffered. After dipping into the bowl, reaching for the cloth, and drying his hands thoroughly, Edward broke the silence.

"How fares the King, my uncle?" Nodding to Agatha that it was her turn now for cleansing, he fixed his eye upon the red-haired foreigner.

"King Edward is well." The man shook out his hands for a brief moment before realizing his error. Quickly, he reached for the towel. "As noted in the missive we just gave you, he hopes that you will consider his request to return to the land of your birth. We will ensure safe passage should you accept his offer."

At this, Margaret stole a glance at Gerhard, but his expression betrayed no feeling. He gave no hint as to how she should react, his face conveying neither pleasure nor suspicion. Instead, the comment hung in the air, echoing indefinitely. No response was given, only the clanging sound of dishes interrupted the silence as more servants appeared with trays of stuffed chicken, sweet pies of pork, and wild rabbit in onion sauce. Margaret had not realized the extent of her hunger until the attendants began slicing and apportioning the food. Small clouds of spices and cooked meat rose from the table and wrapped around her senses. As her mouth watered in anticipation of the first bite, Margaret could almost feel her concern for their conversation evaporating with the scents that lifted up into the air. But she would not be diverted by such temptations. While her eyes followed the chunk of succulent meat placed into her trencher, she kept her mind fixed on the discussion.

Wiping the sheen of grease from his lips with the back of his hand, the burly man spoke. "The time will soon be good for crossing. We have business to tend to in the meantime, but Leofwine, Gyrth, and I will arrange for the crossing to England for you and your family." He dipped his thick fingers back into the trencher, lifting another handful of meat into his mouth.

Margaret watched the man's jaw move rapidly up and down grinding down the portion. When he opened his mouth to speak again, a piece of meat tumbled out and lodged itself on one side of his dangling mustache. Margaret stared at the remnant, waiting for it to fall.

"We can meet again in four weeks' time. In Flanders. The King has arranged for your transport." Even as he reached aggressively into the trencher, the suspended morsel did not slip. He spoke between swallows. "When you arrive in Flanders ... send word to me ... my brothers and I will be lodging ... at The Melusina."

Despite all of his chomping, the leftover food remained embedded in the tendrils of his red mustache, so Margaret gave up watching and shifted her gaze over to her father who sat tall and reserved. Offering only a slight nod of his head in acknowledgement, Edward kept his thoughts to himself, but Margaret's were racing. Clearly, this was a drastic turn of events, she reasoned, but why was the atmosphere in the room so tense? Why was her father not asking any questions of these visitors, questions about conveyances and arrangements and dates and such? Why had her mother barely eaten any of the food placed before her? And why did there seem to be an invisible wall encircling these three messengers, a wall so thick that, despite their welcome news, felt terribly menacing? Everyone looked to be on edge, afraid to speak out, fearful of asking to know more, even though this news should have been received with joy and excitement. And so the hushed silence continued, broken only by the sounds that accompanied the ordinary actions of eating and drinking.

The stiffness lessened when Cristina's nurse, Marta, materialized in the doorway. A plump, usually light-hearted woman, she had raised all three of Edward and Agatha's children with equal measures of discipline and love. Her waist-tied apron sat high upon her chest, directly beneath an ample bosom that a much younger Margaret once believed were the two softest pillows upon which she could lay her head. But Marta was not now the picture of coziness. Her words were tinged with worry and apprehension.

"Begging pardon for the interruption. The child will not be consoled. She has been fed and changed and rocked, but her fever is worsening. She still feels very hot to the touch. After the meal, would you come check on her and help soothe her? I have put her in her cradle just now, so it may be that she will cry herself to sleep, and if that should happen, I will surely send word." Marta, the outer edges of her eyebrows pointing downward in concern, awaited Agatha's reply.

Here was Margaret's chance to escape the heaviness in the room. She jumped up. "I will go," she said, simultaneously pushing her seat away from the table. "I can take care of her, Mama. I know how to calm Cristina."

For Harold, the boredom of being sent on this mission lifted when the young maiden spoke. Now here was a little diversion. The innocence of her voice drew his attention. Her face glowed with youth and freshness, and her body was lithe and supple. He felt a stirring in his loins when he envisioned the untouched skin that lay beneath her bodice and the hidden seal that protected her virginity.

Harold felt his desire quicken when she stood from the table, and he could take in all of her person. Her small budding breasts held the promise of future voluptuousness, and her long, blonde hair, tied back now, would be rather enticing when it hung freely over her naked body. Harold rose from his chair as he watched her make her way around the edge of the table and closer toward him.

Running rather than walking, Margaret moved with such haste that her foot caught in the hem of her dress, and she fell, face and arms forward, onto the ground beside Harold. Turning his back toward the table and away from the people seated there, he bent down toward the ground to lift her. Aroused by her closeness, he placed his hands on either side of her arms and quickly swept his thumbs across her chest.

Margaret felt confused, knowing only that she wanted to break away from his grip. She raised her foot, and with all of the force she could muster, stomped on his.

More out of surprise than pain, Harold released his hold just as Gerhard appeared at her side. Turning Margaret's elbow toward himself, Gerhard wrapped her in a reassuring hug. "Come, child, together we shall go tend to Cristina. Perhaps we can share one of your favorite tales with her, yes?" Sending a knowing look Harold's way, Gerhard ushered Margaret from the room.

Harold returned the glare with fearless indifference, offering some parting advice for the girl. "Be careful, fair maiden. You may run headlong into danger if you do not choose your steps wisely." He smirked to himself when he saw Gerhard embrace the girl tighter. Comfortable in the knowledge that no one else at the table had any notion of what had happened, Harold plunged his fingers into the trencher, not caring if any pieces dribbled down his chin and came to rest in the coils of his hair. *As long as you get enough of what you want, leftovers are expendable,* he thought to himself. *I shall have my fill and care nothing for what falls by the wayside.*

Once they had left the dining hall and moved down the corridor toward Cristina's room, Margaret whispered to Gerhard with contrition. "I have not ruined anything, have I, master? I promise I shall do penance." She looked up at her teacher, her eyes remorseful and uncertain.

He gently tapped her hand. "No need, child. No need."

THE WORLD BECKONS
FLANDERS – EARLY SPRING 1057

It took more than a few taps at the door before Magaret stirred from her deep meditation. Just after dawn she had awakened in the darkness to tiptoe over to a small alcove in the room that served her purpose. Quietly lifting a parcel of their belongings, she positioned it vertically into the corner where the two walls met, creating a makeshift altar for herself. Placing her hand upon the cross that dangled from her neck, she began to pray fervently: *Give ear to my words, O Lord, consider my meditation. Hearken unto the voice of my cry, my King and my God; for unto thee will I pray. My voice shalt thou hear in the morning, O Lord; in the morning will I direct my prayer unto thee, and will look up...*

Neither her mother nor her sister was aware of her movements. Lady Agatha lay exhausted upon the nearby bed, tired not only from the miles they had traversed to get to the inn but also from the unceasing worry that Cristina would not survive to see the next day. The little one had been ill since Christmas-tide, perpetually feverish and battling for breath. Her lethargy made her appear more like a puppet than a living creature, so listless and disengaged was she. Cristina's wheezing provided a kind of ominous cadence to Margaret's recitation as each verse from her psalter seemed to rise and fall with her sister's very existence.

Margaret prayed on, begging for her sister's recovery as well as her family's protection throughout this journey to an unknown land.

There were moments when Margaret's spirits soared with anticipation and delight at what the future might bring, but then her elevated hopes diminished, pulled down by her own rising sense of unease. *Have mercy upon me, O Lord; for I am weak; O Lord, heal me…*

Soon there would be new faces surrounding them, fresh landscapes for her and Edgar to explore, and a grand estate her father could call home despite being exiled from it nearly his entire life. But it was the reason behind his forced absence that made Margaret's blood run cold, causing her lips to tremble ever so slightly in between the words of her prayer. That fear, like a foot callus one tries to soothe by wearing a softer slipper, never went away. Instead, it kept sending intermittent pangs of discomfort, turning her promising steps toward the future into ones of pain.

Another soft tapping at the door finally penetrated her jumbled thoughts. She blanketed herself in the sign of the cross, put her lips to the amulet, and rose from her kneeling position to open the portal just wide enough to see what lay on the other side. Into that small gap poked Edgar's head, and his animated whisper reached out to her, "Margaret, let us go! Father told Master Gerhard we could do our lessons outdoors today. Come, we can get out of this place for a few hours. Hurry!" Visible through the crack, Edgar's single eye brimmed with enthusiasm at the prospect of being liberated from this cell they had been confined to for so many days. After weeks and months of moving freely about the lands of Hungary and Bavaria, it was torture to have been forced to remain stagnant at this seaport in Flanders for so long. But with their voyage to England delayed for lack of wind and their freedom to explore forbidden because of Father's edict about the dangers of port towns, there was little diversion for Edgar and Margaret other than their daily lessons—and even those were carried out in the tiny, stale rooms they had rented in these hinterlands.

"Hush, you will wake Cristina and mother!" Margaret's doubts about Edgar's announcement disappeared when she saw behind him the folded creases of Gerhard's full-length cloak. Accepting now that this trip was indeed sanctioned by their tutor, Margaret added, "Give me a moment, I will be right along."

Closing the door, she moved quietly toward her packed clothing and reached for the simple homespun gown to put over her nightdress. Her mother had cautioned against wearing traditional Hungarian attire, noting that its bright colors would mark her as a foreigner—a dangerous thing when one was living on the road amidst strangers. Mother consoled her that someday there would be a time to don those fancy garments, but certainly not here in this transient town. Delicately lifting her shawl from the corner of the bed, Margaret carried it in a scrunched up ball, not wanting to disturb the quiet with the flutter of air that would accompany her wrapping it around her shoulders. Instead, she held the material close to her chest, turned the knob of the door, and stepped from the room, relieved to hear no interruption in the rhythm of her sister's breath.

*　　*　　*　　*　　*

Once the door was safely closed, Edgar clapped his hands together, "Yay! Let us go!" He spun quickly to move down the lengthy hall of the inn as they made their way past the other rooms toward the front door. With his back to her, he spoke over his shoulder, "We have already picked up bread from the kitchen for breakfast, and Master Gerhard said we could bring it with us and eat it down by the wharf." Margaret smiled brightly at the prospect of being out among the living again, for the days had passed ever so slowly in the dim confines of her room with only her mother's misery and her sister's mortality for company. And even though her prayer life had deepened and she had found richness in such solitude, she would be lying to herself if she said an outing such as this was unwelcome.

Despite the fact that it was still early morning, the town square was bustling with activity. Small tables of trade were being put in place, some already engaged in commerce with merchants and townspeople haggling over the wares. Cheeses and milk, cloth and wool, casks of wine and flagons of ale—everything one could imagine was on display to catch the eye of both native villagers and visitors from newly arrived ships.

Gerhard led the way, and Margaret followed close behind, her hand clasping Edgar's while their eyes wandered freely about the action. Languages of all tongues filled the air, so the universal form of communication became hand gestures and facial expressions as sellers and buyers searched for common ground. Surrounded by a variety of clothing and complexions, Margaret regretted that she had reached for her drab homespun instead of a dress that proudly announced to this vibrant world the colors of her people; for here, in this forum, to be different was to blend in.

Gerhard stepped in front of the cheese seller and took his place in line behind three very sunburned, reddened sailors whose faces were etched with wrinkles that ran like deep carvings across their forehead and cheeks. They were enormously tall and wide-chested, their forearms thick with muscle. Each wore a kerchief bound across the top of his head under which escaped locks of blonde, wavy hair. Margaret sidled over, tilting her ear closer to listen to the husky and abrupt string of words that punctuated their conversation. Edgar meanwhile stood to the side of them, staring in wonder at the picture that was painted lengthwise from the shoulder to the wrist on the skin of the tallest man. The drawing appeared to be some kind of tree, depicted in shades of green and blue. Edgar tugged at Margaret's sleeve until he gained her attention, darting his eyes back and forth from her to the man's arm until she understood his unspoken request. Then Margaret too began to gape at this marvel of art on skin. Soon the stranger became aware of the two pairs of eyes upon him.

The man pointed to the sketch with his opposite hand, "Yggdrasil." This was followed by a tumble of words neither Margaret nor Edgar could comprehend. When his companions finished their bartering, the sailor departed with a nod to Margaret and a pat on the head to the awestruck Edgar who looked as if he had just witnessed a god's return to earth. Edgar's eyes continued to follow the band of men, paying no attention to Gerhard's purchase of additional food for their later meal. His enchantment was broken only when Margaret pulled on his arm and dragged him toward the grasses that led down to the waterfront.

Once the scenery changed, so too did Edgar's mood. Surrounded now by the tall sea grass, he forgot entirely about his encounter with the Viking men and instead began blazing their path down toward the waterfront as if his arms were swords and the reeds his enemies. But Margaret's fascination remained. "Master, what was the meaning of that picture on that man's skin? What is a 'yggdrasil'?"

She waited for Gerhard to simplify this mystery for her, but Edgar had already moved on. Oblivious to all things other than his own imaginative play, he bent down to pick up a fallen branch that now became his newly christened weapon of choice.

"Where shall we begin, my dear?" Gerhard briefly paused to tuck the cheese into his satchel and then resumed his walk. "Those three men were Northmen whose home floats freely upon water rather than fixed upon land. They are one with the sea. It is in their blood. They travel up and down this vast expanse," here he gestured toward the blue waters before them, "to ports far and wide, their fair skin weathered to copper, and their faces chiseled by sun beams." Distracted by Edgar's movements, Gerhard's voice lifted in warning, "Young man, slow down, or you shall lose your retinue and the might of your thaynes. Then you would have but one lone sword with which to confront the enemy."

Edgar stopped, and Gerhard closed the gap between them as he talked. "The image carved into the man's skin is a picture of an ash tree, a symbol sacred to his people. Yggdrasil connected the nine worlds to each other; it is the center of their universe. They believed their gods would visit the tree regularly and that all sorts of mythical creatures—dragons, serpents, eagles, stags—resided on its branches, at its roots, and within its heart. The well-being of the cosmos depends on the well-being of Yggdrasil."

The tall grasses thinned out, and the horizon opened with a full view of the ocean. Overwhelmed by the vista, Margaret inhaled a deep breath of salt air before questioning again. "But why put that image on his skin?"

Gerhard quickened his pace from alongside Margaret to overtake Edgar, placing himself at the vanguard of their troop. "Well, I suppose you would have to ask the man himself his reason for making that selection. But I would venture to guess that, though the tree is sacred, it is still mortal and in need of protection. Like the sailor himself. Perhaps the etching is a reminder to him of the delicate balance between nature and man, omnipotence and vulnerability. Something we must all be conscious of. He can take that awareness with him everywhere, to every land he visits and upon all seas he sails."

The conversation ended just as Margaret witnessed the bustling activity at the waterfront. Boats of all kinds could be seen in the Flemish harbor, some pulling away from land, others sailing toward it. Each bringing its own set of cargo, people, heritage, and culture.

"I never knew the world was so big!" Margaret spoke aloud to no one in particular. But then turning to Gerhard, she added, "For so long, my whole life consisted only of the mountains and lakes surrounding Reyka, but today there is so much more!"

And just like the sacred tree of the Northmen, Flanders seemed to Margaret the center of a remarkable universe. She sailed down the hill toward the waterfront, leaving Gerhard and Edgar in her wake.

*   *   *   *   *

Margaret picked up speed as she bounded toward the harbor, letting the slope dictate her movement. Her arms trailed behind her as she leaned forward, diving headfirst into this new experience. Soon her hair tumbled loose from its ribbon and lifted behind her like a golden cape fluttering upon the wind. As she drew closer to the shoreline, the air grew chill from the combination of the cold sea and the drifting gusts that made the water's surface curl and tumble.

When she reached the pebbled beach, she stopped running. Closing her eyes, she opened her arms to embrace the sea breeze. When she had her fill, she glanced over her shoulder and saw Edgar trundling down the hill with Gerhard not far behind, side-stepping his way. He bent his knees ever so slightly to maintain his balance on his way to the bottom. Impatient and too excited to wait, Margaret rushed back up to meet them, asking, "Master, which one is ours?"

Tugging at his sleeve to usher him toward the water, she gestured with her other hand at the assortment of ships resting in the harbor. Some were long and graceful, equipped with extra space for rowing benches. Larger ones were, strangely enough, beached upon the shore. Some were in the process of being unloaded, while others stood empty, bobbing up and down according to the will of the water.

"Yes," chimed in Edgar, "which one is ours? Do we get to choose?" Edgar's tree branch-sword now served as his hiking stick as he clacked along the stony beach toward one of the landed ships.

"Well, I do believe King Edward has commissioned a vessel much like that one there for our journey," and as Gerhard said this, he pointed to the vacant boat that was tied to the mooring. "But come, let us sit upon the ground here and have our meal while I tell you about our upcoming adventure."

Gerhard's newfound enthusiasm did not go unnoticed—at least to Margaret. Sensitive to such things, she realized her teacher had left his melancholy behind somewhere along the mud-packed ruts imprinted by their wagon. She too had felt a shift in her mood, especially now as they all looked with wonder at the thriving port.

She readily agreed to his suggestion that they eat. Her mouth watered as Gerhard broke off a portion of cheese and placed it into her hand along with a sizable chunk of warm bread. Doing the same for Edgar, he then took a small piece of cheese for himself and leaned back contentedly as they studied the picture that stretched out before them. Margaret waited patiently for Gerhard to speak, as she studied the approach and recession of the water upon the land. Reaching into his satchel again, Gerhard pulled out a jug of watered ale, uncorked it, and took a long, refreshing swallow before passing it on to Edgar. Using both hands to wrap around the belly of the flagon, the boy then raised it to his lips. After a trickle streamed down the side of his mouth and onto his lap, he returned the bottle to its upright position and handed it back to Gerhard who then passed it on to Margaret.

Before raising the jug to her mouth, Margaret found her mind had leapt again. "Does the water ever tire of reaching forward and drawing back? Does it rest as we do each night when the day comes to a close?" She stared at the retreating water, awaiting his response.

Laying the bread down upon his lap, Gerhard rubbed his hands together lightly, dusting the crumbs from his fingers. Then, pointing to the water's edge, he began. "See the wetted sand there and the curving lines that mark the sea's approach? That line continually changes, every hour of the day and night. The water never rests— unlike you or you or me," he singled out each child as he spoke.

"Wait, but no," interrupted Edgar, "I *am* like the sea though! I hate to take naps, and I hate to be told to go to bed. I want to run and play all day! Why can Mama not let me be? Hmmph." He folded his arms in protest, his bottom lip protruding in a pout.

"Do not be a fool, Edgar," Margaret responded. "Most of the time you drop down and fall asleep without even realizing it. Just like the other day. When Master Gerhard had sketched out a map of our new country, remember? Your head dropped lower and lower until your nose landed upon Dover and your spittle flowed right into the sea. You can no more stave off sleep than I can stop asking questions." She returned to the subject at hand. "Please, Master Gerhard, I pray you continue." Margaret leaned forward eagerly, while Edgar remained sullen, knowing that his sister's words were true.

Taking another draught from the bottle, Gerhard explained. "As I was saying, we need the restorative power of sleep to energize us and to keep us going. But the sea gains its strength and its power from the pull of the heavens. The movement of the water is based upon the breathings of the moon, its level tied to its phases. Come." Gerhard returned the flagon and the remaining food back to his bag. Taking Edgar's hand, he motioned to Margaret to follow. They stopped at the edge of the water line and watched the sea bubble and reach further up the shoreline. "There is a union, a bond, between the movement of the ocean and the picture of the moon. At the rising and the setting of the moon, the sea covers the coast far and wide, sending forth its surge. And when the surge is drawn back, the beach is laid bare. It is as though the water follows the breath of the moon."

Margaret considered this, impressed by the unity of God's creation. But Edgar was unmoved by such philosophical talk. "Then why will the moon not breathe faster so that we can get away from this place?" He planted his tree branch into a spongy part of earth, posturing like a king demanding tribute. "We have been stuck here forever waiting for the right moment to sail. When will the moon do its job for us?"

Gerhard gently removed the stick from the sand, passed it back to Edgar, motioning for the boy to follow. Margaret kept up with them as well, longing to hear Gerhard's answer. She too was frustrated by this long delay, especially after having traveled over land so quickly. They made their way over to the wharf and stepped onto the wooden planks of the pier, Edgar tapping the walking stick upon every slat. Gerhard waited until now to answer Edgar, directing the boy's attention to the water level on the pier. "See the watermark here, young man? It is much too high for us to attempt to sail across the sea to your family's new home. Here, give me your weapon."

Edgar reluctantly handed him the pole, "You will not discard it, will you, Sir?"

Gerhard extended his hand, palm open, and shook his head. "No, I am just going to show you something."

Once the stick was in his possession, Gerhard knelt down upon the planks and leaned over the edge, aligning the top of the branch with the wood of the dock and letting the water lick against it. The two children plopped down cross-legged on either side of him, peering down to see what he was measuring.

"Are you touching the bottom there? Is the sea only as deep as my sword?" Edgar collapsed down onto his belly to reach his own arm toward the surface.

In one swift action, Gerhard raised Edgar's arm up from the sea, chastising him. "Do not lean too far over, my boy. The bottom here is much deeper than this stick can reach. Sit back." As he said this, he lifted the branch from the sea and pointed to the watermark. "Take note," he continued, addressing both the young boy and Margaret. "Today this is where the tide stands, and this is much too high for us to embark upon our journey. 'Twould be best if the mark were somewhere down here," and he pointed to a lower point on the pole. "Then, with the right wind, conditions would be favorable for us to make our crossing. Come." Handing the stick back to its rightful owner, Gerhard stood up gingerly, each knee clicking as he drew himself upright. "Let us venture forward to gaze upon our vessel."

Margaret placed her hand in Gerhard's, but Edgar was still busy looking at the residue left behind on his toy, quickly adapting the facts to suit his imagination. "Yes, my friend," he said with the bold voice of a sea captain, "my blade is smeared with the blood of our enemies who have been trying to prevent our departure. But no matter, they have been silenced, and soon Lady Fortuna will shine down upon us so that we can return to our kingdom." He trailed his sister and his tutor, lifting his legs high as if marching toward the preserved sanctity of his ship.

Margaret's excitement grew as she walked closer to the boat that would soon be theirs. "My goodness! Look at that, Sir! How tall is that beam? How spacious it is for our small family!" Margaret's hand lifted to shield her eyes from the sun as she tried to measure the height that the single sail would one day reach. "There is so much room, and we have brought so little with us. We shall have more space upon the water than we have had in our lodgings these past weeks!"

Patting her clasped hand, Gerhard corrected her, "I am afraid, my dear, we will be packed in with other people and cargo—wool, timber, and pelts will take up most of the space in the hull, but we will have our own section set aside just for us. The crossing, if all goes well and tide and wind cooperate, will consume no more than a day for us, and before you know it, you two will be setting foot upon the soil of your ancestors—the realm of England. Just wait till you see the mariners hoisting the sail. Then the true majesty of the vessel will match the nobility of your blood, my lady."

Margaret closed her eyes trying to summon a vision of what the boat would look like when they were underway, but her daydream was interrupted when Edgar jostled her. The boy moved between her and Gerhard, shouting, "Worthless, pirates! Take care and stand back, you two, whilst my sword greets these villains who are trying to board our vessel!" Pushing them aside, Edgar plunged his stick in and through the air with an exclamatory, "Hiiiya! Hiiiya!!"

Caught up in his fantasy, he did not hear Gerhard's warning, "Watch there! You are drawing too close to the edge."

After one particularly strong lunge, Edgar started to lose his balance. He teetered on one foot and began circling his arms in an attempt to remain on the dock. Margaret sprinted quickly toward him, trying to grab hold of him but was left with only a shred of his sleeve when Edgar toppled into the sea with a loud splash. Margaret stood frozen in horror, but Gerhard, without hesitation, immediately jumped in after the boy. He disappeared under the surface until all that could be seen was the churning water at the point of their entry.

Margaret's hands covered her mouth. "Sweet Jesus, help us!" And as the words escaped her lips, the surface broke and her brother's head popped up, followed closely by that of her tutor. Their clothing billowed beneath them, the heaviness of the fabric pulling them toward the murky bottom. Gerhard fought mightily against its force, maintaining a firm grasp on the boy. Edgar's eyes remained shut, but his coughing was a clear sign of life.

"How can I help?" Margaret yelled with urgency, moving down the pier as Gerhard tried to propel her brother and himself closer to land.

Between breaths of air, the old man answered, "Go to the inn. Get two blankets. Do not alarm anyone. We are both fine, just cold. Run quickly." Margaret took one last glance at the pair, noting how Gerhard's legs were in constant motion as he fought to keep her brother elevated upon his shoulder.

Over the rocky shore she ran, hearing Edgar coughing up chunks of kelp and sea water. Back up the hill, through the tall grasses, and across the marketplace, Margaret moved swiftly, paying no mind to the field of daffodils dancing up and down upon the breeze or the lines at the shopping stalls now ten people deep. She did take time to consider how and where she would find the two blankets, deciding it would be best to avoid her own room since her mother was most likely still abed with the ailing Cristina. She would instead go to the men's quarters and lift the two quilts from there.

Rushing over the threshold of the inn, she raced down the hallway toward her father's room, praying not to attract attention. As she turned to her left to face the entrance of his chamber, a red-haired warrior materialized before her eyes, his swiftness incongruous with his size. Launching himself between Margaret and the door, he licked his lips until they glistened. His black eyes swallowed her, dragging her into their darkness.

"Now, what can you be wanting here? Mayhap there is something I can provide you with? Hmm?" He stepped closer. Margaret tried to move further back, but his hands seized her shoulders before she could create any distance. He stood close enough for her to feel his hot breath on her face. She watched the hairs in his mustache flutter and settle.

"My business here is none of your concern. All of my needs are met by God." Her hands trembled, but she spoke with conviction, finding in her faith the power to look directly into the menacing eyes of Harold Godwinson.

He clicked his tongue in admiration of her boldness, but his words contained only disdain. "You may wish to think on that a bit more, wench. In the near future, you will be needing my assistance more than that of the divine. Remember, you are headed into my domain, and you would be wise to count me as a friend when you and the rest of your family find yourselves among enemies."

He fingered strands of her yellow hair as he said this, lifting some of it across the gap between them and raising it to his nose to inhale. His eyes narrowed as he whispered one final warning. "I'd wager you would taste as sweet as honey upon my tongue. If you want to keep those you love safe and among the living, I would counsel you to open your door to me when time serves. Let me have my fill, and there is no favor I would not grant for you. Bear that in mind when you wish to call upon the Lord instead of me when your feet are standing upon English soil."

Margaret thrust her knee, hard and fast, between his legs.

"Ooooh, you scraette," he cursed as he doubled over and crumpled in pain.

She had just enough time to unlatch the door, snatch the two quilts, and dart around his doubled-over body before he could recover. Fleeing from the inn back down toward the waterfront, she felt no need to ask the Lord for forgiveness this time.

A TRAGIC HOMECOMING

Margaret, give me a boost, will you?"

Edgar had been hopping on both feet, attempting to latch his fingers around the edge of the cog's railing, but his feeble jump, combined with the coating of sea spray upon the wood, relegated him to the lower portion of the boat below the line of vision. And what a vision it was! Margaret leaned forward into the wind, reveling in the cheers and celebratory clapping that came from the citizens gathered on the shore to welcome them. The gray skies and wet winds that had been their constant companions throughout the voyage were now as inconsequential as the stray spark that floats from the blacksmith's hammer upon the anvil. Forgotten too were the stomach cramps and subsequent chunks of bile they had launched off the side of the boat, clumps that had dissolved into the froth of the sea.

Margaret reached down toward Edgar, using her arms to lift him until his elbows could rest on the ledge of the vessel. His legs, suspended in mid-air, dangled freely beneath him. "Oh, Margaret. They are happy to see us!" Edgar's mouth opened wide with wonder while Margaret craned her neck from one side to the other, measuring the impressive size of the crowd.

"Look, Edgar!" She pointed to the six banners that their bearers were waving back and forth, keeping time with the pronouncement, "Long live, Edward. Long live the son of Edmund Ironside!" Without taking her eyes off the multitudes, she whispered to him, "They are cheering for Father. Edmund Ironside was the grandfather we never met. Actually, Father did not know him either. He died when Papa was too young to have any memory of him." A momentary shudder rippled down her spine when she considered how the throngs celebrating their arrival today could perhaps be descendants of those responsible for her grandfather's murder long ago. Swiftly, she dismissed the dark thought with a physical shaking of her head, vowing to herself that nothing would diminish the excitement overflowing in her heart.

Unable to point with his finger for fear of losing his grip on the rail, Edgar gestured with his head toward the banners. "What is on the flag, Margaret? It looks like some kind of dragon."

She turned her gaze toward the pennant, squinting her eyes to block out the droplets of sea mist. "It *is* a kind of dragon. You are partly right. But see the arrow-shape tip of its tail? It is called a *wyvern*. It is Father's crest—the House of Wessex, the House of Cerdic—and it is yours too! Someday you shall be king of England!" Margaret smiled broadly when she saw her brother's eyes bulge in disbelief at hearing such a declaration. She squeezed his shoulders in exhilaration until one of the crew members inserted himself between them.

"Best be droppin' down now off the railin' unless ye'd be wantin' to have yer fingers crushed. We're gettin' ready to tie up now, ye see," and with that, the man pulled himself up by his thick forearms to land surefooted as a cat upon the edge.

Despite the narrowness of the barrier, he moved with ease, first running to the front of the boat and then, drawing his arms behind him for momentum, leaping across the gap of water to land upon the dock. Yelling to his mate to toss him the rope, he looped the mooring line around the cleat, while two other crew members repeated the same process for the middle and rear of the vessel. Margaret watched and listened with great interest, noticing how, despite the outward frenzy and confusion, there was a distinct order and rhythm to their shouts and gesticulations.

The crowd roared at the success of the mariners' efforts, and Margaret spun about to find Gerhard, Cristina, and her parents alongside her and Edgar—all of them breathing shallowly with delight over this unexpected welcome. Maybe the people did genuinely consider this to be her father's homecoming, even though Margaret knew deep down that he was returning to a place that was utterly foreign to him, foreign to them all.

Her father and then her mother, who was carrying Cristina, ascended the steps first, while she and Edgar each grabbed hold of one of Gerhard's hands as he stood in between. The biting wind came full force once they stepped closer to the plank, and Margaret was too slow to stop her hair covering from going airborne. Breaking her clasp with Gerhard, she sprinted toward the veil which continued to tumble away from her in a kind of comical dance. Just before it blew overboard on the opposite side, a sailor lifted his heavy boot and stomped on it, halting its get-away. After he retrieved it, he offered her both the cloth and a large gap-toothed smile. "Here ye go, milady. This will suit ye just fine here, but …" he lowered his voice to a gravelly whisper, "mayhap ye can talk to your Papa on the side and tell him to do away wi' that fur-lined pointy cap so's he can blend in a bit more wi' his new neighbors, eh?"

Although he chuckled in a playful way, Margaret drew back at his subtle criticism, fearful that the people's warm display of affection could be hiding a more sinister vein of distrust. With a quick nod of thanks, she ran to the outstretched hand of Gerhard, relieved to be back in familiar company.

Margaret followed her parents and Cristina, placing her feet upon the land that was to become her new home. As the banners kept waving and the people continued cheering, the exiled family stood in place, unmoving and still. The crowd assumed the family was basking in the welcome that enveloped them, but Margaret wondered if their fixity was because her father simply did not know what to do next. No one had stepped forward to greet them or to direct them where to go. There was no indication that they were being received by any dignitary from King Edward's court. And while it was, no doubt, heartwarming to be loved and appreciated by the commoners, Margaret could not help fearing for their future.

When she could wait no more, Margaret tugged gently on Gerhard's arm until he bent his ear down toward her. "Master, what do we do now? Where do we go? What happens next?" Never letting her eyes leave her father, she asked these questions while studying her Papa's demeanor.

"Hush. We just wait. Be patient. An emissary or the King himself will be here directly. Keep your head steady and your eyes warm with greeting while we bide this time." And so they stood before the assembly, silently accepting their welcome as if this were all they were expected to do—for however long the reception would last.

Finally, a thundering of hooves broke time with the crowd's applause until eventually the gathering shifted to make way for five men on horseback, three of whom led riderless mounts and the final two who led ox-drawn carts. The man at the front carved his path through the masses with little concern for how his maneuvering affected anyone other than himself. His wild and wavy red hair escaped out the sides of his form-fitting helmet whose strip of steel ran from the point of the headpiece down to the bottom of his nose. The strip separated the two dark, beady eyes that stared down upon the travel-worn family with cold detachment. When he removed his helmet, Margaret immediately recognized Harold and tried to swallow her fear, but her mouth and tongue were parched. Once again, shadows eclipsed the brightness of their arrival.

"Greetings to you, Edward, nephew of our sovereign king," he shouted as the gathered people grew silent in their yearning to hear the exchange. "The King regrets that he is unable to welcome you himself here at Sandwich, the site that marks your return to your ancestral home." Margaret waited anxiously, feeling Gerhard's grip tighten upon her hand as if to defend her.

Announcing the news more to the crowd than to the family, Harold continued. "I shall escort you to London where you shall be united with our noble leader—God save the King." The people echoed the same blessing and broke out again into applause. Margaret was disappointed that her father's interview with the King would be delayed and looked to Gerhard for his reaction. But his face conveyed nothing. He stood straight and unmoved. Neither the cheering nor the announcement moved him. He remained as cool and as grounded as the marble Roman arch they passed through at Richborough fort. Margaret tugged again at his sleeve and whispered, "What do we do now?"

Gerhard silenced her with a sharp look, and she soon realized why. The people of England were waiting for her father to address them. With measured steps, Edmund Ironside's son moved beyond Harold and his English companions to draw closer to the gathering. He stood before the crowd in his finest tunic, tan cloth embroidered with small blue triangles that stretched from his waist to the bottom hem. His sleeves billowed to the elbow and then gathered tight to his wrist, while a string of cloth buttons ran down the middle of his chest. A light blue sash was knotted around his midsection, the dangling ends of which he pushed off to the side of his hip as he strode forward to meet the crowd.

Margaret had heard him rehearsing this speech with Gerhard many times over, each iteration only slightly better than the last. Unlike she and Edgar whose minds were young and malleable, her father struggled with this new language, his words often garbled and uneven. Even she knew how important it was for him to make a good first impression upon these kinsmen who would only welcome him as one of their own if he could convince them that he was. She let go of Gerhard's hand and pressed hers together in prayer. She could sense the gravity of the moment reflected in Gerhard's posture, his whole body supporting this man he had raised since childhood, leaning forward as if to propel him toward success. She closed her eyes and offered a silent, hasty prayer as her father removed his leather gloves and his fur-lined cap and cleared his throat to speak.

Inhaling deeply, Edward began. "Thank you. Thank you, to all who come forth to welcome me to this land. It has been some time since I wander these sandy shores and green hills, but I never forget the majesty of this country or the beauty of her people. I promise to honor the memory of my noble father, Edmund, devoting my life to the protection of this realm and the glorification of our Lord Jesus Christ. I offer my humble service to his brother and my uncle, King Edward, the ruler of this domain, who was so kind to give me chance to return to this place of my birth. I am very pleased to finally come home."

Margaret's heart burst with a mixture of relief and pride as she watched her father bow three times, to the left, to the middle and to the right of the assembly, as the crowd chanted in response, "Wessex, Wessex," over and over until the distant forest echoed with admiration. But such praise was too much for Harold to bear. He shifted his horse to block Edward from the crowd, hoping to sever the connection that was being made between the people and the newly returned prince. Spitting upon the ground in disgust, Harold pulled

Edward away from his followers and spoke without ever dismounting so that he could command him from above.

"London is nearly a week's worth of travel—weather permitting—what with your possessions and retinue. The first leg of the journey will be by river, up the Stour to Canterbury. We will be housed with the Benedictines at the monastery before we continue our path over land. Provisions have been made for you to sup this evening and stay overnight at The Garland. Someone will come for you in the morning to bring you to the boat."

Harold gestured toward the two oxen. "Have your servants load up these carts with your belongings. The women and children can walk. You and your men can take a mount if you wish. I am going on ahead to get preparations underway." Margaret watched Harold turn his horse abruptly and ride away. As an afterthought, he looked back over his shoulder and shouted, "Leofwine and Father Thurstan will show you the way." Without waiting for either of the men to identify themselves to the group, Harold galloped off toward the inn.

Some of the crowd began to disperse but many who stood closest to the family stayed to observe the next progression of their arrival. Margaret listened as her father gave instructions to his attendants as to which bundles should be placed into which carts, so the scene became busy with activity. Wandering toward her own belongings, she stole a quick glance back at Gerhard and Edgar. Her brother was already prancing about as if he himself had been crowned king, checking out the placement of their possessions on the cart and examining which horse he would take for himself—with Gerhard, of course, holding him steady. And Gerhard had started securing the more delicate pieces to rest safely atop the conveyance. Margaret guessed that the slight curl in his upper lip had nothing to do with the labor he was engaged in.

She sensed his discontent and approached him tentatively. "Master, do you not wish we could find our own way to London and King Edward? Would we not be better off relying on the villagers along the way—people who actually like us—rather than have that awful man in our midst?" But Gerhard did not respond. He shot her a look that forbade her to say more and moved away toward the other cart, leaving her to sift through her own thoughts alone.

Someone else though had heard her conversation, someone from Harold's entourage. A cowled figure sidled up alongside her. Drawing closer, he extended a single crooked finger from his wide sleeve and pointed it directly at Margaret's face. "Woe to you, ungrateful child. Remember, you are exiles in this land." He drew closer. His foul breath made her cough. She felt herself weaken under such contagion.

His words then turned vicious as he latched his bony fingers around her narrow wrist. "Jeremiah speaks of people like you. Heed his warning: *'I will hurl you and your mother who bore you into another country where you were not born and there you will die.'* This country is not your own. Do well to remember that. You are lucky to have Earl Harold's assistance. The man demeans himself in doing so, filthy gypsies that you are. Beware, else this 'homecoming' may turn out to be an eternal one for you and your family."

Margaret tried to free her arm from his clasp, but she could not break his grip. The tips of her fingers began to tingle and turn numb as he continued to hold fast. It was not until someone pulled hard on her elbow, wrenching it away from the odious priest, that she realized she was no longer alone. Gerhard surged in front of the priest, using both hands to push the man away from Margaret and down to the ground. "Lie in the dirt, serpent, the place for those who twist the word of God to suit their own malicious intentions."

Although his hands trembled from losing his temper, Gerhard spoke with clarity. "You are never to come near or to speak to my lady again. Or it shall be you who will be laid to perpetual rest. Men like you propagate evil in this world by distorting the Lord's message. But you have trespassed into the wrong company of souls with your misappropriated warning. *'When a stranger resides with you in your land, you shall not wrong him... he shall be to you as one of your citizens; you shall love him as yourself.'* That is the Christian way to treat the exile." Lifting his foot, he kicked the bottom of the priest's robe, dismissing the fellow with disdain. "Even a monk's cowl cannot hide the hypocrite who skulks beneath. Clearly, you should spend more time learning how to interpret scripture accurately and less time terrorizing the faithful."

Wrapping his arm inside Margaret's, Gerhard marched off with her toward the group that was readying itself for the journey to The Garland. Although the intensity of the moment had passed, she could still feel the energy pulsing throughout her body. Now there were two men she needed to steer clear of—Harold Godwinson and this priest —but, strong though they were, she could drown out their harsh messages with the warm recollection of the resounding cheers from the crowd.

The reception her family had received upon their arrival proved to her that most people in this kingdom liked them, welcomed them. And even if one day in the future the crowd's voice should turn shrill and cold, at least she had one person who would always remain loyal and true. She tightened the knot between their arms and placed her trust in Gerhard.

*　　*　　*　　*　　*

Less than a day in this new country and already Margaret felt everything shifting. Yesterday's sense of wide-open adventure had shriveled, making this new world much smaller and more desolate. No longer did she and Edgar have the freedom to wander as they once did over the hills and streams by Reyka. Kept under close watch and within restricted boundaries, she became more dejected when even Gerhard could not be persuaded to let them go exploring during the free time they had between their arrival at The Garland and the serving of the meal.

Besides limited access outdoors, Margaret was also excluded from being in the company of her father. Although in the past it was true that she had never spent unlimited hours in his presence, at least she had always felt that he would make time for her even when he was conducting a meeting with a tenant or supervising the construction of a new stable. If she needed him, he nearly always pushed aside those pressing appointments to make room for her on his lap. But just as the familiar shoreline had melted away when their boat ventured farther from their homeland, so too did those opportunities to be with him fade and disappear.

Margaret became aware that she was no longer a little girl. Somewhere in her mind she always knew that those private moments between her and her father would naturally recede with the passage of time. That simply was the way of the world. The way of life. Those precious moments would be nothing more than a pleasant memory to recall when she would someday raise children of her own. That was the normal progression of things. And she could accept that. What she could not accept was the abruptness of the fracture, the suddenness of the division. And the shock of that split left her lonely for him.

Ever since they piled up their belongings and set out for The Garland, her father was surrounded by Harold's men. Of course, Gerhard was still with him, serving as translator, and Edgar was there too as he rode in tandem with the teacher, but she was far removed from their cluster. Instead, she walked obediently beside her mother and Cristina, deprived of their company. There were a few times when Gerhard and Edgar would return to her, the tutor sharing stories from history—about Britannia, the Roman invasion, and the surrender of the eleven tribes without bloodshed—but none of this stirred Margaret's usual curiosity, not even the bit about elephants coming ashore sparked her interest. She nodded and smiled out of politeness, but she could not step out from the circle of isolation she had drawn about herself.

Supper at the inn passed in much the same manner. She sat with Edgar, her mother, and Cristina at one long table while her father was seated in the center of the front one, flanked on either side by Harold and that horrid priest, Father Thurstan. Next to them were Harold's two brothers. This time even Gerhard was forced to keep a distance as he was placed three chairs away on Edward's right.

"Look at all this delicious food! What ails you, daughter?" Agatha wrapped one arm around Margaret's shoulder, hoping to shepherd her back into their company. "Why are you not eating?"

And it was indeed a sumptuous feast. Roast duck was served on trenchers of thick slices of dark bread while bowls of carrots, beets, and peas were spaced at intervals atop the table. Before each of them stood mugs of warm ale, while flagons of wine filled the cups belonging to her father and to the other Englishmen. No one took notice of the bowl of parsnips that was served only to Edward.

"My stomach is still unsettled from the sea journey, Mama, but I will try." Margaret used the single knife to slice off a small piece of the meat, and with her fingers, raised the morsel to her lips. Before taking it in, she added, "This *is* a grand display, is it not, Mother? They do seem to want us to feel welcome ...?" She forced herself to chew and swallow even though she had no appetite.

In between chomps of food, Edgar agreed, "Of course they do. Look at all this. Look at Father seated at the front, in the place of greatest importance. They love us without knowing us, and when they know us, they shall love us even more!" He rubbed his greasy hand on his clothing. "I like this place already!" he announced and plopped a carrot in his mouth in exclamation.

Agatha's head gestured to Margaret, "You think too much, daughter. It is that active mind of yours, always trying to dig beyond what is put before you." She paused to take in and swallow a draught of ale. "For once, just accept what stands before you without ruining it with images of doom coming from your head. Tonight is wonderful. Everything about our journey has been good and will continue to be so—as long as you do not try to find fault with it at every turn. Now stop this nonsense and eat. We have many miles yet to go before we reach London." She dipped her fingers into the bowl of beets, plucked out a handful, and plopped them atop Margaret's trencher. "Eat."

Margaret gave a weak smile of agreement and stared down at the food in front of her, thankful that, at that very moment, the faint plucking of strings veered her mother's attention away from her and toward the music of the minstrel.

*　　*　　*　　*　　*

Her voice lifted in confusion. "Father?"

Margaret had been breathing in the musky smell of the woodlands and the flowering anemone that lined their path when she saw her father's body, as it was positioned in the saddle, tilt further and further toward the side.

That morning the family had left the inn and began traveling toward Favreshant, following a path made fragrant by the flowers and plants newly opened for spring. The weather did much to improve Margaret's spirits as the sun shone brightly upon them from a clear, blue-domed sky. An occasional puffy cloud floated across the heavens but never did it linger long enough to diminish the warmth that embraced her. Walking with a bemused smile upon her face, Margaret surrendered to the charms of the countryside, relishing in the way the light accentuated the many shades of green that colored the leaves, the bushes, and the flower stems. A random look toward the front of the cavalcade snapped her pleasant daydream when she noticed the rider near the head of the train—her father—was about to fall.

Abandoning her usual sauntering walk, she broke into enormous strides trying to close the gap between her father and herself. The rapid turnover of her feet upon the soil alarmed the flock of yellowhammers who had been flitting about the blossoms. To escape the disruption, they rose higher and hovered above, waiting for the tumult to settle.

"Father!"

Her shout coincided with the loud thud of his body landing on solid ground, his head coming to rest in a patch of wildflowers.

Before Margaret reached him, she could see Gerhard was already there. He had carefully removed young Edgar from the saddle and then ran toward Edward, dropping to his knees for closer inspection. Margaret skidded to a halt and took the same posture on the other side of her father's fallen body. Hesitantly, she repeated again, "Father…?"

His lips parted but no sound issued forth.

After a quick glance in her direction, Gerhard moved closer to Edward, placing one hand beneath his master's neck and bringing his own closer. "Edward! Edward, can you hear me?" Nothing. "Blink your eyes if you can hear me." Gerhard's voice cracked with worry, his usual composure gone. Because Gerhard had leaned so closely over her father's head, Margaret had to slide further up toward his shoulder to be able to see whether or not her father had comprehended Gerhard's words.

To her relief, she saw his eyelashes flutter—*he understood!* He was still there, he was still with them!

Gerhard continued. "Can you move your legs, my lord? Your arms? Just blink to let me know if you still have some control over your limbs."

The words hung in the air as other people soon gathered around the group of three upon the ground. Margaret heard Edgar sniffling somewhere outside the circle and felt Harold, the priest, and his two brothers glaring down upon them from their seats. None of them had dismounted; instead, they surrounded the trio like a band of highwaymen waiting to pounce on an unsuspecting victim. To Margaret's dismay, her father's eyelids did not flicker.

She studied Gerhard and watched the changing color of emotion move across his face—from confusion to concern, from fear to speculation, from suspicion to anger. When they both noticed the parting of her father's lips, their hopes lifted. Together, she and Gerhard leaned in closer.

Her father's eyes remained open but unfocused, and he whispered gently, more so to the air than to them. "No … feeling …my legs. My feet… cannot feel them… cannot move them… nothing there."

Gerhard was about to respond but stopped when he saw Edward gather his breath once more. Unable to inhale deeply, he spoke in shallow exchanges. "Dizzy … since morn...could not get… legs...to keep hold … of the horse... chest feels … full… crushed.." He paused here for a lengthier break. Margaret could feel her eyes welling up, her lashes wet with moisture. "Cannot… take …. in … air.." With his gaze still focused at some point in the far distance, he whispered in a hushed tone, "Twas… foul… play." Silence and he moved no more.

Margaret felt tears stinging her eyes. They burned her skin as they tumbled down her face until they left small, individual droplets of water on her father's tunic. She watched as Gerhard placed his hand over Edward's face, his fingers gently extending to close each eyelid. Tiny bright-blue flowers with yellow centers formed a soft, decorative pillow where his sleeping head lay. Reminded of Jesus' promise when he created these delicate blossoms, Margaret trusted that the Blessed Virgin would watch over her father's soul. And she also knew that her father—like the flower itself—was urging her to "forget-me-not."

PART TWO

MATTERS OF THE HEART

SUMMER 1057 – SUMMER 1060

CELIA

THE WILL TO CARRY ON

CAEN, NORMANDY - SUMMER 1057

The voice of Ada Renouf droned on, but Celia was only half-listening. There were so many chores she had yet to finish, and the daylight hours were dwindling fast, swallowed up by each gulp of air Ada took as she dived into another subject. From the Duke's battles to last week's storm to her husband's bunions to menacing rabbits, the old woman certainly had an aversion for silence.

"Same time last year, they ransacked the garden just when the berries had grown red, juicy, and plump." Ada folded her arms so that they rested atop her ample bosom. "And here I am, one day thinking how grand the harvest will be with all the pies and jams I would soon be making, and the next I am looking at chewed off stumps and trampled vines. So," her eyes twinkled at her own ingenuity, "this year I moved the patch farther away. To a new spot since the little buggers never venture far from their den. Change of location seems to have done the trick so far. Though two weeks' time will tell whether I will be sharing strawberry watercress salad with you or not."

Celia feigned interest by focusing only on the movement of Ada's lips, occasionally allowing her mind to envision a word or two floating up into the air that separated them. A simple nod of her head at just the right interval kept the woman spinning her tales as the sun dropped lower and lower on the horizon, and the natural light in the cottage grew dimmer. Almost as if her unspoken prayer for rescue had been heard, Celia was grateful to hear Vivienne stir.

Straightening out the folds of her skirt, Celia stood and made her way over to the child. "Hello, *mon petit coeur*. Did you have sweet dreams?" *Interrupted by tales of nasty calluses and mischievous rabbits, perhaps—?* she almost added.

Over a year had passed since her father's death and Simon's departure. Vivienne, now two years old, had nearly outgrown the pallet upon which she lay, but Celia had not the heart to switch the child over to the larger bed that had belonged to their parents. She liked to think she avoided making the change because she treasured Vivienne's baby days, but in truth, it was the haunting memory of caring for her invalid father on it that kept her from switching. As she lifted the child to her shoulder, the other voice kept filling the room.

"But 'tis only a nuisance to deal with furry garden thieves; 'tis quite another to deal with human ones." Ada pushed her chair away from the table in order to face the center of the room where Celia jiggled Vivienne up and down on her shoulder.

Celia's interest was piqued. "What thieves?"

Pleased at her own self-importance, Ada pointed her finger past the doorway of the cottage. "Well, you know the Beaumont family and their bevy of livestock? Tsk, tsk. A week never went by without your father having to walk one of their stray sheep back to their farm. Well, this time there will be no returning for some four or five heads of sheep… ever. Totally gone they are, and 'twas not the first farm to suffer the consequences of such a visit." Ada looked down at her crusty fingers and began flicking the dirt from one of her nails, waiting impatiently to be asked to go on.

This bit of gossip far outshone the bunions and the bunnies; indeed, it was even more exciting than the news of Duke's achievements, mainly because William's battles involved places far away and unfamiliar. Vivienne wiggled her way out of Celia's arms and trundled over to Ada, coming to an abrupt halt by slapping both of her hands in triumph on the vast expanse of the woman's lap.

"Well, just look at you now! Practically running to come see your old friend!" The woman caressed Vivienne's head, softly stroking the baby's wisps of blonde hair. "I brought you into this world, my love, and 'tis my joy to see how much brighter it has become because you are in it!" A wide grin spread across the child's face, but from both corners ran a thin stream of drool that puddled on Ada's apron.

"She is teething again, I am afraid." Celia approached with a cloth. "The past few days she is been a bit feverish at night and quite irritable during the day. Constantly chewing her fingers, her rag doll, anything she can get her mouth on." Celia moistened another cloth by dipping it into the pitcher of water. Rolling the cloth into a ball, she handed it to Vivienne who seized it and waddled away into the corner of the room where her doll lay. "Tell me more about this sheep thief."

"Well, it seems the rogue has been stalking the fields for a few weeks now, but no one can catch him or find where he is hiding. Some think it may be more than one person. Maybe the King's soldiers or Martel's. I suppose we are the ones being punished because of William's boldness, I guess. Anyway, just a few weeks ago, the Levesques—who live but a day's journey from here—caught the man in the act, but the villain stabbed old Basil to death with Basil's own knife. The son Tomas managed to wrest the knife back and sliced his way down the man's leg, but he beat Tomas senseless with a hayfork to his head and then escaped. The neighbors organized a search but found nothing—save a trail of blood that eventually disappeared altogether." Ada began fussing with her kerchief, tucking in the stray, curly hairs that had escaped above her ears. "'It was quiet for a while until we heard of the raid late last week at the Beaumont farm. It is a good thing you do not have a herd of sheep or cattle here."

"Yes, only the one goat, which is good, I suppose." Celia looked around at her humble surroundings and felt a sense of relief. "There is nothing here to tempt a thief to pay us a visit." She opened her arms wide and swung her head around the sparsely decorated room as if to validate her claim.

"That may be true." Ada stood up, taking her shawl off the back of her chair and wrapping it about her shoulders. "But just the same, if I were you, I had keep a shovel within reach, just in case the scoundrel has any designs on stealing something other than wooly creatures." Her eyes rested on the child in the corner who grasped her doll in one hand and held the wet cloth in the other. "If you hear anything or need anything, no matter what hour of the day or night, you come right down the road to me, and we will take you in—both of you." Her soft, pudgy hand grabbed hold of Celia's chin, forcing the girl to meet her gaze. "Now you promise me, young lady, that you will not take any chances, yes? You will come to me and my Hubert? We will take good care of you both. It has been a long time since we have heard a child's laughter in our home, and we'd welcome the sound." With a kiss atop Celia's head, she sealed her promise and walked toward the door. When her stout body filled the portal, she turned back once more to add, "Now mind me, Celia, eh?"

Although Celia nodded in silent agreement, Ada did not budge from the door. Clearly, she was not yet convinced that Celia would seek out anyone's help. Putting aside thoughts of thieves and blood and sheep, Celia recalled all of the work she still had ahead of her. In the heartiest voice she could muster, she said, "Of course," and with those two words she sent Ada Renouf on her way and liberated herself to tend to her remaining chores.

*　　*　　*　　*　　*

A loud pounding blended its way into Celia's dream. The sound grew in intensity as she visualized each shovel of dirt she dropped into the earthen hole. Her thoughts became frantic. In her dream, she had mistakenly buried her father alive, and he was slamming his fists against the thick coating of soil she had leveled upon him. The sweat on her upper lip dripped into her open mouth as she dropped her shovel in horror. Collapsing onto her hands and knees, she began clawing away at the dirt in a frenzy to get to him. She had to get to the noise. She had to get him free. She must rescue him and bring him back to her.

But the pounding was not coming from her dream. It came from her door. And it only stopped when Ada Renouf and her husband broke the latch and burst into the cottage. "Celia! Wake up! Hurry!" The woman grabbed Celia's shoulders, shaking her back and forth.

Celia's nightmare had turned her mind upside down. Rather than digging deeper into the grave, she was instead scratching her way to the surface of consciousness, slowly becoming aware of the ache in her low back and the stiffness in her fingers. The acrid smell of smoke hung in the air as she blinked her eyes repeatedly until the kindly couple came into focus.

Ada was wearing layer upon layer of clothing, her round face dotted with blotches of red, her breath coming in short gasps. "Get up, girl! Grab only what is necessary. We must run!" The older woman threw a shawl upon the bed and tossed another onto the floor that would serve as the sling to carry the baby. Her husband Hubert lifted Vivienne from the other pallet and handed her off into Ada's seasoned hands.

As the woman began fashioning the pouch for Vivienne, Celia bolted upright and jumped from her bed, darting about the room to retrieve the few items of importance that she owned. "What is going on? Why are we running away?" Seizing Vivienne's feeding bottle, some clean rags for changing her, her mother's locket, and Philippe's carved horses, she thrust the items into a sack.

"There will be time later for explaining. It is no thief. It is the King's army. Burning and killing. Come, let us go!" Ada was nearly screaming at this point. Hubert offered his hand to Celia to take her sack of belongings so that she was free to fasten the baby's sling to her body.

Ada revealed more. "Emil alerted us. They kidnapped his three sisters. When his father tried to stop them, they cut him down. Emil's mother collapsed, and they trampled her with their horses. He escaped and ran to alert us, just as we are now doing for you. Come!" Ada pulled Celia from the room, dragging her out the door to follow behind her husband.

Tucking the babe in close and cushioning her head with the palm of her hand, Celia looked up into the sky as soon as she exited the cottage. Flames of orange and red reached toward the heavens in a demonic dance driven by the wind. Smoke billowed in the distance above, its tentacles extending closer to where they stood. The Renoufs, each carrying a sack of goods over their shoulder, waddled more than ran. Despite their lack of speed, Celia knew she would never desert them. She would not break her bond with the people who had just saved her life and her sister's as well. Without Simon around, the Renoufs were the only ones who knew her and were willing to protect her. Celia focused on the sound of their feet trampling the twigs on the ground and the stilted, labored breathing of the couple in front of her.

Although the night-time sky was alight with danger and the smell of burning flesh hung in the air, they dragged themselves forward, creating distance between themselves and the village. Soon they were beyond the homesteads and fields, but still they kept going until they came upon a grove of trees, a possible haven. As they moved deeper into its recesses, the forest seemed to offer a protective canopy for the refugees. Sensing this, they communicated in unspoken words, slowing to a walk and looking around the bower for a place to rest. Noticing a small section curtained by hanging branches, Hubert went down upon his knees to go inside and investigate. He silently gestured with his hands, "Wait here," before crawling inside.

Celia loosened the carrier to get a good look at the child. Ada stepped closer to put her hand on Celia's shoulder. The woman gazed at Vivienne. "Look at ... that face. So peaceful ... and angelic." Detaching her hand, Ada dipped into her pocket, pulled out a cloth, and began dabbing the sweat off her face. Because of her size and the many layers of clothing she was wearing, her face shone purple like a plum, and her chest continued to rise and fall as she struggled to catch her breath. "Looking at her ... you would never know ... we just escaped from Hell. That we had come ... nearly face to face ... with death."

It took a few moments for Ada's heart to settle, and when it did, her emotions then took over. She cried out against the unfairness of it all. "Why is this happening? What have we done to deserve this? They ravage our homes, kill our people, destroy our land. But why? Henry's troops and Martel's want to teach the Duke a lesson. Only he is not the one being schooled. We are. They have come to destroy us —people who have no claim to castles or titles. People who only wish for peace. People who are content with a decent cup of wine, enough food to fill their belly, and a few friends round the fireside for companionship. Yet we pay the price for their vanity and greed." Pushing the cloth up against her eyes, Ada wept bitterly.

Hubert popped his head out from the leafy bower, signaling to them to come inside and join him. Celia, who had laid the baby on the ground, lifted her to her chest and walked with Ada toward the opening. Getting down on all fours, they crawled into the space and settled themselves within its safe confines. The pungent smell of smoke had not penetrated their little room, so they breathed in the scent of wet leaves and moist dirt, a welcome change from the air that had singed their throats. Despite this improvement, Ada was at her breaking point.

"Everything we have is gone, Hubert." She whimpered like a wounded animal. "We are too old to start over again. What shall we do?" She pulled the cloth away from her face only to bury it in her husband's chest. Hubert said nothing. Instead, he rocked her from side to side, holding her in his arms, letting her give way to grief. When her sobs subsided, she lifted her face to lock eyes with Celia.

"Hubert is too old. He cannot build a new cottage for us. We have no children, no sons to call upon. Where will we go? What shall we do?" The enormity of her situation engulfed Ada again in sadness. Celia wished she had words of comfort to offer as her own mother often did for her in days gone by. But the futility of the Renoufs' situation mirrored her own. How could she provide any type of solace when she too had to face the same stark reality? Where would she and Vivienne go? What would they do?

As only those mired in misery know, Celia provided the single answer available to her at that time. Reaching out to grab Ada's hand that dangled by her side, she clasped it tightly. "I do not know what the future will bring, but we have each other, do we not? We will figure this out together. Vivienne and I will not leave you. If Simon's house is still standing, we can stay there until he returns from battle. He will help us both rebuild. I know he will."

Ada's face cracked into a partial smile. "You are so kind to us. Thank you, *mon cherie*." She enveloped Celia in an emotional embrace.

After giving them some time, Hubert patted each woman affectionately. "This may not be the best lodgings you will ever find, but it is good enough for now. There is nothing further we can do tonight other than pray and be grateful we are alive. Everything will look better in the morning. I am certain of it." He kissed the top of Celia's head and then stood beside his wife as Celia handed over the child into Ada's arms.

"I am just going to fill these flasks with water from the brook. Can you mind her till I come back?" Celia held up three containers as she spoke.

"Of course." Ada brushed her lips against the crown of Vivienne's head while the baby cooed softly. "No! Wait! You can not do that. You can not venture outside again!" Ada grew more alarmed. "Absolutely not. You cannot go out there alone. If you must go, then Hubert must go with you." She turned to her husband. "Hubert, she must not go alone. Not with the devil out there, skulking behind every bend and shadow. Go with her."

When Hubert nodded in agreement, Ada felt a measure of relief. She nodded to them both, giving them permission to leave together and then began swaying back and forth, keeping time with the melody she hummed into the ears of the innocent child.

*   *   *   *   *

It happened so fast.

Celia was dipping a third jug into the stream when a shriek pierced the air.

The shrillness of it startled Celia. It was Ada. She dropped the bottle and spun around.

"Wait!" Hubert shouted. "I am coming too! Wait!" Ignoring his plea, she sprinted back to their hiding place.

She paid no mind to the branches and brambles that scratched her arms as she pumped them faster and faster toward the source of the cry. Her eyes narrowed with focus as she leapt over buried roots and fallen twigs, hurdling over hewn trunks that remained fixed in the earth, stubby reminders of former growth. Thanks to the many years she had spent roaming the woods with Philippe, she knew its secret pathways as well as the lines on the palm of her hand. Another chilling scream made her quicken her pace.

Racing with abandon, she did not see the hidden vine whose tendrils caught beneath her foot. She stumbled and fell face down, her left cheek hitting the ground with a thud. As she took a few deep breaths to gather herself, the metallic taste of blood filled her mouth from where her teeth had pierced her tongue. With little time to consider her own pain, she pulled herself up and resumed running.

As she drew closer to their secret spot, she somehow knew that her life would never be the same again. It was a funny feeling—to be living the moment and yet be fully aware that it would impact her forever. It was as if she were both inside and outside of what was occurring.

Upon arriving, she saw that the area was no longer hidden. The hanging branches had been ripped away and cast aside. They now lay on the ground, strewn about in uneven piles. With no thought for her own protection, she darted through the widened opening.

She crumpled to her knees at the sight, thrusting both fists into her mouth and biting down hard on her knuckles. Before her lay Ada Renouf, the bloody stump of her neck leaking red droplets into an expanding pool of liquid. Her kerchiefed head, fully detached from her body, lay a distance away, tilted a little to the side as if considering something of great import. The woman's eyes were wide open, eternally searching the ground for some missing item. For a few timeless seconds, Celia remained suspended, unable to do anything. The brutality of what lay before her blocked her capacity to think. All she could do was stare.

But something clicked in her brain. "Vivienne?" she cried.

"Oh, my God. Oh, my God. Vivienne, where are you?" Her hands and knees became stained with blood as she crawled around the confines of the wooded space. Their sacks had been emptied of belongings, but she lifted up the bundles anyway just in case there was some trace of her sister. Doing her best to avoid making contact with Ada's body parts, she left a red trail behind her as she scoured every inch of the covert, calling out her sister's name with ever increasing panic. In the deepest corner of their shelter, she spied a small piece of fabric jutting out from beneath a fallen tree branch.

Holding her breath, Celia inched her way closer to the fabric, praying that the child had scurried there to hide. Perhaps she had found safety there? Celia whispered tenderly, "Vivienne? Do not worry, *mon petit coeur*. Sissy is here. Do not be frightened. It is only me."

Her heart ached with desperation as she extended her arm toward the cloth, her fingers tingled with the anticipation of finding a living child beneath that green canopy. She made contact with the remnant and tugged at it gently. It gave way too easily. No living treasure lay within. With mounting dread, Celia slowly began to pull. Instead of plucking her sister from danger, Celia found only the child's plaything—a rag doll, lifeless and wet from Vivienne's teething. She brought it to her face, moistening it further with tears.

*   *   *   *   *

She must not give up. She needed to keep going, keep searching. As long as there was no body, there was still hope Vivienne was alive. Casting the doll aside, she pushed herself off the ground, ignoring the red splotches on her skirt and the rusty smell of sweat, blood, and worry in the air. Outside the enclosure came a rustling of leaves and heavy footsteps. She snatched a tree branch from the ground and waited beside the entrance to greet her uninvited guest. Coiled and ready to spring, she listened.

A familiar voice broke the silence. "Celia, are you in there?" Hubert called out to her.

How lucky he is not to know the truth, thought Celia. She wished she could protect him from what he was about to see. Dropping her club to the ground, she knew there was nothing she could do to shield him from the horror that awaited.

Hubert yelled once more before stepping over the fallen branches by the entrance. Then he froze, fixed to the spot as he surveyed the gore. Overwhelmed, he collapsed to the ground. Celia assumed he had fainted until she noticed the dagger lodged in his lower back.

What kind of monster was this man who let Hubert see his wife's mutilated body first before stabbing him? The thought instilled anger in her more so than fear.

Grasping the club once again, she marched toward the opening, her voice hysterical with rage and grief over the loss of all three of her loved ones. "You bastard! Come get me too! Kill us all! What are you waiting for?" She yelled even louder, spinning her head side-to-side. "Come out where I can see you! Where did you put her? Where is my sister?"

No one emerged. No one stepped forward. The killer or killers lurked somewhere in the forest, but none took claim for the carnage. The stillness was broken only by the warbling of morning birds heralding dawn. In frustration, Celia pounded a fallen tree trunk with her club until sweat ran down her neck and the wood began to splinter. After the club completely snapped in two, she picked up both halves, pivoted off one foot, and thrust each one into the distance. She no longer cared about protecting herself. "Where are you, you cowards?" she sobbed. "Kill me too." She collapsed in grief to the ground. "Come," her voice choking with misery, "and kill me too."

Nothing. No response.

Still hoping and waiting for death, she crawled back inside the enclosure and looked upon the two dead bodies. Two lives stolen. And for what reason? What harm had they ever done to anyone, and yet this was how they were forced to end their days? At the receiving end of a blade sharpened by greed and power? She knelt down and pulled the dagger out of Hubert's back. After wiping the blood on his clothing, she shoved the knife deep into the pocket of her cloak to keep for herself. Placing both her hands on the side of his rib cage, she flipped over his body. The leaves crinkled beneath him when he landed on his back. Standing up, she moved toward his head and reached down to grab both of his arms. Then she dragged him closer to where his wife's body lay and placed him by her side. She struggled with what she had to do next, not wanting to even look upon the severed head, but she knew she must somehow restore it to its proper place. Looking around the small room, she saw the cloth that had been emptied of the couple's belongings and moved to go pick it up. Once in hand, she shuffled reluctantly toward the head, focusing her eyes in the other direction. When she felt she was near, she dropped the cloth onto the body part, but could not bring herself to touch it.

She looked toward heaven. "Please, Lord. Help me get through this." With a deep breath, she tucked the fabric around the back of the head and carried it toward the paired bodies. Gently, she placed it atop the open neck where the blood had since congealed. She decided she would not remove the cloth.

There was nothing more she could do for them, for these two friends who had rescued her and tried to do the same for Vivienne. Thoughts of her sister compelled Celia to pray once more. Raising her interlocked hands, she begged. "Please, Lord. When will this be enough? Help me get through this. If she is alive, show me how to find her. Help me. Help my soul. And if she is gone, grant me release through death."

Celia's eyes were closed as she sent her petition to heaven. She kept them shut while she prayed for a miracle, fully aware that the longer she waited, the less likely it would be for her wish to come true. Her sister was gone. What more was there to say or do?

When the morning birdsong was interrupted by the sounds of steps and a thud, steps and a thud, she figured it must be another villain or soldier—their identities had become interchangeable. He was approaching her hiding place. She just wanted to get it over with. She would offer no resistance when he thrust his blade into her body and thankfully ended her suffering. She was ready. She welcomed the end and slowly opened her eyes. But instead of death, she was granted a new lease on life.

In front of her was the miracle she had wished for. Little Vivienne staggered toward her on her unwieldy toddler legs. Not seeing the two bodies behind Celia, the child pointed to the rag doll flung into the corner and uttered the single word, "Mine."

*   *   *   *   *

How quickly tears of sorrow can transform to ones of joy. Celia squeezed and squeezed her sister's little body to prove that the child was real. She needed confirmation that Vivienne was flesh and blood and not some exceptionally vivid dream. Replacing hiccupping sobs with laughter, Celia felt silly with elation, while Vivienne, clutching her doll to her chest, seemed confused by all the fuss.

Celia was careful to prevent her sister from seeing the bodies. She lifted her into her arms and carried her outside the enclosure. "Where were you? Where did you go?" Pushing the stray hairs away from

Vivienne's face, she tucked them gently behind the child's ears. The child was too preoccupied with her doll to answer, so Celia kept the monologue going. "You must not *ever* leave me again, *ma bichette*, without telling me! You understand? You must tell me always where you are going. Do you understand?" She did not wait for the child's reply. They had to get away from this place of blood and death.

Aside from each other, there was nothing more to gather up and take away with them. Everything they had—except the two containers of water that she had left by the stream—was gone. With no time or equipment to properly bury her kindly neighbors, Celia prayed for the repose of their souls and guided Vivienne toward the stream to retrieve the flagons and continue their journey.

Despite the smoke that came from the smoldering ruins of cottages and lost dreams, daybreak came as it always did, unaffected by man's atrocities. Nature paid no mind to man's propensity for evil as the gray haze eventually dissipated into the expanding blue sky. The birds too carried on with their usual twittering and foraging, and as the sun rose higher, its rays shone in between the tree branches, dappling the ground with splotches of light.

But Celia could not sweep aside her brush with death as readily as did Nature. Haunted by her thoughts, she could feel her hands tremble as she lifted the bottles from the stream and placed them into their traveling sack. Slinging the carrier over her shoulder, she bent down to lift Vivienne to her chest when the child spoke.

"We going?" she asked. "We going where? There?" and she used her doll to point back toward the forest area they had just left.

When Celia kept walking forward without answering, Vivienne became insistent. "We going *there*?" Her voice raised in pitch on the last word. The truth was that Celia did not have an answer. Where were they going? Where could they go? Who would take them in— two people without a home, without family, without possessions?

How many others were destitute like them? Even though she had no clear destination in her mind, she put one foot in front of the other and just started walking. She kept it simple—one step, then another, then another. Despite the briskness of her stride, she kept a keen eye about her, glancing around the foliage for any signs of an intruder. Vivienne must have sensed a purpose to Celia pace because she stopped asking any further questions.

The snap of a twig. It came from behind. Celia stopped and waited. Then nothing, save the chirping birds and Vivienne's nonsensical gibberish. Cautiously, she resumed her stride, but there it was again. The sound of movement, footsteps crunching the leaves upon the ground. Then silence. She turned around abruptly, the suddenness silencing the child's song. But Celia saw nothing.

She changed direction, veering off the trampled path toward the right, heading deeper into the forest. Each time she came upon a thick tree trunk, she ducked behind it and waited. Nothing. A few more paces and then another stop. Could she outrun their pursuer? Probably not. She must remain hidden and hope he passed by without noticing them.

Squatting closer to the ground, she put her sister down and scoured the earth for large rocks. Spotting two oversized ones a few trees away, she grabbed Vivienne's hand and pulled her over to the spot. Clutching a rock now in the palm of each hand, she hushed the child and waited.

Nothing seemed to happen for quite some time, but then she heard it again. More footsteps. From her low vantage point, she saw first a pair of spindly legs. They moved cautiously—a few steps and then a halt. It was somewhat unbalanced, more side to side than purposely forward as if the person had been out carousing all night. After a few lateral steps, the stranger paused before resuming his unsteady gait.

Compromised or not, he still posed a threat to her and Vivienne. She remained alert, ready to launch the rocks if need be.

The child sensed Celia's intensity. She nestled in closer beneath her sister's arm, ducking her head to breathe in the security she found there. Celia continued to watch. As the man's body became more visible, she saw the reason for his faltering steps. A blood-stained cloth encircled his stomach, the darkest portion of it resting above his left hip. His right arm hugged close against the wound, as if to keep his insides in place. As his right foot stepped forward, his left had to be coaxed by his guiding arm to keep up, thus making his movements uneven and slow.

This was no time for pity. Whether commoner or soldier, he embodied danger and must be removed. If she took the chance to strike him now, two things could happen: her throw could miss him entirely and they would be caught and killed, or she could hit the target and live to see another few hours.

It would serve her conscience well to strike him before she saw his face. Let him remain anonymous. But the distance between them was too great and confidence in her accuracy was slim. So she continued to watch, gently lifting her arm away from Vivienne and shifting her position so that her left foot was slightly in front of the right, primed for throwing.

As the man drew closer, his neck and then his head came into view, and she saw not the bold face of a seasoned warrior but the skittish look of a beardless teen. Dropping both rocks to the ground, she cried out, "Emil? Emil Valentin? Oh, my goodness, Emil, is it you?" Tears of relief wet her eyelashes as she darted toward the boy who nearly collapsed from exhaustion into her arms.

For different reasons, each was grateful to have found the other. Celia was going to embrace him in welcome but thought better of it, thinking of the pain he must be in. Soon Vivienne trotted over to join in the celebration, but she too stopped short. She pointed to the bandage. "Boo boo? You have bad boo boo. Sissy, kiss and make better?" She tugged Celia's hand with her plea.

"Yes, we will make Emil all better, little one. I promise." She tapped the child on the head and then opened the sack to offer the flagon to him. "Here," she lifted it from the sack. "Drink. Come, sit down."

Taking the bottle with his left hand, he took a full swallow, handed it back to her, and wiped his lips with the back of the same hand. His right never moved. He held it in place, fastened to the left side of his body.

His eyes softened as he spoke. "There is no time to rest, Celia. All is gone. My sisters have been kidnapped. My father killed. My mother trampled to death. Our home, the entire village destroyed." His face was smudged with dirt and grime. His hair hung flat around his face, wet and moist from sweat. With a shaking hand, he grasped his forehead, squeezing his temples in anguish. "I had a horse—at first. But they cut me and took him." He looked down at his left side. "They will pay for this, Celia. They will pay for what they have done to us, to our people." His eyes, young and innocent no more, narrowed and clouded over with vengeance. As he straightened his posture, he grimaced in pain. "Come, we shall travel together, Celia, the three of us. I realize I may not look very strong right now, but I am. I am fueled by hatred. Hatred for King Henry and his army. I will protect you, guard you both with all that I have."

"Oh, Emil," Celia bent to kiss his free hand, "of course we will go with you. You are our savior. We are alive because of the Renoufs. They came for us, helped us escape. And that was because you alerted them to the danger and saved them. But now they are gone. Oh, Emil, they were killed. Both of them. It happened so fast. I could do nothing for them, and they did everything for us. So we are alone now,

Vivienne and I. We have no home, and nowhere to go. We would be grateful to have the chance to travel with you, to pay you back in some way for the good you have done for us. Let me help you as we go along." She lifted his hand to her cheek, caressing it there. Her eyes closed in gratitude.

Vivienne, too young to fully understand everything going on, intuitively sensed the power of the moment—the man's offer, her sister's tears, the idea that they would all be together. Wanting to do something for Emil, she broke her promise not to stray and wandered away a short distance toward an old tree stump where a patch of lavender wild flowers grew from its base. Plucking one, she held it carefully in one hand and cupped it gently with the other. When she returned to Emil, she extended her gift to him. "For you?" she said in a soft whisper.

Because of his wound, he could not bend down to thank her, but he accepted her token and smiled grandly. "Thank you, my lady. And would you like to go on an adventure with me? You and your sister? Both of you. Would you?" His eyes glistened with the promise of better days ahead.

"Oh, yes," she bobbed her head up and down emphatically. "Celia, we can go, yes?" Celia blinked back her sorrow and nodded silently. "Where we go?" Vivienne asked.

Emil glanced at Celia first before answering the little girl. "We are going to a castle. Would you like that? We are going to see Duke William and Lady Matilda." And to Celia, he added. "There you will find shelter, and I an army. A place for your safety and a sword for my vengeance."

Celia lifted Vivienne into her arms once again while Emil continued to hug his side. Although his steps were still unsteady and his pace rather slow, he moved with determination, holding fast to the purple wildflower he clutched tightly in his free hand.

*   *   *   *   *

Putting one foot in front of the other eventually became easier, thanks to the group of fellow travelers who had come to join them. All refugees. All displaced. All in need of food and shelter. And a journey that should have taken a few hours wound up lasting two days as they walked only at night and had to go very slowly because of the number of children in their company and their lack of conveyances— no horses, no carts, no wagons. Just themselves, their poorly shod feet, and their flickering hopes. Emil managed to recognize a familiar face or two and was thus able to beg for a chunk of brown bread and some beans or nuts to later divide among the three of them. And Celia kept the group supplied with fresh water, filling the bottles from the river.

Despite the group swelling to over twenty people, the three remained together, never straying more than a few feet apart whether moving or resting. Now that they were nearing their destination, Celia let Vivienne do a little walking beside them. Looking up at Celia, Vivienne's eyes danced with joy and twinkled with light even though darkness enveloped them. "I walk with Chloe too?" she pleaded.

It was too dark for Vivienne to see Celia shake her head to say no, so instead Celia whispered it curtly. Fastening a cloth around Vivienne's waist, Celia tethered her to her wrist, leashing her up like a farm animal. "No, we cannot go looking for Chloe now. We must keep moving ahead." She finished tying the knot. "When we get to where we need to go and it is time for rest, then you can look for your friend." Celia continued to march forward. No one could see the look of dismay on the child's face, but the drooping of her head wordlessly conveyed her feelings.

They moved on in silence for quite some time with Celia alternating between carrying her sister and letting her walk on her own. The trio almost always found themselves at the rear of the cavalcade because of Vivienne's whimsical behavior and Emil's debilitating injury. But that night the sound of running feet came from behind them, and then a single whisper of "Vivienne?"

Soon, the whisper was followed by a voice filled with agitation. "Get back here, Chloe! How dare you run from me! Stop right there, you little toad, or I am going to toss you into the boiling pot with the stew!"

Vivienne stopped in her tracks and yanked on the rope to gain Celia's attention. "Chloe's coming now, Celia! We go to her, please? She is right there," and as Vivienne pointed toward a distant tree, she leaned as far as her restraint would allow. The tether tightened and Celia softened.

Why deny the girl this companionship? Have I learned nothing? Facing the world alone makes everything so much harder. Nodding to Emil, she told the child, "Yes, we can go to her. Come."

Once reunited, the two girls giggled and held hands as Celia and Chloe's mother continued moving north toward Duke William's nearly finished castle where, with his help and that of Lady Matilda, they could all make a new start together. With hearts lightened by friendship, they carried on, mile after mile, ignoring the discomfort because they had each other.

Eventually, the velvet darkness gave way to a rose colored sky glowing with promise. The fortress stood resolute before them. Amidst the rubble of the town, its round towers remained, daring the enemy to test its fortifications. Bathed in heavenly protection, it seemed impenetrable.

Finally, Celia could stop worrying about their fate. They would find protection here. Their hunger would be satisfied. Their weary bodies would find rest. Without consciously deciding so, the group quickened its pace to match its rising hopes as the wooden drawbridge stretched out invitingly before them. Vivienne still had her hand fixed to Chloe's, and Celia looked over the girls' heads to speak to Chloe's mother.

"We have made it, Rowena. It was not an easy journey, but we have made it." Celia smiled broadly, blinking back tears that wanted to fall in memory of family and friends who were not as lucky as they. Still keeping a determined eye on her daughter, Rowena reached over her protruding stomach and across the gap to squeeze Celia's hand.

"We have, my dear, we have. Can you see anything? I am too short, but you are long and lean and must have a better view. Can you see what is going on at the front?" Rowena stretched her neck to its full length and bobbed her head from side to side. The extra weight she carried from pregnancy made her movements awkward. "All I can see are the legs and bodies of the people directly in front of us. Ugh." She squeezed Celia's hand tighter. "Tell me, love. Tell me what you see."

Celia marveled at the strength of the woman beside her. In less than a month, Rowena would be bringing another child into this cruel world, and she would be doing so without the comfort of home or the support of a husband. On that fateful night, Felix had thrust Rowena and their daughter from their beds and pushed them toward escape while he stayed behind to distract the vandals. He never reappeared. Now Rowena and Chloe were all alone, their fragile future balancing on how things would go once they arrived at the Duke's residence.

Celia raised herself up onto her toes and swiveled her head in and out of the breaks between the people who were ahead of them. "I see . . . yes, I see Duke William's soldiers. They are in the center of the bridge. They are embracing our menfolk. And . . . over to the right, there are some tables with baskets of food. Servants are standing behind those tables, handing out what appears to be bread and cheese." Celia kept up with the moving crowd by continuing to walk mincingly on her toes. "I see people crossing through the gatehouse now. Praise God, let this nightmare be over." She turned toward Emil and tapped him on his arm. "If we should get separated, how shall I find you? We owe you our lives. I must repay you somehow." Her blue eyes warmed with gratitude.

Despite the excitement, the young man slowed down and stopped. "Celia, you owe me nothing. It was you two who kept me going. After all the savagery, I kept asking, Why? Why let me live? Why were all those I loved killed and yet not myself? Were it not for your need of protection, I would have given up, crawled into my grief and let my wounds usher me into the next world. But you made me keep going. I had to ... for the sake of you both. So do not thank me. I must thank you for restoring my will to live." He reached down to kiss her hand.

"When we get through the gates," he continued, "I need to seek the surgeon. Once I am tended to and he gives me his blessing, I shall be leaving to join William's army wherever they may go. My sorrow is gone. Dried up. Vengeance has taken its place. My heart cannot rest until my sword drips with the blood of King Henry's men." He cupped his two hands over hers. "Let this then be my farewell to you, Celia, and someday when your sister is old enough to bear the weight of such heavy memories, let her know that her spirit beats on in the heart of this soldier." He released his grip on her hand. "I shall think of you often, *mon sauveur*." With that, he ducked away before Celia could respond. She watched him hobble toward his chosen destiny before letting her gaze rest upon the two little girls whose hands were still clasped together. Perhaps they too were walking toward their destiny, bound together for the days to come.

A PLEDGE FOR THE FUTURE

CAEN, NORMANDY – DECEMBER 1060

The water in the large vat had begun to boil. Small bubbles increased in number and frequency. Celia reached down and hoisted up the heavy bucket filled with fermented urine that would serve to bleach the dirty household linens. Needing to wait for the water to return again to a boil, she moved away from the basket of soiled clothing and ambled over to the stable to breathe in the memory of better times.

Not that her current situation was bad. She crossed over the threshold and into the barn. Vivienne was thriving, she herself had steady work, and they both had food, shelter, and each other. Celia's feet crumpled the leftover strands of straw that littered the narrow walkway which ran up and down the stalls.

"Hello there, beauty." She wrapped one arm beneath the thick neck of the roan-colored mare and laid her cheek against its mane. She breathed in. Coming here was both her solace and her torment, for it brought back sweet thoughts of the days she had spent with her father as well as the anguish of knowing those days would never return.

When she was barely up to Papa's knee, he had her sitting atop Honey, the gentle pony who moved with an intuitive awareness of Celia's vulnerability. Even when Celia had grown bigger and taller, she still chose Honey to be the one she rode over the hills and meadows of the countryside, never wanting to abandon her first friend. But the time did come when she had to leave the small pony behind, and her father carefully oversaw Celia's gradual progression from one mount to the next. Soon she was as fine a rider as anyone in the entire village. But in moments like these, her mind drifted back to those first days of wonder when, despite Honey's diminutive stature, Celia felt on top of the world. She believed herself to be the duchess of the county and had no doubt whatsoever that she was the center of Papa's world.

That was all gone now. Her mother's death while birthing Vivienne was the beginning of the end. And although Papa lingered after her mother was gone, his heart had turned to dust the moment hers stopped beating. Celia breathed in again, deeper this time, letting the scent of the animal ease her wounded soul. She sighed.

Young Philippe had been ripped away from her as well. In a more practical state of mind, she could acknowledge that his apprenticeship with Jacques was actually a blessing. But when she was feeling wistful and melancholy, as she was now, she could not see the positive side of things. She simply could not muster the discipline needed to crawl out of the pit of loneliness that now swallowed her whole. Simon's departure hollowed out her heart and sank her spirits even further. All that was left were she and Vivienne, forced to fill up the hours with only each other for company.

Celia moved her arm from beneath the horse's neck to stroke the long white line of fur extending from its forehead to its velvety nostrils. Her mind veered back again, this time to that horrific night when they were forced to take to the road in fear. Witnessing the destruction of everything they had ever known—the houses, the livestock, the crops, the people. The loss of Emil's entire family. The brutal killing of Ada Renouf and her husband. Then the frightening journey she was forced to take with only ghosts for company, where the snap of every twig and the screech of every night animal confirmed Death was pursuing them from the shadows.

She made her way to the side of the horse and ran her hand across its body from shoulder to haunch. Long, slow strokes calmed her mind as her thoughts turned slowly from despair to hope. She was here. In this place. For two years now. And so was Vivienne. They had survived thus far anyway. Questions about the future beyond the next day she shut down. It was impossible for her to imagine anything but the immediate present. So she contented herself with the situation they were in now, and let the past return to being buried.

She smiled tentatively now as she breathed in her father's presence, treasuring also the years she had spent with her mother and the good fortune that had come Philippe's way. She prayed for Simon's safety and whispered a blessing upon the Renoufs and Emil for delivering her to this new life. And with that, she could dawdle no longer. It was time for her to go back outside to check on the water in the vat.

The sound of approaching footsteps interrupted her musings. "Why did you not ask me to help you carry the water to the tub, Celia?" A chubby stableboy poked his head into Brigette's stall. "You know I would have brought it up for you." His saucer-like brown eyes widened with the disappointment of rejection.

"Oh, Cantrell," she said kindly, "you are much too busy with your own tasks to stop and do those that are mine." Celia brushed past him, exiting the barn to return to her laundry station.

Cantrell hovered beside her like a fly buzzing near a morsel of food. "It is no bother, ever," he protested. "I can help you any time and still not fall behind on my own responsibilities." His closely cropped black hair was cut unevenly on one side, and his thick nose turned up a bit like a piglet's, but Celia found him a pleasant young man—if somewhat annoying in his devotion to her.

He raced to get in front of her. "Maybe I can stir the pot for you? Here let me help." He dropped to the ground to pick up a large stick that he could use to stir the clothes around in the bleached water. He held the stick, eagerly awaiting Celia's nod of approval.

She giggled. Strands of her shiny black hair loosened and escaped from under her bonnet as she shook her head from side to side. "Cantrell, you are always too kind to me. Please, please, go take care of your own work and know that I am fine. Besides," she glanced at him sideways, "I would not want Mallory to think I am trying to steal her man away from her!" Celia winked mischievously at him, her blue eyes shimmering and dancing in shared confidence.

He stood taller, trying to make himself appear more independent. "I am nobody's man, Celia. I have told you that before. And I am not hanging around here much longer if I have my way. You know why? Because Duke William is going to take me with him on his next expedition. I am sure you have seen many of the soldiers coming back already, have you not? Returning from Varaville, Tillieres, and the like? They're getting ready for another battle, I am certain of it. And now with the King and Martel both dead and buried, there is no telling what the Duke will do next. The time is right for the army to move into other parts of France." Cantrell puffed himself up with confidence. "And I will be there with them, wherever they go, to extend the Duke's power."

He picked up a single piece of hay and began splitting it in two with his small fingers. He looked down at his hands in shyness. "But if I may, I would like to be *your* man, Celia. If you would have me. If you would wait for me." For a brief moment, he raised his doe eyes to take a peek at Celia who was too busy stirring the pot to take him seriously.

"Look, I have told you before, I am not getting mixed up in any weird love triangle. I am not interested in love. You may not think there is anything between you and Mallory, but she sure does, so you had better set the record straight if you do not want anything to do with her." Celia's patience had worn thin. Why did men have to be so foolish? Friendship was fine, but why did they always try to push for more? She had never done anything to encourage the boy. His request downright irritated her, as did his soft and dreamy manner of speaking and his fantastical visions of their shared future together.

Celia was aware of Mallory's jealousy. The girl resented Cantrell's kindness toward her and Vivienne. Since Celia first arrived, Mallory considered Celia her rival. Such competition made Mallory hide in doorways or behind shrubs to spy on Cantrell. And her later confrontations with him often ended with her storming off in a huff. Too bad those confrontations did not have the impact Mallory had intended. Cantrell looked upon her absence with glee, not pain.

Despite all of that, Celia had to be honest with the young man. The past two years had taught her something about loneliness and survival. "I will tell you one thing, Cantrell. Even if you may not have deep feelings for her just yet, give it time. Time to see if it grows. If you break her heart now, you may end up closing off your own in the process. And that is no way to live." She continued to move the stick in large circles inside the tub, making sure that all of the linens were fully submerged. Cantrell considered her advice but offered no comment. She figured his mind was not expansive enough to understand what she was trying to tell him.

Had she been talking to Cantrell or to herself? Maybe she should have given more time to Simon. More time to focus on the companionship they shared. Perhaps she had closed off her own heart in the process of denying his. Oh, what did it matter now? She needed to finish her tasks. She would let the fabric soak and head back down to the river to fill more buckets for the other vat for the rinsing. But a disturbance in the distance interrupted them both. Together they turned to look up the hill and saw men riding toward the drawbridge. Duke William's gonfanon flew high in the air before them.

Cantrell squealed, "More soldiers! I must go!" He tossed aside his torn hay stick and ran to greet the warriors, but Celia did not share his excitement. These men were probably no different from the ones who had slaughtered her neighbors and destroyed her village. The only distinction was the banner they rode under. She lifted up the two empty buckets and walked downhill toward the riverbank.

Neither she nor Cantrell had been aware that they were being watched.

Engorged with envy, a housemaid dropped the soiled rushes she had been carrying. She propped up her thick arms on her hips and lowered her head like a vulture considering its prey. Cantrell belonged to her. And no one else. She decided right then that someone needed to be taught a lesson.

*   *   *   *   *

Despite it being early December, the river water was not as cold as Celia had expected it to be. No ice chips floated through the current, no frost covered the rocks that poked through the surface. Even so, her hands were still raw and chapped—if not from the temperature, then certainly from the position as laundress to the Duchess.

Her fingers throbbed from mixing together lard and ashes in order to make the lye soap. The muscles in her back and shoulders ached from all the carrying, stirring, and draining that needed to be done in order to clean and dry the clothing, sheets, and tablecloths used in the castle. Dragging wood to heat the tub and tending the fire required consistent vigilance. But at least it freed her to be outdoors, allowing her the chance to catch Vivienne at play.

Celia dropped the second bucket into the river. She would need to make three more trips in order to fill the rinsing tub. Despite the heavy lifting, her eyes sparkled when she thought of her younger sister. The child was growing so fast. Celia shook her head in disbelief, not only at Vivienne's development but mostly for the child's resilience, her untainted joy for life. For someone who had endured so much loss, Vivienne shockingly absorbed none of its corresponding despair. The child was so trusting and had such abiding faith in people's goodness that even the roughest scoundrel viewed himself in a better light once Vivienne shined her smile upon him.

Celia knew it was through God's infinite grace that she and Rowena had been able to pair up two years ago on that night of ruin. Her good friend now served as one of the nursemaids here at Caen, so Celia could rest easy knowing that Vivienne, along with the other displaced children, was in Rowena's loving care.

When the weather was mild, Rowena let the children frolic in the meadow which afforded Celia the opportunity to set up her station closer to their playground. On colder days like this, the children still came outdoors but for shorter periods of time and for more directed activities: a scavenger hunt for specified objects, a prescribed hike around the estate, the identification and discovery of animal tracks. These activities—so brief in duration—kept Celia on alert for when their paths would cross. She rejoiced that at night she and her sister could stay together, but when the sun rose each morning, they each went off to their respective places. Once again, there was a rhythm to their days here at Caen as there was in their old homestead, and Celia was grateful for such predictability and structure—both of which kept her from fretting over what the extended future would bring.

She walked unevenly uphill toward the awaiting vats, her right arm stronger than her left. She leaned a little toward the left side because of the disparity. As she drew closer though, her nose twitched in disgust. *What was that smell?* she thought to herself.

Before she arrived at the boiling cauldron, Cantrell came running down the hill from the drawbridge, his short legs churning, arms pumping up and down. "Celia! Celia! Someone knows you! Here, look, he is coming! He says he knows you! He has come back!"

Like a rolling boulder that picks up speed on the decline, Cantrell was nearly right upon her when she put down her buckets to look beyond the stable boy. From a distance, she could see only a tall, stiff figure coming toward her. Dressed in chainmail and wearing the conical helmet of a knight, the man seemed determined in his stride and focused on his destination. Celia actually looked behind her toward the river to see if maybe the stranger had someone else as his objective, but there was nothing there save the cascading water that darted in and around the rocks.

Cantrell reached her and pulled at her sleeve. "He is coming! He is coming for you. Said he is from your village." The young man stopped abruptly. "Eeeeww, what is that smell?" He crinkled his nose and left her there to go check on the heated vat. "Did hemlock get mixed in with the wood or something? It smells awful!"

Celia's eyes did not stray from studying the approaching warrior. She spoke distractedly. "I am not sure ... I just noticed the stench myself ... and was ... about ... to check it ... when you ... came ... rushing ... down."

Cantrell gazed into the pot. "Oh, no, Celia. Someone has ruined your work!" He turned his face away from the tub in disgust.

Celia was forced to pull her attention away from the nearing soldier in order to investigate what had happened to the linens. She took one glance into the pot and immediately dropped her head between her legs. Dry heaves racked her body.

Cantrell tried to soothe her. "Somebody mixed in chunks of manure with your linens. But do not worry. I can fix it."

She took her anger out on him. "Get away from that and get away from me. For the hundredth time, I do not want or need your help!" She held her breath this time before peering again inside the tub. In it, the clods of dung were breaking apart, darkening the water to a brownish-yellow, leaving fecal residue on all of the clothes inside.

Cantrell's eyes lowered to stare at the ground as he kicked aside a stray pebble with his foot. "Well, if you do not want me to help here, the least I can do is find out who is responsible for committing so foul an act. You will let me do that, won't you?" Looking up, he realized he was about to lose his place to the warrior who was drawing ever closer.

Celia dismissed him, wishing to be rid of the stable boy. "Of course. Go see what you can find out."

The truth was, though, she did not really need Cantrell's help in figuring out who was to blame for the deed. Celia already knew. And she also knew that person would pay mightily for having crossed her.

*   *   *   *   *

The soldier carried no shield and had no sword sheathed by his side. His conical helmet sat upon his head, its visor lifted. His dark brown eyes studied Celia intensely as he took his final steps toward her. In a voice heavy with disappointment at her indifference, he spoke as he walked. "Celia? Do you not know me?" He extended his right hand toward her.

She stopped lifting the stick that she had been using to pull the soiled clothing from the water but made no motion toward the stranger. Instead, she left his hand suspended in the air and turned her back on him to wash her arms in the other bucket of clean water.

"I am sorry, sir," she spoke over her shoulder without looking at him, "but I do not know any knights in the Duke's army. The only men I know are my brother, who is still a young boy, and a former neighbor, who would only be a foot soldier. Not a knight such as yourself." Still facing the other direction, she wiped her hands and arms on her woolen skirt. "Cantrell must have told you my name, but I am afraid that is probably all you really know about me. So if you would be so kind, I need to get on with my work here."

The man dropped his hand but would not leave. He removed his helmet and tucked it in the crook of his arm. His face was lined and ruddy from weathering, and an old scar that traversed his cheek to his jaw was now joined with fresh nicks and dents that dotted his forehead and face. Thick auburn hair, parted down the middle, lay straight in bunches cut short just below the ears. He stepped closer. "Come, look at me, Celia. You must know who I am. I bring word of Philippe to you"

"Philippe?" She turned around quickly and met his gaze. Tilting her head ever so slightly, she spoke hesitantly.. "Simon? Is it ... could it be?" She ran to him. "Oh, Simon! I am so sorry. I did not recognize you. I could not tell." She wrapped her arms around his chest and rested her cheek against the cold links of his chainmail in the space just below his heart. "I did not think it could be you, dressed as you are."

She chided herself. "Oh, how could I not recognize you? How could I not tell? Oh, Simon. You have come back! It has been so long. So much has happened . . . " She pulled away to look up at him, her eyes searching his with deeper yearning.

Her questions ran unbridled. "How is Philippe? Where is he? Is he here? How did you become a knight? Are you hurt? How did you find me? Did you hear what happened to our village, to . . ."

"Slow down, slow down, little squirrel!" He held her at arm's distance so that he could take in her presence. "I will tell you all I know and answer all of your questions, and you shall do the same for me. But first," he lifted his nose in the air, "let us set about making this situation right. Is this a new way to bleach clothing, substituting manure for soap?" He smiled at his teasing.

"Hah! Funny, aren't you?" She playfully swung the stick to tap him on the leg. "No, this base trick was done by someone who will soon regret ever tangling with me."

"Oh, ho! Well, whoever it is will learn not to make the same mistake twice, I daresay! Let me lighten your burden as we talk." Simon gathered more wood from the pile and brought it to the second tub so that they could start the cleaning routine all over again.

Celia breathed a sigh of relief that, at least for a little while, she was not all alone.

*   *   *   *   *

Once everything had been set up anew and the soiled garments rinsed clean, Celia dropped them into the boiling water to bleach them a second time. The ease of conversation flowed just as it had done in bygone days when Simon had taught her how to hunt and fish.

"Yes, Philippe remains with Jacques, and the two of them are in constant demand because of their skill. Duke William relies heavily on his mounted warriors, and much of the army's success can be attributed to Jacques' ability to keep the horses healthy and strong."

Celia stirred the clothing. "I am relieved to hear that my brother is safe with Jacques and not directly on the battlefield, though I am sure he is pushing for it to be so."

"You are right about that, Celia. On one occasion, the old man actually had to resort to using old leather reins on your brother to keep him from grabbing a mount and dashing headlong into the fray." Simon continued to scour the inside of the soiled pot with lye and fresh water.

Celia laughed. "I can believe that. Yes, I do believe that. Philippe always had a grand vision of himself. Even in the pasture outside our little cottage, he walked the land as if it were his own kingdom." She looked up at Simon with interest. "Tell me about Varaville. How did you defeat King Henry?"

Simon stopped cleaning for a moment. "Well, let me tell you something about the Duke. He is a man who knows how to bide his time and then strike. And the force of his personality is so strong that he can convince his men to remain patient and do the same." Simon shook his head in amazement. "He may be the only leader I have ever met who can keep the fire burning inside an entire legion yet hold back the stray sparks until he gives the signal for a full blaze to ignite. No one ever questions or goes against his orders."

He dived back into his work. "And holding back is a very hard thing for a warrior to do when all he wants is to put his anger in his blade. You cannot imagine how enraged, how desperate, how frenzied we all were, having to sit idle and watch Henry's men destroy the very villages and houses we wanted to protect. But wait we did, trusting in William's promise that we'd soon strike in a way that would be unanswerable and final."

Celia rested her chin upon the top of the stick, mesmerized by his story. Her interest spurred him on. "We were a mobile force, and at the time, I was but a foot soldier, as you said earlier. William made us hold off—despite the screams that echoed in our ears, despite the smell of scorched farmland that assaulted our noses, despite the bodies strewn randomly over the ground that our eyes could not avoid. Our fury grew to such levels that it demanded release. And then the moment came."

He finished cleaning the soiled tub and stepped away from it, looking at Celia to measure her approval or disdain. She gestured for him to go on. "Some of Henry's troops had already crossed the river

Dives. And just when the waters began to rise, William gave the signal. Swords raised and banners flying, we attacked their rear guard with such ferocity that the water turned red with blood. Desperate, their men ran toward the crossing, but the bridge was old, and the boards cracked under the weight of the throng. I saw it shake until it finally collapsed, dooming them all to a watery grave. Those who did survive lived only long enough to be felled by blade or club or arrow. It was a cunning move—to hold us back and wait. Such forbearance made our swords sing with vengeance. A resounding victory it was for us."

Shaking his hands dry, he reached down to grab the rope that lay at Celia's feet and began tying it at either end to a tree. "Here, let me draw the line for you."

Celia started hanging the clothes one by one so that they could dry. "You know, Simon, you are speaking only of the joyous end result, nothing of the gory details. Surely, it could not have been so pleasant a fairytale as this." She snapped the linens to whisk away the moisture before hanging each of them on the line.

"Ah, you are ever still a most practical maiden, Celia. The world has taught you to be so." He looked away from her toward the river. "Of course, there was hardship. There was suffering. There was doubt. There was pain. But who can consider such things in a feverish moment? When the panic intensified on and around the bridge, it is true there were a good many bodies that would never rise with the coming morn. There were men and parts of men lying bloodied at my feet. The same fellows I had supped with the eve before, the ones who had playfully motioned for more wine, now lay mutilated on the swampy bank, crying out in agony to be put out of their misery. Their pleas haunt me still in the dark corners of my silence, but I choose to keep the memory of our brotherhood in my heart rather than the vision of their corpses in my mind. So I bury their grisly images and cherish their valor instead. But this is our reunion, Celia, and as brief as it may be, I would rather spend it considering pleasant days ahead than mournful ones that have passed."

He walked down further to the place where she was about to hang the next piece of laundry. There was important news he wanted to share with her, but he did not want her to think him haughty. He shifted his weight from one leg to another while he planned out how he would share with her his good fortune. He cleared his throat. "For certain exceptional deeds I performed at Varaville, I have been given a mount and am now part of a conroy." He forced himself to stop fidgeting even though his heart was racing with expectation and hope. "I have armor and shield and even a new sword. Speaking of something new, I have brought something for you as well." He walked back over to where he had placed his helmet and purse, and from the sack, he pulled a velvet pouch. He returned to where she was standing and handed it to her. Resuming his position on the other side of the clothes line, he held his breath, hoping that he had pleased and not offended her.

He felt the need to justify his present. "It is just a small gift, really, something that had been left behind in one of the abandoned estates we passed on our way back to Caen. Most of the soldiers took the spoils that remained—silver goblets, gold coins, bejeweled brooches, and rings. But when I saw these, I thought of you, and how a woman of your beauty deserved such things." He studied her.

Celia pulled the strings of the pouch and looked inside. "Oh, Simon. They are exquisite!" She pulled out a brush and comb made of pure ivory, the bristles of the brush soft but firm. In the winter sunlight, the bone color of the set deepened with richness. "Simon! How thoughtful! I honestly do not know what to say! Can you imagine me—the one who never stops babbling when I am with you —to be without words? Not just because of the elegance of such a gift but because of your sweetness in thinking of me." She lifted the pouch close to her chest while casting her soft, blue eyes upon his face.

Her look was so enchanting that he had to break away from it and gaze down at the grass beneath his feet. His voice quavered. "How can I not think of you, Celia? Knowing what had happened to our lands? To our homes? I worried every day about you and Vivienne, but I could secure no word of your safety. Until today. I nearly squeezed the life out of that young stableboy when he told me that you were here." He turned shy again, as if he were a child afraid of being reprimanded rather than a warrior who had just cheated death. "You know, Celia, I have been gifted a plot of land in Dives-sur-Mer and will settle there once my military service is completed." He had the courage to lift his gaze from the ground back to her face as he shifted his feet back and forth on the opposite side of the hanging line. "I hear the fishing there is quite good. Perhaps we could—together— throw my net into those waters some day?" His brown eyes were soulful with yearning.

His longing matched her own. She so wanted to be protected and cared for—and in Simon's arms, she knew she would find both—but at what cost? He would want something in return, would he not? And that something would involve much more than companionship. The prospect of taking that next step into marriage meant the inevitability of intimacy and the subsequent birthing of children. As taut as the rope that ran from tree to tree, the noose of commitment tightened around her throat so that her response was choked into silence.

Simon's proposal simply danced away upon the air just like the linens that snapped, rippled, and lifted with the breeze.

*　　*　　*　　*　　*

Celia's encounter with Simon unsettled her. It was so much easier to focus on the present moment than to envision a picture of the

126

distant future. With her first set of laundry done, she sought out Rowena.

The children were sitting in pairs on the floor of the room, sorting out winter berries they had picked. Most of them were gathered in the center, save one boy who sat near the door all by himself, working happily on his own. Rowena walked from group to group, kneeling down to engage them in discussion as to what they had found and where. With Grace, her youngest child, wrapped in her arms, Rowena then asked Vivienne to hand out small woolen pouches for the children to use as containers for each type of berry.

Celia stood still in the doorway, wanting to remain unnoticed. She observed Vivienne's head bob up and down as the child skipped joyfully from pair to pair. Swirls of curly blonde hair peeked out from beneath her bonnet, framing a pink, heart-shaped face that glowed with health and innocence. Vivienne's eyes were nearly translucent, like the delicate shell of a robin's egg in early spring. Celia once again took pride in the life she had given her sister, a life where she was protected from the wolves lurking outside the door. It was Celia who kept that door latched. It was she who leaned her own body against it to prevent it from opening. Willingly would she give her own life to ensure the preservation of her sister's.

Watching the child move about the room with such joy was worth every night Celia went hungry, every death she witnessed, every secret she kept hidden. This was her reward for such sacrifices.

Rowena looked up and saw Celia standing there. "Come in, my friend! Come see what we have collected!" She placed little Grace on the ground next to one set of children and was about to usher Celia into the room when Vivienne darted in front of her and blocked her way.

"Slow down, *mon mignon*," Rowena said gently.

Vivienne wrapped her tiny arms around Celia's legs, burying her head in her sister's waist. "Celia! Come over, come see our berries!" The child gestured toward the vacated spot where she had been partnered with her best friend Chloe.

Rowena touched Vivienne's bonnet. "Wait, Vivienne. Let me greet Celia first, and then she shall go and inspect your findings."

"All right," she responded good-naturedly before she wagged her small finger at Celia to signal her sister to bend down to her. Once there, the child caressed both sides of Celia's head and kissed her on the cheek before trotting off to finish distributing the pouches.

"First round of laundry done, eh?" Rowena asked.

"Yes, just thought I had take a quick break before starting up again," Celia's eyes went to the boy off to the side. "What happened with Andre? Misbehaving again?" She asked the question matter of factly, fully expecting to hear that the boy was in trouble yet again. Andre often acted out as abominably as did his arrogant mother Jeanette, one of Matilda's ladies-in-waiting. Jeanette constantly reminded everyone that, had her husband not perished at Val-es-Dunes, she herself would have been a duchess, giving orders rather than following them.

Small waif though he was, Andre had an enormous opinion of himself and hated whenever anyone else was singled out for praise. He destroyed their crafts when he was jealous and pushed around the younger ones when he was being willful. Sometimes, he even threatened Rowena when forced to partake of any activity he did not like, saying he would report her to his mother who would then, in turn, inform Matilda.

"He has the fungus again," Rowena whispered, lifting her chin in his direction. "Watch. He will start pulling and scratching at his head any minute now. His hair has just grown back after the last bout with it. I sent for his mother, but she is with Matilda. They are checking on the progress of the women's abbey, so she will not be returning until late afternoon."

Rowena ushered Celia over to one of the tables in the back corner of the room and pulled out both chairs. "Come, sit." She took the pitcher of wine and poured it into two cups. "I had to put him off to the side because I do not want him to spread it to the other children. Sadly, it hasn't been a problem keeping them away because nobody likes him anyway. I would feel sorry for him if he were not so incorrigible and if I did not hate Jeanette as much as I do. He is too young to see his mother for the witch she is, but I keep hoping to instill some sense of proper behavior by praising him publicly when he does good and pulling him away from the group and reprimanding him privately when he does wrong. I have seen a slight change for the better."

She took a sip of the wine. "But today's situation is not really his fault. What can a child do when his mother cares more for herself than for him? His head will need to be shaved again before he can return though."

She put down her cup and reached across the table to pat Celia's hand. "And how are things with you, *ma mie*?" The woman's smile was warm and inviting.

Celia felt bad complaining like this to Rowena, a woman who had it so much worse. She was raising two daughters all by herself while still grieving over the loss of her husband. Yet, she soldiered on. And not only that, Rowena had absorbed none of the bitterness which often accompanies such tragedy. Rowena spoke often of Felix and did so with a lilt in her voice and a gleam in her eye, as if the man were simply tending to his sheep and coming home later for dinner. She had kept his memory alive for both Chloe and Grace in such a way that the girls carried only laughter and smiles inside them rather than resentment and sorrow. Knowing Rowena to be far wiser than herself, Celia leaned upon her for comfort and direction.

"Well, two things have come up actually. Two things that I need your opinion on." Celia heard Grace starting to fuss, so she went over to retrieve the child and then plopped her into Rowena's arms. "Mallory is at it again…"

"Oh, no!" Rowena interrupted. She bounced Grace up and down in her lap. "Whatever is that girl's problem?"

"I thought I had taught her a lesson about tangling with me when I poured warm lard under her bed sheets for a 'soothing' night's sleep, but I am afraid she has done it again. This time she put manure into my cleaning tub when I was not looking. So I must come up with another form of restitution. But it has to be something more long-lasting than a single uncomfortable night. Something more enduring, yes?"

Grace was still fussing, so Rowena placed her finger in the child's mouth and let her gnaw on it. "Hmmm. Well, we have to give this one some thought and come up with something really good. Why she thinks you would even be interested in a fellow like Cantrell makes no sense to me! With your looks, *mon cherie*, you could have the Duke himself if you so desired!"

"Oh, shush, Rowena! You know how I feel. I will not be turned into a breeding mare—" Her words escaped her mouth before she had the tact to realize what she had said. "I am so sorry, Rowena. You know I meant that only for me. There is clearly something wrong with me, inside my head, I guess. I just do not have any wish to be a mother—not that there is anything wrong with being a mother—it is just that it is wrong for me, that is all." She folded her hands and rested them on the table, begging Rowena to understand her intent.

"No offense have I taken, Celia. I know how you feel about marriage and men, and I know your words were intended only for you." She looked over at Vivienne and then back at Celia. "You do realize though that you *have* already been a mother, and a rather outstanding one at that, for these past few years, do you not?"

"That is different though. I did not have to endure anything for Vivienne to come into this world. My mother bore the burden of that and look what became of her." Celia's voice cracked. She cleared her throat.

"Which brings me to the second thing I wanted to talk to you about. Simon, the neighbor I told you about, the man who helped me carry on after mother's death and father's surrender? Simon is back."

Celia spoke so sadly that Rowena was confused. "So what is the problem then? Are you not glad to see this man?"

Celia looked down at her hands on the table as if ashamed. "I am happy. That is why I am worried. I am happy. I let him know how thrilled I was to see him safe and alive, and now he thinks there is something more to that."

Grace had drifted off to sleep in her mother's arms. Rowena removed her finger from the baby's slackened mouth and wiped it on her skirt. "Do *you* think it means more than that?"

Celia wanted to slam her hands against the tabletop in frustration but held back for the sake of the napping child. "I do not know, Rowena. I just do not know. I know that I missed him. And I know I could readily go with him and bring Vivienne with me to the new estate he has been promised when the fighting is over. But I would want to go only as his friend and not as his wife, and I do not think that he—or any other man for that matter—would want to throw in his lot with a woman and her little sister unless there was something in it for him. So I think I had rather stay here and be under no obligation to anyone than be forced to give away all of myself to another."

Rowena looked at Celia with tenderness but made no comment. The minutes passed, laden with unspoken words, while the chatter of the children continued in the background.

Celia asked pointedly, "What do *you* think I should do, Rowena? What would you do?"

Rowena exhaled deeply, curling her lips and closing her eyes. "I cannot tell you what to do, Celia, just as I cannot tell you how to feel. You must follow your heart as I once followed my own. In the beginning, I never had passionate dreams about Felix where I would wake up in the morning panting with desire for him. Nor did my voice catch or my hands tremble when I was in his presence. You know, all the things poets sing of in their verses. But Felix was steady and reliable and trustworthy. He fluttered my heart not with yearning but with laughter. He was so clever and so amusing. I came to adore his antics and drew strength from his ability to make the toughest of situations more manageable.

And he loved me. Oh, how he loved me, deeply, so deeply. I knew that no matter how ugly and unappealing I thought I was, how irritable and cranky I would behave, or how wrinkly and toothless I would one day become, Felix would always see me as the light of his life. When you feel a certainty like that in another person, a magical thing sometimes happens. You find your own feelings growing and expanding, and soon your heart is overflowing with a love that goes beyond storybook traditions. Now even though he is gone, when I wake up each morn, I am grateful to have heard the echo of his laughter in my dream the night before. And that echo readies me to take on the new day because I carry inside the foundation of his belief in me.

So I cannot tell you, *mon tresor*, what you should do. I can only tell you this. Do not close off your heart to a man who wants only to give himself to you. Do not deny him that chance. He may be satisfied with just being able to serve you and nothing more. And who knows? Perhaps some day your affection for him will intensify to the point where you will embrace him not just as a companion but as a true partner in life, in all of its aspects."

Celia pondered Rowena's words, remaining still without responding. She wondered if it could be like that. Perhaps they could just go along as they were—she and Simon—without attaching any definition to their alliance. Then she could let the future unfold day by day. After all, he was heading back to battle anyway, so she needn't take any action at the moment. Her meditation was broken when Andre yelled out to Rowena from the doorway.

"Rowena, my hair is on fire with itching. I must go to the river—now!"

The boy's announcement made something click in Celia's mind. She sprang from her chair inspired by the flash of a brilliant idea. In answer to Andre's call, she turned to Rowena. "I will take him. Relax and stay here with the children. I have just thought of a way to solve my first problem."

While nothing had to be done for the moment with regard to Simon, the time was ripe for exacting revenge on her manure-bearing enemy, Mallory.

*　　*　　*　　*　　*

Mallory stared at the clump of hair in her hand. Strands that were once rooted to her head now filled the teeth of her comb, looking lifeless in her palm. Her bottom lip quivered at the thought of repeating the process and getting the same result.

133

What was happening to her? She was frantic with worry. Her thick, chestnut brown hair was her crowning glory. Even those who disliked Mallory agreed it was the one saving grace that compensated for her grating voice, perpetual scowl, and nasty temperament. Indeed, if someone viewed Mallory only from behind and saw her flowing hair cascading down her back, they would think her somewhat desirable—that is, until she turned around to offer full view of her face and a glimpse into her foul disposition.

Her scalp itched beyond belief. She wanted to plunge her fingers into her head and pierce her skull in order to get at the source of the stinging irritation. But she was afraid of losing more hair. Necessity defeated vanity, and her fingers dived in.

More batches came loose.

When the urge subsided, she reflected on her situation in horror. Soon all of her hair would be gone from her head. Tears of anger ran down her cheeks. How did this happen? At this rate, her head would be a barren dome just like the eggs she cracked for breakfast. Sitting on her bed with her back to the doorway, she brooded.

To have this happen, just when Cantrell seemed to be showing interest in her, was just so unfair. Was it not two days ago when he had left on her bed the beautiful ivory comb she was now holding, left it alongside his stable gloves that secretly announced his gift? Her heart had surged with happiness in celebration over winning the battle for his affection. He had pledged his love for her as surely as if he had placed a ring on her finger. What an evil twist of fate it was then that this token of admiration had become her instrument of torture as it ripped out her one claim to beauty. She raged at life's cruelty, realizing she would not be able to see him now for weeks. She would have to remain distant from him at least until she was not quite so bald.

Just then, Jeanette, one of Matilda's ladies-in-waiting, swept into the room, arms bent at the elbows, hips swaying from side to side as if she were too important a person to visit the living quarters of a mere chambermaid. Somewhat cross-eyed, Jeanette often had to tilt her head sideways in order to address someone straight on. Despite that imperfection—and the brown rot that edged one of her front teeth—the woman believed herself to be a paragon of nobility. And the arrogance she carried was meant to smother the confidence of anyone who dared occupy the same space with her.

"What are you still doing here?" Jeannette scolded her sharply. "What is the reason for your delay?"

Mallory, still sitting and hunched over with her back to Jeanette, answered gruffly. "Go away."

"Look at me, wench, when I am talking to you!" Jeanette's voice squeaked with impatience, her hands firmly placed on her hips, her nose lifted higher in the air. "The rushes need to be changed in all of the bedrooms. I said, 'Look at me!'" Jeanette stomped over to the other side of the bed.

"The Duchess is very upset with you. The rushes are starting to smell—Wha—what is this?" Jeanette stopped short when she looked at the floor beneath Mallory's feet. There, strewn upon the ground, were blobs of brown hair lying drab and limp. She shifted her head to the side as she beheld the few individual strands that still remained attached to the girl's head, tendrils that were separated by huge blotches of milky white skin that were barren and empty.

"Oh, my . . ." were the only words Jeanette could muster.

Outside the door, two women had overheard the exchange between Jeanette and Mallory. A stifled giggle from one of them reached Jeanette's ear. "Who's there?" she demanded, turning from Mallory toward the door. Stepping into the hall, she summoned the pair who had started running away. "You two, stop right there. Get back here this minute." But the two sped up, scurrying down the hall until they could turn the nearest corner, leaving a trail of laughter behind them.

Jeanette was angry—not because she felt sorry for Mallory who had probably been victimized by the two. Truth was, she could not care less about the chambermaid and her hair loss. No, Jeanette was incensed over the fact that her directive was ignored. So she stored away the idea that one or both of these women had something to do with Mallory's situation and hoped that such information would one day benefit herself somewhere down the line. Should the Duchess ever need someone to complete an unsavory task, Jeanette knew exactly who to recommend for the job.

She went back to Mallory who was once again scratching her head vigorously. Jeanette felt no emotion as she watched gobs of hair continue to fall. "Shave off the rest of those greasy strings, put on a bonnet, and get going."

*   *   *   *   *

For two days straight it rained, coming down with such intensity that it was driven sideways by the wind. Simon was running out of time. It was his own fault. Why had he waited until the last minute to do this? Filling the days and hours leading up to this night with empty chatter? Now it was the eve of his departure and his last chance to speak to Celia of serious matters. In the morning he would be leaving with the rest of the men. He had to put things in order before saying goodbye.

He preferred not to speak to her within the confines of the castle where someone could be tucked away in an alcove or passing through a hallway and overhear him. Whether it came about due to his prayers being answered or the random turning of Fortuna's wheel, his luck thankfully changed by late afternoon when the rain stopped after supper. Through Rowena—who had been recognized by one of the archers as a former neighbor—he sent word that Celia should meet him by the copse of trees down by the river. And there he waited.

As soon as she came into view, he could hear her already shouting, "Simon!" with a mixture of joy and concern. His eyes grew wide at the sight of such beauty approaching him. Self-doubt and insecurity clanged upon his heart as he realized the incongruity of their pairing. An oversized, ugly farmhand daring to converse with a captivating woman who had the elegance of a lady? He should laugh at the folly of his own boldness, were he not acquainted with Celia's lack of pretense.

She wore a hooded cloak of forest green that billowed out to the sides as she ran down the hill toward him. His heart swelled with pleasure to see her dashing toward him like this, calling out his name with such happiness. *If only it could always be this way,* he thought to himself. Her hood bobbed up and down so that he could see her hair flying out beneath it. She drew closer and slowed her pace so as not to overtake him. Her eyes, now bluish-green, sparkled when her lips broke into a warm smile of greeting.

"I am so glad you sent for me, Simon! I did not know how to find you or get word to you amidst all the men encamped on the grounds." She linked her arm in his, tacitly urging him to walk with her. "I wanted to go from tent to tent and ask for you, but Rowena forbade me to do so." She laughed at the idea of someone restraining her. "Rowena was afraid that after two weeks of boredom and so many days of foul weather, the men would be restless and eager for action." Celia stopped walking to look up at him as if he could help her recall something. "What was it she said?" She appealed to him as if he had been in on their conversation, and then squeezed his arm tighter. "That is it! Rowena said, 'It takes nothing more than the tipping of a penny candle near a hay bale to set a farmhouse ablaze!'" She started walking again, pulling him toward the water's edge. "So that is why I am so glad you sent me a message to meet you tonight."

He tapped the hand that was interlocked into the crook of his elbow. "She has a keen eye to observe such things, Celia, and she is right. We are all eager to get moving again. Sitting around is not good for simple-minded men."

A lone nightingale warbled from the tree above as they continued to match their steps together. "Where are you being sent?" Celia asked.

"Saint-Evroult. The Duke removed the abbot there because of his kinship with the Giroie family. But many in the region are sympathetic towards Abbot Robert de Grandmesnil. Before taking holy orders, he was a former soldier, so there is a strong likelihood that trouble is brewing." He stopped walking and pulled his arm from hers only to reach out and grab both of her hands.

"Celia, I know we have spent some time together during this break, and we have talked a good deal about many things . . . conditions in the duchy, Matilda's abbey, Cantrell's obsession with you, Mallory's 'fungus'... I could go on and on. But tonight I want to revisit something more important than all that. Something I brought up to you the very first day I saw you here, the day we worked the linens together."

She started to draw away from him and even took a step toward the water before he seized her shoulder and spun her around to face him. "No. Do not walk away from me Celia. At least, not yet. You may decide to do so later, and that is fine, but grant me the chance to confess my sins and purge myself of this guilt I have been carrying for many years. Then, if you decide to walk away, I must accept it. Because I will know that I have shown you everything I am. And if that is not good enough, then so be it. I deserve this chance to fulfill my penance."

He put both hands on her shoulders, and when she dropped her eyes to the ground, he gently touched her chin with two of his fingers in order to make her look directly at him. "I need you to know everything about me. I am a sinner, Celia. A murderer. Only it is not what people think. I did not kill Giselle, no matter what others may say." He dropped his hand, breaking their connection. Then he stepped away from her and began telling his story.

He folded his arms across his chest, seemingly addressing the river itself. "She showed up on Bertram's doorstep—Bertram, the master weaver—without announcement, without notice. She would come to be his apprentice, sent there when her community in Barbillon was devastated after Val-es-Dunes, when the bloated bodies of the fallen floated downstream and blocked the mill there. Long before that, her father and mother had died of a fever when she was young, so she was raised by an older brother. The same brother who then fought for the rebels and presumably died in the battle, but not before arranging for her to be taken in by Bertram, a distant family friend.

"Most people kept their distance from Giselle for fear of being associated with the rebels. She was too wild for girls her age— sometimes sneaking out on summer nights to bathe in the river under a full moon. I saw her there once, her black hair, sleek and shiny as an eel's skin, swept back off her face. Her shoulders, just breaking through the water's surface, glistening with droplets that flashed and sparkled under the moon beams. I fell under her spell. I could not help myself. I watched and waited nearly every night, hiding behind trees just to catch a glimpse of her radiance. I believe she knew I was there, for I can say now that she seemed to be performing for me. I know this to be true because she later revealed she had been dismissed from her apprenticeship. Told to leave by the mistress of the house who had sniffed out Giselle's sensuality and the advances she had made toward Bertram. Soon she would have nowhere to go.

"At the time though, I did not question my good fortune. So when she reached toward me one night and beckoned me to join her, I plunged in without hesitation, ignoring the grating voice in my head asking, *why would she ever want me?*

"She was untamed. Feral. So different from myself. I did not analyze our pairing, so glad was I that she had agreed to be my wife. But from the beginning, everything was marked by deceit—I had started it off that way by concealing myself from view because of my own lust. On our wedding night, she denied me her bed, saying she was ill. Her 'illness' persisted over a week and into the next, though I saw no signs of fever or chills, no cough, no stomach pains. I soon realized there was something more deeply wrong with her, with us. A fortnight later, she took care of my needs on one occasion, but never, ever did we make love.

"I resigned myself to her ways and savored the fact that at least the house was no longer silent. But before the month was out, she began spending large amounts of time away from the cottage. Said she was busy collecting herbs and wild flowers in the forest, yet her basket always came back empty. I chose not to confront her. I was weak. I hate myself for it now.

"The truth was she had been meeting up with a Breton soldier, a mercenary who, with his companions, had been hired to fight on behalf of King Henry—after he had turned on William. Two months into our marriage, she announced she was with child, both of us aware it was not mine. Doubt and vengeance consumed me. I became suspicious of every villager who crossed my path. I agonized alone, not even able to broach the subject of the father's identity with Giselle herself.

"There were times when I wanted to wrap my thick hands around her delicate neck and choke her until she confessed, but then I remembered the innocent child in her womb, the babe who had the right to live. As she got further along, I began to make preparations for the child's arrival, cutting wood and building a cradle for the little one. If I could not be a husband to Giselle, at least I could be a father to her baby. I soon found my heart filling with joy again instead of anger.

"Giselle grew restless. I convinced myself that it was the strain of her condition. There was such venom in the words she directed at me. She belittled me, called me hideous to look at, mocked my happiness by calling me a fool, too dumb and too weak to satisfy his own wife, making her look elsewhere for a real man. When she was nearly full term, we had a terrible fight, and she jumped aboard my skiff to get away from me. Said she was leaving me. That I would never see her or her child again. That she could not stand being in a world that had me in it. She called me simple-minded, which I probably was because I would have forgiven her of everything had she stayed.

"I knew she was going to meet her lover, so I followed on foot, running through the woods, close enough to the river's edge but hidden from view. Eventually I came upon an encampment, a group of men sat around a fire pit—two were whittling, one was drinking, two playing dice. Another two stood off to the side engaged in conversation. I crouched down and waited.

"At the sound of rustling in the brush, each man stopped, their bodies tense with anticipation. I could see the fingers on each man's hand slowly extend and reach toward a weapon as they readied themselves for conflict. But emerging from the darkness was no enemy soldier. It was Giselle. At her appearance, the seated men began to snicker. All five of them turned toward the two standing men, both of whom had their daggers drawn.

One of the standing men spoke. "'Tis a foe of a different sort, is it not, Neven?' he laughed derisively. "You cannot plant a seed on fertile ground and not expect a harvest come due." He pushed the man's shoulder in Giselle's direction.

"Another of the fellows chimed in. 'You have left enough bastards sprinkled throughout the countryside to form your own regiment. When they're of age, you can ditch the French king and hire them out to fight for William, one of their own kind!'

"The man named Neven cuffed the back of the head of the other fellow and marched purposefully toward Giselle, grabbing her elbow and turning her about. In order to follow them, I had to go backwards, away from the gathering, and then cut back closer to the water. The delay put me at a disadvantage because when I found Giselle and the soldier they were already engaged in a heated argument. I was too far away to hear exactly what they were saying, but I could see she was on her knees, hands extending up and reaching toward him. Based on her hatred of me, I guessed she was begging him to take her away with him. His face twisted with impatience and disgust.

"He said something harsh and abrupt and turned away from her. In desperation, she reached out and grabbed the hem of his coat. The gesture infuriated him. He spun back toward her and struck her face with the back of his hand. I fought the urge to jump up and defend her, burying my desire to retaliate. I could not quiet my breath as I panted with rage. When she refused to let go, he pushed her to the ground and spit upon her face. As he raised his leg preparing to kick her exposed stomach, I could wait no longer.

"My fury had no bounds. It was bad enough to see Giselle's face bruised from the blow, but the child he was about to harm was my child, regardless of whose blood ran through its body. And it was to protect that child that I struck him down. I cannot explain what happened exactly. All I know is I could not stop. I struck his face so many times my knuckles crunched and broke under the force of the impact. Even when he was no longer moving, I grabbed his collar and slammed his head repeatedly on the ground, not registering how it flopped up and down as lifeless as a rag doll.

"I came to myself when I heard a scream penetrating my skull. I was no savior. She saw me as the Devil himself. She cursed me and went to him. Kneeling upon the ground, she lay her cheek against his mangled face. When she looked back up at me, her eyes narrowed with loathing. Her cheeks were stained with his blood.

"I could not fathom what I had done, shocked at my own capacity for evil. I did not see her take the dagger from his hilt. I only saw her get back into the boat, taking with her all I had ever wanted in this world.

"I dragged his body to the shoreline, removed his coat, placed a large rock on his stomach, and tied the arms of the jacket around his body in order to weigh it down. I then rolled him into the water and watched it sink.

"As you know, everyone—myself included—assumed Giselle had run away, disappeared as mysteriously as she had arrived a year ago. Most people said good riddance, but I was crushed. And I was not pretending. All I had ever wanted was a chance to make a good life for us and for the child. I wanted nothing more in return, only the bond of a family. A day later, the boat washed up on shore, a pool of rusty liquid lapping back and forth in the hull with the rise and fall of the current. And then a week later her body was found, stab wounds punctured her belly.

"I am not sorry for what I did to that man. He deserved it for breaking Giselle's heart. But I deserved some form of punishment as well, for I too broke her heart even though I had never intended to. I have been living in purgatory ever since."

A deep silence ensued. He finally turned back to face her. "I am not asking you, Celia, to save the likes of me. Some people are just not meant for heaven. But I know that my penance would be more bearable were I able to offer you sanctuary and a measure of peace.

"I have learned much from all this. I have learned that you cannot force someone to love you, just as you cannot make them stop loving another. I have learned that the harder one tries to force those feelings on another, the more that person drifts away. So I am not asking for love, Celia. I am just asking for warmth. The opportunity for us both not to be alone. And if the time should come when you do find love, I swear on my honor I will not stand in your way.

"I am not so foolish any more to look for love when it is not there or think I can make it appear like magic from nothing. Passion grows from a tiny spark within, a spark that can be lit only by the person himself. It is not possible for one to kindle it in another."

He looked down at the ground under his feet, feeling too unworthy to meet her gaze. "I will be leaving with the troops in the morning. And I will not ask you for your heart, for I know it is not me you think of in the moments before sleep. But I do ask you to consider settling in Dives-sur-Mer with me. I can build a separate space for you and Vivienne on my land. I just want to have someone to care for, to work for. The days are long and the nights even longer when one is alone."

Celia remained still. Was there something wrong with her that his brutality did not frighten her? Her opinion of him had not diminished at all. In fact, despite the violence, she admired his unwavering devotion to the dream he had envisioned, a devotion so strong that even a vicious woman like Giselle could not weaken it. His heart remained true to the end.

Delicately, she reached out to him; this time it was her feathery touch that rested gently upon his chin, lifting it up for him to look at her. She saw a tear had formed on the outside rim of his eye. His spirit matched his words. A slight shift occurred inside her. She let her hand travel downward from his face to clasp his hand. She could feel the power that lay beneath his calloused skin. Her eyes studied the thickness of his wrist and the muscles that ran through his forearm.

The clouds above them tumbled across the sky, driven westward by the wind, until a crescent moon peeked out from behind the gray patches. She breathed in. That was all he was asking of her. A little sliver of herself. Nothing more than that. She could still retain so much of herself without disappearing into him.

The breeze lifted her hair from behind her ear, driving the strands across her face. She pushed them to the side along with her hesitation. Moving her eyes from their hands to his face, she whispered, "I will wait for you, Simon. I will be here for you when you return."

His eyes fluttered as he blinked in disbelief and joy. The movement caused the tear to topple over the edge and trail down one side of his face. He placed his other hand to rest upon her own. "That is enough for me. We will find our way together." His voice, thick with feeling, did not break.

Like the glowing orb that chased away the thinning clouds, she pushed aside all of his doubts, and the two embraced, bathed in the light from above.

MARGARET

TO HEED A GREATER CALLING

THORNEY ISLAND, ENGLAND - 1058

Sometimes after daily mass and before the hunt, King Edward would send for the children. Focused more on spiritual matters than earthly ones, he cared little for his conjugal responsibilities, so his interaction with the three exiles was the closest he would ever come to being a father. Beyond the familial satisfaction he derived from spending time with them, he basked in the contented glow of knowing he was saving three little souls.

One of the spare chambers of the castle had been converted into a schoolroom of sorts, and despite the green veneer of mold on the stone walls and its confined, windowless interior, the room was alive with energy. Gerhard was supervising Edgar's latest architectural feat —the building of a weight-bearing bridge made of sticks—while Margaret (who had already finished her translation of Cicero) was plaiting Cristina's mousy brown hair. Margaret's fingers moved gracefully and efficiently in and out of the braid, as she occasionally dipped her fingers into the nearby mug of ale to wet down Cristina's coiled tendrils that fought against such restriction.

The children took no notice of the door opening nor did they see the royal servant nodding at Gerhard, but when their tutor cleared his raspy throat, they each came to attention. "Tis time, everyone. The King—" he stopped abruptly, overtaken by a coughing spell that came from deep inside his chest. Harsh and grating, the spasm brought no relief, and the cloth he brought to his mouth in hopes of expelling the agitation remained empty and dry.

Edgar abandoned his sticks and rushed toward him, rubbing Gerhard's back in the same manner that Edgar's own mother had often done for him. But the stubborn Swede would have none of it. He waved off the boy with one hand, and then, when that did not work, he physically pulled Edgar away and back toward the table where the project lay. Holding up a single finger directing them to wait, Gerhard left the room presumably to secure a fresh mug of ale.

Margaret and her family had been at King Edward's court for a year now, but for Margaret, things still did not feel right. It was not as if she were yearning to go back to Baranya, but at the same time, she did not feel at home here either. She felt out of place and different. People stared. Some whispered. Most shunned them. "Cristina, do sit still. I am nearly done, but if you keep fidgeting, it will come out, and I will have to start all over again." She tugged harder on purpose to get her sister to sit still.

But it was not really Cristina's behavior that irritated her. It was Gerhard. Something was wrong with him, very wrong, and yet whenever she asked him about it, he gruffly put aside her question. When she tried to confide in her mother about his condition, Agatha turned her away, saying she had more pressing issues to consider, like how to keep her son alive and safe amidst a den of serpents.

Margaret's eyes burned when she thought of how much worse this foreign land would be if she had to surrender yet a second person to the grave. Still raw and fresh was the wound in her heart. Her ears heard the echo of the stone slab closing on her father's coffin. The grating screech of the rock raked furrows into her heart, leaving trenches of pain in its wake. She could not go through that again. She must do something to save her beloved teacher. She could not lose him too. Hastily, she finished making the braid and rushed from the room until she came upon Gerhard in the hallway, leaning with one hand against the stone wall. "Master, are you all right? May I get you something from the kitchen?" She tiptoed up behind him, gently placing her hand upon his back.

He turned his face from the wall to smile at her, but his attempt was interrupted by another paroxysm of coughing, reassurance smothered by the cloth that sealed his mouth. With an aggressive movement of his hand, he pointed down the passageway in the direction of the Great Hall, silently urging Margaret not to keep the King waiting.

A cold, clammy sensation washed over her as she gazed at him, her mind seized by yet another unwelcome vision. These had been occurring with more frequency of late, fleeting sights of things yet to come. It happened on the voyage from Flanders to England, and again at her father's burial. And now it was happening once more—the slow tingling sensation that began in her gut and then extended straight up through the crown of her head. A chill that pulsed through her body as her eyes pierced the veil of reality to witness a deeper truth. For a brief moment, she could see beyond the exterior of the fabric that Gerhard held to his mouth to glimpse the thick clots of blood that soiled its other side. The crimson goblets that dotted the cloth had spidery tentacles extending from their centers and reaching toward each other, until they linked together to form a single, solid banner that heralded imminent death. Squeezing her eyes shut, she halted the vision, desperately commanding her mind to banish such thoughts. Grounded once again in reality, she left behind the world of prophecy and acted upon Gerhard's urgent gesture by rushing back into the schoolroom to gather up her brother and sister.

"Edgar, Cristina, come. We must not delay. The King has sent for us. We are lucky his Highness has put aside time to be with us."

Reaching out one hand for Edgar and the other for Cristina, she stood between them as the threesome made its way down the hall.

Moving his free hand with a flourish and bringing it to rest upon his chest, Edgar announced, "When I become King, I shall be too busy fighting wars and piling up treasure to waste time teaching children about Scripture." The boy lifted his chin arrogantly.

Releasing her clasp on Cristina, Margaret slapped Edgar's hand. She whispered intensely, "How dare you utter such words, you foolish boy! Nothing in life is certain, least of which is our position here at court. Just a simple word from another counselor, and we would all disappear—from this land or from the world altogether. Earl Godwinson hates us, so does Father Thurstan. Almost everyone here looks upon us with suspicion and mistrust. With a single judgment, we could all be wiped out, and your vain boasts about the future would remain what they are—nothing but words upon the wind." Edgar dropped his eyes toward the ground.

"Besides," she continued, reconnecting her hand with Cristina's, "about the only thing we *can* rely upon is God, and so we must place our faith in him. The King's lessons remind us of that! *For those who love God, all things will work together for the good.*"

Edgar's remorse was short-lived. "Easy for you to say." He pulled away from Margaret, leaning against the wall facing her in defiance. "You like sitting in a room and praying. And that is good for you because that is all you want to be someday. Well, no one's stopping *you* from doing what you want to do, are they? You want to go live in a cloister, then go do it, but do not force me to give up what I dream about. They took the kingship away from Father, but they will not do the same to me." He took a deep breath. "So if you want to make me sit for my 'lessons' with a King who does not even want to rule, I will do it, but do not expect me to be excited about it. And when his milky white hands and his long, spindly fingers turn the pages of the book we are reading, I want you to know that I do not care one bit about what we are studying or what he is saying. All I will be thinking about is how those hands have never—and will never—feel the rush of raising a sword in defense of his people. So there is nothing that he can teach me that I care to learn."

Having spoken his word, Edgar moved back toward Margaret's outstretched hand and yanked it down to meet his own. She said nothing as the three resumed their path down the corridor in silence. When they arrived at the closed pair of chamber doors that led to the Great Hall, she fixed her eyes on her brother. "Remember your place. Warrior or not, the King imparts divine wisdom, something we all should lean on during these unsettling times. *For many plans are in a person's heart, but the Lord's decree will prevail.* Remember your place."

Dropping their hands, Margaret pushed open the door aware that the man on the other side was the only person keeping them from the grave.

*   *   *   *   *

All Edgar could think about was how the King was a stretched out version of the albino bull-calf they had raised back at their estate in Baranya. When it was born, Edgar remembered how the creature seemed to glow in its peculiarity. With light pink skin and eyelashes of bright white, the calf seemed to look as if it had just come out of the boiling pot, scalded by the heat. No matter how he tried, he could not get the image of that animal out of his head whenever he looked at his sovereign king. Despite his height and slender frame, the King seemed to be as frail and otherworldly as that calf. White wisps of hair fell in individual strands about his head, lifting and shifting with the slightest movement of air. His splotchy skin seemed overcooked in some spots and downright raw in others. Clearly, it was a skin victimized by the outdoors—burnt to a crisp on sun-filled days and tinged with streaks of blue veins on wintry ones. It amazed Edgar that Margaret could sit so spellbound in the man's company when all he himself could do was imagine His Majesty chewing the cud, pieces of grass mixed with spit, splashing and mashing around his yellow teeth.

The King sniffled and addressed them in a stuffy, nasal voice. "And that is why I have commissioned the building of the new church upon this sacred ground. Saint Peter was always quite special to me, especially in my youth. Have I mentioned to you all that it was he who saved me when my horse stumbled from a dangerous cliff?" He placed his hand over his heart as he spoke. "It was my spontaneous prayer to him that saved us both that day." Satisfied now with his spiritual testimony, he waited for his awe-inspired tale to impress his three listeners, but the room remained uncomfortably quiet. When Margaret leaned slightly forward, it appeared as if at least one member of his audience actually cared about what he had just said, and that was enough for him to resume the thread of his story. "And this new structure shall rival the beauty of the monastery in Jumieges, will it not, Reginald?" Turning toward his counselor for confirmation, Edward's white hairs floated upward with the wind that resulted from his sudden swivel.

While Edgar continued to gaze in the distance and Cristina studied the lines in her palm, Margaret sat riveted, listening to the words of the King. She then rotated about with interest in order to hear the Norman clerk's response.

At the mention of his name, Reginald who sat at the nearby desk quickly looked up from his paperwork and, in his earnestness to please the King, hurriedly put aside his business. His hair was cut short, shorn well above his ears and forehead. His dark complexion and dark eyes stood in contrast to Edward's ghostly aura, and his unusual accent confirmed Margaret's suspicion that the man was no native of this country. "But, of course, my liege, it shall be the greatest abbey in all of Cristendom. A true testament to the magnitude of your faith. A visual display of your devotion to Saint Peter and to all of the saints." Reginald bowed his head in deference to the King, his eyes closed in solemnity. "A thousand pilgrimages to Rome could never equal the impact this structure shall have on the faithful of this land. Our Holy Father, Pope Stephen IX—God rest his soul—knew this to be true. His divine approval of this endeavor confirms how you, milord, shall be remembered and honored for all posterity."

While Reginald maintained this submissive position awaiting the King's word, Margaret tingled with excitement at being privy to such discourse, especially since the subject of their conversation dealt with the soul's journey toward heaven. She felt no interest or pull toward temporal matters; she had already committed herself to God, fully aware that meaningful sustenance came only from the contemplation of His word and the study of the saints. She could envision the rounded arches of the future church, sturdy and strong, encapsulating the kind of faith that moved mountains. How incredible to be part of such majesty, to be allowed to be in the presence of the man who was the primary force behind its conception and creation. Edgar just yawned.

"A grand undertaking, is it not?" Edward concurred with his chancellor. "But what do those papers there have to say about the delay regarding the supporting columns of the undercroft? Why have they not yet been completed?" Agitation edged the King's words.

Raising his hands palms facing up, Reginald answered in the voice of a parent who is forced to repeat the same correction to his child over and over. His tone seemed to imply that this was a common occurrence between the two men. "You know how these things take time, my liege. Your vision touches perfection, and perfection requires superior materials and master craftsmanship. Of late," he lifted up the parchment and waved it toward Edward, "the poor quality of the Yorkshire limestone has put a halt on construction of the pillars. You know that we must not do anything to tarnish the purity of your conception. Nor would we ever compromise your unblemished legacy by using inferior materials. That would be a grave transgression on our part. Therefore, we must wait for the proper stone to be delivered, knowing that excellence is required to fulfill a project that carries with it such profound implications."

Fully aware that the King's political power had recently been clipped, Reginald embellished the construction of the abbey until it approached the magnitude of a continental war. Church building was all that remained under King Edward's jurisdiction. It was the only undertaking where he could impose his will. A project like this must seal his legacy for generations to come just as combat did for war chieftains. With no battle cries of victory echoing throughout the countryside and no noteworthy alliances made during his reign, the Church of Saint Peter had to serve as a substitute for those other secular accomplishments.

Placing his long, bony finger upon the tip of his chin, Edward remained silent, deep in thought. He gently tapped his index finger against the translucent skin below his bottom lip, pondering the situation. "I have half a mind to ask William for access to the stone at Caen. After all, the Romans did the same here centuries ago. Most of our builders are Norman anyway, and they would be more than familiar with Caen's texture and quality." With even greater determination, he said, "Yes. It is decided. That is what I shall do. Reginald, send a missive to the Duke. I shall dictate it to you now."

Edgar could not shake his boredom. All this fuss over a building. Could there be anything more dull than this? Just as he was about to yawn again for a third time in succession, the doors burst open. Filling the space was the wide body of Harold Godwinson. The man paused for a moment to survey the room, and then strode assertively, chest broad and chin uplifted, toward the King. He was trailed by his cleric who moved with the quickened steps of a rat, scurrying behind Harold's shadow as it would hide from candle in an otherwise darkened room.

Already Margaret had darted from her seat, scooping up Cristina and pointing her little sister toward the door. At the same time, she motioned with her head and her open hand, tacitly conveying to Edgar that it was time to leave. The last thing she wanted was to have any interaction with the Earl or his vile companion. Aside from the physical repulsion she felt from being in his presence, she knew in the deep recesses of her mind that this was the man who murdered her father. She had no real proof other than the vague outline of a vision she had experienced after her father had breathed his last. At the tomb in St. Paul's Cathedral before the slab sealed his resting place, she saw her father reach both hands to his throat as if he were trying to dislodge something stuck inside. Poison. And the man who did it would stop at nothing to ensure the success of his plan. They—her entire family—were not safe with a man like Harold nearby.

Unconsciously, her upper lip curled into a snarl when she thought of how he had turned her carefree existence into one riddled with doubt, suspicion, and fear. And all for power. For the opportunity to wear a crown that rightly belonged to her father after the current pious King—who had been so kind to her and her siblings—had departed from this world to find his place among the saints in the next. With Cristina already out the door and Edgar close behind, Margaret curtsied with a quick, "Thank you, my King," and spun toward the exit, but not before a bony, grayish-colored hand reached out from its billowed sleeve to seize her shoulder.

"'Tis unseemly to move with such haste before being formally dismissed by our sovereign. One would think you and your siblings would have more respect." Father Thurstan's bulbous eyes in their blood-lined sockets shifted back and forth from Margaret to the King. His sharp fingernails, like needles, pierced her flesh.

Before she could make amends, King Edward spoke dismissively. "Let them go. Their lesson was over anyway." To Reginald, who had stood protectively closer to the King once Harold had entered the room, Edward added, "I shall dictate the contents of that letter later today." Noticing Harold's curiosity intensify, Edward purposely tagged on, "The letter to William of Normandy," just so he could enjoy the Saxon's face turn red with irritation.

As Margaret rushed out the door, the last words she heard came from the Earl. "My brother Tostig has returned, and he has brought with him the newly crowned King of Scotland."

Edward paid little attention to Harold's announcement about the coronation of his northern neighbor, offering only a passing comment. "Well, as St. Augustine once said, 'tis a greater felicity to have concord with a neighbor than to subdue him by warfare." Then, dismissing the topic from his thoughts, Edward turned his thoughts to more pressing matters such as how to secure the proper stone to complete his most sacred project.

Quite pleased that Edward's mind remained up in the heavens, Harold carefully considered how his brother's relationship with King Malcolm could further secure Harold's own powers on earth.

*   *   *   *   *

Once she had started, Margaret ran right past Edgar and Cristina and kept the pace going as she sprinted down the long corridor, beyond the schoolroom and their bedchambers, until she came to the stone staircase. Behind her, she could hear them giggling as she tip-tapped two feet upon each wide step as if her toes were scorched on a hot griddle. Eventually their laughter faded away as she raced from

155

the confines of the castle to the open fields that lay beyond, fields edged by long grasses and clumps of soft rushes.

It was an exquisite April afternoon, unusually bright and warm. The sun had traveled past its central point in the sky, signaling it was later than mid-day. The mudflats of low tide had dried up and disappeared so that the boggy ground was now solid and firm. Pockets of yellow, purple, and pink wildflowers dotted either side of the sandy trail, their stems lolling from side to side as if woozy from sleep while their colorful petals danced along with the wind in energetic bursts of movement. Margaret slowed her speed to breathe deep of the scented air that blended the musky fragrance of the flowers with the moisture of the Tyburn.

Two sets of legs came charging, eventually coming to a halt on either side of Margaret. "Aaagggh. Could not get out of there fast enough," Edgar complained between puffs of breath. "How many times does he have to tell us about his horse and St. Peter?" Edgar moved past Margaret, taking out his frustration by slicing the tall grass with his outside hand. "I was actually glad to see Earl Godwinson, if you can believe that!"

Margaret seized Edgar's wrist and spun him round to face her. "Stay far, far away from that man. He wishes only ill for you, for all of us."

Defiantly squirming his way out of her hold, Edgar challenged her. "Why? I need not fear him. The King has already told me he has great plans for me. Harold can not do anything about that, now can he? Not unless he wants to be hanged as a traitor for going against his King's wishes." The tall river grass that had edged either side of the narrow dirt path gave way to a cluster of trees. Just a little further on was their favorite; its trunk sat firmly planted on one side of the trail while its branches seemed to reach up high and then dip down and around, bending as if to embrace the opposite side of the road in a kind of leafy hug. Edgar reached for one of its branches.

"You are such a fool," Margaret felt compelled to correct him. "Have you not listened to what Gerhard has told us? The King wields little to no power over Harold. That card has already been played. He exiled the Godwins once before, but they raised a huge army and came back. And the King could do nothing to stop them. Harold and his family rule the country more than the King does. At least that is what Gerhard says." Margaret leaned up against the base of the tree to watch Edgar climb nimbly from one branch to the next while Cristina sat under the boughs, laying down the wildflowers she had collected into batches of yellows, purples, and pinks.

The tree's unique shape meant that it never really crowned but instead formed an arch. Its branches bent and curved to touch the grass on the other side, creating a kind of magical doorway from which a person could look in a northerly direction toward the open landscape. As Edgar crouched tight, moving hand by knee, hand by knee toward the highest point of the tree, Margaret called out to him. "You know what? If I were you, I would be careful. Not just up there but everywhere. Harold can easily ignore the King's plans for you since all the power rests with him and not with our grand uncle."

Having delivered her warning, Margaret walked down the incline toward the banks of the river where a single patch of pure white sand opened before her. The water was not foamy or brackish; rather, the gentle sway of its movement welcomed her in hues of pale to rich blue. The sunlight pierced the surface, illuminating the sand at the bottom so that Margaret could see clumps of tiny fish darting feverishly from place to place in their frantic search for food. She enjoyed watching their frenzy as they moved in unpredictable patterns yet still remained together. There were no large rocks to lean upon, so she tucked her skirts beneath her and sat upon the ground, gazing out on the sparkling water while her fingertips reached deep into the pocket of her skirt to lift out and unfold the pages she had transcribed from scripture. She began thumbing through the passages, reading an excerpt here and an excerpt there, until something made her stop and look up.

The vibration of the earth beneath her feet told her someone was coming. She kept the verses in her hand as she stood up to investigate. On the edge of the northern horizon, two men on horseback emerged, and soon their full bodies came into view. Margaret silently observed them, but Edgar, who had stopped climbing mid-branch, shouted out to her, "Finally, some excitement!" At his words, Margaret left the shoreline behind to rush back toward her siblings.

The riders drew closer. A sense of ease flowed between the two. They seemed to be brothers, either by blood or fellowship. Both men were helmeted, but the one who rode lower in the saddle was thicker in girth and seemed to defer to the other. The other exuded power as evidenced by his upright carriage and sweeping observance of the region before him. Unlike his companion's horse, this man's steed was draped in a bright yellow cloth featuring a crimson lion. Margaret felt a ripple run down her spine as, once again, important emissaries had arrived. Her thoughts hearkened back to that fateful day just a little over a year ago when Harold and his entourage arrived at Baranya with "good news" that ultimately brought death.

The travelers had not yet arrived at the tree, but Edgar was already crawling between the bright green leaves that were moist and bendable in their announcement of summer. In one quick move, he dangled from the uppermost branch with both arms extended and then let go and crashed to the ground, landing in a squat upon the spongy surface. Before Margaret could utter a word of caution, he was sprinting away.

He shouted as he ran. "Hello. I am Edgar, son of Edward. Who are you? Where are you coming from? Have you come to see the King?" His words were loud but choppy because of his unsteady breath.

Margaret followed Edgar until she could gain a better look at the two visitors. The visors of their helmets were raised, and she saw the serious look in the eyes of the heavier fellow, his brows gathered together like a pair of clouds that collide during a storm. The other, his blue eyes as clear as the sea that flowed nearby, had an expression of calm intensity.

The taller of the two men dismounted and removed his helmet completely. As he bent down to address Edgar at eye level, Margaret felt a slight skip in her heart. Of its own volition, her hand pressed down on her chest as if to quiet and steady its rhythm. She saw a thick mane of long, wavy reddish-brown hair tumble down to the man's shoulders, framing his ruddy complexion and those piercing eyes. Bristles of red whiskers pushed through along his jawline and chin like spears of spring grass breaking through the earth. His belted tunic was sleeveless, and Margaret stared involuntarily at the knotted muscles that pulsed and lengthened as he tossed the reins toward his companion.

"'Tis close enough fer me to walk from here. I will be along soon." Deep and rich was the voice that sat upon the air with its commanding authority. "Water the horses and wait fer me by the stables. Together we will meet wi' the King and yer brother, aye?"

The shorter man nodded and left, guiding the second horse alongside his own. After watching his friend leave, the remaining warrior then turned to the boy. "I have indeed come to see the King. And am I to imagine that ye are the Aetheling himself, the hope o' all Saxons throughout the land?"

Edgar's chest expanded. He raised up his chin at being addressed in such a manner. Placing both hands upon his hips, he lowered his usual high-pitched voice to match the masculinity he hoped to convey. "That I am."

"Well, now," the man said as he bent one knee down to the ground, "may I introduce myself to ye then? My name is Malcolm, son of Duncan. And that fellow who just left us is Tostig Godwinson. We have come from battle and are here to tell yer grand uncle a bit o' good news, news that I will share with ye first, my worthy prince. The Dunkeld line has been restored in the North." Edgar, uncertain of what this announcement might mean, looked at Malcolm with even greater admiration. "It would be my wish that we two could become friends." Malcolm extended his hand in Edgar's direction and left it suspended there while the young boy chewed his bottom lip, pretending to give Malcolm's offer deep consideration when all the boy really wanted to do was shake it enthusiastically.

By this time, Margaret had moved closer to the pair, coming to stand behind the kneeling man. Edgar was the first to heed her presence. His eyes lifted up toward her as if to ask what he should do. This change in the boy's gaze did not go unnoticed by Malcolm, a warrior trained to detect signs of danger. Immediately, he withdrew his extended hand, snatched the dirk from his belt, and swung round to confront the intruder.

Margaret squealed and jumped backwards, her eyes fixed upon the knife. In that instant, she could not know she was not the victim here. For although she stood before him without weapons or war gear, he was the one who had lost. Without shedding a single droplet of blood, he knew he had been conquered by a pair of emerald eyes that bore into his heart deeper than any dagger.

His hand trembled as the sunlight flashed erratically off the unsteadiness of his blade. Matching her look of shock with one of astonishment, Malcolm witnessed the young maiden falter, a move that coincided with the soft flutter of her pages drifting to the ground.

She paid no mind as to how they had slipped from her fingers so carelessly. His gaze held her captive. The connection between them held fast, like a rope encircling and cinching them together. Neither moved nor breathed.

Margaret broke the spell first when she leaned down to gather up the fallen pages that lay beside her feet. Before she could get very far, Malcolm was again on his knee, raising the sheets to her in offering. "I am so verra, verra sorry, my lass," he apologized in earnest. "I had no' thought 'twas a fine lady such as yerself who was movin' behind me." His hands shook and the pages rippled as he held them out toward her.

She cleared her throat that seemed clogged with emotion. "Thank you ... Malcolm, son of Duncan." Her eyes rested on the scarred hand and thick knuckles that clasped her writing before she reached out toward him to accept this token. Her fingertips lightly brushed against his as the exchange was completed.

"'Tis my pleasure, milady." He felt tongue-tied and foolish before this young girl and wondered if she could detect his frailty. He stood up and then bowed to her in deference. "Let it be said that I would be obliged to be o' service to ye in more important ways beyond the mere retrieval of yer book."

. Looking around to acknowledge the splendor of their surroundings, he smiled amusedly and said, "And what 'tis this great work that ye are writin' that can rival the message o' nature's beauty in a meadow such as this? Surely, it must be o' great import fer ye to choose to study dry pages rather gaze upon yon windin' river and the billowy clouds above?"

Margaret found more of her voice. "Oh, yes, milord. Nature's bounty *is* glorious, but God's word surpasses all temporal glamour. For these scenes will come and go," she swept her hand over the landscape, "they will enthrall and disappoint, but His message endures forever."

Malcolm's eyes flashed with interest at the depth of her faith. He wanted to linger here with her, all afternoon if he could, just to be in her presence. The melody of her voice charmed him, her words like velvet so soft upon his ears. He felt himself drifting into a kind of reverie just listening to it.

Everything about her was perfect. Her green eyes gazed freely into his, rich and full of innocence, and her lips turned up at the corners in a look of perpetual joy. The two long braids that hung down on either side of her face had loosened, allowing a few stray strands to float around like wisps of yellow silk. She wore no shawl or covering, so he could see the beginning contours of her shoulders as well as her long, delicate neck, accentuating her vulnerability even more. He longed to touch her, to let his finger trace a path from her face to her neck to the more private places that lay hidden beneath the fabric of her dress. He imagined a future intimacy between them where he would hold her in his arms, taste her lips, and ultimately have her as his own. Such thoughts were improper to consider, for she was too sweet, too angelic to be claimed. What had he done to deserve an encounter such as this, a chance meeting with so divine a creature? How he wished he could take this moment and make it his forever!

Edgar's footfall went unnoticed. He marched over toward the two, feeling rather disgruntled at having been supplanted by his sister. He wondered what it was about Margaret that was distracting this man who had so recently been interested only in him. Displaced and out of sorts, he sat down cross-legged in a huff, and when the two continued to pay him no mind, he began to gather up a few stray leaves that had drifted to the ground, pulling apart the stems of pairs that had landed together.

In his full posture, Malcolm stood before Margaret like a column of stone that dwarfed her in size. The crown of her head came barely to his collarbone, and her frame seemed incredibly fragile next to the width of his chest and the spread of his shoulders. Speaking with a gentleness in stark contrast to his physique, he asked, "Would ye read somethin' o' it to me?"

At first, she doubted his sincerity and thought perhaps that he was mocking her piety. But after peering more closely into his eyes, she found reassurance and began to turn the pages. "Of course. This is from Matthew's gospel. *'Again, the kingdom of heaven is like treasure hidden in a field, which a man found and hid; and for joy over it he goes and sells all that he has and buys that field. Again, the kingdom of heaven is like unto a merchant man, seeking goodly pearls: Who, when he had found one pearl of great price, went and sold all that he had, and bought it... '"*

As the soft breeze tickled the reeds at the water's edge, so too did her words dance lightly upon his own thoughts. When she paused to look up at him, their eyes met again. Tacitly, she asked if she should continue. He could form no words. He had lost the power to speak. So taken he was with her beauty and virtue. Assuming his silence was her answer, she started to fold up her pages.

Abruptly, he gathered himself and croaked the word, "Wait." He opened his hand toward her. "Please. Dinna' stop." He swallowed purposefully so that his speech could flow more freely. "I know nothin' o' heaven nor hell, but I do know what it may feel like to come across a pearl o' great price. Fer that is just what has happened this day to me. What is yer name, milady?" He made no move toward her save with his eyes which reached across the gap between them to touch her soul.

She blushed pink before answering. "My name is Margaret. My family and I reside at the court of King Edward—God bless his soul for the mercy he has shown to us. My father died but twelve-month ago. Edgar is my brother. I have a sister too, Cristina. She is over there counting her flower petals, and my mother is inside the castle tending to chores. This is our new home, but it does not feel very much like one since it was here that we lost our father." She faced him boldly as she spoke her truth.

Malcolm paused for a bit, digesting her words. He then strode away from her to lift the young boy up from the ground. Placing his hands under Edgar's arms, he raised him to a standing position and said to them both, "I too know what it is like to have lost a father. I have endured the same long and lonely hours as ye have, wishin' fer the return o' a savior who never seemed to come. Orphaned I was, left alone to fight fer justice in the name o' my father." He placed his hands firmly upon Edgar's shoulders. "And there were many a dark day and many a dark hour, but trust me, ye'll get through them. Fer ye may not know how or when, but justice will be served, so long as ye stay strong in yer heart and true to yer purpose." Clapping him on both shoulders for emphasis, he winked at Edgar as if to seal their secret.

During Malcolm's speech, Edgar's eyes had filled at the mention of his father's name. Not trusting his ability to speak, he only nodded in agreement. Malcolm understood quite well the pain that gripped the young boy's heart as it was not very long ago when he too had felt that same vise about his own. Reaching out to tousle Edgar's hair, he then announced, "And now, I must be going. 'Tis time fer me to pay homage to yer sovereign King and bring him good tidings from the North." He began to turn toward the direction of the castle.

"Wait, King Malcolm. May I go with you? I am done climbing trees and running about. It is time for me to seek justice as well. Perhaps you can tell me how. How did you do it? Find justice, I mean. How did you make them pay for your father's death?" Edgar sped after him, tapping the powerful warrior on his lower back in order to gain his attention.

Malcolm turned a glowing smile upon the earnest lad. "Will ye no' walk wi' me to the castle? I can tell ye all about it as we go," and turning toward Margaret one last time, he added, "And ye, fair maiden, someday ye shall come visit my kingdom, and I will show ye wonders ye canna' find in any book."

Again, Margaret blushed. Pressing her pages close to her chest, she hoped to slow her racing heart. She spoke no words, but Edgar answered her curiosity for her when he shouted, "What kingdom do you speak of, milord?"

Although it was the boy who asked the question, Malcolm locked eyes with Margaret and spoke only to her, "I am the King o' Scotland. I come from the North. 'Tis a wonderful kingdom, a powerful kingdom, but it lacks a certain beauty, it does. I believe I have found that beauty, and I am certain that once it is in my possession, I shall have the grandest kingdom i' the land. Come on lad, let us go see the King." He began walking away, Edgar at his side, but took one last opportunity to glance over his shoulder at the maiden he had left behind. And deep inside his soul, he made a private vow that, one day, he would never part from her again.

*   *   *   *   *

Malcolm could not concentrate. Typically known in battle as a man of keen awareness, he was unsettled by this feeling. His thoughts were frayed and disjointed. Usually when most men panicked, he moved with calm. His actions were always definitive, his decisions marked by clarity. Yet here he was, just as feeble as those timid soldiers, unable to function during the simple act of eating.

Individual words from the conversation swirled about his head. Fielding questions about old Siward of Northumbria and then

Lulach's brief reign, he answered succinctly, leaving the rest of the details to Tostig. His thoughts were elsewhere.

He forced himself to keep his gaze downward, afraid she would be frightened away if he looked too intently at her. But staring at his dish and the charred brown pieces of meat made no difference. All he saw was her countenance. Between intermittent replies, he shifted his eyes to study his hands and fingers—thick, scarred, and callused—and chided himself for imagining this delicate lady across the table would want anything to do with a warrior like himself. Titles and land, which he had and which nearly every woman coveted, probably meant nothing to someone as pious as she. Her heart seemed impervious to worldly temptation.

With his first wife's death, he was free again to wed. Indeed, his counselors had been pestering him about forging another marital alliance. Suggesting various "worthy" options, they encouraged him to consider the security and expansion of his kingdom. A few vows before God and man, and he would have another wife. The act itself was rather simple. Take a woman (or more accurately, her territory) to bed and thus bring power and glory to Scotland. For the time being, he had been able to put off their recommendations since more pressing matters were at hand—like deposing an impostor and restoring his own right to rule. But now, there was no cause for further postponement. And with that immediacy pricking him, he just now realized his good fortune. God had arranged the perfect match for him, and she sat only a few feet away. He need not look any further. That he wanted her, there was no doubt. That she would satisfy an alliance his advisors desired, there was no question.

He looked up.

She glowed with beauty, enlivening the room with a freshness that reminded him of dew drops shimmering upon the spring leaves. He wanted nothing more than to join her in that private sphere and leave behind the staleness of the room and the conversation. A creature of light she was, and he yearned to feel the warmth of her upon himself.

"Is that not so, Malcolm? Eh? My friend, is that not so?" Tostig nudged him with his elbow.

Tostig's physical prodding broke the spell. Malcolm swiveled his head from Tostig to King Edward and back, trying to regain some semblance of awareness. Thankfully, his companion rescued him by supplying more bits of information. "You know, 'twas their march south that done them in, aye? Near Aberdeenshire." Tostig winked in confidence at Malcolm, providing the necessary thread Malcolm could weave into the discussion.

He could not trust himself to look at Margaret and remain on task. Instead, he leaned forward to address the King who sat two chairs away with Queen Edith in between them. "Aye, your majesty, 'twas an unsettled summer day, taken by moments o' sun and storm throughout the battle. Southeast o' Essie, we occupied the mound o' Lumphanan, which gave us a better vantage point to survey the tyrant's retreating army." His blue eyes glistened with intensity as he recalled the details. "The only sounds i' the air were the clashing o' swords and the cries o' the wounded. When the weather did turn and the downpour began, streams o' water red from blood gushed from the hill to the valley below. The cursed traitor tried to bide his time by playin' the coward, hidin' himself beneath the dead bodies o' two o' his own fallen soldiers. But a restlessness i' me and a hunger fer justice drove me on to scour the area i' search of the villain who had killed my father and usurped my birthright." He turned to his companion. "What was it, Tostig, that I told ye brought me to him? Do ye remember how I said 'twas the strange movement below the mound that drew my eye?"

After taking a swig of ale from his cup, Tostig answered. " 'Tis true, my Lord, just as he says. The pair of bodies appeared to be waking from sleep, shifting and moving every so often as if to shake off their slumber. That is when our man here, Malcolm, reached down and seized the leather jerkin of one fellow and thrust him aside. And there, lying out in the open for all to see was the usurper himself. With his sword pointed at Macbeth's throat, Malcolm dragged him by his hair over the rocky ground to the nearby stone for execution. Before the scoundrel could utter a single word, Malcolm sliced his head from his body and raised it aloft for all good soldiers to see!" Tostig clapped him on the back as if to recreate the triumphant moment.

King Edward nodded in approval. "You have learned well the ways of vengeance, my boy. But am I right in saying your thirst for righteousness remained unquenched? I seem to recall reports coming back that all was not over. Your mission did not end on that field in Lumphanan, is that right?" Edward tapped his cup to signal his servant for more ale.

When the talk then shifted to the brief reign of Macbeth's son Lulach, Malcolm wished he could signal Tostig to tone down the gruesome details about their role in the murder of the ill-fated ruler. *She will think me a monster*, he thought, *a creature unfit to be i' her presence. How can I convince her otherwise? I must not lose this chance to make her mine.* He had to present himself as worthy of her. *Saint that she is, perhaps she will take pity on me fer being the sinner I am? One whose soul is i' need of saving?* As Tostig continued on about Lulach—the simple-minded idiot they ambushed near Strathbogie—it was clear to Malcolm that, in front of her, he need not act or pretend at all. Sinner was a role that suited him well.

*   *   *   *   *

Her shoulders were tense. She could feel them straining higher, pitched upwards close to her ears. Her hands she kept folded, one inside the other on her lap. She could not stop the outside hand from pulling at the fingers and squeezing the knuckles of the other. Why was she so tense?

Present but not present, she took an account of the events that brought her to this moment. It was not too long ago when she and her family had sat at table with strangers from a distant land. And now here she was again, finding herself in similar circumstances. Only this time there was no heaviness in the air as there was when the three Englishmen came to Baranya—that cold-hearted trio who issued only commands and directives, their silences thick with unspoken threat. But with these two visitors who sat across from her, such was not the case tonight. So why then was she so tight through her neck and back? She breathed in deeply, wanting to release the strain and absorb the good fellowship instead.

When she finally started to relax, she marveled at the ease with which the visitors interacted with her great uncle and his advisors. There were no furtive glances exchanged between Malcolm and his companion. There was no pretense in their conversation. They were forthright and spontaneous with their words, the cadence of their speech pleasant to the ear. No, these two were so very different from the three travelers who had disrupted their lives in Hungary with their cold sneers and bitter commentary, men who ultimately sent her father to his grave.

She settled in to study the men more deeply—well, in truth, her interest rested upon only one actually, the blue-eyed, fiery haired warrior who sat directly across from her. Earlier she had noted the beam of intensity that flashed from the center of each eye, a single ray that could cut away all deception and expose a person for who he truly was. For the present moment, that power lay hidden, his gaze fixed upon his place setting. His face was ruddy and weathered from the outdoors; the whiskers along his jawline and chin varied in color from flecks of gold and auburn to maroon and deep brown. Some of them had begun to sprout squiggly hairs that ran in small half-circles, marking him as one who reflected the wantonness of nature. No doubt he was raw and untamed, the stories shared around the table attested to that wildness. But when she had encountered him in the meadow earlier that morning, she knew there was another side to him, a tenderness that lay beneath that force.

Under the table, she clasped her hands together in prayer. *"Mother Mary, have you sent this man to be our protector? To provide for my brother's safety in this land marked by shadows and suspicion? I put my trust in you. Let him be that ray of hope that either brightens our future here or lights our way back home to Baranya."* After this private contemplation, Margaret decided she would visit the monastery for the singing of Lauds at dawn and place her entreaty before God.

*   *   *   *   *

She swung her legs across the edge of the bed and touched her feet upon the floor, immediately pulling them up when she contacted the cold stone. After lacing up her shoes of leather, she tiptoed toward the clothing trunk to grab another layer of skirt and a heavy shawl. Although Margaret tried to make as little noise as possible, Cristina began to stir. Her head lifted up from her reclined position, her face partially covered by hair that had come undone during sleep. In a voice thick from slumber, she asked, "Where are you going so early?" Cristina rubbed her eyes and glanced over at their mother whose body faced the wall, her back rising up and down without any break in its rhythm.

Margaret moved closer to sit upon Cristina's bed. "I often leave the chamber at this hour. It is just that you are usually so deep in sleep that you never hear me go." She rearranged the creased blanket so that she could tuck it under Cristina's chin. "Would you like to join me for

Lauds? Morning office is about to begin." She squeezed her sister's toes gently beneath the covers.

Cristina slid her feet away from Margaret and sat upright. "No, thank you. I have already found my savior." She tilted her head toward another room in the castle rather than to heaven above. Her smile promised mischief.

Margaret moved up the bed, drawing nearer to Cristina's face. "What is that you say? Need I remind you there is only one savior?" She playfully tugged at one of Cristina's misshapen braids and then the other. "Is your devotion so fickle that you bury it in the bottom of a chest as soon as a more colorful piece comes along?" She gestured toward the clothing trunk in the corner. "What is this business— 'You have found your savior'?"

Folding her arms across her chest, Cristina refused to be deterred. "Look, Margaret. You may decide to take the habit and openly declare your vows, but I shall keep mine in private . . . while I am busy being Queen." Her eyes were more alert now, sparkling with challenge. With one announcement, she erased all the conversations they had shared about joining the convent together—their sworn contract to retreat from the outside world to enter the spiritual one. Sisters who would become sisters.

"Queen? Queen of what? Queen of where? Have you lost your mind and soul at once?" Margaret shook her head in disbelief, refusing to take her sister's words seriously. "No amount of wealth is worth forfeiting an oath, Cristina. None. Remember that."

"Whose Queen? Why Malcolm's Queen, of course! He is newly crowned. He told us so this evening. And every King needs a lady by his side to help rule the land. So why not me? I have an ancestral name. And one day my brother shall be King of England! What better wife could he want? And maybe, when I have been living in Scotland with him for some time, I shall sing a melody sweeter than any of those performed at Matins, Lauds, Vespers, whenever!" She pulled the blanket over her head, dismissing Margaret from her presence.

Stifling her disapproval, Margaret left the bedside and moved toward the chamber door. Before leaving, she turned back one last time. "I will pray for your soul."

No response came from beneath the blanket.

*   *   *   *   *

With the outside world still silent and the sky awash in the gray of pre-dawn, Margaret listened to the crunch of the gravel beneath her feet. *How flimsy are the oaths people swear,* she thought. She could not fault Cristina for her fantastical promises. After all, the girl was still very much a child. But what of the oaths made by grown men? Like Harold Godwinson's vow to King Edward to bring her family safely to this land? Her father had barely set foot upon the soil when they had to bury him beneath it. And what of the King's promise to shelter them here and name her brother as his successor? Would Edward's words be as changeable as the weather itself on this dreadful island?

Her steps quickened as she drew near the construction of the new church dedicated to St. Peter. Despite its unfinished state, a flag of crimson and gold still flew proudly from its rounded arches, rippling and twisting in the early morning wind. Its bright red background taunted the soft pink stripe of approaching dawn, and the yellow of St. Peter's crossed keys and Edward's ring shone brighter than the frail rays of the barely risen sun.

The masons had not yet arrived, so the arched entrance way yawned emptily, quiet but inviting. Wooden lattice work within the arch was still visible, while above it rested one full set of stone. Beneath the top tier, another was only a third of the way completed. Off to the side was the large wheel and pulley that would hoist the carved boulders from the ground to the area above. Tall ladders, spaced at distinctly measured intervals, stood vacant, awaiting craftsmen who would scurry up their planks to reach the tops of the wall. No other castle dweller was making this journey with her. She was alone both on the path and in her thoughts.

In her lessons with the King, Margaret had heard all about the Benedictine monks who resided at St. Peter's and was comforted in knowing that they were part of the same sect she had grown close to in Baranya. Their traditions were familiar to her—the way they moved about in their hooded cowls and black habits tilling the soil, helping the needy, and praying at specified intervals. All of this provided her with a sense of continuity that was otherwise absent in this unpredictable country. Adopting their motto "pray and work" as her own, she too tried to follow a regimented schedule, turning away from selfish desires to surrender completely to God's will. The solitude of the chapel filled her with grace, and the hypnotic rhythm of their chants ushered her toward peace.

Ever since she was a little girl and first heard the sweet voice of Jesus coming through the Scriptures, she had made the decision to turn her life over to Him. The question she continually pondered was, how could she best serve Him? In the limited world of her youth, she started simply by bringing a light heart to all of her chores and by remaining kind and patient even in the midst of her siblings' worst tantrums. As the years passed, she was awed by the serenity of the mass, inspired by the breaking of the bread and the sharing of the Eucharist. She imagined that tiny piece of divinity growing larger inside her, and God's word like wind upon an ember, fanning the glowing spark until it blazed with glory.

Yearning for an even deeper connection, she gained permission from her parents to spend an hour or two each day working in the kitchen of the monastery in Baranya, helping to serve the community its meager repast. To the monks, Margaret was just another set of hands, another worker. They paid as little attention to her as they did to the broth in their bowl. The food they savored was of a spiritual kind, and the visions they saw were celestial not earth-bound. Blending in so easily, she soon became acquainted with the rhythm of their days, a pattern that revolved around specified hours of prayer and devotion. The more time she spent within the walls of the abbey, the more liberated she felt from the constraints of the world. She had found her calling.

Now, after this total upheaval in their lives and their vulnerable position in this new country, she felt the urgency of her longing. She waited impatiently for the day when she could bid farewell to the noise, distraction, and intrigue that made her head dizzy with confusion. In the silence there was tranquility, there was clarity, there was beauty, and there was infinite love.

She seated herself in the last pew of the old church and felt the edges of her veil lightly touch her shoulders, a gentle brush that steered her away from the threats that lurked outside this haven. The monks did not mind her intrusion. Swept away by their singular devotion, they barely noted she was there. But there was one priest, however, who was always keenly aware of her presence.

Last spring while she sat in sorrow upon the grass outside the abbey, Brother Tobias came upon her in her misery. Her mind was in turmoil, her brow furrowed with worry. She kept reviewing the sequence of past events over and over in her head. Carrying her father's lifeless body back from Favreshant. The stone slab above his tomb at St. Paul's being sealed shut forever. Having her family thrust upon King Edward, a veritable stranger who knew nothing really of their father or the magnitude of their loss. Every bitter detail. They had no one in this country they could trust, no familiar faces they could turn to for assistance. Even Gerhard had abandoned her of late, so sick was he that he had taken to bed and refused to accept any visitors. And so Margaret sat there outside the church all alone, pulling at her fingers one-by-one, agonizing over their future and what was to become of them, what was to become of her. She broke her gaze away from the wringing of her hands only when she heard the rustling of robes as someone walked up to her from behind.

Squatting before her, Tobias reached down to quiet her hands. His touch was warm and welcoming. Though small in stature, he was filled with immeasurable grace. His soft gray eyes reflected a serenity matched by the soothing quality of his voice.

"My child," he tilted his head toward her as he spoke, "the Lord feels your pain. He sees your suffering. You must trust in His ways." He nimbly sat down on his knees in front of her, the sandals of his feet crossed beneath his body.

"Love is eternal. It bridges the gulf between this world and the next. The gap you feel between you and your father need not be there." She looked up at him, startled that he knew of her loss. "Yes, I am aware of your suffering. Close the chasm of doubt with the certainty of love. You must have faith in the life to come."

He smiled at her with a knowingness that was foreign to her, a confidence that had escaped her. Despite the fact that she had been praying unceasingly since the moment her father had fallen from his mount, she had found no tranquility in her heart—not until this priest came to comfort her. He shifted his position to sit beside her. They remained like that, side by side, for quite some time. In the stillness, she found a measure of contentment.

And then, like a thin trickle of water that later fills a goblet to its rim, his voice rose in prayer. Beginning softly and then growing stronger, he began singing the words of *Deum Verum*. The melody lifted her up from the well of darkness to see the fullness of light. *"Quoniam Deus magnus Dominus. Et Rex magnus super omnes deos.*" With his eyes remaining closed, he interlocked his fingers in prayer and raised his head to the sky above.

Margaret too ascended toward the heavens, her heart welling up with joy. She knew that there was no death, not for believers in Christ. But Tobias helped her truly believe it. She need not dwell on her father's absence in this world, for it was a world both superficial and fleeting. One that was so insignificant when compared with God's promise of eternal life.

Thus began the deep friendship between Margaret and the diminutive monk with the indomitable spirit and angelic voice. To celebrate the arrival of each season, he brought her cuttings from their gardens: holly and ivy at Christmas, birch boughs in May, red roses for garlands at Corpus Christi in June, white lilies for saints' feasts. And when times were more somber—like when Cristina took ill again —it was Tobias who provided her with a remedy. Tucking into Margaret's hands a pouch filled with thyme leaves, he instructed her to brew a special tea that would ease Cristina's coughing and allow her to breathe freely again. After two draughts, her sister was cured and her health restored.

So it was Brother Tobias who had extended Margaret the invitation to keep praying with him—and with his community—at Lauds each morning. He understood her precarious position at court and witnessed her desire to be not of that world. As all the monks filed in and she waited that morning in the back of the church for the service to begin, she offered a silent devotion of gratitude to the man who had taught her about one oath that would never be broken— God's promise of immortality to those who trusted in His word.

But as it had happened a few times before, Margaret felt one of her visions coming on. A sharp pain penetrated the space between her eyes, piercing her with its demand for attention. She fought against it. Squeezing her eyes shut, she tried to block its force from coming through, but it refused to be pushed aside. The vision would come. Behind her eyelids, forms began to take shape. The outline of a man appeared, one that resembled the Scottish king who had come so recently into her life and that of her family. She shook it away. Soon another image fought hard for expression. She held it at bay by focusing instead on the opening words of the service: "*Domine labia mea aperies et as meum adnuntiabit laudem tuam.*" She tried to fix her attention on the verses being sung, but it was no use. The music turned eerie, from chanting to moaning until it overcame her with its haunting sound.

A young girl cowered in fear, raising her hands above her head to ward off the blows of the oar. Her threadbare dress hung off one shoulder, exposing her skeletal collarbone and shoulder. Her hair, wet and matted, clung to her skull, falling in lifeless brown strands as drab as the dead reeds that bordered the water's edge. The only sign of vitality about the child were her blue eyes which, at one time, must have glistened with laughter and joy, but were now clouded with pain.

"Ye ignorant wench! Ye've cost me a day's work with yer carelessness! Can ye not do the simplest of tasks without something gone amiss?" The spittle from his mouth flew freely as he slapped the oar against her exposed skin with greater force.

"Aye, go ahead. Keep crying out like that, why don't ye? Ye sound like a sick cat, mind ye. No one's coming fer ye, ye know. Who'd want to save an English she-devil like yerself anyways?" Her pale, thin arms were already speckled with bright red splotches in areas where the paddle had come down hard upon her. "Good fer nothing, pig. Too ugly to even warm my bed."

The young girl tried to find her voice. She tried to plead with him. "Please, master, please. I swear I did not loosen the line. I did not even touch it." She could not add that the fishing line must not have been tied properly in the first place. No, she could not say that because that would shift the blame on him, and in Giric's household, the blame must always rest on her.

"Should've left ye on the pile with the other dead bodies to wash away with the tide. Why did I bother paying good coin for a dumb bitch such as yerself?" He used the back of his hand to wipe his mouth and push his long, greasy hair off to one side. That momentary pause was all she needed to run.

For the last five years, she prayed for death. But it did not come.

It was not that way at first. At first, she did not pray for death. She prayed for rescue. But no savior ever came. So then she prayed for escape. The saints heeded her call. Her first attempt came two years into her bondage. It did not work. She was stripped, tied to the mooring, and whipped fifty times—five for each year of her life. It took months to heal, her portion of food so meager, her body so weak. Once the physical pain subsided, she dared to hope again.

She dreamed of home—of the way the sun's rays caressed her island of Lindisfarne, especially on summer nights when patches of gold shimmered on the water, and the tide rose to tuck them all in at night: Kenneth, Harry, her eight-year-old self, and newborn Avery. She could taste the sweetness of Mother's pudding gliding smoothly down her throat, especially the way she would swish it around inside her mouth for a few extra seconds just to delight in its flavor a little longer before swallowing. She grew warm inside, remembering the evenings when Papa would sit with them by the hearth and tell stories of their forefathers who had come to settle on the Holy Island. Her eyes grew damp, not just from those glimpses of her past life, but mainly because she knew she had completely disappeared, vanished. Her identity was gone. Her single wish was for someone to call her again by her name. Evelyn. That was her name. In this barbaric place, she was nothing but a slave, a she-devil, a wench, a bitch, a pig, an idiot, a slut. No one here had ever addressed her by her name.

She had tried once more to escape. The second time she made it as far as Belhaven, but she was headed the wrong way and the hounds came for her. One mongrel latched onto her ankle so fiercely that the skin around the bone was torn off. Tossed into Giric's cart like a sack of grain, she used her own hands to stanch the blood. Once back in her cell, she ripped part of her dress and applied it as a bandage. She could not walk for weeks. Infection set in. No one cared. Despite the sting, she used sea water to heal the wound, but the foot never sat right again. She could no longer drop her heel to the ground. She never ran away again. She could not, even if she wanted to.

She thought of all of these things in the split second in which Giric had stopped beating her. Since no savior was coming and escape was not possible, she renewed her prayer for death.

Scrambling from the boat to a standing position, she commanded her legs to move as fast as they could in their lopsided fashion toward the band of trees that lay beyond the shore. "Take me, Lord. Take me. Evelyn. Take Evelyn home!" She stumbled along with her head tilted back and her chin pointed up to the heavens, blocking out the sound of Giric's footsteps speeding up behind her . . .

The vision went dark.

Margaret's head felt full, her stomach queasy. Her limbs felt like stone, dragging her down deeper into the darkness of her vision. She had to fight the rigidity of her posture to bring her awareness back to the room. She then reminded herself of where she was. Not in her room but in the church. But there was silence now. The chanting had ceased. Had she blacked out for the entire ceremony? Pulled away from it by the horror of her own imagination? Who was that poor girl? And what did Malcolm have to do with the girl's plight? Or the girl's ultimate fate? Even though Margaret had returned now to her own time and space, she could not ignore the throbbing pain in both of her arms. With trembling hands, she rolled back her sleeves and gasped when she saw the red welts on her skin. She panicked. Visions do not do this. They may leave insight in their wake, but not visual evidence. How could this be? She shuddered at what this might mean.

Margaret continued to blink her eyes, rapidly and continuously, in an attempt to shift her mind from inward to outward awareness. The monks were now walking past the altar, exiting the church in order to begin their daily chores. And as was his wont, Brother Tobias blazed his own path by moving in the opposite direction from the others, heading down the aisle toward the back of the church in order to greet her.

At the sight of Margaret, his upturned nose lifted even higher as he broke into a warm, elfish grin. But his steps were not as spry as they usually were. By his side, Tobias guided an elderly priest who was leaning on his arm for assistance, thus slowing his movement and making his pace more deliberate.

Like a startled rabbit, Margaret rushed to quickly pull down her sleeves before they drew closer. Although she would normally have shared this strange experience with the kind monk, the presence of the outsider relegated her to silence. She had not seen this priest before, this man with the ruddy face and tonsure of pure white. Most distinct about his appearance were his eyes, so pale blue they seemed almost translucent. Those eyes—never moving, never shifting, never seeing —were fixed somewhere faraway.

She brought her cuffs to her wrists when the two stopped alongside her pew. "I bid thee good morning, Lady Margaret," Tobias said cheerily, bending at his waist in deference to her, his oversized cowl drooping lower than his chest. He then looked up at her face. "I trust this day finds you … well?" He hesitated in his greeting. He could see she was visibly upset, her serenity replaced with agitation. "What ails you, my lady?" he fastened the priest's hand to the top of the pew so that he could envelop Margaret's in his own.

Before she could speak, the visitor tilted his head to the side, responding to more than just her physical presence. He spoke to the air above her head. "There are many ways to answer a calling. Heed the signs. Not all paths lead to the cloister." His words hung in the air.

What was she to make of that? What did this man know of her? Of her vocation? And why was he telling her to "heed the signs"?

Brother Tobias who normally came to her rescue in times of spiritual struggle only confused her further. "Yes, Father Timothy, this is Lady Margaret, the person you desired to meet."

Margaret spun her head from the old man back to Tobias. She was about to question the monk as to why this stranger should wish to speak specifically to her. She had no role in anything, no claim to anything, no answers to anything. Tobias went on.

"She is the daughter of the recently deceased Edward of Wessex, the Exile who returned to his homeland after such a long absence from its shores. She and the rest of her family have been received at court and remain under King Edward's protection. And like our pious monarch, Margaret too is guided in all things by her faith. Indeed, she prays with our community every morning and spends her days in fasting, study, and contemplation." Tobias placed his hand on her shoulder to bid her to rise.

For some reason, she felt very small and fragile in front of the blind priest who dominated the encounter with his presence. When she saw his fingers fumbling toward her, she clasped them in reassurance that she was right there beside him. His lips broke into a warm smile as he addressed her with sincere admiration. "My sweet, sweet lady. I have traveled many miles and many days to speak with you. A journey that ends for me here, as I shall not live long enough to make the return. Come, let us sit."

As he shuffled his feet closer to the pew's opening, Tobias touched the old man's back tenderly to guide him. Margaret slid over and resumed her position in the pew, never breaking the bond between their interlocked hands.

He raised his head, continuing to look above her own. "You shall be a leader, caretaker of the poor, sick, and orphaned. Your descendants shall rule for many generations. Answer the call when it comes. Do not presume to know the ways of God before that call arrives. Keep your mind and heart open. When the time comes, place yourself in His hands. He will show you the way. Remember the words of Our Lady at the wedding feast at Cana: 'Do whatever He tells you.'"

Mystified over the connection between her most recent vision and this man's words, Margaret could do only what he suggested. Wait. Cast aside all doubt. Ignore the need to figure things out. Surrender to God's plan and hearken to his voice when he summoned her.

In that moment, she felt her spirit grow in grace, the burden of worry lifted. She placed her distress before the altar, emptying herself of her need to control. She would be the Lord's vessel, used by him in the way that He felt best. She felt powerless in the presence of this priest, this messenger from heaven.

Their conversation was not yet over. Breaking their connected hands, he dug deep within the folds of his robe to pull out a reliquary in the shape of a crucifix, one that fit the length of his palm. It was made of dark wood and finely decorated jewels. On that nearly black cross rested the body of Christ formed in ivory and outlined in gold. Father Timothy searched again for one of her hands, opened it, and placed the gift inside. "Go ahead," he said, "it opens and shuts like a chest. Go ahead. Look inside."

She did as he commanded.

"Inside there is a true fragment of Christ's cross, preserved from the wood that stood upon Golgatha. Many, many years ago it belonged to King Alfred of Wessex. Your grandfather, Edmund, carried it on his person throughout his battles against the Danes. When his body came to our abbey for burial, the Virgin Mary begged me to remove the relic from his tomb. She said it had to be returned to one of Saxon blood. I held it in secret, awaiting Divine Providence for direction. For many years, I heard nothing but silence between the syllables of my own prayers. Only when news came of your father's return to England did Mary speak to me again and bless me with the fortitude to perform this mission.

"It was Our Lady's desire then to bestow this gift upon your father, but my journey from Glastonbury took many weeks, and I arrived too late. I reasoned that the boy, your brother, should naturally be the one to carry it now, but Mary has been absent from my meditations. Until last night. It was then that I was told to leave it in your care." His voice quivered with emotion, so joyous was he to have found the person deemed worthy to possess this symbol of unwavering faith and new life.

"Therefore, I give this Black Rood unto you, God's chosen one. Bless you, child. And whatever calling He bids you to follow, do well to advance his heavenly kingdom here on earth." Making the sign of the cross upon her forehead, Father Timothy then turned aside from her and reached out for Tobias.

The young monk nestled the man's arm within the crook of his elbow and smiled upon Margaret with eyes that communicated admiration and wonder. "Blessings upon you, Lady Margaret," he said very softly as if not to disturb the grace that had settled upon the young girl. The two men then began their slow procession toward the altar, leaving Margaret to sift through her thoughts in private.

She cradled the precious object in her cupped hands, gazing at the wood of the cross, trying to conceive of the mission that had been placed upon her. With each inhalation of breath, she brought acceptance into her heart, and with each exhalation, she set forth her intention to see that mission fulfilled. She remained that way until the silence of the church began to echo in her mind. Closing shut the case that contained the holy relic, she wished her future could be laid out for her as simply and as quickly as the snapping of the box. But as soon as she heard herself trying to impose her own wish for a fast resolution, she took another deep breath and committed herself to the old priest's message: surrender. "Not my will, but Thy will be done," she whispered aloud.

Blessing herself, she started to walk out of the church ready to greet the new day with obedience and trust—but then stopped in her tracks and scurried back into the pew. Collapsing upon her knees to offer one more prayer, she said aloud, "Dear Lord, use me in a way where I may glorify your name. And may one of those ways involve bringing Evelyn home to Lindisfarne. Amen."

Now Margaret was ready to begin the day.

LESSONS TO BE LEARNED

THORNEY ISLAND, ENGLAND - 1058

"Come."

Father Thurstan gripped Edgar's shoulder, digging his fingers into the boy's flesh as he pulled him away from the common room toward the stairs that led down into the shadows. In the darkness was a single chamber beneath the chapel that served as both storage place and study. Edgar hated these meetings with the priest, meetings that were forced upon him because Thurstan had convinced the King of Edgar's recklessness. The boy lacked humility, refused to be obedient, cared only for his own selfish needs. Who better to teach him those lessons than Thurstan himself, a man of the cloth known for his austerity, sternness, and self-denial? So now, instead of running around the grounds and playing outdoors with his two sisters, he had to endure these private tutoring sessions with this taskmaster.

It was almost as if the priest had two faces, Edgar thought to himself. Kind of like the flat fish he had seen at the dock in Flanders. The one that had both of its eyes on one side and then none at all on the other. Father Thurstan was like this to Edgar. In front of King Edward, the priest was smooth and agreeable, but in the King's absence, Thurstan's watery, bulging eyes would fix themselves on Edgar, penetrating him with a glare so cold and so mean it made Edgar's skin feel like gooseflesh. His hands and legs quivered like ripples on the water.

"What is your problem?" Father Thurstan released his grip on Edgar's neck only to smack the back of his head with his open hand. "You move more slowly than a worm slithering uphill." He struck the boy again. "You would think a young man your age would show some respect and keep a decent pace so as not to waste the valuable time of a scholar of the Church such as I." This time, after the smack, Father Thurstan lifted his leg off the floor and bent it at the knee to shove it into Edgar's lower back, sending the boy tumbling down the final three steps.

Landing on his hands and knees before the locked study door, Edgar felt the priest's foot intrude beneath his stomach. "Get out of the way, imbecile. How do you expect me to open the door with you lying there, choking on your spit like some drunk peasant?"

The force of Thurstan's foot flipped Edgar over and onto his back. He watched the priest sift through the keys fastened to his belt to find the one that fit. Edgar stared at the man's profile. He felt his stomach churn, not just from the blows but from the prospect of having to endure another hour in this man's presence. Needing to transcend the horrible experience awaiting him, Edgar removed himself mentally from his circumstances and entered into his own internal monologue where Thurstan's words could not touch him. As he watched the priest fumble with his keys, Edgar studied the jailor's pocked face, the skin dotted with mini-caverns of all shapes and sizes, his beak-like nose hooking down toward his pointy chin as if the two were straining to touch. Indeed, Edgar believed that very well may happen—sooner rather than later—since Thurstan's few teeth could not anchor his mouth to any fixed shape. His lips caved in further and further, erasing any impediment between nose and chin.

"Get in," the man reached for Edgar's clothing and lifted him to stand, thrusting him across the threshold with a hard shove. The room smelled of rotten cheese, sweat, and an unemptied chamber pot. Once again, it made Edgar wonder, how could the King be so fooled? How could this wretch hold a position of such high authority? Personal confessor to Harold Godwinson? Respected theologian to the King himself? How could this be? There were street mongers who were more honorable than this pretentious scoundrel.

"Sit." Father Thurstan extended his crooked, arthritic finger to point to the single wooden chair and desk that leaned against a stone wall damp and streaked with mold. There were no windows in the room, no hearth either, only a single straw-filled pallet raised above the floor by four blocks of wood in each corner. A tall podium stood across from the chair and upon it balanced Thurstan's bible. Using the remaining light that came from the open door, the priest grabbed the flint and iron from the top of the podium and sat on the mattress. Taking the tin from the bedside table, he placed it on his knees and struck together the flint and iron until sparks descended into the tin. While Thurstan concentrated on the friction he was creating, Edgar felt the sound of each strike like a knell counting down the seconds to when his real misery began.

Thurstan preached only of man's depravity, his propensity for evil, his mere existence an abomination in God's eyes. And although Edgar did not believe this description applied to most men, he did agree that it fit Father Thurstan quite well. Base, vile, and offensive to God, the priest was talking about himself and did not even know it. Edgar watched Thurstan lift the tin to his face and blow upon the sparks. He caught a glimpse of the rotted teeth hidden behind the priest's lips and shuddered to think of the foul breath circulating in the room every time the man pushed out a blast of air.

Satisfied with his progress, Thurstan lifted the candle, hovered it over the tin until the wax melted, and watched as a flame sprung up, allowing him to light the wick. But the light only served to magnify Edgar's distress even more. Cobwebs clung to the corners of each wall. The soiled mattress was dotted with brown smudges he hoped to be dirt. He smelled the rancid odor of urine coming from the container beneath the bed. And from time to time, his eyes caught a flash of movement as a rat darted past. Looking around his surroundings, he found himself more imprisoned than any criminal ever was, mainly because there was no specified time limit to his sentence. These lessons could go on indefinitely, or for at least for as long as he and his family remained at court in this foreign kingdom. Forced to exist under the presence of such a merciless warden, Edgar did what all prisoners do: he plotted out a plan to secure his freedom, thinking of a way to get out of these lessons. What game would he have to play to convince King Edward that he had been reformed and no longer in need of such instruction?

Father Thurstan carried the candle over to the podium, placed it on the left corner, and opened his bible. "Today you shall hear the story of Elijah and the prophets of Baal." His lips pulsed inside and out, nose and chin drawing together and splitting apart, as he generated the saliva in his mouth needed to read.

Rather than show the disinterest he really felt, Edgar leaned forward, placing his hands on his knees with feigned eagerness. Believing this to be his only means of escape, Edgar lied.

"Please, go on, Father Thurstan. I am ready to learn." And while he despised himself for not being the warrior he had imagined himself to be, Edgar was also learning that some wars are better fought with brains rather than brawn.

*   *   *   *   *

"Cristina, give me a push to get started, will you?" Margaret looked over her shoulder as she stood upon the wooden swing that was fastened with ropes to the tree branch above. "Put down your dolls for a second until you can get me going."

A few yards behind the tree, Cristina sat bathed in sunlight, her knees tucked up behind her as she moved her two straw figurines down an aisle she would made with pebble borders. "Wait, Margaret. They are getting married. Let them get to the altar first, and then I will come." At the front of that aisle stood a mound of stones, behind which stood a single stick in the grass that would serve as the celebrant for the ceremony.

Margaret clicked her tongue in disappointment. "Tsssk. Well, as soon as they have said their vows, then come and give me a shove." The dappled sunshine spotted Margaret's hands with light that had penetrated in and around the leafy ceiling. The air was fresh and sweet with the fertility of the season, and a sky of blue stretched from one point of the horizon to the other, wrapping the girls in an azure embrace. Margaret began singing an old tune from home, her thoughts of Baranya bringing comfort not sorrow.

As I went with half a penny to the fair

And I bought with half a penny one hen there

Then my hen says: Cluck, cluck, cluck

Little-broody, sweetie biddy

I still have my half penny . . .

She continued to stand through the next stanzas which told of purchasing a chick, a drake, and a turkey before she called out again to her sister. "That is an awfully long wedding ceremony, Cristina. Your guests are going to fall asleep, and your couple will grow old before their time!" Although Margaret laughed, she was growing more impatient with each passing minute.

"Just a little bit longer. They forgot the rings. I have to go find some. Hang on." Cristina unfolded her legs and scampered over to the tree trunk, searching for small leaf stems that would bend without breaking.

"Oh, just forget it," Margaret snapped impatiently. She settled down to sit onto the wooden seat so that she could pump her legs herself in order to become airborne.

Thrusting her toes up toward heaven and bending her knees with her heels facing behind her, she rose higher and higher toward the blue dome above. Straightening and bending her legs over and over, she sang with greater enthusiasm as she used her "half penny" to buy a goose, a pig, and a sheep, each purchase lengthening the refrain as she rose higher and higher. She lost all need for Cristina as she reached the desired height. Carefully, she unthreaded her arms from behind the ropes to place them in front, and then launched herself into the air, giggling with triumph as she landed on her feet, only to topple over onto her side, onto the soft grass of the meadow.

With her song still unfinished, she darted back to the swing, unconcerned that her maroon-beaded snood had fallen from her hair and lay upon the ground. Repeating that same routine, she soared once again, singing the words of the rhyme with new purchases of both a goat and a colt. As she came to the final verse, she sat poised on the edge of the swing ready to launch in coordination with her final acquisition at the fair. By this time, Cristina had put aside her dolls and joined in the singing, clapping her hands in anticipation of Margaret's jump. The two girls shouted together:

As I went with a half penny to the fair

And I bought with half a penny a young lad there . . .

At that declaration, Margaret flew from her perch again, her hair untethered, her spirit free. Then after landing in a crouch upon the ground, she opened her arms to receive Cristina. The two joined her in laughter as they rolled around together, crushing the soft blades of grass beneath them. "I want to do that too, Margaret! Let me try. Come on, push me, Margaret. It is my turn now!"

Margaret dusted herself off and stood up. "Oh, so *now* you are interested in the swing just because it is your turn, hmm? But what about me, little one? You left me to fend for myself when I needed a favor from you. That does not sound very fair to me, now does it?" And with that, Margaret playfully chased her sister, "*Ciroka maroka! Mit foztel? Kasat.*" Recognizing the opening words of the tickle song, Cristina sprinted away. She could not run very fast though, so choked was she with giggles that she simply gave up and fell to the ground at just the thought of being tickled.

As Malcolm strode across the meadow, he heard their mingled laughter and saw the two sisters tumbling around on the grass. He smiled without telling himself to, feeling warm inside at having been gifted this vision unadulterated joy. He considered the wonder of the moment. With so many concerns weighing heavily on the minds of this displaced family, it was refreshing to catch them having fun. He did not wish to disturb them. He knew his intrusion would jar them from the memory of better days, so he silently turned around and started to retrace his steps back to the castle. It was Cristina who saw him first.

"Hello, there, King. Hello, King Malcolm. Come back. Do not go away." Cristina untangled herself from Margaret's arms and began to run toward him. "Come back. Do you not want to meet your new wife?"

Margaret looked up immediately with alarm, her brow knitted as she tried unsuccessfully to reach out for Cristina's arm as if to pull her away from such a fantasy. Malcolm too was startled with surprise and disbelief, staring at the child as if she were some kind of soothsayer who had delivered a most welcome prophecy. But Cristina had meant none of that.

"Over here. Come over here. See?" She picked up one of her straw dolls. "This is you." She lifted the other. "And this is your new wife. She is now the Queen of Scotland. She is not from your country, but the people do not mind. She does have royal blood, you see, and she loves you very much, so she won't even miss her old home. That is because Scotland will be her true home now." Her eyes looked down in disappointment. "But they forgot the rings, so I had to stop the ceremony to go get them." She waved over to the tree to where she had been searching for her leafy jewelry. Holding up the one doll, she asked, "So, do you love her? Is she not perfect for you?" Cristina's lips quivered, her eyes widened with hope as she awaited Malcolm's response.

Margaret watched this mountain of a man transform into a gentle poet, his raspy voice as soft and welcoming as the soft petals of a yellow rose. Pushing aside his scabbard, Malcolm bent down upon one knee to be eye-level with Cristina. He pointed toward the doll.

"Ah, sure now. There is naught more any man can ask fer than a lass whose heart is pure and filled wi' love fer him. 'Tis no doubt he would be honored to take her as his Queen, but," he raised his thick, red eyebrows in question, "would she be happy living amongst strangers i' a new land? I would no' want to break her heart wi' yearning fer her old home, ye ken." He fixed his gaze directly at Margaret while he waited for the answer. Margaret tilted her head, trying to get a sense of the meaning behind his words.

Their silent exchange was missed by Cristina. She was too busy placing the figures before the stone altar to notice anything had transpired. With her eyes upon her imaginary chapel, she answered Malcolm with confident assurance. "Oh, no. She is already living among strangers in a new land, and she is so lonely here because no one really wants her around. They're all so mean, and so sneaky, and so busy with themselves that she does not have anyone to turn to. But not you. You are her true friend. And she trusts you. So if you have those two things, that is when you have love. She is not scared of leaving as much as she is scared of staying—without you." Cristina looked toward him and smiled, her dimpled chin lifted up in complete approval. "But I have to run now and find their rings." She scooted away toward another tree and started sifting through the dirt, leaving Margaret and Malcolm together alone.

*   *   *   *   *

Neither one of them moved, their stillness a contrast to the vibrant natural world around them. Birds hopped from one branch to another, some warbled to new companions as they landed close beside them. Others took to flight, rising to race with the clouds that shifted and glided across the sky. Gentle breezes lifted the leaves, flipping them from one side to the other, breaking the silence with their rustling. Grey squirrels chased each other, up one tree and down another, pausing long enough to sit upright, lift their noses, and catch the scent of the other, only to dash away yet again. But Margaret and Malcolm did not talk, frolic, or move as they stood facing one another in the meadow. Their fixity spoke of wonder, curiosity, and fear.

Without shifting her gaze from his face, Margaret felt her hand rise involuntarily to touch her loosened hair. She blushed, realizing how slovenly she must look. Not one to miss a sign, Malcolm walked swiftly toward the dislodged hair covering and retrieved it. Keeping the distance between them, he extended his arm across the gap, handing her the maroon netting.

Words did not come freely to either of them. Hers were lodged in her throat, his locked behind the teeth that bit into his bottom lip. Coughing to clear the blockage, Margaret uttered a simple. "Thank you."

Their hands did not touch, but for a brief moment the netting bound them until he relinquished his hold. With eyes brimming over in adoration, he stopped biting his lip to speak, "Will ye' walk wi' me, lass? O'er down by the river's edge?" He lifted his chin in the direction of the shoreline as if to convey how simple it would be to spend more time together in mutual wonder.

Margaret, who had been studying the hair net in her hands, raised her eyes to him, the thick lashes lifting to reveal a pair of emerald gems that sparkled and glistened with anticipation. "Of course." Surprised at the conviction in her own voice, she added more softly, "I would like that."

Needing both hands to wind her thick yellow hair into a knotted bun, she passed him the snood. "Can you hold this for a moment?" Her fingers moved quickly as she gathered up her mane and twisted it round and round, tucking in the bottom to anchor it in place. Then taking the hair net from him, she stretched it around the crown of her head and down over the back until it felt secure. He could not stop himself from staring in wonder at her extraordinary beauty. So helpless and overcome with feeling was he that he reached toward her without deliberating over whether or not it was right to do so. He lifted one strand of gold that had escaped from the netting. His rough fingers brushed against the softness of her neck as he placed the lock of hair within the covering. He felt a rush of heat coursing through his body and wondered if she had felt it too.

"The piece came undone." He was relieved, pleased that she did not pull away from him or jump back with alarm. Clearly, she was not afraid of him. He had that in his favor, no doubt, but dare he imagine that she may think fondly of him? She took the strand and tucked it in more tightly to the twisted bun, then led the way downhill toward the water.

The intensity of the moment had passed, and they soon spoke more freely. "How long do you plan to remain here in England?" Margaret lifted her skirts as they moved along the rocks by the shore.

"No' verra' long, I am afraid." He stooped to pick up a few flat rocks that he jiggled around back and forth in his hand as the two continued to stroll. "Lady Fortuna may have smiled upon me thus far, but I wouldna' wish to risk her favor by appearing ungrateful and abandoning my responsibilities fer too many weeks. Tostig must leave too to return to his earldom. The people o' Northumbria remain cold to his rule. 'T'will take some time fer him to win them o'er, and he certainly canna' do that the longer he stays here. We will ride out together."

He turned to face the water, placing one rock in his hand and tossing it out to skim upon the surface. "Ye must come someday to visit my land, my kingdom. The sky is ne'er so rich and blue as 'tis on a soft summer day i' Inverness. And the meadow, it smells so sweet. 'Tis almost like a hint o' honey dancing on yer lips. Especially when the whin bushes are i' bloom, and the hillside is blanketed i' such yellow that ye feel as if yer walking amongst clusters o' sunlight."

He glanced over at her to measure her interest. Satisfied, he continued. "And the trees, they're like canopies suspended magically above ye, their thick, green leaves rich i' color and abundance. And if ye find yerself feeling a mite bothered by the heat o' the sun, ye just take yerself up a bit higher to the hills and mountains where the breezes blow much cooler, and the air is edged wi' a crispness that invigorates ye all o'er again."

As he faced the river, his mind caught up in the reverie of his vision. "From the summit, the whole world stretches out below ye, and ye can see all the colors o' the vista—purple, pink, blue, yellows and green—encircling ye all the way 'round. Makes ye feel as if yer the ruler o' the universe. I would like fer ye to come and see that. To come and sense that. To come and feel like ye are Queen o' the land."

He continued to gaze out over the water, letting his proposal hang between them. He waited for Margaret to say something, but she offered no reaction. Intuitively aware of what he was suggesting, she rested her hand in the pocket of her skirt, grasping and squeezing the gospel book she kept there, clinging to it as if it were a lifeline leading her to a safer destination. When he was answered with silence, he dropped another rock into his right hand and resumed throwing.

"And what were that song ye were singing, lass? The one to yer sister? I have no' heard that tune afore now."

Margaret blushed at the silliness of the song. She tried to deflect his interest. "Oh, it was nothing really. Just a little rhyme we used to sing back home … in Baranya. I should have been doing more reading, that is what I should have been doing, rather than playing foolish games with Cristina."

His voice was soft. "I would no' say 'tis foolish to make yer sister laugh and be joyful. The world is filled wi' too much sorrow to be mad at yerself fer spending time being happy on a sun-washed afternoon. And the song was a merry one, least it sounded that way to me. I speak many languages and understand many foreign tongues, but I had no' heard words like that 'afore. And as fer reading, well, perhaps ye'll take the time once again to share that gift wi' me when ye can, fer I canna' cipher the words on the page so well as I can those spoken upon the air."

She smiled at him in agreement. "Of course. I had be happy to. But now it is my turn to ask you a question." Margaret looked first for his approval before continuing. After he nodded, she said, "When you engage in warfare, do you make slaves of the conquered? When your army is triumphant, I mean . . . "

Her question disarmed him. It seemed so out of place in this pleasant setting amidst such feelings of warmth. He knew his answer would disappoint her. Still, he must be honest. "Yes." He wished he could end the discussion there, but her eyes told him she wanted to hear more. "That is often the practice."

He had never questioned the procedure of taking captives, whether exchanging them for ransom or selling them on the market. Why was she forcing him to examine his conscience like this? "Why do ye ask?"

Her eyes bore into him; she did not look away. "It is not my business to tell you how to run your army or your kingdom. I simply ask out of concern for those who have no power to determine outcomes. Those who are abandoned and mistreated. They are not much different than myself. Wouldst thou harm me, my lord?"

She was not trying to charm him. Her question was sincere. He felt a rush of affection for her, and he could not control his need to tell her of it. "Aaaah, Margaret. I told ye once afore. Ye are a pearl o' great price. Something to be treasured and cherished. I would ne'er let ye be harmed."

"Can you think well of that when it comes to others? For truly, they are no different than I. Would you grant me that, good sir? Would you give it deep consideration?"

Standing here with her, he had only one thought, which was to give her anything she desired. "I shall." And so with two words, he was ready to abolish the longstanding strategy of subjugation. The truth was that from the moment he had met her, he had become a slave himself, powerless to determine his own fate, as she had argued. She ruled over every aspect of his world and did not even know it.

Searching his mind for less sensitive topics, Malcolm asked about Edgar. "And where is the young Aetheling today, lass? I would have thought he would be out here wi' ye and yer sister, or mayhap he is riding one o' the King's fine horses on this lovely afternoon. There be some spirited colts and a few docile fillies from which to choose i' Edward's stables. I still remember some o' them myself as I was wont to spend many an afternoon out riding through the countryside here when I was a young lad under the King's care." He bent down to select a few more choice rocks to add to his collection.

Margaret's grip on her book slowly loosened. She sat down on a large boulder and watched Malcolm gather the pebbles. "Oh, no. Edgar's not riding, nor is he allowed to come play with Cristina and me. The King has decided Edgar needs more schooling on account of his wild behavior. So he remains at the castle for a few more hours taking his lessons."

Malcolm continued to toss, increasing the distance with each throw. "Well, I suppose that punishes Master Gerhard too in a way, does it not? If I had my guess, I am sure yer tutor would much rather be out and about amidst the sunshine. Northmen, such as he, much prefer the fresh air o' the meadow to the stale smell o' a dank castle, no? At least all the ones I have ever encountered felt that way. Even in the harshest o' winters, they're out there. They seem to thrive most when they're no' confined to interior space, whether they be walking a meadow, climbing a mountain, or sailing upon the sea. Ye canna' restrict a Northman's need to roam, no matter the man's age."

Margaret watched Malcolm step and release each rock. She was impressed at the speed and force with which he threw, and how he was more interested in distance rather than finesse. "I am afraid Gerhard hasn't been able to be with us of late. It has been a fortnight since we have last seen him. He has taken to his bed and will not accept visitors—not even ourselves." She looked down at her own hands in her lap, kneading them with concern. "I have tried to gain entry. And Edgar too, but the servant who brings him water and food says he does not wish to be disturbed. I told Mother, but she said she already knew of his malady and that it would be best if we just stopped pestering him and left him alone to heal. But I do not think loneliness helps anyone to heal, do you? So even though that is what we have done, we still have had no word of his improvement."

Margaret stood up and drew closer to Malcolm. She nearly reached out to touch his non-throwing arm but decorum held her back. Instead, she sought him with her voice. "Unless . . . do you think you could check on him? Maybe they would let you in to see him, I mean, since you are so much more powerful and important than we are. Or at least, maybe the servant can tell you what is really going on? And then, perhaps, you could give the attendant a message for Master Gerhard from me?"

Malcolm stopped what he was doing to look into her eyes. They were glossy with sadness, her voice heavy with feeling. He knew he would do anything for this woman. Even a small task such as this he welcomed, for it could open the door to greater, more significant ones in the future. He wanted to serve her, to be the man she could count on, the one she could trust. "I welcome the chance to help ye, milady. I will go see him tonight. Would ye like to write him a missive first, one that I can bring wi' me when I go to his chamber?"

When her face broke into a smile, a single tear escaped from ehr glistening eyes. "Yes, yes, that would be perfect. I have been longing to talk to him for quite some time now. If you could visit him and deliver my message, I would be truly grateful."

Without thinking, he caressed her face with his hand and let his callused thumb wipe away her sorrow. "Well, then, 'tis settled. I will come fer the note 'afore supper." He looked down upon her with tenderness before asking, "But then who's giving our boy Edgar his catechism? If 'tis no' Gerhard, then who?"

Margaret did not answer right away. She was too lost in wonder over how she had warmed to his touch. What a comfort it was to have someone to protect her, someone as brave and powerful as this man who could seemingly toss boulders with a flick of his wrist. In a world where she had lost the man who loved her most and was slowly losing another who tried to fill that void, Margaret had felt so alone.

Like a small skiff on a vast, tumultuous sea, she foundered, feeling the hours and days slip away as she drowned deeper into resignation and sorrow. But perhaps safe harbor was only an arm's length away. Dare she sail toward it?

She decided she would by confiding in him even further.

"Poor Edgar. He is now forced to study with Father Thurstan. I have only met the priest a handful of times, but every encounter has been awful. He is Earl Godwinson's private confessor, but if you ask me, he is in need of a confessor himself! His wickedness is so great that one time …"

Malcolm seized Margaret's shoulders, interrupting her before she could finish. "Father Thurstan, ye say? Father Thurstan? That villain has been skulking 'round the castle since the days when I was young."

He pulled back in horror and released his grip. "I am so sorry, lass, fer getting carried away and doing that—fer touching ye like that. Can ye forgive me? It's just that ye're right. The man is pure evil is what he is, and I canna' let yer brother be subjected to the kind o' instruction Thurstan gives. I still bear the scars o' his teachings. Thankfully, they are but physical ones and no' the kind that plague the mind as they did when I was a lad. Fer years, I would wake up from nightmares o' being back in that dank chamber o' his. 'Twas below the chapel, ye ken, down the stairs into the bowels o' the castle, a fitting place fer such vermin as he."

Malcolm's eyes narrowed with anger. "Even today, whenever I see a staircase leading down to a darkened landing, I feel like I am back there again, a little boy dragging himself step-by-step into misery." He spoke contritely. "Again, I am so sorry, lass, fer reacting this way, but ye do no' understand the kind o' danger Edgar is in. I wish I knew how King Edward could be so fooled by men such as Thurstan. The kind that show one face when the light's shining on them and another altogether when they are in the shadows."

He looked over her head toward the castle. "I must take leave o' ye immediately to see the King. Edward must put an end to these tutoring sessions, and he will—once I tell him what I know they consist o'. Mayhap I should have done that years ago when I was i' Edgar's place. But it seemed pointless since I was able to deal wi' Thurstan myself. I was lucky to be at an age where I had enough strength i' my own hands to fight off the bastard and free myself o' his presence forever. But Edgar, he is too young to be able to defend himself against such a one."

Malcolm dropped the remaining rocks onto the ground and rubbed his hands on his kilt before going down on one knee to reach out for Margaret's hand. "Do no' forget I will come fer yer letter fer Gerhard afore supper. I will make certain that he gets it, and I will wait to see if he has an answer fer ye as well. In the meantime, I shall go confer wi' the King." Slowly, he bent down his head to brush a kiss against her hand, and from that lowered position, he locked eyes with her for a brief moment before turning away and heading back up the hill toward the castle.

As his figure began to fade in the distance, Margaret felt worry cascade over her. Once again, she was a tiny vessel caught in a maelstrom, the currents of intrigue swirling about her. This time though when waves of panic began to seize her, she did not turn from them. She faced their onslaught and breathed deeply. She would not wait for rescue. She would take matters into her own hands. And the first step was to free her brother from Thurstan's control. Patting the gospel book in her pocket, she moved confidently in the direction of deliverance. With each stride, she prayed for forgiveness about the lie she was going to tell. She hoped that Jesus would understand.

*　　*　　*　　*　　*

Father Thurstan was done reading. Edgar tried to keep his attention on the content of the passage, but his mind kept flitting about. It took nearly all his concentration to keep his hands folded on the desk when all they really wanted to do was reach down and swat at the vermin that came menacingly close to his feet. He wiggled his toes and flexed his heels to keep them away. When he did try to concentrate on what Thurstan was saying, the message was blurred by the man's ugliness. Edgar got lost in the man's caved mouth, studying his protruding and receding lips that dripped saliva at the edges. Occasionally, the hint of a tooth would push through, the image of rot so vile that Edgar found himself blinking repeatedly as if to erase it from his vision.

"Do you hear me, boy? I will ask once again: What have the prophets of Baal learned?" Thurstan stepped in closer without invitation.

Edgar cleared his throat. "Sorry, Father. I was just thinking it over."

Thurstan roared. "Thinking it over? A village idiot would not need to 'think it over'! It is right there in the text! There is only one God. There is only one Lord."

"Yes, Father." Edgar added casually, "I was about to say that before you answered the question for me."

Thurstan's eyes squinted in rage. ""About' to say? 'About' to say? You were given plenty of time to respond, young man. Do you have the nerve to fix the blame on me? Accuse me of speaking hastily?" Thurstan edged even nearer to the desk.

Edgar pulled back in fear. "No, Father. That was not my intent. I just wanted you to know that I had the answer. Surely, it was my own fault for not getting it out faster."

The priest was now right in front of him. "The prophets of Baal were calling upon the wrong Lord, the wrong leader. Put out your hand, boy. There can only be one Lord, just as there can only be one

King. Lay your hand flat on the desk. For that, *"Elijah brought them down to the brook Kishon and slaughtered them all.'"* The priest raised the bone pen in his hand and brought it down with force into the web between Edgar's thumb and index finger. The boy screeched in agony, barely able to restrain his urge to escape.

"Now, tell me again, what have you learned?"

A bead of sweat trickled from Edgar's temple as he watched the blood pool beneath his impaled hand. "I … have learned … there is … only … one God." He uttered the words with gaps of breath in between, trying to control his anger. The calm tenor of his speech hid his overwhelming desire to pull the bone pen from his hand and plunge it into Thurstan's neck.

Nodding his head in approval, the priest leaned in toward Edgar, letting the hot steam of his breath choke the air around them. "In time, you will also come to learn that things here are no different from those in Mount Carmel. There will be only one Lord here in England after King Edward is gone. And anyone who dares put forth a rival to that Lord shall perish. Edward's successor will be a native of this land and not some foreign-born impostor without a brain in his head or a—"

Hearing a noise from the doorway, the priest stopped mid-sentence. He turned to look over his shoulder.

Margaret had been at the top of the stairs when she heard Edgar's cry. She raced down the steps and burst through the portal to find Thurstan hovering over her brother with his face turned toward her.

"Who do you think you are? Barging into my study? Disrupting my instruction?" His words dripped with loathing.

In the time it took for Father Thurstan to shift his attention to Margaret, Edgar pulled the bone pen from his hand and sprang out of his chair. But Margaret was not ready to leave just yet.

"And who do you think *you* are, tormenting my brother like this?" She shoved the priest with the force of all the hatred she had for this country and its corrupt noblemen. She watched with cold indifference as he toppled over and fell upon his side, his head coming to rest just inches away from the filled chamber pot.

"Go, Edgar. Run. Get out of here."

The boy sprinted away. Margaret moved over to the fallen priest. "The King has sent for my brother; just wait until Edgar tells him about the kind of lessons you teach. As a matter of fact, Malcolm of Scotland is with the King right now, sharing his own experiences when he was your student, those many years ago. This will put an end to your despicable 'instruction.'"

Thurstan scrambled to his feet, knowing that he had to stop his secrets from getting out. He darted toward the door to block her exit. "You will not say a word, nor shall your brother. Otherwise, you shall never know what drink or what morsel of food shall be the last to cross your lips. You are too foolish to understand how things work in this kingdom. You need to know that we do not take too kindly to exiles—something you could surely ask your father about . . . were he not sealed away in a stone vault." The priest folded his arms triumphantly, delighting in his power over her and over anyone who stood in the way of Harold's ascension to the throne.

"You are the Devil's man." Margaret was struck by a mixture of rage, fear, and desperation. "I fight you with the power of the true Lord." She had to figure out a way to get past him and out of that horrid place. Reaching into the pocket of her skirt, she drew forth her gospel book, and holding it with both hands, she batted the priest on the side of his body. "You blackguard. You hypocrite. Twisting the words of God to fit your fiendish plans and schemes. But His justice shall rain down upon you, and one day you shall be forced to answer for your sins."

She kept striking him even after he fell to the ground and covered his head with his arms for protection. When he cowered far enough away for her to open up the door, she crossed the threshold and turned back to offer a final warning. "'*God will crush the heads of his enemies…those who persist in guilty ways.*' Read the true word of God, and stay away from my brother. From all of us."

Margaret fled up the steps, eager to distance herself from such evil, but she knew she had not gotten away unscathed. In her encounter with Father Thurstan, her spirit had stepped into the shadows. And in the hours and days to come, she would need to atone for choosing that pathway into darkness.

*   *   *   *   *

Gerhard lay on his back in the gloom. He felt the heaviness of it pushing down upon his chest as he remained flat on his bed. The absence of light mirrored his own loss of hope.

His skin was gray and ashen, his bones as brittle as a sparrow's. He had not enough energy to lift his head and had taken no food for days. Each morning the servant came in with broth and returned later to remove it, the contents untouched. His body ached, every joint locked in place and unable to bend. It had come to the point where he could barely roll over to relieve himself, the agony of standing too great. But all the pain, the constant throbbing, and the ripples of cold that flushed through his body did not trouble him as much as the misery weighing down his heart.

He had failed. It kept coming back to him as an inescapable truth. He was his lord's protector, and he had failed. After all of the years of overseeing Edward's schooling, his journey into manhood, his illustrious military career, his prosperous marriage, the raising of his three children, Gerhard fell short when it counted most, practically handing over Edward into the hands of his enemies. Gerhard took no pleasure in any of those past accomplishments. They had all been

205

washed away as Gerhard drowned in grief over the loss of his "son" and disgust over his own ineptitude. The man he was supposed to guide, shield, and defend now lay buried and rotting in a frigid tomb when his star should have been at its zenith for all to behold.

For a brief time, Gerhard did attempt to rally himself after Edward's death. He tried to believe that redemption was his, as long as he could ensure the safety of his ward's three children. But Gerhard had no faith in himself any longer. He knew he would fail at that too, and so, on some level, he felt it better to not even try. His absence from them was hard to endure—on both sides, he was certain—but it was definitely better than being with them only to blunder again, driving him down even deeper into that dark abyss that was swallowing him whole.

A soft tapping at the door confused him for a moment. He wished it had been the final rattling of his heart. But it was not. His suffering would continue. The small stub of a candle danced up and down, coinciding with the arrival of the servant who drew near.

Gerhard's eyes struggled to focus. The attendant's face was blurry to him, but Gerhard could see a paper in his hand. The servant brought the parchment closer to the candle to shine a feeble light upon it.

"A missive for you, sir." The man tried to offer it to Gerhard. "The Scottish king delivered it himself and is waiting outside the door for your response."

Gerhard had no strength to open his hand, nor did he have any hope of being able to read the letter. Licking his dry, cracked lips, he mumbled, "Read it."

"I barely know my letters, sir, but I will try." The servant nodded and went down upon one knee, placing the candle on the ground for a better angle of light. He bent lower and read in a stilted fashion:

We long to be with you, Master Gerhard. Please let us—or at least me—come visit. Your absence weighs heavily on our hearts. Remember the proverb you taught us?

"A broken spirit dries up the bones."

We do not mind if you are tired. We do not need lessons, nor do we need to play. We just want to sit with you.

I have nowhere to put my love when you are not around. And I become bitter and afraid when I have only myself to turn to. Please let me visit—I can bring you food, ale, anything—only do not leave me alone like this without knowing how you are.

- Margaret

Gerhard felt the sting of tears. One by one, they left a trail of moisture down his cheek, navigating their way through the grizzled whiskers along his jawline. Parting his lips once more, he whispered, "Send him in."

*   *   *   *   *

Malcolm stood outside the door pacing back and forth awaiting Gerhard's reply. To be truthful, he was thinking more about Margaret's absence from dinner than Gerhard's answer to the letter. He had been looking forward to seeing her when Edgar had told him she would not be in attendance. The boy spoke with an openness that was refreshing to see at court. It was the young man's innocence that allowed him to speak with such candor. He had not yet learned the practice of hidden meanings or the art of leaving certain words unspoken.

Forthright in his explanation, Edgar told Malcolm everything. "No, she is not coming to dinner. My sister is too busy making up for all her sins. She has much to make up for too. At least, that is what she said. And when she gets like that, nobody can convince her otherwise. She will probably kneel on pebbles for a week or something. And then she will go without sleep and probably starve herself in the process. But," he added matter of factly, "she did tell me to give you this." That was when Edgar had handed him the letter.

Now, here he was, marching outside Gerhard's door, wondering about the saintly girl who had captured his heart. The door creaked open, interrupting his thoughts.

"He wishes to see you," the servant said without emotion, handing Malcolm the candle.

Malcolm ducked quickly through the low arching door. Once inside, he slowed his pace to match the solemn atmosphere that hinted at impending death. "I am here, sir, at yer service—Malcolm, the emissary chosen by Lady Margaret to deliver ye that message." When Malcolm heard a slight rumble coming from Gerhard's throat, he knelt on the ground next to the bed in order to hear what the frail man was trying to say.

Malcolm offered further information. "Milady has tried to contact ye 'afore now, but she has been turned aside time and time again. She felt that, mayhap, I would be granted permission to bring her words to ye, and that seems to have come to pass. So may she come visit ye? It doesna' have to be fer long. Just so she can sit wi' ye fer a wee bit?"

The silence lengthened. Malcolm waited patiently until he heard a muffled sound coming from Gerhard's chest. The old man was trying to speak, but it was not easy. Malcolm wished he could help. He wanted to reach in and pull the words from Gerhard's throat. He could not bear to witness such struggle like this.

"I… cannot… see… any of them… I am… ashamed…" The syllables came out slowly, drenched in sorrow.

Malcolm watched the teardrops descend down Gerhard's face. He was never one for pretending, so he did not lie to the old fellow and speak of recovery or a return to the world of the living. The man was readying himself for death, of that there was no doubt.

"'Tis no shame in having done all one can do to ensure an outcome, even if the outcome was no' the one ye wished fer. The striving fer it is where true honor and nobility rest. And i' my eyes, ye've performed yer duties nobly. 'Twas no fault o' yer own that their father was called home to God. When a man's time is up, there is naught anyone can do to stop that moment from coming. So as fer shame, I will hear none o' that."

Malcolm's eyes softened as he thought of all of the people he had known, all of the soldiers he had served with who had crossed into the next world. "But I will tell ye something further. Something about saying a proper farewell. We dinna' know how long we will be permitted to grace this world. But when the hour draws near fer us to go, we owe it to those we leave behind to face it head on. There'll be no burrowing ourselves into a hole somewhere to just disappear. Those that love us have earned the right to say good-bye 'afore we leave them to go. There is naught they can see o' ye that can damage the memory o' love. Love doesna' twist or bend or disappear like that. 'Tis steady and strong and unbroken. But to be denied that final farewell leaves gaps o' mystery that can wind up being filled wi' fear, sorrow, and resentment. Let her come and bid ye a proper farewell. Ye deserve that, as does she."

Gerhard heard Malcolm's voice, but it was nothing more than a whisper. The tutor was already far, far away. At the mention of Margaret's name, he was back on the ice again, skating with her upon Lake Ilmen in Baranya. Only this time instead of the frail old man he was, Gerhard was young again, gliding over the frosty surface with ease. As he moved in a direction opposite from Margaret, he noticed spidery cracks beginning to spread upon the area where he skated. His apprehension grew. He turned back to make sure that Margaret was safe. She was not. Just a short distance in front of her, a hole had opened. The icy water waited hungrily to suck her under.

Despite his youth and vigor, he would never get to her in time to save her from drowning in the frigid water. He saw her try to skate away from the chasm, but chunks of ice kept breaking away, expanding the hole faster than she could fly. The surface became thin and more fragile. He watched as she was being pulled backwards. Her arms flailed as she began to lose her balance. Just as she was about to tumble in, another figure—tall, strong, sturdy—materialized from the crystalized air. He defied the ice beneath him. Wrapping his thick arms around Margaret's waist, he swept her away from peril and carried her back to solid ground. He remained there with her, standing bravely by her side. The two joined together as one, looking at Gerhard with a mixture of love and release.

It was his time. Now the cracks had widened near himself. He heard the shards of ice crumble and saw them disintegrate into the murky depths below. He felt himself slipping into the beckoning water. Right before submerging, he managed to deliver one final message. In a faltering voice tinged with regret, he said to Malcolm, "Tell her …I am sorry… so very sorry…Take care of her … for me." Then he was gone.

In Malcolm's hand, the light from the candle trembled and flickered. Its glow cast a shadow upon the lifeless body that lay stretched out on the bed. Placing his hand upon Gerhard's stilled heart, he ushered him toward peace. "I will, good sir. I will."

PART THREE

LAYERS OF INTRIGUE

Winter 1060 – Spring 1064

CELIA

THE FORCE BEHIND THE THRONE

CAEN, NORMANDY – WINTER 1060

Celia loved the snap of the freshly laundered tablecloth when she held it from its ends and whipped it into the air. The sound reminded her of how daily problems could vanish just like wrinkles on the fabric by dint of concentrated effort. Once the linen was smooth and clear, she carefully matched the edges together and folded it into perfect creases. Finished with one, she reached for the next, but then stopped. With her hand hovering over the basket, she lifted her head and waited. Something told her she was not alone.

Her intuition was confirmed when she turned from her work to face the doorway. There stood Jeanette, her crossed eye scrutinizing Celia's every move.

"You startled me." Celia spoke with detachment.

"Well, do not be so sensitive then." Jeanette drew closer and snatched the piece Celia had just folded. "Hmm. Adequate." She tossed it carelessly back onto the table. "Though I do think a bit more lye would make it whiter. You will need to do better than this." She sifted through the pile, rumpling up the work Celia had done. "Come. We have to go."

Celia would not be intimidated. "I do not recall asking for your opinion regarding my skills, so busy yourself with some other servant who either cares what you think or is too meek to say she does not."

Most of the time, Celia was able to limit her interaction with Jeanette simply through avoidance. Everyone knew the woman to be a scheming manipulator who had slithered her way into the Duchess' inner circle, a circle that could enlarge or shrink based on Matilda's whim. With her position founded upon shifting sand, Jeanette was constantly looking to solidify her worth by sabotaging someone else's. All of the maids and servants knew that when Jeanette felt threatened, she would fabricate some tale of ineptitude or negligence and then gloat while she watched her rival lose favor with the Duchess. Girls who had shown great promise soon found themselves relegated to jobs like tannery assistant or garderobe cleaner—places where they would have no further chance of engaging with Matilda. In that way, Jeanette kept herself relevant.

"Go where?" Celia would know this before agreeing to go anywhere with the woman.

"To meet with the Duchess. She commands it. She awaits us in the Great Hall." Celia took note of Jeanette's emphasis on "us," clearly an assertion of her own importance.

This was a strange summons indeed, but Celia would not display her worry in front of Jeanette. Dropping her chin to her chest, she kept her head down and rearranged the folded tablecloths before moving towards the door. She had met Matilda on a single occasion, the day when Her Grace had welcomed all of the homeless villagers to Caen. Since then, Celia had seen the Duchess only from a distance, which was fine with her because she had no desire for promotion or power. Thoughts began swirling in her head. *Why does she wish to speak with me? Have I done something wrong? Is it something to do with Vivienne?* Burying these troubling questions, she followed Jeanette without speaking.

When they arrived at the hall, Celia saw the Duchess perched on a large, ornate chair which was raised on a high platform. Her delicate hands held the fabric she was embroidering, her fingers guiding the needle in and out to form the pattern. There was a calm, steady flow to her stitches just as there was a palpable air of self-possession about her. The Duchess looked up when she heard movement near the doorway. Jeanette entered the room and curtsied in deference. Celia waited at the threshold.

"Here is Celia, Your Grace. The servant you wished to see." She gestured with her hand in Celia's direction and then moved toward the right side of Matilda's chair where she would assume her place of importance.

Matilda's light brown eyes sparkled with authority. "That will be all."

In front of the Duchess, Jeanette hid her disappointment but threw a nasty glance Celia's way before exiting.

"Come in, Celia." Matilda rose from her chair and placed the sewing on the vacant seat. Everything about the Duchess was dainty —her small stature and light footstep made her seem more fairy than human. The skin on her face shone bright and radiant as if it had just been scrubbed with water from a cold spring. Complementing her full lips and slender nose were a pair of luminous brown eyes that gazed out upon the world with keen intellect.

Celia was still in her curtsied position when Matilda came close enough to tap her shoulder and latch her own arm into Celia's. Guiding her to sit on the bench positioned against the wall, she motioned for Celia to sit while she herself began walking slowly about the room.

"I understand you have had some difficulty with Mallory, one of the chambermaids."

Celia's mind flew across gaps in thought to make connections. Is this why she had been summoned? Mallory must have told on her. Despite the sweetness in the Duchess' voice, Celia knew she could not admit to what had been going on between her and Mallory. She must simply avoid telling the truth.

She opened her hands, palms facing up. "I am truly sorry, Your Grace, but I do not understand." She shrugged her shoulders in confusion. "I have no issue with Mallory." That was easy to say because it was the truth. Mallory initiated the mischief, Celia had just responded to it. "Indeed, she rarely occupies my thoughts. I am too busy performing my duties to concern myself with anything or anyone else." Celia widened her eyes large enough to feign complete innocence. "There are no problems between Mallory and me. How can there be when my heart is filled only with gratitude for what you and the Duke have done for all of us here? You are the reason for our survival."

"Ah, but who said 'problems'? I merely mentioned 'difficulty.' Are there problems then, between you and this girl?" Matilda stopped walking to pause right in front of Celia where she could study the girl's reaction.

Celia corrected herself. "Difficulty *is* what you said, Your Grace, of course. But no, I have neither difficulties nor problems with Mallory." A true statement because, in Celia's mind, Mallory was never any real threat. Nothing she herself could not handle.

"Hmmm." Matilda removed her veil and shifted her single braid from the back of her head to rest upon the side of her shoulder. She pulled off the ribbon at the bottom and then began replaiting her hair, blending in the strands that had escaped. Her fingers worked fast and efficiently, keeping pace with the observations she was making in her mind.

Celia met Matilda's gaze without faltering even though she could feel her insides churning. How could she continue to feign innocence? But she had to omit the truth. She must. She could not risk losing her position here, could not risk being told to leave. She tried to hold herself together. The stillness felt like mud sucking her downward. She knew she was burying herself deeper under the mire of her own fabrications, but she was committed to do so if it meant protecting her sister and herself.

"You impress me, Celia, and not just for your creative ways of exacting revenge. The fact that you can look me in the eye and portray fallacy as truth, well, that is even more impressive." Matilda's stare was unrelenting.

The Duchess continued. "Do you take me for a fool? Do you think I am unaware of what is happening under my own roof?"

The mildness in her voice was gone. A steely edge took its place. "Let me tell you this. My husband would never have arrived at his position of power were it not for the efforts of his devoted wife, a wife who is more attuned to the comings and goings of everyone in this castle than even the Duke himself."

Matilda dropped all pretense. "I know about the lard. I know about the manure. And, most importantly, I know why Mallory is bald."

Celia had to find a way to redeem herself. She must beg forgiveness. Dropping from the bench to her knees, she bowed her head in supplication. "I am sorry for not being forthright with you, Your Grace. I admit I—"

"Silence. I am not interested in hearing any apologies. I am no priest and this is no confessional. Take care of that on your own time when your conscience becomes too much to bear." Reaching toward Celia's clasped hands, she commanded, "Get off your knees and sit back down."

Celia did as she was ordered and watched the Duchess march back toward her chair laden with authority. "You are not here to be chastised, foolish girl. You are here because I actually like your methods. I admire the way you handle your affairs. And, I especially enjoy how you can remain calm under interrogation amidst building tension. These are invaluable gifts for one to possess, and that is why I want to make you one of my private attendants. Once there, you can do more than launder the linens, although your new tasks will still require you to remove filth to a certain degree—the filth that infiltrates this court." She grasped both arms of the chair as evidence of her determination.

Celia was willing to agree to anything as long as she was not going to be expelled from the castle. "Most certainly, Your Grace. Whatever it is you require. I would be honored to be of service to you."

Leaning forward, Matilda focused her large brown eyes in order to pierce Celia's own. "Is this your genuine feeling, or are you telling me what I wish to hear?" Her shrewdness proved she was well acquainted with the sugary words of flatterers.

"Your Grace, do not doubt me. I lay my heart bare to you. My sister and I owe everything to you and the Duke. Command me how you will."

Matilda relaxed her posture, softening her grip on the chair. She reclined further back. "The games played at court are complex and calculated. A friend one day is an enemy the next. That is why I need ears to hear and eyes to see in those places where I cannot go. That is what you shall do for me."

Celia had questions she wanted to ask but did not want the Duchess to think she was balking at this assignment. She decided to limit them to just one. "Is there any place you wish me to frequent in particular, or any people you specifically want me to be attentive to?"

"See. This is good. You are asking the right kind of questions. My dear, you were made for this kind of work. I knew I had a viper in you. Undetected, you strike without fanfare, without prior notice. Swift and potent." She thought about Celia's inquiry. "Of course, I want you to be sensitive to all of the people who visit the castle as well as all those who reside here. But for the moment, I want you to monitor the conversations and activities involving the Count of Maine and his sister. We have provided them sanctuary and have welcomed them into our family, offering them betrothals to our own daughter and son. The county of Maine is of great concern to my husband, and it is our wish that it be returned to our family."

Casually, Matilda picked up her embroidery and began pushing the needle in and out of the fabric once again. "Things are stirring in that region. With the death of Geoffrey, his Anjou estate is now in the hands of his two nephews. They may try to reach out to Herbert to thwart my husband's wishes for the future. Avail yourself of the girl. The pair are very close. He will confide in Marguerite if an alliance with the two nephews is proposed. Gather information. Lurk in the shadows. Linger at the table. Hover in the meadow. It is information I seek."

She continued to speak as if she were addressing the material in her lap. "My husband is a man of action—a genius in the field and ruthless in victory. I suppose I am that way too within my own sphere of power. But the beauty of it is that so are you. I heard and saw what you did to Mallory. Sometimes people need to be taught a lesson. They need to learn that there are some individuals one should never cross. Mallory will not trouble you again. And her punishment was especially delicious—quick and oh, so memorable."

She lifted the hoop to examine what she had completed so far, her eyes evaluating the quality of her work. "My husband has set his sights on securing Maine, taking back what is rightfully his, and I want to see his design come to fruition. So remember. Watch. Listen. And report. That is what I ask and what I expect of you. Jeanette will show you your new accommodations."

With these words, Celia's audience with the Duchess was over. She bowed and headed for the door. Before leaving, she took a final look back and watched as Matilda bit the excess thread with her teeth, satisfied with the stitches she had completed.

*   *   *   *   *

Celia knew she did not belong. She knew it and so did all of the other women in the room. There was not a drop of noble blood in her ancestry. Who was she anyway? Some vagabond who had wandered in from the road. And now she found herself surrounded by daughters of barons or counts, girls who were never forced to plant their own food or dig a parent's grave. But neither she nor any of them would ever say a word about her being an outsider in this assembly. No one dare challenge Matilda or her decisions.

For Celia, the hours crept by slowly. Companionship, conversation, entertainment—all dreadfully dull. She never thought she would say it, but she preferred the frenetic pace of the last few years to this tedium, this comfortable but boring existence. Gone were her chapped and cracked hands from all the washing, cleaning, and cooking. Instead, a pair of soft, supple ones rested feebly in her lap. Doing nothing. Useless. They yearned for motion. She forced them into stillness to mask her impatience.

It was that hectic pace that made the past years fly by. When there is no time for leisure, there is no time for thought. One is subsumed with survival. And while the thought of survival still lingered in the back of her mind, most of the time it never plagued her to the extent that the prospect of having no food in winter did.

All of the women were seated together, forming an arch that stretched out from its central figure of Matilda into an open semicircle. The Duchess, from her raised chair, presided over the group, while Marguerite sat on a stool in the middle of the room, plucking away at her lute. The *chanson* she sang featured the joyful reunion of a mother and son, but the singer herself reflected no such joy. Pale and washed out, Marguerite was so weak and frail that the lute overwhelmed her body. It engulfed her figure in the same way that life had swallowed her strength. Celia could see that it was a visible struggle for the girl to get the lyrics out of her mouth. She had to suck in deep gulps of air just to create the thin, nasal sound that hurt Celia's ears but somehow enchanted everyone else's.

The song involved a little boy who had wandered off into the forest, leaving his mother distraught. Happily, the child is later returned by faeries and the two rejoice at being brought together again. Celia forced her lips closed to hold back a yawn. She had heard this *lai* many times before, and truth be told, those earlier renditions were far superior to this current one.

With Marguerite still languishing in the melancholy portion of the tune, Celia looked with disdain at the eyes around her that had swelled with tears. She mocked them silently, thinking about how this was what they cried over. An imaginary tale. They knew nothing of the real sorrows of the world. Of flesh and blood children wrenched from their mother's arms when soldiers come pillaging. They had not heard the shrieks borne of separation that pierce so deeply they clang upon the heart for eternity. They knew not of such things. With their brightly colored gowns and milky white skin unsullied by cut, wound or scar, they mistook fanciful tales for reality. With nothing but air inside their head, they had as much substance as dead leaves carried away by the slightest wind. And when the melody eventually shifts to the joyous part of the song, they will be swept away yet again by the felicity it recounts. Their fake tears magically vanish into the air, leaving behind no trace of real sorrow.

Celia believed Matilda was different though. She was not like the empty vessels who populated the room. Today her gown was rose in color, a soft shade of pink that accentuated her dark hair and soulful eyes. But Celia had come to learn there was not anything soft about Matilda's character. Her will was forged of iron, unbendable and cold beneath that outward beauty. Although the singer occupied a seat of attention, it was still Matilda who dominated the room. One need not plunge into the ocean to be aware of its current.

Matilda's face assumed a look of interest, but Celia believed it to be just a facade. Even though her eyes smiled with the richness of cinnamon, Celia knew the Duchess was continually measuring, evaluating, and planning. Far different was she from the aimless fools who sat around her. Over these last few months, Matilda devoured every morsel of information Celia delivered. Minor or otherwise, the Duchess welcomed it all. There already were a few times when Celia knew she had truly pleased her sovereign, like the day when she handed over news that Robert de Grandnesmil was planning a papal visit to Rome to overturn his expulsion by the Duke. On that occasion, Matilda's eyes flashed like a lightning strike. Grateful beyond words, she spontaneously undid the clasp of the brooch fastened to her own shawl and fixed the jewel upon Celia's own. Sometimes Celia learned of the outcomes brought about by her information—like the siege of Saint-Ceneri or the naming of a new abbot at Saint-Evroul—sometimes she did not. Either way, what did it matter? As long as she kept the Duchess satisfied.

The more involved she was in this kind of intrigue, the more she learned that worthwhile information was rarely exchanged in the dark corners or private rooms of the castle. Strangely enough, the best locations for significant discoveries were in the most unlikely of places: the water trough outside the stable, outdoor celebrations and gatherings, marketplaces and selling stalls. She much preferred being at one of those sites now rather than stuck in her chair listening to the story of some farfetched reunion involving elves and sprites. She needed to get out of there.

As Marguerite continued to whine her way through the melody, Celia decided she could take no more. "My stomach is unsettled. I beg pardon," she whispered to the jailer beside her—Jeanette. Crouching down low to make the least disturbance possible, Celia tiptoed out of the room. Jeanette's nostrils flared, and her nose went up into the air as if trying to detect the scent of an ulterior motive.

Celia had no need of the privy. Free of it all—Jeanette, the insipid musical performance, and the dim-witted ladies in attendance—she sought out a healthy dose of real life, a reunion that involved the friendship and goodwill of Rowena and the love and tenderness she felt for Vivienne. At this time of day, she knew where she would find them both, and who knew? Perhaps in that open and innocent setting, she might even find a secret or two worth sharing with her sovereign.

FEALTY REWARDED

CAEN, NORMANDY - AUTUMN 1062

She had never seen the Duchess behave this way. Her usual composure and confidence were gone. She moved about frantically as if in a perpetual state of emergency.

Duke William was ill, extremely ill. Celia overheard that nothing was working. The apothecary's weekly visits had turned into perpetual care, and still there was no improvement. Despite all of the tonics, bloodletting, and bedside prayers, his condition remained the same. The once mighty warrior was wasting away. According to his servants, he was nearing death. That explained why Matilda was crumbling.

This is what she and Rowena were discussing when they met together one evening. Rowena put out some bread and a thick wedge of cheese. Their work done for the day, they sat at the small wooden table in Rowena's room as a single candle embraced them in a warm yellow light.

Rowena took a sip of wine, savoring its taste before speaking. "Is there nothing they can do for him then?"

Celia reached for the bread, broke it in two, and offered a piece to her friend. "The surgeons have no answer. No one has seen him, other than the Duchess and his advisors, but there are rumors of course. I have heard rumblings that he can no longer sit up and is barely aware of his surroundings."

Rowena took a bite, but then paused and held up the bread mid-air at the description of the Duke's situation. "Now that *is* frightening. No one has ever seen him falter. Think of all the times we have caught glimpses of him riding about the region, surveying his lands or returning from battle. Such an imposing figure. How very sad to see him so vulnerable!" Rowena returned to her wine. "And how fares the Duchess?"

Celia left her food untouched. "Matilda has come undone. Confused. Disheveled. She won't let anyone prepare her toilet. She wears the same gown and has not combed her hair for days. She wanders about lost in thought when she is in our company—which is less and less these days. Most times, she is at prayer, either by his bedside or in the abbey."

Rowena reached across the small table to squeeze Celia's hand. "What will happen to us all if William does die? Where would we go? We have found a measure of contentment here, have we not? Both you and I. And just look at how far you have come. People say you are favored by the Duchess. But even so, if he should pass away, what would she do? What would happen to us both? It troubles me to think of having to leave this place and take to the road again."

Celia felt the same flood waters rising in her own heart, a sea of worry that threatened to drown them both. "I know. There is to be a ceremony tomorrow at William's bedside. He has summoned all of the noblemen to swear allegiance to Robert, his son. The Duke is naming him as his successor. If Robert is accepted by them, then perhaps there will be no change in our situation here." She reconsidered. "Well, not with yours but perhaps there will be with mine, for Matilda would soon be supplanted by Robert's wife, if and when he marries. Matilda would not need as many ladies tending her then."

"But still, you would have to be among the ones she retains. In any case, let us hope then that by that point all of William's troops will have been called home, and Chloe, Grace, and I can come live with you and Simon in Dives-sur-Mer someday." Rowena brushed the crumbs from the table into her hand, walked toward the aperture in the wall, and sent them sprinkling out through the open casement.

"That too is a dream of mine, Rowena. To see us all together when Simon returns. I thought I would have received word from him by now, but he must not have been able to send a message. We will have such a happy home if you come join us. And how it would ease my mind if I had you there with me to help with the more—shall we say, practical details involved in wedded life."

"Of course, *mon tresor*. I can give you as much or as little detail as you like!" Rowena sauntered over to Celia and rested her cheek on the top of Celia's head, embracing her from behind. "Speaking of little details, I just realized I left the box containing my beads and ribbons outdoors by the children's play area. Will you come with me while I retrieve it?' She grabbed her shawl, and after Celia nodded, Rowena tossed over Celia's as well.

"The girls made bracelets today. I had to keep them busy while I walked the boys over to Cantrell for a lesson on how to chop wood. Poor Cantrell, he looked positively exhausted, probably from having to be around Mallory so much more now since he does not have you to break up his day. His 'chance' meetings with you—which he most certainly pre-planned—gave him something to look forward to, I daresay. But now, he just drags himself around the place, showing little interest in anything. At least teaching the boys does help. Gives him distraction and a break from her." Rowena held open the door, waiting for Celia to join her.

Outside the warmth of the castle, they could see their breath even though it was not yet winter. The trees were bare, their branches reaching out from their trunks as if trying to recapture a vibrancy that now lay dormant. Shafts of moonlight peeked through the limbs, creating patches of hope amidst the blackness. The ground beneath them, layered with fallen leaves, was now coated with a white sheen of frost that made each step they took crackle and crunch as if the leaves themselves were in pain. It was a night for cold thoughts.

"You are lucky to work with children. Their lives are rounded out with hope. As one grows older, expectation fades away." Celia could barely remember her own carefree childhood, so much had changed. Now only wistfulness remained. "Death is never far away, is it, Rowena? I fear it is encircling the palace more so now than ever before."

They continued to walk downhill closer to the river. "The Duke's illness makes you think of this, eh?" Rowena asked.

"That, and . . ." Celia broke off and reached out her arm to stop Rowena's forward movement. "Did you hear something?" Her blue eyes shifted back and forth, scanning the immediate area.

"When?"

"Now"

"No." Rowena tilted her head and listened. They both waited in silence. "I do not hear anything."

Celia gradually agreed. "Maybe it is just me. I probably just imagined it." They resumed their journey and soon came upon the box with the trinkets. "Anyway, it is not just the Duke. First, it was Marguerite. Then her brother Herbert. Now it seems as if the Duke is next. And then, who knows? Perhaps Matilda. She seems lifeless already, a mere shadow of her former self. Clearly she loves William more than I had ever thought."

"More than you and everyone else ever thought, I am sure. Royal marriages rarely engage the heart. But their union is—" Rowena stopped abruptly. "Now I *did* just hear something. Just now." She whispered intensely. "Who would be about at this hour?" She clutched the box tightly to her chest.

"Start heading back. I will go see."

"Have you lost your wits? Leave you out here alone? No, I will not go back without you. Who knows what danger lurks out there!" Rowena pulled on Celia's sleeve.

"You do not understand, Rowena, this is what I do. I must go see who is there. I will not do anything beyond that. Nothing that will endanger myself. Observe, listen, and report. That is what I do. You go on ahead. I will meet you back at your room." Celia tapped Rowena's hand in reassurance. "Probably just someone come to relieve himself in the woods, nothing more. Go on ahead. I will be along soon. Promise."

Rowena hesitated. "I do not like this, Celia. I do not like it at all. But I shall abide by your wishes because I know I would be a hindrance to you should I remain. Do not fail to come visit me again later when you are done out here. If you are not back soon, I am getting Cantrell to go find you and drag you back inside—and then you will have Mallory's jealousy to deal with all over again." Although her tone was curt, Rowena kissed Celia's hand and spun around to make her way back to the castle.

Freed from worrying over her friend, Celia moved silently through the shadows, careful to avoid areas illuminated by moonlight. From tree to tree, she darted between the gaps to find refuge behind each trunk. Her footfall was so soft it seemed as if she were gliding over the ground. Soon the sound of conversation grew louder, and she was able to detect two voices. One male, one female. The pair was on the move, and Celia followed in pursuit. She watched first, then plotted her way, hoping to get close enough to hear but far enough to avoid detection.

Stretching her neck from behind the tree, she could see the woman. She was squat and thick, her black cloak dragged on the ground, the hood pulled over her head. Judging from the fabric and style of her garment, she was no peasant. Celia felt she recognized the body to be somewhat familiar, but she reserved judgment until she could hear the stranger's voice. The man was wiry and tall, his tunic barely coming to his knee and the exposed portion of his legs thin like twigs. He wore no boots, only simple shoes made of cloth. Despite not having an outer garment, he seemed impervious to the cold, so hungry was he for the woman's information.

The two passed the livestock pens and the barn and then stopped outside the granary which, because of its raised structure, blocked out the moon. They were enveloped in darkness.

"I have told you already, this is the end."

"You are certain of it?"

"Aye. There will be no coming back for him from this point on."

That voice . . . the woman's voice. She had heard it before.

"This will please my lord." The man sounded happy as well.

"As it should. If he strikes now, no Norman will stop him from seizing Maine, at least no one here. Everyone will be too busy mourning the passing of the Duke to care about land acquisition."

"This is tremendous news indeed. With the assistance of Geoffrey, the region will belong to my lord. And then who knows? Perhaps even the land of his uncle shall come under Walter's banner. I shall set out immediately. Take this for now." The man removed a ring from his finger and gave it to the woman. "Should all this come to pass as you have just described, there shall be even greater reward for you."

Celia held her breath as she committed their words to memory. She watched the man head back toward the stables, most likely to grab his mount and deliver this information to "Walter," his master. Meanwhile, the woman stepped out from the shadows to examine the ring more closely. The moonlight reflected off the jewel to illuminate the traitor's face in a soft glow. Even in the darkness Celia could see the crossed-eye sparkle with gratification.

Celia backed away and, once at a safe distance, ran back to the castle without stopping. Pausing briefly to check in with Rowena, she reported directly to Matilda's private chamber. Because of the nature of Celia's work, she was the only consort always granted access, regardless of time of day. But when she arrived at the room, she was greeted by a solitary attendant, Caroline, one of the more sincere ladies-in-waiting.

"I am sorry, Celia, but the Duchess is not here, of course." Caroline found it difficult to contain her grief. "She spends every moment now at her husband's side. They say it is only a matter of time." The girl dug into her pocket drawing out a cloth to dab away her tears. "If it is something urgent, you can find her there."

Celia could spare no time in comforting Caroline—it was not in her nature anyway to do so. In haste, she left Caroline behind. With the sconces in the hall still lit, she was able to move swiftly down the corridor without fear of slipping on the moist, uneven stones beneath her feet. When she arrived at the door of William's quarters, two soldiers stood guard at the rounded entranceway which was closed to visitors. Both men were equal in size, but she chose to address the one with the gentle, gray eyes.

"Please, you must help me. I have urgent news for the Duchess. I must speak with her."

"No one is permitted entry." The guard on the right gave his partner no chance to respond. He spoke the words flatly without feeling.

She ignored him. "Yes, I know that. I understand that to be so." She continued to speak only to the gray eyed sentinel. "But perhaps you could ask the Duchess to step outside ever so briefly. It will take but a moment." When she saw him shift his gaze to look upon her, she hurried on, "Tell her it is Celia. Tell her I have important news."

She had chosen well. The soldier did not look to his partner for approval. He lifted the latch on the door and stepped carefully inside. The remaining guard continued to scowl.

Slowly the door opened, and from the narrow gap, the Duchess slipped out and extended both of her hands to grab Celia's. Leading her a safe distance away and out of earshot, she stopped and brushed aside her tangled and untamed hair. Her rich brown eyes searched Celia's face.

"You have served me well, Celia, but I doubt that any news you carry can mean much to me—unless it involves a remedy for my husband, some divine elixir that can restore his vigor." Matilda shook her head as if to rid herself of such morbid thoughts. She started again. "Nonetheless, the world is what it is, and the future is not for ourselves to know. Therefore, I must protect myself against any threats that shall arise in the upcoming days and months if I do find myself alone. Tell me the information you have to share."

Until that moment, Celia had not realized just how much sturdier she was compared to the fragile Duchess. Weighed down by grief, Matilda seemed as limp as the straw doll Celia once fit into the palm of her hand when she was a little girl.

"Go on. What do you have for me?"

"Your Grace, there is a traitor amongst us. A traitor who is spreading news of the Duke's illness to his most bitter enemies. It happened just now, by the granary."

Matildas's spirits surged. Her listlessness melted away, and in its place, a new sense of purpose emerged.

"Tell me at once."

She recounted every detail she had witnessed, especially careful to accurately repeat the names "Walter" and "Geoffrey."

Matilda began to pace back and forth. "Already the vultures are circling, quick to claim their territory now that death seems imminent. But whether my husband lives or dies, I shall not let anyone seize what rightfully belongs to our family. That province is ours, twice over, by virtue of Marguerite's betrothal to our son Robert and Herbert's to our daughter Adela. Walter of the Vexin has no claim to our land, regardless of what alliances he makes."

Matilda stopped pacing to stand before Celia. She locked eyes with her so intensely that Celia felt bound by a spell that would not permit her to look away. "You have given me more than news, my dear. You have given me new life. Tomorrow I shall take my planned journey to the church at Cherbourg and deliver the donation and relics the Duke has bequeathed. There I shall place his gifts on the altar and pray to Our Lady that she return my dearest to me. She shall answer my prayer. She must answer my prayer."

Matilda's voice grew stronger. "When—not if—my husband's health is restored, the conquest of Maine shall serve as a stepping stone on his path to glory. And once that county is secure, he shall set his sights on even greater lands that are rightfully his. Let Walter think he is invincible, trusting the word of his spy and believing he will succeed his uncle as King of England. My husband will prove him wrong on both counts. Ruler of two kingdoms my Duke shall one day be." She brushed her lips against Celia's cheeks, kissing her on either side.

"And as for our cross-eyed informer, I will bring her with me to Cherbourg." Matilda's face was cold like marble, her brown eyes resolute with vengeance. Then, like the snap of a fire spark, the look vanished and she smiled angelically once more. "But alas, she will not be with us on our return."

As she turned to go, Celia called out, "I shall pray for the Duke's recovery and for your safekeeping, Your Grace."

With her hand on the latch, Matilda paused to smile once again before returning to the darkened room where her husband lay clinging to life. Celia watched the Duchess disappear behind the door, wondering what manner of fate awaited Jeanette; indeed, what manner of fate awaited them all.

ALL FOR HER

ROUEN, NORMANDY - SPRING - FALL 1064

Celia unwound her hair from its bun, the weight of it now released as it tumbled down to tickle her bare shoulders. Sitting on the bed in only a linen shift, she closed her eyes and willed her cares to melt away. Slowly, very slowly, she rubbed her fingers against her skull and massaged the roots, soothing the strands once pulled so tightly. Caroline and Juliette, were still busy with the Duchess, so she relished the quiet for however long it would last.

The faint scent of rosewater floated upon the air as she moved her hands to the back of her neck to lift her heavy, thick mane up and down. When she finally did open her eyes, her gaze landed on the chipped wooden comb that lay beside her. A pang of sadness struck deeply.

She had sacrificed Simon's gift on an altar she herself had built, an altar that honored vengeance. And now she had nothing left of his. Not one shred of the affection that had linked them together. The last time she had seen him was nearly four years ago, and all she had to fill up those months of absence was her own guesswork as to where he was and what battle he was fighting. She gathered up all of her hair to rest upon her shoulder and reached from the comb.

In her former home, there were other tokens from him, but those items were gone now. His mule cart, the fishing traps, one chopping axe—everything had been destroyed in the fires that raged before

Varaville. And those objects were gifts too, gifts that helped her survive when there was no one but herself to rely on. She closed her eyes once again as she ran the comb slowly and rhythmically through her hair from the crown to the ends. Her mind wandered.

Last she heard, Simon's regiment was in Maine. After the Duke had miraculously recovered, the campaign began in earnest. William laid claim to a series of castles, and then set his sights on Le Mans. But the surrender of Le Mans was long over, as was the defeat of Walter of the Vexin, and still no word from Simon. Perhaps he had returned to Caen? Maybe he was with Vivienne and Rowena right now, and they would explain to him how she was forced to come here to Rouen as part of the Duchess' retinue? She paused, placing the comb in the palm of her other hand. Yes, that was the vision she would cling to in her mind. She had to. Otherwise, she would wallow in despair.

And still, she felt the emptiness growing. Normally at this hour, she would be brushing Vivienne's tangled curls while they exchanged stories about the day. Their conversation would continue after the candle was extinguished, as they lay next to one another on the pallet they shared. After some time, two voices would dwindle to one with Vivienne drifting off to sleep during Celia's retelling of some sunny moment they had shared together.

The world was a cold place indeed when one was forced to exist in it alone.

She jumped back with surprise when the door to her room opened abruptly. Caroline shoved herself inside, slamming it shut in a single motion. Her eyes were wide with excitement, her chest moved up and down as if she had just run a race.

"By Our Lady, what is it, Caroline? Have you been chased by a ghost?" Celia put down the comb along with her musings.

"Oh, my goodness!" Caroline remained standing with her back against the door as if to block anyone from entering. Her breath was shallow, her words choppy. "Our soldiers . . . they have ransomed . . . two Englishmen . . . important ones . . . from Guy of Ponthieu . . . They just . . . brought them . . . to the Duke!"

Celia failed to see the reason for Caroline's distress. "So? Is William receiving them now?"

"And Matilda as well . . . she is with him . . . She dismissed us . . . from the room."

"Well, how did she seem? Was she worried? Angry? Happy?"

"Happy . . . yes, more than happy . . . kind of . . . triumphant." Caroline was starting to regain her composure. "She mumbled something about . . . catching a rat . . . without having to use any bait."

None of this made much sense to Celia. "Any idea who they are?"

"The men? One is a priest and the other one, I do not know but I think he is related to the English king. Matilda was short with us, but that was because she was hurrying to get to William."

Celia still could not make any connection between the prisoners' arrival and Caroline's excitement, but regardless, an event like this would surely afford her many opportunities to listen, observe, and report. "I suppose then that things will be interesting for all of us over the next few weeks."

Feeling more steady, Caroline stepped away from her post at the door. "But that is not all." She came closer to Celia. "There is someone here for you too. A soldier." Caroline had gained her composure well enough to begin teasing Celia. "He was asking around to see if anyone knew you. When I heard him say your name, I told him I knew you. Do you wish to know more?"

Celia's heart fluttered. *No, this could not be!* she thought. It was as if her previous reflections had willed Simon into existence! Now it was her turn to be short of breath. She dared not hope. "Where?"

Caroline smiled with the joy of having the upper hand. "Hmmm. Wouldn't you like to know!"

"Caroline—!" Celia had no patience for such games.

She conceded. "All right, all right. He is in the buttery, next to the Great Hall. He said he would be waiting there or down the stairs in the beer cellar."

Celia grabbed her tunic from off the bed and pulled it over her head. She did not bother to tie back her hair so eager was she to get to Simon. She had so much to tell him. So much had happened since they had been together. So much since he helped her undo Mallory's treachery. So much since she had pledged her word to him.

Purposely jostling Caroline as payback for her teasing, Celia ran out the door and went flying down the hall. The corridor was empty of guards. Busy with the hostages, she imagined. She sprinted with an enthusiasm she had not felt since she was a little girl. Back when the world offered adventure not misfortune.

Finally she arrived at the arched entrance to the room. Against the left wall, seven barrels were stacked—four on the bottom, three on top. The brown containers blended with the light from the sconces to create an orange glow in the room. There, with his back to her, stood a lone soldier. Even before he turned about, she felt the crush of disappointment. His shoulders were too narrow, his body too slender. The anticipated reunion she had hoped for was not to be.

In a flat, emotionless voice, she said, "I am Celia."

The young man froze at the sound of her words and remained with his back to her a second or two longer before slowly turning around.

When he turned, she saw his blue eyes sparkle with excitement and mischief.

"For once, you have to catch up to me instead of the other way around!"

The little boy who had constantly yearned for his sister's attention, who had begged to be included in her games, who had struggled to keep pace with her when she ran from him, that little boy was now fully grown, and here he was, the lean warrior towering over her.

Neither one of them had yet moved. Both were frozen with shock and disbelief.

"Philippe? My Philippe!" The words sputtered out in between sobs of joy. She darted toward him to close the space that separated them and then squeezed the arms that dangled far past his waist. He had sprouted so tall in these intervening years that his legs came up to her chest. Although his face still retained the blush of boyhood, his impressive height made her feel like one of the silly acrobats who performed at court.

Philippe's helmet, along with his sword and shield, rested on the first step of the staircase at the other end of the room. His blue and gray tunic ran down to his knees. Over it, he still wore his long-sleeved chain mail. A brown leather belt was cinched multiple times around his midsection, and his black boots were caked in mud. Despite being a soldier who defended or seized castles, Celia still saw him as the child who had built them with riverside pebbles.

"Dear, dear brother of mine! You have grown up without me! How dare you do that?" She reached out to tousle his short hair. "Praise God we have found one another again! Come, let us fill in the gaps of these years. I will fetch us some wine, and you can tell me how much you have missed me!" Not wanting to let him out of her sight, she gripped his hand and led him to the kitchen where she seated him by the hearth. After handing him a cup of wine, she pulled over another stool and sat next to him. In the fireplace, the embers still glowed.

"Celia, you are a good sister to me. I do not deserve such kindness. I am a brother who has failed you." Philippe dropped his head and stared at the hearth. He kept his face from her, but his voice revealed the strain.

"I am full of shame. You shouldered every hardship alone, and I did nothing. So busy was I serving Jacques that I never thought beyond my own needs, my own concerns. I did not ask about you because I did not want to know. I did not want to be held back from pursuing my own desires. So selfish was I. And then, when I grew wise enough to realize my wrongdoing, it was too late to make amends. My responsibilities as a soldier prevented me from doing so. I wanted to get back, please believe me when I say that. I wanted to get back to all of you. But as a man with no name, no lineage, and no anchor, I had not the power to stem the tide of battle. Every time I thought I would have the chance to get back home, the army tightened its grip and pulled me back in. But please know that I was haunted, tormented over how I had failed you."

Now he lifted his head to look directly into her eyes. "I thought of you and Papa and Vivienne every single day. And I prayed for all of you every morning and every night while I waited for the day—this day—when I could confess these things to you." He bent down upon his knees in front of her, placing his head in her lap. "Sister, I am so sorry for leaving you."

She placed both hands upon either side of his face and looked upon him with compassion. Traces of the innocent boy still remained beneath his soiled skin. With his reddish hair shorn so short on top, his eyes dominated his face with the same look of wonder that he had worn all those years ago. Save for the stubble that appeared sparsely along his jawline, his skin was still smooth as a baby's, the dimple in his chin as deep as it was in youth.

"Brother of mine, let us not dwell on what could have or should have been. The past is dead—thank God—and deserves no further consideration or time. Rather, let us be grateful that we are together, now, in this moment. You are alive and well, and so am I. And so is Vivienne who grows steadily and is smarter at her letters than you and I put together!"

She brought her hands down from his face and rested them on the table. "I would bring you to her right now, but she is not here. She is back at Caen with Rowena—oh, wait—you have not even met Rowena. She is like a second mother to Vivienne. She has two daughters of her own, Chloe and Grace. Her husband was killed by Martel's troops. I met her after the loss of our home. We were all searching for shelter."

Philippe went back to his seat, slapping his hands on his legs in frustration. "You see? That is exactly what I mean. I should have been there! I should have been there to protect you all." He spoke of himself with disgust. "I should have not left you alone."

"Stop! You are behaving more like a child now than you ever did back then because you insist on being doubly foolish and stubborn! Do you not realize I would not have accepted your protection back then? You were nothing but a nuisance to me. I told you that every day when we were growing up, and I am reminding you of that fact now. Anyway, we did have help, so stop torturing yourself. The Renoufs came to our aid and Emil, of course." She thought of something. "Emil, yes! Have you seen him in your journeys? Have you crossed paths with him at any time?"

"Valentin? Emil Valentin? Yes, I did hear of him. Not that I was able to speak with him, but he was with us when we were sending a message throughout the countryside surrounding Le Mans, as we went about building alliances and intimidating rebels."

"Sending a message?" Her voice took on a sarcastic edge. "Let me guess what that means. You forced innocent people—like me and your sister—to become homeless. Is that what you soldiers call sending a message? Why must such messages be delivered to those who have nothing to do with waging war? Those who gain nothing from it but misery?"

"Sister," his voice matched hers in irritation. "I do not create the strategy. I merely enforce it. And not all confrontations end in destruction. Take Le Mans, for example. The surrender came about ceremoniously. The Bishop and the clergy marched out fully robed, carrying their Gospel books and crosiers. No blood was shed."

"Oh, yes? And what about the guts that spilled out from the bodies of the people, huh?" Celia's lip thinned in anger. "Do you not see the folly of it all? Soldiers serve a leader's vanity at the expense of commoners like us. Do you not understand?"

"And what am I supposed to do? Find a patch of land to plough until the next battle scorches it black and useless? Watch my wife and children starve because there is naught but grass or hay to eat? Of course I understand. But this is what I am, sister. This is all I have. And I thank the vain leader I serve—as should you—that I am still on this side of the grave, and I hope it remains that way. And so I will continue to fight—without remorse—on his behalf."

His tone softened. "Strangely enough, I did seek you out, Celia, to be chastised by you. Not for the policies of war but for my own sins with regard to neglecting you, father, and Vivienne. I do not wish for us to entangle ourselves in philosophical discussions that are beyond our power to redress. I just wanted to tell you that I am sorry about the past, and that I love you and miss you and hope to return to you someday when these wars have ended. But, after listening to you now, perhaps I would be unwelcome." Philippe pushed his chair away from the hearth and readied himself to leave.

"No, wait." She grabbed his forearm. "I am sorry for my harsh words. I guess I have not grown up very much at all. I am still that domineering sister who tries to command her brother into doing what she thinks he should do and behaving how she thinks he should behave." When her hand made contact with the braided chain mail, she fought the impulse to draw it back. "I know that you are doing what you must, as I too do the same. There is no accusation in my voice. I love you, brother. Everyone must make decisions in order to survive, and who am I to question yours? If you only knew the dark sins etched upon my own soul, you would be the fitter judge of us two."

"I do not judge you or anyone, Celia. That is not my calling. But while I remain here at Rouen, let us come together with a lightness in our hearts to reminisce about the laughter we shared in the past and plan for the peace we shall have in the future when we shall all be together again." He reached out his hand toward her and pulled her in for a warm embrace.

While she was standing, Celia took Philippe's cup that he had placed on the mantelpiece and refilled it. She offered it to him. "How long can you stay? And—fool that I am for waiting this long to ask— what brings you here to Rouen? Are you responsible for those two English hostages?"

"Yes, we took them from the Count and brought them here." He took a gratifying swallow. "They were lucky enough to survive the shipwreck, but ill-fated enough to wash ashore on land belonging to Guy. The Count had the two Englishmen locked up in his chateau at Beaurain and was ready to collect their ransom for himself. Once William got word of what happened, he sent us to liberate them."

"Interesting. They must be rather important for the Duke to have intervened."

"That they are. Apparently, they were sailing here to negotiate the release of hostages with William himself. Members of their own family—a brother and nephew, I think, of one of the men. But a storm caught them unaware and dumped them into Guy's hands. So we went out and retrieved them. My men and I could end up staying here in Rouen for quite some time—at least until the Duke gives us orders to go elsewhere. Maybe we will be commissioned to bring these men back to England."

Celia had to extend her arms high in order to place them on her brother's shoulders. "Philippe, how far you have come from those days when your little legs could not spin fast enough to match your sister's speed. Now look at you. Clearly, you are a respected warrior if you are among the first to be called for a mission like this!" She patted him twice in praise.

"The Duke has never forgotten me, Celia, from that first meeting when I nearly ran him over. Do you remember how it was back then? When he offered to make me one of his cavalrymen? He has never forgotten that encounter, and neither have I. Without a father to serve, I look upon him now as my father, and I shall do his bidding in the same manner I followed Papa's commands when my legs were much shorter and my arms much weaker."

Unable to sit still, Celia started poking at the embers in the fire, stirring them around a bit. "Were you in great danger on this mission?"

"No. The men I serve with are like brothers to me. I may be the youngest, but I have proven myself worthy. Without going into details that will annoy you again, let me just say that each of us would lay down his life for the other and have done so in the past. This assignment was just an exercise of logistics. We went to Beaurain,

Guy recognized William as his overlord, we demanded the hostages, Guy released them. The priest—Father Thurstan is his name—well, his gratitude lasted less than a stone's throw from Guy's estate. Almost immediately, he started threatening us with retribution from the English king and damnation from God Himself if we did not arrange for their transport home. The brawny, red-haired captive—Harold as he is called—he rode in silence, but we had to remain vigilant. We kept him encircled, for he looked bold enough to attempt escape. But then, we reasoned, where could he even go? He had no knowledge of the landscape and no reason to believe anyone in the region would be sympathetic to his situation. So we managed to arrive here without incident and delivered them to the Duke and Duchess. What happens next is up to the Duke."

She put down the tool and leaned against the table to face him. "Well, brother, I for one shall hope that the two foreigners remain here as guests at Rouen for many days so that you and I can spend lots of time together." She wondered how she could bring up the subject of Simon without revealing the deep feelings she had for him. "Where are you staying?"

"In the barracks where the castle guards sleep. My fellows are there now. And how shall I find you tomorrow?"

"I am one of Matilda's attendants."

Philippe lifted his eyebrows as if very impressed. "Obviously, she must not be aware what a shrew you were to your own brother!"

"No, no! I am not that way any more. The years have mellowed me. And I am not that important, really. But I am at her disposal, so I do not rightly know where I will be—only that I will somehow be attached to her." Now she thought of a way to slip in Simon. "Yes, no more days laundering the linens and spending most of my time outdoors as I once did back at the castle in Caen when I came upon Simon our neighbor after the triumph at Varaville."

Philippe did not react, so she had to push further. "Have you—did you—have occasion to run into Simon, our former neighbor, by any chance? Last I saw him was about four years hence . . ."

"Simon? The fellow with the scar? The one whose wife washed up dead? Oh, I am afraid he is dead too. I saw him from a distance at the surrender of Le Mans, but we never talked. Weeks later though, when I looked for him after we set fire to Geoffrey's castle, someone said he was wounded in the siege. Never heard of him again. Guess we will never know what really happened between him and his wife."

Philippe had no idea of the impact of his words. He stood up to say good night. "Come find me tomorrow, Celia. Might be easier that way. I will be tending the horses. Look for me by the stables." His eyes glistened with relief and joy. "It is so good to see you again, sister. So good to know I have finally found my way home to you."

Celia leaned up against the stones of the hearth to steady herself. Her voice trembled a bit. "I am glad too, brother." She stepped away from the wall and pulled back her shoulders to stand tall. "I will look for you at the stables." Embracing him with all the love that remained in her heart, she sent him on his way.

Alone, she stared into the glowing embers, watching the light grow dimmer. Soon all would be ashes. Just like her dreams.

*   *   *   *   *

The irony of the situation did not escape her.

She who had once scorned religious zealots and the mindless worshipers that followed them now found herself among their ranks. She had become one of those people who searched for life's meaning and had somehow found traces of the answer in the hushed solemnity of a church.

Although the sun was shining outdoors, the inside of the cathedral was still dark, and she relished the comfort found in its shadows. From her seat to the right of the high altar, she tried to quiet her mind.

245

Ever since she had learned of Simon's death, nothing seemed to matter. Everyone she had cared for had been torn away.

Spending time in the cathedral helped. She would not call it praying exactly; that would be too devout for her. It was more a quality of being, not praying. Surrounded by images of faith, she let worry give way to acceptance. To her left was the long nave, edged on both sides by windows of stained glass—reminders that light could be found if one were willing to look up. True, Simon was gone, as were her mother and father and even Philippe, but the belief that she would return to Caen and be with Vivienne again was her dominant thought when she sat before the altar and breathed in the lingering fragrance of incense.

Celia knew the child would not be feeling the same emptiness over their separation, and that realization brought relief not resentment. No, Vivienne would be running and skipping, learning and exploring, snuggling in with Chloe and Grace and sleeping soundly through the night. At least her younger sister still believed in the promises offered by a new day, even though for Celia, dawn had lost its luster.

When she felt herself slipping beneath the rising waters of self-pity like this, she adjusted her course and visited the church. Here she could redirect her energy toward action and possibility. She would be of use again, and that was a good thing. The Breton campaign was yet another success for the Duke with Conan handing over the keys to the chateau at Dinan. With many of the Norman soldiers now back at court, Celia would have plenty to keep her busy. Conversations to overhear, letters to intercept, couriers to monitor. There would be feasts and celebrations where personalities would be on display. She could listen, observe, and evaluate. By being useful, she could return to being the kind of person she once was. A warrior. A fighter. Someone whose determination could make circumstances shift to match her vision of the future. Serenity came not from surrender but from conviction. Nothing would stop her from getting back to Caen and Vivienne.

She jumped from her seat when something sharp stabbed the fleshy part of her shoulder. Spinning around with a jolt, she came face-to-face with the English priest who had just poked his bony finger into her back. He looked down upon her with disapproval as if her presence tainted the purity of the church.

"Why did you do that? What do you want?" She clutched her shawl against her chest and glared at him without panic. Her blue eyes pierced him with accusation and spite. "You have no right to interrupt a penitent conversing with God. Last I checked, the cathedral is open to all and not just to those who jangle the keys."

She faced him without fear, but inside, she chided herself for not being vigilant. How did he get so close to her without her noticing? Sneaking up on her without sound, he was no different from the vermin in the castle who appeared from nowhere and then squeezed into some secret recess to elude capture. She wished he would disappear like that now.

His shifty black eyes took delight in her discomfort. "I do not want anything from you. Perhaps I should be asking, what do you want of me?" His pointy chin nearly touched his nose as he worked his toothless mouth up and down. He looked at her arresting beauty with disgust. "You have the look of a sinner to me. How many men have lusted for you? How many of them have had their way with you?"

He wanted her out of the church as quickly as possible. "Confess your transgressions to me. I cannot promise an easy penance to someone of your reputation, but going to the grave unshriven will guarantee eternal damnation." He tried to reach for a lock of her hair. "Imagine all that beauty shriveled up in the fires of Gehenna."

She matched his cool reserve. "Why would I seek absolution from a sinner worse off than myself? You should be worried about your own predicament in this realm and not mine in the next." She continued to stare at him a moment longer before tossing her nose up at him in disdain. "Filthy Englishman!" She would have spat upon the ground were she not in a church.

She kept her head held high and her shoulders back as she walked with dignity down the long nave. Waiting for her at the end of the aisle was Earl Harold. He stood immovable, arms locked across his chest. He moistened his lips as she drew near. His red hair was parted down the middle, the top portion—greasy and unwashed—adhered tightly to his head. He sidestepped to block her way.

"Now where are you off to, young maiden, with such determined purpose?" His wiry, russet-colored mustache trailed beyond his lips, and his arms rose as if readying to seize her shoulders.

In one swift motion, she ducked lower and away from his grasp, leaving him with empty air to embrace. "What I do and where I go is no concern of yours." She quickened her pace and crossed over the threshold into the safety of the outdoors.

Harold laughed with amusement as he walked up the nave to join Father Thurstan. "Now there is a lively one, aye?" The two of them stood facing one another with the altar between them. "With that body, she would warm any man's bed, I warrant. Feisty too. Makes for great sport beneath the covers."

"Oh, get your mind off the carnal, will you? Come now, we must figure a way out of this detestable place. Whether the Duke speaks it aloud or not, we are his prisoners here. Look at the amount of time he has kept us in this God forsaken kingdom, making us dance to his tune and play his little war games. And Lord knows, William is rather notorious for the way he treats his guests. Need I mention the man and his wife who were enjoying his hospitality at Falaise? They both wound up dead." Thurstan drummed his fingers upon the marble altar.

"But we are not Normans. He dare not cross me. I am brother to the Queen of England, the closest consort of the King. He will not risk enraging an entire country by murdering us. Furthermore, he has given me his word that we can return home." Harold waved his hand dismissively at the priest.

Thurstan scowled. "In order to conduct a private conversation like this, I know we had to concoct the excuse of my hearing your confession, but perhaps you should do just that. Excessive pride is a grave sin, my lord. Your previous comment reeks of vanity."

"'Tis not a sin if what is being said is truth. Is that not so? I defeated the Welsh-Bretons on the island. And now I have defeated them again, here on the continent as well. I rescued two men from quicksand and got knighted in the process. I do believe that gives me the right to be bold enough to state the truth. Come now, Father, you know I am more than ready to sail for home, and the Duke knows it too. He will not risk an outright war with England by keeping us here any longer. His little skirmish in Brittany is over, and I am no more impressed with his horseback warriors than I was when I heard minstrels singing songs of them."

Thurstan pondered Harold's claims. "How do you know for certain that he will send us home?"

"We have discussed it. On the ride back from the battle. He has already made the arrangements. The ship will be outfitted on the morrow."

"And what about Hakon and Wulfnoth, your nephew and brother? Will he release them to us? Can we bring them both home?"

Harold fidgeted uncomfortably. The truth was, he did not know William's intentions for certain. "He said we would discuss the terms later on tonight. But if we are denied our request at this juncture, we can come back another time for them—with King Edward's permission, of course—and bring more soldiers and a sea captain better skilled at handling storms."

"The King's permission? You mean like the way you had Edward's permission to embark upon this journey in the first place?" Thurstan's sarcasm made Harold wince.

Thurstan shifted the conversation in another direction. "No matter. What is done is done. You must set your sights on the future." He leaned in closer to speak in a conspiratorial tone. "Speaking of King Edward, his days are numbered. He grows more and more detached from worldly affairs. You must consider what will happen next."

Harold placed his hands upon his hips and puffed his chest wide, his voice full of bravado. "The boy Edgar is no threat. He is too young to be of serious concern."

"True. And even if the Witan should rule in his favor, you could be Edgar's regent if necessary. But that will not be necessary, I am certain of that. No one has a claim as strong as your own."

"What about the girl?"

"What girl? Oh, heaven save us! Are you thinking again with your loins instead of your head?"

"No," Harold laughed, "not that girl. Not the one you rudely interrupted with your words of damnation. I am referring to the Saxon girl back home. Edgar's sister. She is of royal blood as well."

Thurstan shook his head to disagree. "Margaret? The Witan will never side with a woman." He snorted at Harold's foolishness.

"The Scot wants her though. Malcolm. If they should marry, he could make a legitimate claim for the throne, backed by troops at his disposal. And Malcolm's friendship with my brother could give him greater military strength, should Tostig turn on me. And let us not forget Hardrada, the Norwegian. The three of them could form an alliance against me."

"Well then, we must keep a close eye on the Scot. He has always been an insufferable human being, ever since he was a child. Incapable of being civilized. A barbarian through and through. Illiterate. Dumb as a stone. He actually deserves a hypocrite like Margaret—all sweet and pious on the outside but a Jezebel within. Even so, we must be sure to thwart any union between the two. No one can stand in your way."

"And no one shall. We will feast this evening and set terms with William regarding our departure tomorrow."

Father Thurstan revisited his earlier offer. "One last chance . . . since we are here anyway, of course." The priest gestured to a nearby seat where Harold could atone for his sins.

"I have done nothing for which I need to be shriven." Harold's resolve was unshakeable.

Thurstan conceded. "Let it go then, for now. But there may be need of it someday . . . should you feel compelled to pay back our Norman host."

With a mischievous twinkle in his eye, Harold grinned knowingly at his partner in crime. He then went down upon one knee. Thurstan took this invitation to rest his gnarled hand upon the earl's head and say, "*Voluntas nostra fiat.*"

The two men laughed in fellowship as they walked out of the cathedral together, oblivious to their unseen guest.

For unbeknownst to them, Celia had doubled back earlier and used the outer door at the bottom of the cellar steps to enter the crypt located beneath the high altar. Once inside, like the priests who prayed over the entombed dead by listening in to the mass taking place above, she had opened the grated peephole and overheard every word.

*   *   *   *   *

Matilda and her servants were working in earnest to prepare for the evening's festivities when Celia came rushing in. She noted how the Duchess moved about the room with a sense of giddiness, as if joy spouted directly from her person like water bubbling from a fountain. She discharged every one of her commands with a pulsing desire to find perfection.

"Eduard, bring me that strongbox. Caroline, go get the cloths for the tables. Where are the tapers? Oh, Juliette, place the candelabras at either end. Yes, that is it. Now go find the tapers." When Matilda caught sight of Celia, her hand stopped pointing in the various directions, and her arms opened toward her in welcome.

"Celia! Have you come to help?" Matilda winked at her in secret understanding. She could feel Celia's urgency.

"Eduard, give the strongbox to Celia instead." Once Celia received it, Matilda directed her toward the dais. "Come, Celia, come. Bring that with you. Here, come follow me." She gestured to an area beneath the high table.

Celia followed the Duchess' lead, and the two women bent down to look at the area under the table. Matilda pointed. "There. Slide it over. A bit more. Yes. A little more. See if you can align it so that it rests in front of the large chair behind you. See it? Make sure it is out of sight and beyond reach of the Duke's legs."

Matilda nodded with approval. "Good. Right there." She rubbed her hands against each other almost as if she were clapping them together. "Well done, my dear. Yes. Now, I wonder . . . with what else can you help me?" Her pink lips broke into a warm smile, and her eyes grew wide with anticipation.

Celia glanced over her shoulder as if to communicate the need for greater privacy. She offered only the cryptic words, "I have news."

The Duchess immediately grabbed Celia's wrist and pulled her way from the frenzied preparations. In an alcove beyond the Great Hall, Celia told Matilda everything. As if perfectly timed, the sound of boots striding down the corridor coincided with the conclusion of Celia's tale. Matilda raised her finger to her lips, silencing Celia as the noise drew closer. Gesturing with her hand to tell Celia to stay put, Matilda stepped forth from the niche to learn the identity of the passerby.

Her voice gushed with happiness. "My husband!" She exulted upon seeing the Duke towering over her. Raising herself up onto her toes, she caressed his face with her delicate hands. He was clean-shaven, but his skin was swarthy from exposure to the outdoors. He wore no crown or ornament upon his head, so his black hair cut round like a bowl framed his face in strands that were straight and thick. His size made it impossible for him to fit inside the hiding place with them, so Matilda reached into the recess to draw forth Celia.

Placing Celia's hand into William's, she introduced them to one another. "Husband, this is Celia. She is—"

"...the daughter of Artur Campion. Yes, my love, I know of her already." He turned to Celia. "And Philippe's sister as well, yes?

She nodded and then curtsied before him.

"You must be quite proud of your brother, no doubt. He continues to serve me well. Brittany was yet another engagement where his contributions helped bring about our victory."

Matilda tapped Celia's shoulder to get her to rise from kneeling. Then she took Celia's hand along with her husband's and stood between them, directing them to the door leading into the courtyard. Turning to William, she said, "Dearest, you will not be surprised then to hear that fealty runs in their blood. Celia has been as indispensable to me as Philippe has been to you. And this recent occasion proves this to be so."

When they reached the arbor, she gestured to William to sit upon the bench. Out of deference to her, he did so without questioning.

"Listen to this, my love. Celia, tell the Duke exactly what you just told me." Matilda placed her arm around Celia's shoulder to encourage her to speak freely and without fear.

Details tumbled forth uninterrupted as Celia told of what transpired between Earl Harold and Father Thurstan. During her recitation, she kept her eyes fixed upon the Duke in order to assess his reaction. She watched his face transform as the ocean does before a storm begins to roll in. At first he listened with detachment, nodding his head at certain intervals, but when talk shifted to King Edward's successor, William's eyes erupted with outrage. Waves of betrayal washed over his countenance as his mind searched for a way to restore justice.

"And that is all I heard, Your Grace."

William did not speak. He was too deep in thought, calculating how he could use this information to his advantage. His wife stepped in.

"Well done, Celia. A token of our appreciation will be sent to your room before tonight's dinner." Matilda's brown eyes warmed with gratitude. "You are free to go now."

Unsure of the exact impact her report would have on events that were to follow, Celia felt relief at being dismissed. "Yes, Your

Grace." She left the arbor feeling rather pleased with herself, not only because Matilda and William obviously valued her service, but also because her information placed the two Englishmen in harm's way. And that satisfied her most of all.

After Celia had departed, William spoke openly to his wife. "Did you receive the strongbox?"

"I did." Matilda joined him on the bench. She started stroking his hair until she settled her hand on the side of his cheek. "The relics are inside, and the box is positioned beneath the section of the table where the Earl will be seated."

He placed his hand atop hers and moved it from his cheek to his lips. Kissing it, he said, "If we are forced to fight for the English crown, then it shall be a holy war—one that the Pope must sanction." He returned her hand to her lap and rose to a standing position. "That will cover us when it comes to Harold, and as for Edgar, I have no worries about the aetheling. His age renders him useless. Even if he is chosen, it will still come down to Harold. But the sister? This Margaret? We must watch and see about this possible union between her and the Scottish king. That is an alliance I had not thought of and one that must be considered."

Matilda joined him in standing but only came up to his chest. Wrapping her arms around his waist, she rested her cheek against his tunic. "Do not trouble yourself over that, my beloved. I have the perfect person to infiltrate that circle. Just convince the Earl that he too stands to benefit from the information our agent will ascertain, and then she—our agent—can travel with them back to England."

Bending down to rest his chin upon Matilda's head, William felt her strength of purpose seep into his own. "My dearest love, you know I was schooled in war since childhood. Never have I backed down from physical confrontation. Combat, the spillage of blood, the shrieks of pain—all of it enthralls me. But battles waged with words, well, that is a different matter altogether. For that, I defer to your expertise. May the oath sworn tonight ensnare Harold in a trap he cannot escape, and may the presence of our informant at the English court keep us abreast of any threat to our future glory."

Tilting her head towards his, she looked at her husband with total confidence. "Leave it all to me."

*　　*　　*　　*　　*

"Why must I be seated right next to you?" Caroline whined with disappointment, and her head drooped in defeat. "I feel like a troll beside the fairie queen."

All of the women were placed together at the same table. Mixed in with them were knights who were, as yet, unwedded. The women blushed and batted their eyelashes attempting to gain favor with their warrior of choice, but their coquetry went unnoticed. The girl in the blue dress eclipsed them all.

Juliette leaned over toward Caroline and whispered loud enough for Celia to hear. "You are right. We are all trolls here, whether we sit right next to that one or a few chairs away. It is just not fair. If I had a dress like that, I too would be the center of attention." She crinkled her nose in envy.

"Oh hush, both of you!" Celia leaned into the table and turned sideways to face them both. "I have no desire to listen to these men and their false narratives of personal glory. Such fabrications bore me. So stop dwelling on your petty jealousies and tap into your feminine charm instead. Pay them attention. Fawn over them. Make them feel good about themselves, and soon they will recognize that you two are the ones worth competing for."

Celia felt the need to spur Caroline and Juliette into action because it was true—the men were staring at her unapologetically, and it made her terribly uncomfortable. She wanted neither their attention nor their admiration, so she assumed an air of haughtiness that made her unapproachable. It worked. Her one word answers fostered a coldness that made the men seek warmth elsewhere, and Caroline and Juliet willingly satisfied that need. The two women unabashedly praised the knights for their embellished feats and encouraged them to tell even more.

Celia knew she made a striking appearance, but that was through no intention of her own. It was the gown itself. It transformed her from background attendant to peerless lady, the reward for a job well done. As soon as she had stepped into the dress of dark blue and pulled her arms through its long, dangling sleeves, she felt her identity change. The gold thread embroidered throughout the fabric sparkled from the reflected candlelight, and the material itself embraced her body in all the right places, brushing against her skin with the softness of a whisper. She had never owned anything as luxurious as this and doubted if she would ever find occasion to wear it again. The bodice, cinched tight, went across her chest in a straight line, accentuating her shapely bosom.

The Great Hall was filled to capacity, making it a challenge for the serving maids to navigate their way in and around the tables. The dining areas were split up by rank. Closest to the door were common tables where squires, a few waiting women, and heralds were seated. Celia, along with Caroline, Juliet, and the other ladies-in-waiting were placed together with the various knights to form two tables that filled in the center of the room. At the High Table sat the Duke and Duchess, William's closest advisors, and the two Englishmen. Harold occupied the chair placed directly on William's right, and then next to the Earl was Father Thurstan.

Two courses of the meal had already been served, the first consisting of chicken brushed with oil, garlic, and sage, and the second pork smothered in a sweet mustard sauce. Side dishes of buttered peas and leeks seasoned with pepper and coriander dotted the tables at evenly spaced locations, accompanied by baskets of bread, the finest and whitest of the loaves reserved for the High Table. Wine and ale flowed freely, and keeping pace with such indulgences, conversation soon became less measured and topics more bawdy.

Despite Celia's initial discomfort at being treated like an alabaster goddess, she eventually softened to the lively atmosphere in the hall and found amusement in the argument taking place between two brothers who sat across from her.

"You shall never win a maiden's heart."

"Oh? And what makes you the authority on that? I see no woman on your arm, eh?"

"Well, for one, just look at yourself. Your teeth are spindly. Your hair is thinning. Your back is hunched over. Soon you will be nothing more than an aged infant, slabbering spit down your chin and begging for your breeches to be changed."

"Well, last I checked, teeth, hair, and a crooked back have little to do with satisfying a woman. And in that department, there is nothing about me that is soft."

At this, Celia blushed and stifled a giggle. The two continued.

"Still, what woman will ever get beyond that ugly face of yours to see the hidden 'beauty' you speak of?"

"It just may take a bit of persuasion, is all." The elder brother gestured toward Celia. "Take this pretty damsel here. What is your name, love?"

"Celia."

"Celia!" He reached across the table nearly toppling over his wine goblet in the process to signal for her hand. "If I promised you pleasure beyond your wildest dreams, would you consent to being courted by a fine fellow like me?"

Before she could answer, the younger brother slapped the elder's hand. "You would have to drag this lady off her horse by her braids and throw her to the ground to get her to consent to being with you! And you have not the daring nor the charisma of our Duke in order to pull off something like that, so I doubt she would take well to such rough wooing. No, the Bellamy line would come to an end if you were its only remaining son. But thanks to Lady Fortuna, there is yet another whose heart—and other organs—are pulsing with Bellamy blood."

Now he turned his attention toward Celia. "So, my dear lady," he glanced over at the musicians who were readying to play, "would you dance with me when occasion calls? I do not hobble or limp. I am not losing my hearing, nor do I drool with my mouth open when I am thinking. Years of marital bliss could await us both if you will grant me this first dance?"

The elder brother seized the younger one's arm, bent it at the elbow, and twisted it behind his back. The younger one yelled. "Stop, stop. I surrender. You are not as bad as I said. At least you are not a doddering fool—yet. But I still get to dance with Celia first. Tell me this can be so, dear lady."

She was amused by the silliness of the two men, grateful to have been freed from the snares set by the spiteful women at the table. First, she addressed the younger brother. "Of course I shall grant your request, good sir." Then, with a wink toward the elder one, she said. "And when the musicians change the tune from something jaunty to something sweet, I welcome the chance to partner with a man who takes pleasure in that which is mellow and slow."

In that way, Celia satisfied both petitioners. But before any musical note played, the Duke stood up and raised his arms high above the clamor. The clanking of glasses, the movement of bodies, and the noise of conversation slowly diminished, as people started looking around the room to discover the reason for the growing quiet. William's voice then filled the silence.

"Lords, ladies, knights, and yeomen, my dear people of Normandy. I have important news to share. Over these last few months, we have been blessed by the presence of our English friends, but the time has come for them to bid us farewell and sail for home."

Father Thurstan darted his eyes over the assembly, measuring the crowd's reception of this news. Harold turned his chair slightly to the side so that he could gain full view of William, cynically taking note of the Duke's flair for theatrics.

William was impressive not just in size but also in manner. His deep voice boomed as if he were on the field of battle rather than in a hall with guests, his words echoing back as if they had bounced against war shields.

"Come, my friend." William gestured with his hand towards the other side of the dais where Harold was seated. "Come stand before us so that I can share with all those here my appreciation and gratitude."

Celia's mind quickly shifted from the lightness of the earlier banter to the gravity of this formal announcement. Her focus was now entirely on what was taking place at the high table. She noted a furtive glance exchanged between Harold and Thurstan, and then saw the priest nod ever so slightly at the Earl, as if telling him to acquiesce to William's request.

Silence blanketed the room. There was no eating, no drinking, no talking. All eyes were fixed on the red-headed foreigner as he lumbered his way around the table to stand before William, his back to the audience. Although a bit older than the Duke, Harold matched him in vigor as well as in girth. The length of his hair was markedly different not just from William's but from all other men in the room. Harold's streamed down from the crown of his head to his shoulders, wild, messy, and untethered. His feet pounded the floor so loudly that it seemed he was marching with a heavy load upon his back. When he stopped his forward advance, he came face-to-face with the Duke, only the table stood between them.

Celia moved her chair to get a closer look. She peeked over at the Duchess, but Matilda betrayed no emotion. The woman looked as cool as if she were alone in her private chamber, quietly embroidering by the fireside. Her eyes were steady and still, her disposition calm. How different Matilda looked from everyone else in the room whose faces conveyed varying degrees of curiosity, confusion, and worry. No one dared even breathe for fear of breaking ceremonial decorum.

Unlike his wife, William was intensely engaged in the moment.

"It has been an honor and a privilege to offer my hospitality to you and your men, Earl Harold Godwinson. And it is my hope that we will continue to strengthen this bond of friendship and fealty in both word and deed. A few weeks ago, I delivered your regiment from captivity at the hands of Count Guy de Ponthieu and brought all of you safely here to Rouen. I then invited you on campaign with me in Brittany where we fought side-by-side like brothers against the enemy. To which, in recognition of your valour, I bestowed the rank of knighthood upon you. And now, to solidify the fellowship I wish to maintain with you and your family, I offer you the hand of my daughter Adela in marriage."

When loud cheers broke out among the audience, William stopped speaking altogether for a few moments to let their approval be heard. Even more importantly, the pause was taken so that William's generosity toward Harold could be duly noted.

It was now Harold's turn to respond, and he did so in a clear, loud voice.

"I thank you, Your Grace, for the kindness you have shown me and for the promise that our futures shall be bound together by the union of our two houses through marriage."

Again, applause and celebratory shouts rang through the chamber.

"Very good. This is very good, I say." William then leaned a bit further toward his guest, his chest now over the dais. "Then, as your protector, your commander in battle, and your future father-in-law, I ask you to kneel and place one hand on your heart and one on this table to take the oath of homage, as an expression of goodwill and gratitude."

Not many could see the momentary panic in Harold's eyes, but Celia detected the hesitation along with the brief glance in Father Thurstan's direction. The priest closed his eyes conveying Harold's need for obeisance, and with that, the Earl moved into place. He repeated the words fed to him by William:

"I promise ... on my faith ... that I will pay homage to you ... by showing fealty ... in good conscience ... and without deceit."

As soon as the words were delivered, Harold stood up and lifted his head high to match William's powerful stance. Celia watched Matilda's facade give way as she exhaled noticeably and blessed herself with the sign of the cross. The Duchess' reaction made little sense to Celia, nor did Celia understand the magnitude of the scene she had just witnessed. Her only thought was that the moment was very intense indeed and that something beyond her scope must have transpired.

William spoke once more. "With the pact between us further strengthened, from both my actions and the Earl's oath, we send him forth upon the sea bound for England. Once there, he will share news of this accord with his King and the people of his realm." William then offered his open, weaponless hand toward Harold. In this ritual gesture of a handshake, the Duke showed all in attendance that the two men were inextricably bound together. "Now," he motioned to Harold to return to his seat, "let the music begin!

When the lute player plucked the first notes of his tune, the young knight raised his eyebrows at Celia and motioned for her hand. She smiled back. This was his dance, and she must not go back on her promise. But as she moved toward the open floor with her hand in his, she could not help feeling that some deeper choreography had already taken place, one orchestrated by the Duke and Duchess relying on words not melody for its art.

*   *   *   *   *

"Oh, no, Your Grace." Celia was flustered and confused. She could feel the panic surging in her body. "Please, please do not send me away. I cannot leave Normandy. I cannot abandon my sister. She is all I have."

Matilda was unmoved. She sat erect in her raised chair, staring down at Celia without sympathy. Her words were crisp with authority. "Your concern for your sister is touching but quite unnecessary. It is not as if you would be going away forever." She drew out the last word to lengthen its sound.

Celia twisted her fingers in anguish. "Surely someone else would be better suited for such an assignment? I am just a simple servant girl who was lucky enough to be in the right place at the right time on a few choice occasions. I am ill-prepared for this. I have never traveled abroad; I know not how to blend in. How would I ever gain anyone's trust? Please, please do not send me away."

Matilda's impatience was starting to show. A frown line cut the space between her eyes. Her lips were drawn thin and straight. "We have gone over all of this once before. You are the perfect fit for this plan. That is why you were chosen."

From her seated position, the Duchess looked down into her lap and started straightening some of the creases in her dress. "There is nothing to be afraid of. The girl is not a monster. From what I am told, she is quite the opposite. Pious and innocent. She will be pleased to have a friend like you—one as devout as she, one who also plans to take the veil. Once you gain her trust, you can keep us informed as to any communication she—or her brother—receives from the Scottish king. All the while, you must continue to convince her of her true calling. Reinforce her belief that the convent is where she belongs."

Matilda tilted her head as if to ponder other outcomes. "And . . . if we cannot get her to agree to being locked away in a cloister, then at least we will know ahead of time if, and when, she will bind herself to Malcolm. That way we can be fully prepared if they make a move for the English crown—whether for himself or for that brother of hers."

Celia braced herself for the punishment that would likely ensue. Dropping to her knees, she lay her chest flat upon the ground in supplication. "I . . . I cannot do this, Your Grace. This girl will see right through me. I am more sinner than saint. There is no way I can convince her otherwise." She gathered her breath and continued. "I am unworthy of the kindness you have shown me over these past years. I did not deserve such generosity then, nor do I dare to hope for it now. Turn me out. Cast me aside. Remove me from your service. I will take my sister and relieve you of the burden of our care. I will take my leave of you now and be gone."

When she finished speaking, she raised her head from the floor so that she was upright but still kneeling. When the door opened, a swath of light projected into the room from which a shadow appeared on the ground in front of her. Before she could stand and face the portal, the shadow was filled in by the living, breathing form of the Duke.

His voice filled her with dread. "That is right. You will get your belongings and be gone. But you will go where I tell you to go." He stood at his full height, invading the space between her and the Duchess. The tips of his boots came so close to her folded knees that felt the need to slide herself carefully backwards a few inches.

Matilda stepped down from her chair to join him. Gently touching his forearm thick with muscle, she played the role of intermediary. "Dearest husband, Celia is merely afraid of disappointing us. That is all. That is why she is reluctant to go. But I am certain you can help her to see she needn't worry. Won't you?"

Matilda lifted up her face to William's and nodded at him, signaling that it was his turn to take over the discussion. Before relinquishing the reins completely, she spoke to Celia once more. "Get up."

The two of them then looked at Celia with shared resolve. She noticed their clasped hands, a unified front that could not and would not be breached.

Taking the cue from his wife, William laid out the terms. "It is settled. You *will* go to England—that is, if you ever want to see your sister again. She is under my power, and she will remain my hostage until I am satisfied that you have fulfilled your mission. If you choose to run away or if you perform the task half-heartedly, your sister will disappear. Hostages do have a way of disappearing, do they not, my dear?" He turned to his wife for affirmation.

Matilda picked up the thread. "And what a pity it would be to see so beautiful a child reduced to rags and enslaved to some filthy plowman somewhere."

Celia despised them both. Her hands shook with rage.

"My love," William patiently corrected his wife, "you know I am not fond of enslavement. Better it be to dispose of the urchin immediately. We have had a good deal of success in the past with tainted food or adulterated drink, have we not? Quick, tidy, and effective."

Celia had heard enough. Dropping to her knees once more, she lowered her head to kiss the ground before the Duchess' feet. "I will do as you wish. I will go to England. I will discover all I can about this girl and her brother and her suitor. I will not fail."

Hearing Celia's acceptance, Matilda reverted back to the sweet sovereign she was purported to be. "There, there, my girl. I knew you could come around to our way of thinking. I told you some time ago you were special. But sometimes even a viper needs to be reminded of where and when it needs to strike."

Celia wanted to scream out loud to drown out the Duchess' compliment. Matilda's words made her feel dirty and ashamed. She hated how she was forced to perform for them like some marionette at the mercy of another's pull. And she despised herself even more for being too powerless to free herself or her sister from their demands.

But what else could she do? And did it really matter anyway, if she continued to be a sinner while she pretended to be a saint? If she must send the Saxon girl to the convent or her grave, then so be it. She felt nothing and owed nothing to this stranger. In fact, she hated this "Margaret" already because it was she who would determine whether Vivienne lived or died.

William kissed his wife's cheek with heartfelt admiration. Wrapping his arm about her waist, he guided her toward the door. Before leaving, they stopped long enough for him to add, "The boat departs at dawn. Do not fail to be there." The Duchess tucked her arm in his as they moved together as one.

In the empty room, Celia sat alone with her shame. She did not move for quite some time, reviewing her predicament over and over again. There was no decision to be made. She had no freedom to make one. Their will would be done. Was it shameful to commit wrong in order to preserve a greater good? She did not believe it to be so. There was no disgrace in that. What did it matter anyway? She had no choice.

Swiftly and stealthily she would work, embodying the spirit of the perfect novice—obedient, contemplative, kind, patient—qualities normally foreign to her. Indeed, she would be so convincing that a figurative halo would glow about her head. Benevolent confidante. She would make the Saxon girl forgo marital vows for solemn ones, binding her to the church and not a king.

Tomorrow it begins. She would ride across the sea to keep Vivienne alive here. Her success depended on her ability to fit in, her capacity to blend in seamlessly with her new environment. But is not that what vipers do best? Teardrops borne of helplessness melted away as her lips turned upward in a knowing smile. The white veil would disguise her true intent. She rose to her feet as Sister Celia, leaving behind any trace of the woman she once was.

*   *   *   *   *

The day was gray and overcast. A thick fog encircled the harbor. Droplets of precipitation clung to the railing of the boat and made the deck slippery. Celia's shawl was weighted with mist. The veil covering her hair pressed down upon her skull, heavy with moisture.

She would not cry. This was not a final farewell. She would come back to these shores, she would make certain of that. Although the weather pressed down upon her, she refused to surrender to its gloom.

The Earl and the priest looked upon her as just another piece of cargo they were bringing back to England, her worth yet to be determined. The Earl's nephew, Hakon, was with them, newly released by William in an act of good faith. The boy was proof that their visit paid off in some measurable way. None of them, including Celia, waved goodbye to the observers on land who watched their departure. The oarsmen dipped their paddles into the murky water, and the journey was underway.

Celia was to be admitted into Wilton Abbey, posing as a close relative of the Duchess. She carried with her forged letters of commendation from the prioress of the *Abbaye Aux Dames,* the Benedictine nunnery in Caen. The letters spoke of her deep spirituality and keen memory for scripture, qualities made evident during her postulancy. Daughters of high ranking noblemen often studied at Wilton, thriving under the exceptional tutelage of the chaplain, Father Goscelin. Some even chose to remain sequestered there forever by taking final vows. The Duchess' decision to send Celia to this convent was a logical one and would not be questioned.

A companion also traveled with her, a man who had the look of a fresh-faced youth. Although he was well past thirty years, no whiskers sprouted upon his chin. His innocent look, squeaky voice, and spry movements made it seem as if he had not yet reached manhood. Joseph was his name, and he was posing as an acolyte ready to serve Father Goscelin. To Celia, he would serve as the conduit between her and the Duke and Duchess.

She watched Joseph standing at the front of the boat eagerly facing the future. She forced herself to do the same. If she had any hope of returning to Normandy, then she must master her assignment in this new land. She fixed her gaze on what lay ahead. The rhythmic sound of the oars carving through the waves kept pace with the commitment she whispered repeatedly to herself. "Someday I will return."

Because she was facing the other way, Celia did not see the rider on horseback who had pulled up hard on the reins once he had arrived at the Norman coastline. The animal snorted and spun his head from one side to the other, irritated at having had to stop so abruptly. Removing his helmet to gain a better view, the man squinted his eyes through the spray of mist to watch the boat drift away. He kept vigil until the boat seemed nothing more than a brown dot in the distance. A single tear ran down the creviced scar upon his face, blending in with the wetness that settled on his skin. Seemingly resurrected from the past, Simon died all over again when he realized he had come too late. Celia was gone.

MARGARET

BOUND BY LOYALTY

PALACE OF WESTMINSTER – AUGUST 1063

Edgar's palms were clammy. He wiped them on his tunic to erase what he was feeling inside. A dull pain throbbed between the thumb and forefinger of his hand. It was always this way whenever Father Thurstan appeared. And here the priest was, standing at the door of the King's chamber. *The man was inserting himself again,* Edgar thought, *trying to keep His Majesty away from me.* These meetings with the King served as Edgar's last hope. They were the only proof that he was being thought of as the aetheling and not some homeless beggar looking for a hand-out.

Edgar knew how delicate his position was at court. Just exactly what the King had in store for him was still a bit of a mystery. He had not been permitted to witness any charters thus far. He had not been granted any estates of land that would indicate he was the heir apparent. No formal declaration or announcement had ever been made about succession. That was what made these conferences with the King so important. They were the slim threads of the rope he clung to, the rope he would use to pull himself from anonymity to importance. But once again, here was Thurstan trying to shove him back into the pit.

At the sound of Thurstan's knock, the King turned to the doorway. "What is it, Father?" Edward sighed with impatience.

Brushing the boy to the side, Thurstan stepped in front and bowed to the King in feigned servitude. "I beg your Majesty's pardon, but I bring important news, outstanding news, in fact, just delivered by courier. It comes from Harold, your loyal subject." He rose to stand upright. "Perhaps we should consult in private?" he asked, extending the parchment in the King's direction.

Edgar pressed his sweaty hands together, hoping he would not be dismissed. Whatever news Thurstan had of Wales was surely to be of great significance. Edgar desperately wanted to stay, but ultimately it was up to the King. As if in answer to Edgar's unspoken wish, the King responded curtly, "The boy stays. Read it to me. To us." Edward then folded his arms across his chest, his head tilted upwards to the ceiling as if trying to envision the scene the words were about to describe.

Thurstan hid his disappointment by looking down at the missive. He squinted his eyes and cleared his throat, but still his voice croaked like an ailing bullfrog. Just the sound of it brought back awful memories of the dark hours Edgar was forced to spend listening to the man distort scripture passages with his false tongue.

"Dearest King, honorable leader of our blessed land, a land that now includes the regions both north and west of Wessex,

I send you tidings of our success. We have captured the Welsh fugitive and subdued his people. I will come bearing proof that this rebel shall never again raise his sword against our people."

Thurstan scrolled up the paper and smiled contentedly as if he himself had been part of the triumphant army.

The King looked directly at Edgar. Lifting his chin with pride, he declared, "You see, my boy, I knew my plan would work. It was battle tested. It had worked once before, you know. It was the same land-army and ship-army maneuver we employed years ago against

Macbeth when we secured the throne for Malcolm. I knew we would not fail."

It took much self-control not to smirk in disbelief, for Edgar knew how little the King had to do with anything involving combat. The man spent too much time contemplating the world above to be able to strategize about the one he lived in. Edgar found it quite amusing that the King took credit for Malcolm's victory when the only body and blood His Majesty cared about was the eucharist. Edgar found a gap between the stones on the floor and safely fixed his attention there.

Thurstan ingratiated himself further. "Of course, Your Majesty. It was a genius move back then and a genius move again now. Sending Harold with the fleet around the southern coast and Tostig with the mounted troops through the northern uplands was masterful, simply masterful! Just look at the results. The Welsh have been brought to their knees. They have renounced Gruffydd and despise him for abandoning them. I am certain Harold will find the villain and deliver him to you as prisoner."

Thurstan's voice lifted with enthusiasm, but all Edgar could think was how the man was always performing to fit whatever audience he faced. A man who could never be trusted. Why did the King not see this? Was he completely unaware of Thurstan's hypocrisy? Or did he know and just not care? Perhaps the King was so often up in the clouds with the saints in heaven that he had lost touch with noticing the demons on earth.

But Edgar's thoughts were proven wrong when the King next spoke.

"Of course, the brothers are an interesting pair, are they not?" Edward walked toward the head of the long table and sat down, his question dangling before them unanswered. He waited with his arms folded upon his chest.

When Father Thurstan said nothing, Edgar felt uncomfortable with the silence. "Your Majesty, do you mean Harold and Tostig?"

Edward ignored Edgar's question. "How many times did I send Harold to quell the border? And how long has it taken, hmmm?" He scowled at Thurstan. "More than eight years already, is it not? Treaties, fortifications, raids. And still nothing. Gruffydd has had his way with us for all that time." He unlocked his folded arms, slapping his hands on the table as if an idea had just struck him.

"It was not until Tostig joined Harold that we secured a victory of sorts. And is it not interesting that Tostig himself has never needed assistance from anyone? Is that not something worth noting, Father?" Edward glared at the priest with a searing indictment. "Tostig has managed to keep the Scots under control all on his own, hasn't he? With just a little support from the bishops, he has been able to maintain good relations with Malcolm. Tostig did not need his brother's help in order to fulfill his King's wishes, did he now?"

Thurstan was not pleased with the direction the conversation had taken. He quickly seated himself on Edward's right, thinking that proximity would help him maneuver inside the King's thoughts. "That may be true, my King, but remember, Gruffydd is much more dangerous than Malcolm. Gruffydd has no conscience, his scepter is stained not just with enemy blood. For Jesus' sake, he killed the uncle of the man he now fights alongside! His alliances last only so long as they are useful to him. Look at his history. He slaughtered Aelfgar's uncle to maintain Rhyd y Groes. He killed Iago to get Gwynedd. He stole Hywel's wife after he seized Dyfed and then did away with Hywel. He murdered Gruffydd ap Rhydderch to retake Deheubarth. Need I go on and mention the slaughter at Hereford? The Welsh pose a much greater threat to us than do the Scots. Recent events prove it. You cannot compare the two borders, my liege. Tostig's region is much easier to tame than Harold's."

When the King's face flushed red, Thurstan saw he had overstepped his place and softened his voice to conclude. "Of course, my King, enemies are enemies. And regardless of who those enemies are, they always pose a threat. But when it comes to comparing the two brothers, I believe it may be somewhat useful to consider the differences between their foes."

Despite the priest's gentler tone, King Edward stood abruptly, crashing his chair against the wall. "Who cares what you believe? Did I ask you what you believe?" He narrowed his eyes and began to wave his arms in frustration. "You twist the facts to suit your purpose, and I will not have it. I will not have it, I say! If Tostig were fighting the Welsh all these years, he would have put Gruffydd's head in my lap as I had Rhys ap Rhydderch's eleven years ago! Instead, I am hearing that the man has fled to Ireland. Foiled once again, and the scoundrel safe in Ireland!"

Edward's face deepened in color from red to purple with rage, the thin vessels on his cheeks nearly burst through his pale skin. Marching around the table, he drew closer to Edgar. The boy had remained standing throughout the discussion and was now tucked in tightly near the corner of the hearth.

"And what say you to all this, young man? Whom would you entrust with your most important military engagements? Which of the brothers would you choose?"

Thurstan looked over his shoulder, his dark eyes warmed to see Edgar squirm under the King's ire, forced into as tight a corner as the one in which he stood.

In those few seconds, Edgar searched his mind for the proper way to get out of this trap. In his heart, he wanted to side with Tostig and please the King, especially since Edgar actually liked the northern Earl. His one interaction with Tostig was a pleasant one, coming as it did a few years ago when Malcolm came to announce his defeat of

Macbeth and Lulach. Moreover, Edgar despised Harold. He had disliked the man from the moment he arrived at Baranya and stole their father from them with both his summons and his poison. If Edgar rekindled Thurstan's hatred by not choosing Harold, then so be it. Ever since Malcolm had intervened on Edgar's behalf, the priest had doubled his efforts to find ways to harm him. So what difference could one more offense make? Edgar decided he would tell the truth.

Gathering himself, he looked directly into the King's eyes. "If you are asking my opinion as to which brother is more worthy, then—"

At that precise moment, the door to the chamber flew open, and immediately the room was infused with the scent of sweat, earth, and blood. A bold warrior strode in carrying a sack in his hand. When the man sent a gloved hand to loosen the cheek flaps and remove his brass-trimmed helmet, a pair of black eyes pierced Edgar with their intensity and then turned to rest upon the King.

Harold made his announcement as he walked confidently toward the King. "Your Majesty, I have fulfilled your request." Using only one hand, he placed the soiled and weathered helmet with a rattle upon the table. His hair was wet and matted to his head, his face spotted with traces of mud. Thurstan swung around in his chair to smile upon his favored one.

Harold dropped to one knee and lowered his head. "My Lord, I could not stop nor rest until I was again in your company. Of our victory at Rhuddlan, I am certain you have already heard. But what you do not know is that our kingdom is now secure. England will never again be ravaged by that Welsh devil, for I bring proof he is abiding now in Hell." Harold raised the sack and offered it to the King, but Edward made no move. "Behold, the head of Gruffydd!"

The bag hung in mid-air as if by magic. Edgar looked from the King to the priest and back again. He measured the reactions of the two.

King Edward pulled back a step and brought his hands to his chin, looking like a woodland creature startled by a noise. Meanwhile, Thurstan savored the moment, grinning with pleasure at his devotee. The priest nodded to Harold, indicating that the Earl should proceed.

Rising up from his knee, Harold stood tall and plunged his hand into the sack. With a flourish, he pulled out the bloody stump of his enemy's head, holding it aggressively by the hair. King Edward slid his hands to rest upon heart and stumbled slightly backwards until he leaned against the stone wall.

Edgar himself did not cringe or shy away. He could not stop staring in wonder at the severed head. The skin was ashen and blotchy with gray patches, the neck rimmed with dried blood where the blade had struck. As for the face, one eye socket was completely empty, while the other contained a bulbous eye frozen forever in spite.

Harold continued to hold the head aloft, tightly clutching its black hair. The strands were so long that the head swung back and forth as it dangled. Thurstan, amused by the boy's fascination and the King's timidity, walked boldly toward Harold and embraced him. With one hand, Harold patted the priest on the back, and with the other, he extended the head away from Thurstan's body but closer to Edgar's space. Spellbound by the horrific image, Edgar tilted his head back for a closer look.

The King recovered. "Praise be to God, for He hath delivered us of our enemy. A sight such as this gives me great pleasure." He attempted a feeble smile.

Turning away from the grisly sight, the King rubbed his hands against the sides of his robe as if to rid himself of the bloody vision. "As planned then, we will entrust Wales to Gruffydd's half-brothers, Bleddyn and Rhiwallon. They have sworn oaths to us in the past. We will ask them for hostages and tribute. May this triumph usher in a period of peace and prosperity for all my people. In the words of St.

Augustine, let us *'have concord with a good neighbor'* as we shall now have with both Wales and Scotland."

Father Thurstan thought it wise to take this opportunity to restore himself to the King's good graces by praising him. "Indeed, your Majesty," he gushed, "clearly you have been chosen by God to be the sole ruler of a vast and powerful kingdom. Your sovereignty now extends from Northumbria to Wessex and from East Anglia to Wales."

Thurstan then picked up the empty sack from the ground and walked over to Harold, opening the pouch wide enough in order to receive Harold's gift. "And with Aelfgar the traitor dead and Edwin his son installed in Mercia, all we must do now is remain vigilant so that no bond can ever again be forged between Mercia and Wales." He cinched the bag closed and handed it back to Harold.

To his King, Harold showed deference and devotion, but Edgar sensed the man was already plotting something. His intuition was confirmed when Harold, after picking up his helmet and tucking it under his arm, paused for a moment by the open door.

"I believe I have a way to do just that, my liege. A way to ensure that Mercia will not stray from the crown again. But of that I will speak later, after I have shown the people what happens to those who defy our King."

King Edward, relieved that the grotesque head was no longer near, gestured the sign of the cross as if to bless Harold on this holy mission. The warrior nodded, and with message firm in hand, walked out the door.

*   *   *   *   *

Lost in reverie, Margaret moved slowly down the abbey steps, giving her eyes time to adjust from the solemn chapel to the bright outdoors. The summer heat warmed her body with the same intensity she felt during midday prayer. She gazed up at the sky, noting the sun at its height and how its fullness mirrored the perfect image of divine splendor.

Her concentration was broken though when she noticed a swirl of movement around her. Sounds of celebration drew her back down to earth, compelling her to leave heaven behind. Craftsmen put down their tools, women cast aside their chores, all were making their way out of the courtyard—walking, skipping, or running towards the bridge that spanned the river, a bridge that granted entrance to or exit from the palace. Curious, she allowed herself to be swept up in their excitement, letting the thrill of the crowd be the wind that would carry her to some unknown but desired port.

Bodies clanged together, sweaty arms pumped up and down. Strides were long and full or short and choppy based on the spaces between people. Margaret rushed ahead toward a full-bodied woman in front whose heavy breathing proved how unaccustomed she was to exertion. The stranger's face was already flushed, her white bonnet crooked and about to fall off, were it not for the sizable ear that anchored it.

"What is going on?" Margaret sped up so that she could fall in step with her.

The woman let out a panting breath, "Ha!" She had to inhale with each word she spoke. "As…if…I…know?" She winked at Margaret. "Must…be…something…big…though…right?" The woman's smile revealed an empty space where her front tooth had been chipped near the top.

Margaret's question infused the woman with even greater enthusiasm as she propelled herself beyond Margaret, elbowing those ahead of her to beat them to the prize. Margaret did not try to keep pace with her. She continued to move quickly but chose not to match the urgency felt by her former traveling partner. Behind her, someone on horseback shouted, "Make way! Step aside! Make way!" Those who obeyed the command leaned toward one side, pushing Margaret off the path towards the right and onto the grassy shoulder.

Once safe from being trampled, she looked back to see a cream-colored palfrey maneuvering through the crowd with a four-step diagonal amble, its head held high, nostrils pulsing. Thinking she may have recognized its rider, she whispered hesitantly, "Tostig?"

Looking more carefully, she saw the man's thick, muscular body and took note of the heavy black brow that spanned the bridge of his nose and partially shaded his eyes. "Tostig!" she said again, this time with conviction. She jumped back into the swirling current.

By the time she made her way across the group, Tostig had passed beyond her, but she would not have to go far to catch him because the crowd was already slowing down. The destination must be at hand. When those around her changed their speed, she placed herself right beside the horse and called up, "Tostig? Tostig? Is that you?"

He looked down. His hair, bound with a leather strap around the top, swung freely at its ends when he faced her. "Margaret! Sister of the aetheling, good day, fair maiden." He reached down his hand and sought hers. "Why are you here amidst such chaos?" He raised the back of her hand to brush it with a kiss. "Why are you not in the peaceful solitude of the church?"

He grinned at her with the kindness of a brother trying to shield his sister from harm. "Mayhap your angelic self has come to sanctify us sinners gathered here?"

She slapped her hand against his leg. "You make me laugh at my own unworthiness, Tostig! I have plenty of my own sins to account for, you can be certain of that!" She pointed at the crowd in front of them. "But the truth is, I do not know why I am here or what I am hastening toward. I just followed along. Can you see from up there? What is going on?"

"Come," he squeezed his legs firmly against the horse and bent sideways at the hip. Wrapping both arms around her, he lifted her up as if she were as light as an empty bucket. "There you go!" He placed her in front of him so that she could have a better view. "Can you see now? And just look who it is. My wonderful brother, regaling the people with tales of his own success. Quite the showman, is he not?"

At the mention of Harold's name, Margaret's giddiness faded away. The crowd formed a half-circle around him, and he stood at its center. Raising a single arm above his head, he quieted the chatter.

"Good people of the realm, I bring welcome news of our campaign in Wales. Their army is destroyed. Their fleet burned to cinders. Their people conquered and humbled." He pounded on his chest. "We shall never again be troubled by their butchery!"

Voices surged. Whistles and cheers filled the air as men slapped one another's backs and women embraced.

Margaret studied the victor. He *was* a great performer, a man who exuded heroism. But she knew better. She knew that beneath that bravado was an impostor whose insecurity fueled his hunger for power.

Tostig was disgusted. "You hear that? Sounds like he alone won the battle. All by himself. Hhhmph."

She turned her head back toward Tostig. "Why not go up there and stand beside him? Here, wait. Let me slide off." She made the move to slip down from the side of the horse, but Tostig grabbed her shoulder.

"No, do not bother. I am not interested in speeches or adoration. I have no feel for either of those things. Give me a sword, and I will make people follow. Not like this minstrel who weaves stories from threads drawn from imagination rather than truth."

Harold quieted the crowd again. "Our borders are now safe. Those of you familiar with that region need no longer fear the midnight raids of Gruffydd and his men. Never again will we suffer the shrieks of our countrymen that so often roused us from sleep, seizing our hearts with pain and anguish. "

"Oh, spare me, dear brother," Tostig dismissed Harold sarcastically. "As if this man ever had a care for anyone other than himself—no thought for even members of his own family! Every move he has made is with one goal in mind: his own advancement. You know what he did? He had stone pillars built for himself just west of the Wye and had them inscribed 'Here was Harold the Conqueror'! Meanwhile, if not for my men who came down from the North, my brother would still be licking the boots of that Welsh fiend, handing over to him even more treasure and more land!"

Tostig's rage frightened her. Two men with such power to wield? Not only would they destroy each other, they would sacrifice hundreds of others as well just to come out on top. Behind her eyelids she could feel a throbbing sensation—as if one of her "visions" was struggling to come through. She blinked repeatedly to hold it back.

A burly man in the crowd yelled out. "And what about Gruffydd? Word is he got away. How do you claim such things if the bastard is still on the loose?"

"Yeah, yeah," the crowd seconded the man's accusation, but their criticism did not deter Harold. Rather it offered him the opportunity he had been waiting for.

Striding over toward his horse that was tethered to the wooden railing of the bridge, he countered, "His own people have renounced him. He abandoned them in their hour of need. For too long, their lives and their land have borne the price of his vanity." He rummaged through the saddlebag to grab something.

Tostig rested his arm on her shoulder as he stretched it forward and pointed his finger straight in Harold's direction. "Oh, you will not want to miss this, my lady—so long as you can stomach it."

"Put your worry to rest, dear people of England. For behold, I deliver you the news you so desperately desire. Here is what is left of that traitorous bastard. I give you Gruffydd ap Llwelyn!" Raising the head high into the air, Harold slowly turned from one side of the crowd to the other in order to give everyone a glimpse of his supremacy. Horror switched to glee as the people clapped and roared in exultation.

Carrying his gruesome token, Harold marched along the bridge to the opposite end away from the palace. The mob trailed behind, eagerly anticipating his next move. Tostig chose not command his horse forward. "I think we can both guess what will happen next, can we not?"

Harold had gone too far a distance for Margaret and Tostig to be able to hear his words, but they could see what was taking place. Someone had handed Harold a long, slender stick with a sharpened point at its end. After more joyous shouts from the crowd, Harold thrust the spike—no longer bare—high into the air with Gruffydd's head affixed to the top. Taking the rope supplied to him, Harold tied the stick against the railing near the entrance of the bridge. The crowd rejoiced to see the trophy.

"Well, Margaret," Tostig clicked his tongue in feigned disappointment, "looks like the high point of the show is over." He affectionately tapped his hand against the horse's neck. "My brother has firmly 'planted' his role as savior into their minds. It will be his name, I vow, they will be crying out for someday. Unless someone were to set the record straight. But that someone has other business to tend to at the moment, which means I must bid you farewell and head back North. Shall I bring you to the palace, my lady?"

Margaret slid down from her seat. When she looked up at him from the ground, she had to raise her hand to her forehead to block the sun's glare. "Thank you, Tostig, but that is not necessary. I do not think I am ready just yet to head back. Please know that I will keep you and Lady Judith in my prayers and will petition the Lord for peace and contentment amongst your people." She lovingly stroked the side of the horse that would be carrying Tostig many miles away.

Softly, he touched her hand. "You have not made any mention at all of Malcolm, Lady Margaret, yet you must know he never stops speaking of you. May I bring him a kind word?"

She considered the request. Squinting up at him, she replied, "Yes. Of course. Tell him. ... tell him that I hope the *whins* are in bloom in Inverness and that he can taste their honeyed smell upon his lips."

"I shall relate those very words to him. Farewell, Margaret. And may God be with you always as he is with his other angels on high." Tostig turned his horse about and began riding away.

Margaret stood alone, far removed from the frenzied crowd. The serenity that had anchored her had been ripped away. Against the backdrop of nature's beauty stood this chilling intrusion of man's inhumanity to man. Both sides—friend and foe—were equally responsible for this destruction. Cruelty, violence, pain, malice—her heart choked from having to witness the poison that ran in men's blood. And most crushing of all was the idea that Malcolm, as king and protector of his own land, was probably no different.

*   *   *   *   *

By the time Edgar found her, the crowd was gone. The sun dipped lower in the horizon, taking away the earlier warmth with its descent.

The bridge itself was empty, save for the graven image that remained its lone sentinel.

Margaret was seated on the grassy knoll, head bowed and eyes closed as she fingered the petals of the flower she held in her hand. She was in the world but not of it. Edgar's long strides slowed as he came closer and saw her deep in reflection. Not wanting to jar her too rudely, he tried making enough noise to draw her out from her meditation.

"Hello, sister."

Her eyes flickered and opened. "Hello," her voice thick from disuse.

"Were you here for … that?" he nodded toward the suspended stick.

"Aye."

"I got to see it up close. In the King's room." He wanted to tell more.

"Well, I did not see it up close. Nor do I care to."

With that subject closed, Edgar looked around for something else to do while he thought of what to say. He took from his pocket a small piece of wood and his knife and sat down to whittle.

"Well, at least one border has been quieted." Little pieces of shavings trickled onto his lap as the knife ran up and down the wood.

Realizing she would not be returning to prayer anytime soon, she gestured toward the wood, "What are you making?"

"It is supposed to be a dragon, but it looks more like a bird." He moved the piece around in his hand, looking at it with disappointment.

The stillness was broken when sounds from the far end of the bridge reached their ears. The clip-clop of hooves on the wooden planks was sure and steady. Margaret and Edgar both looked up from their seated positions and watched the horses closing the gap. The wagon they pulled formed a self-contained square, and as it came nearer, they could see it held one passenger, a woman.

Margaret's eyes softened. "Who is that?"

The young girl looked like a frightened deer, her body tense and slightly hunched, her eyes wide and alert. With her hands wrapped firmly around her chest, she leaned up against the wooden rails of the cart in order to maintain her balance as the wagon bumped along the wedges in the bridge.

"I think you mean, 'who are they'?" Edgar countered, and Margaret realized her brother was right.

Tucked in close to the girl's bosom was a tiny infant, its delicate head covered in a dusting of black fuzz. The woman's ivory skin shone like a beacon—even from this distance—but it was pulled tight across her face from worry and suspicion. Like the child's, her hair was also dark, as black as a raven's plumage. A single braid ran down her back, still thick and heavy despite the wavy curls that had come undone because of the jostling.

When the wagon passed right next to them, the girl flashed her green eyes their way, scowling at Margaret and Edgar with hostility as if warning them to stay away. She then turned her shoulder to protect her babe from their view.

Margaret wanted to call out to the wagon and reassure the woman that she and Edgar meant no harm. But as the driver directed the horses to veer toward the palace doors, there was no time for Margaret to speak. Mother and child moved onward, fear and distrust riding along with them.

Margaret felt hollow. How could the girl think that Margaret or her brother would hurt her? The stranger's opinion left Margaret dejected.

"Poor soul," Margaret turned to Edgar. "I wonder why she is being brought here…"

Edgar was uncomfortable discussing this with his pious sister. He fiddled with the dragon-bird, moving it back and forth from one hand to the other. He pocketed his knife.

"I know how you do not like to hear such things, sister, but she is a Welsh prisoner. Not part of the group who will be sold into slavery —because those captives have not yet arrived—but she may as well be."

She grabbed his hand to stop it from moving. "What are you saying?" Her eyes canvassed his face, searching for meaning.

Edgar studied her grip. "Remember how I told you earlier that I had seen the 'trophy' up close? I was in the room when Earl Harold was talking to the King. He said his army seized a good number of Welsh prisoners who would be sold as slaves. But that woman? Well, since she has been separated from the rest, it is probably because she is special, I bet. I heard the Earl say that they had Gruffydd's widow in their possession. I am guessing that is who she is."

Slowly, Margaret let go of Edgar. Her hand dropped to her side. Recalling the image of what now "welcomed" visitors to Westminster, Margaret realized the horror the young girl must have felt when she crossed the bridge and saw her husband defiled like that. Her people had been tortured and enslaved. Her husband killed and dismembered. And what fate was awaiting her, awaiting her child? Margaret shuddered.

"She needs a friend. Someone who can offer some small kindness in a world that has given her so much pain. I will speak to Queen

Edith and ask permission to pray with Gruffydd's widow. She and her child must feel so very alone. Perhaps praying together can bring her some measure of comfort."

Having chosen a clear course of action, Margaret stood up and dusted from her skirt stray blades of grass. Before she walked away, Edgar reached out for her.

"Be careful, sister, about making promises that we can not keep," he spoke hesitantly but tenderly.

"What do you mean?"

"We may not be able to give her much comfort is what I mean." The next words he spoke were tinged with regret. "Harold plans to take that girl as his wife."

Margaret felt her chest tighten. This was a fate far worse than Margaret could have imagined. She must pray for some form of divine intervention. God must intercede where devils tread.

"You are right, brother. We wield no power at this court. We cannot guarantee her deliverance. But as St. Paul writes, if we are equipped in the armor of God, we can take a stand against the devil's schemes. Faith is what has kept us both safe and alive up to this point. And it shall be the same for this woman and her child."

Margaret turned to go, but then had one final thought to share. She pointed at his whittling. "Do not be a brother to dragons, Edgar. Make it be a dove instead."

Not quite catching her meaning, he stared at the object in his hand. By the time he looked up, his sister was gone.

*   *   *   *   *

An orange glow encircled the poet who sat before the hearth, his harp balanced upon his left knee. The light lifted him from the ordinary setting of the room to bring him closer to the world of legend. Holding the instrument steady with one hand, he plucked away at the strings with the other, releasing the melody onto the air.

His shield bore the image

Of the Virgin from above

Her strength he had in hand.

He sought to protect the people he loved

With her power, he was fully in command.

There upon Badon Hill

Where all the Saxons lay wait

Arthur led the advance on his foe

Letting Mary guard his men and their fate

From his blade, oh the blood, it did flow . . .

The man's voice rang clear and pure, like a skylark announcing break of dawn. Its candor cut through the surrounding distractions, sending an irrefusable invitation to journey to another world. Every listener, unable to resist the bard's call, followed the shaft of sound that charmed them back to days of yore. Margaret too fell under his enchantment, reliving Arthur's role as *dux bellorum*—leader of wars. The room transformed into the battleground of Badon Hill, the enemy loomed large and threatening. Unintentionally, she found herself holding her breath as the suspense grew.

With the final note shimmering upon the air, the crowd sat spellbound before slowly breaking into applause. Margaret clapped her hands together as well, showing her admiration not just for the content of the story but even more for the beauty of its delivery. She remained still, her ears desperately trying to cling to the voice that was so angelic.

Edgar, like most guests in the hall, quickly forgot the performance and returned to the business of eating and drinking. He, Margaret, his mother, and Cristina were all seated on the same bench across the table from other guests who had been invited to celebrate in this recent victory over the Welsh. At the front of the room on the higher platform was the dais where sat King Edward and Queen Edith. On the King's right was Harold, and to the left of the Queen were Leofwine, Gyrth, and Father Thurstan. A seventh chair, placed next to Harold and noticeably empty due to Tostig's hasty departure, gave Harold dominion over that entire end of the table. Leaning one way to confer with the King, then to the other to shout toward those seated at other tables nearby, Harold was never without words—most of the conversation focused on his own accomplishments in Wales.

The ten other tables spread about the room shared in the congeniality of the celebration, and although the food delivered to those tables featured fewer dishes than the ones delivered to the dais, there was still plenty to choose from. Most people agreed there was more food set before them that evening than they would normally have seen in a fortnight.

From the far end of the bench, Edgar leaned closer to Margaret. "Sister?" No response.

"Sister?" He repeated more loudly, stretching his neck out over the table to get a closer look at her face. All he saw were her green eyes, glazed over and staring straight ahead, seeing something where there was nothing.

He waved his hand in front of her. "Are you in there, sister?"

She nearly lost her balance on the backless bench at this invasion of her personal space. "What? What is it? Did something happen? Did I miss something?"

Margaret's mother felt the commotion. "Stop, you two. Do not start bickering here. We do not need to direct any attention our way. Mind my words." Agatha's face was twisted with irritation, a look that thinly masked her underlying grief.

Margaret took this moment to notice how her mother had aged. Her once brown hair now had streaks of pure white running through it, bolts of worry and doubt that sprang from the crown of her head where such thoughts originated. Without father around, her mother had lost her smile. Her eyes, once round and bright with amusement, had shrunk beneath the heavy lids which carried the weight of their unknown future.

Sensitive to her suffering, Margaret reached out her hand to place it on her mother's arm. "Yes, Mother. We will not cause any trouble."

To Edgar, she said, "Now what was it that was so important? I was savoring the minstrel's music. I just wanted its beauty to linger..."

Edgar drizzled some honey over his piece of bread and lifted the morsel into his mouth. "He is really a *skald*, you know. But the King will not call him that, of course." He munched on the bread. "Trying to move away from anything associated with the Norsemen, I guess."

She bent closer to her brother to whisper. "I bet Harold believes the song was for his own benefit—whether sung by minstrel or *skald*. I bet he views himself as rather legendary after his defeat of Gruffydd."

"Hmmm. I do not know. Probably." Edgar held a biscuit out to her. "Want one?"

"No, thank you. I do not have much appetite these days." The single platter which stood at the center of their table was empty.

Nothing remained of the roasted lamb but a layer of greasy fat and a few soggy carrots floating in it. Everything had been picked apart and placed into trenchers that were to feed two people, but Margaret's hand had never reached into the one she shared with Edgar.

Edgar popped another piece of bread into his mouth. "You fast too much. You are going to blow away with the next gust of wind, I bet." Nodding over toward the dais, he posed a question. "Speaking of the Earl, did you ever talk to Queen Edith about visiting Gruffydd's widow?"

"I did earlier. She was preparing the King's robes for this evening. Laying out his tunic of royal purple and polishing his jewel-encrusted staff. She thought I had come to fill her in on events at Wilton. The Queen remembers it well from the days when she was there. I think she expected me to speak of my schooling—of embroidery and music and overseeing domestic duties—so she was rather surprised when I asked for permission to pray with Ealdgyth. That is her name by the way. Gruffydd's widow. The Queen was so busy she granted my request without hesitation. I think she just wanted to be rid of me."

Taking the small cloth that lined the basket of biscuits, she snapped it clean of crumbs. "I thought we would have seen Ealdgyth here at the feast, but I guess she is even more of a prisoner than we imagined!" Margaret reached into the basket. "I think I will take some of that bread. Queen Edith set no restrictions as to when I could or could not visit the widow." Pulling out two pieces, she wrapped them in the cloth and dropped her hands beneath the table.

"Mother, I am not very hungry. Is it all right with you if I go?" Careful not to lie, she spoke only what was necessary to gain permission to leave.

As soon as her mother nodded in assent, Margaret scampered away.

*   *   *   *   *

Her footsteps echoed along the long corridor that ran from the Great Hall past the private chambers of the King and Queen. Unlike the walls in the feasting hall which were covered with fine embroidered tapestries, here they were bare and dark. A single torch hung from its sconce at the beginning of the hallway and then another one was placed at the end so that the streaks of dirt and moisture were visible only in those locations.

As Margaret drew closer to the second torch, she saw the winding staircase that led to the upper rooms where Ealgdyth was supposedly being kept. Still holding the gift of bread, Margaret placed her other hand on the cold, damp wall as she carefully made her way up the twisting steps. The space was so narrow only one person could fit at a time, and even she—a rather slender and small person—found it rather confining. When she reached the top step, she marveled at the size of the large man now standing guard outside the widow's room. How in the world did he squeeze his way up those same stairs to arrive at this level?

The sound of her approach alerted him, but he soon relaxed his stance once he saw her. His dagger made a scratching sound as he returned it to its sheath. It swung a bit back and forth on the side of his body as it dangled from his belt.

"There'll be nothing up here of interest to you, my lady. You'd best be going right back down those steps and on your way."

He moved from his post to block her advance, repositioning his body to encourage her retreat. His chest was as broad as a keg of ale; the tops of his arms, jutting out from his sleeveless tunic, were thick and round.

Despite his intimidating posture, Margaret graciously refused to be turned away. "You need not worry, my good fellow, this visitation has been sanctioned by the Queen herself." She motioned to the cloth. "See? I have come to break bread with Ealgdyth and to pray with her. I am to visit her each morn and eve for such a purpose." She smiled sweetly in his direction, her manner straightforward and casual.

The sincerity of her voice and the innocence stamped across her face were nearly enough for the soldier to step aside. Add to that the mention of the Queen's name, and he was convinced. He nodded his head and granted her passage.

Margaret knocked on the door first before grasping the latch handle to push it open. At the same time, she announced herself softly, "Good tidings, my lady. My name is Margaret. I am the grandniece of the King. I bid you good evening . . ."

When the door creaked open far enough, Margaret craned her neck around its edge and saw Ealdgyth whip her head over her shoulder to face her visitor. With her back still turned to the door, she glared at Margaret with aggression, her dark eyes aggressive and slanted like a cat's. "What do you want?"

Margaret could see the girl was extraordinarily beautiful. Her rich black hair tumbled down far past her shoulders, rippling in thick, abundant waves unhindered by kerchief, tie, or ribbon. No wrinkle or blemish tainted her ivory skin which glowed with a vibrancy that outshone the candles in the room. Her lips were full and pink, warm and accustomed to smiling, even though the words coming from them were ice cold.

"I have brought you some bread from the feast," Margaret lifted the cloth and took another small step forward. "I was hoping we could pray together, if that would be agreeable to you."

Slowly Ealdgyth shifted her body on the bed to turn a little closer toward her visitor. She laughed mockingly, "Pray? Pray to whom? To the God of armies? The God of kings? The God of monks and priests and bishops? The God who listens only to the petitions of men and hearkens not to the cries of women? Save your prayers for yourself, foolish girl. I will not waste my breath calling upon a God who delights in sending only more misery."

She lowered her lips to caress the hair of the babe she cradled in her arms. "'Our Father who art in heaven . . .' Ha! What does He know of the agony of women, of wives, of mothers? He is no different from the men he created—manipulating, tormenting, and punishing according to His own whims."

Margaret swallowed the girl's pain, trying to understand her bitterness. She knelt down before the bedside and gently laid the cloth next to the mother and child, making a silent offering of companionship without judgment.

Ealdgyth was taken aback by Margaret's serenity. Even so, she still lashed out. "Get up off your knees. I already told you there will be no praying today. Or any day, for that matter." Ealdgyth repositioned the baby so that her arm was free to reach down and take a piece of bread.

"At least they do not starve us here. Someone brings food at morn and supper. And yet I am always hungry." Gradually her tone was softening. Margaret's grace was smoothing out the rough edges. "Little Nest needs only me for nourishment, but it seems I can never get enough myself. Strange is it not, how the body demands survival even when the mind wishes otherwise?" She licked the honey off her fingertips after eating the first biscuit.

"So why are you *really* here, hmm? Have you come to convince me to be grateful to that cur? To be honored that he has chosen me to be his plaything, his toy? Well, you can forget it. Just be on your way. Tell your 'granduncle' you have failed in your mission. Tell them I hate being an acquisition, an object passed from one set of hands to another. I will not feign gratitude for being forced to do what I would never choose to do."

When Ealdgyth saw Margaret gaze upon her with pity, her voice turned shrill. "And do not look at me like that, silly girl. Your fate will be no different than mine, so feel sorry for yourself too while you are at it then. Better yet, why do you not follow through on your plan and head to the chapel anyway—only pray by yourself instead of with me and beg for a future that does not include suffering a scoundrel's seed entering your body and losing every dream you have ever had."

Gruffydd's widow jumped up in anger, breaking her connection with the nursing child. Stunned at the abrupt detachment, the babe squirmed and writhed in frustration until Ealdgyth helped her latch on again. She held her tightly to her breast while she paced back and forth in the room. Margaret meanwhile had risen from her kneeling position to take a seat upon the bed. She leaned forward with her elbows on her legs, eager to listen to whatever story Ealdgyth wanted to tell, whatever burden she wanted to discharge.

Very gently, she probed, "Mayhap it is grief that has led you to this loss of belief, this loss of trust in God—which is understandable given the circumstances. Your land, your people, your husband, they have all been taken from you. That surely gives you the right to question your faith and God's role in allowing such terrible loss."

Ealdgyth's scornful laugh sent a chill down Margaret's spine. "My land? My people? They were not mine and never were! And as far as my husband goes, I hope he is rotting in hell! One that matches the wretched pit he threw me into when he took me as his wife!"

Margaret's hand involuntarily raised itself to cover her open mouth. She had assumed that Ealdgyth was heartbroken over recent events, yet here she was actually pleased about it all.

Relishing Margaret's shock, Ealdgyth gloated. "Did not foresee that, did you, naive one? Well, it is the truth. I am glad I am out of that dreadful place and free of that vicious fiend."

Ealdgyth's voice cracked as did her rage. In its place flowed a stream of sorrow. "You would not understand. No one understands. I was a child, a mere child when he took me. I should have been singing nursery rhymes and collecting wildflowers. Instead, I was sent to a grown man's bed to be torn asunder. And my father condoned it. He made the union happen. The two of them conspired together to do this. They ripped away my innocence, trampled on my heart. They crushed any dream I ever had about love. "

Margaret sat motionless, staring at her hands folded in her lap. Whatever could she say to all this? It was true that she did not know exactly what took place in the bed shared by husband and wife when the shadows of night fell upon them, but Margaret guessed that between Gruffydd and Ealdgyth it must have been awful. A violent theft where the object stolen could never be recovered again. She lifted her eyes to look up at Ealdgyth, their luminous green color filled with a mixture of compassion and anguish.

Ealdgyth shook her head to reprimand herself. "And why am I telling *you* all this? A total and complete stranger?" She smiled at such odd circumstances.

"Well, if you can take a lesson from me, then here is some advice. Join a convent. Pledge to be a novice at some abbey—choose one that is lenient with rules so you can be in charge of yourself. Then you can do what you will. Secretly take a man to bed if you wish, or keep your sacred vows and remain chaste. It is quite appealing to have such authority, is it not? Not many women have that luxury—only nuns and harlots. One calls upon God, the other worships payment, and by doing so, their needs are satisfied."

The babe had fallen asleep in Ealdgyth's arms, so she carefully laid her near the top of the bed, and in a gesture of sisterhood, sat down next to Margaret. Sensing a lessening of tension, Margaret spoke. "Not for the reasons you said, but I am taking the veil and entering the convent. It is the only place for me. I decided that some time ago.

"But as for why I am here, well, when I saw you yesterday, saw how you were forced to come here in that cart, my heart was heavy with sorrow. And then it nearly stopped beating altogether when you looked at my brother and me as if we were the next ones who would cause you pain. On the bridge, I wanted to yell out to you that not everyone here in this court is self-serving and cruel. That is why I asked the Queen if I could come and pray with you and be a friend to you, to you and your child—if you will let me."

Ealdgyth shook her head at Margaret's rose-colored outlook. "Oh, my dear girl. I wish the world were as simple as you say. You believe that there are good people and bad people, and that it is easy to discern which is which. But even I, with my limited experience of the world, know that the line between the two is blurry. Those whom I thought were good, the people I believed in and loved, they ultimately cared more for their own advancement than for me. They cherished the riches of the world more than the little hand that reached for their own."

Staring at the ground, Ealdgyth thought of her father Aelfgar, the man who had willingly sacrificed her for power. "My father may not have held the knife, but he pushed me into the arms of one who did. And Gruffydd carved his way so deep into my soul that I shall never be whole again."

Drawn to the young girl's suffering, Margaret wanted to reach out and embrace Ealdgyth—offer words of comfort, devise a concoction that would remedy all the pain and erase the misery that was to come.

But she had no words, no antidote, no solution. So she remained still, praying silently to the Virgin Mary for direction.

Ealdgyth was not finished speaking. "I would bang on the doors of the abbey at Wenlock and beg admittance if I did not have my little Nest to care for. She is the one thing that is totally mine, and I will not let her be taken from me by anyone. At least, that I can try to control." She pushed her hands against the bed and stood up.

"So, my new friend, Margaret, perhaps speaking with you has done me some good. Shall we pray now? Maybe there is some saint up above who would hearken to my prayer? Hmmm? What say you? Would they listen to my request? And what if my prayer is an impossible one? For it is impossible, is it not, to pray that I not be forced to wed again? It is futile to wish for that, is it not? My value is not in who I am but in what I represent—and as the widow of Gruffydd and sister of the Earl of Mercia, I exist only in terms of property and alliances. It is a hollow life when one's worth is measured only by titles and dowries. To never be asked about one's feelings, desires, or dreams. It leaves a person empty inside."

Ealdgyth was not sentimental over the truth of her situation, but Margaret was. So moved was she by the widow's predicament that her eyes grew misty. And that sadness grew even deeper when Margaret thought of the awful future that awaited Ealdgyth. To be forced into marriage again with yet another cruel man who cared nothing for Ealdgyth herself? Margaret did the only thing she could do: she called upon her faith.

"Things may look impossible when we view them with our own eyes, but remember, with God all things are possible."

"Ha! And you need to remember what I said before. I will not pray to Him."

Margaret brushed aside the comment and offered an alternative instead. "Then let us call upon Our Lady to intercede for you."

She took Ealdgyth's hand and guided the widow to kneel next to her facing the bed. With the tiny babe sleeping peacefully before them, Margaret folded her own hands together and bowed down her head. "We fly to your patronage, O holy Mother of God; despise not our petitions in our necessities, but deliver us always from all dangers."

Joined together in the stillness, Margaret soon felt a jolt of energy pierce the center of her forehead in the space above her eyebrows. Her arms tingled from the shock and her clasped hands were pulled apart. Ealdgyth felt Margaret's body shift. "What just happened? Are you all right?" She put her arm around the girl's shoulders and felt a warmth not there before.

"Your brother is the Earl of Mercia?" Margaret spoke as if in a trance.

"Yes, Edwin took possession of the title upon my father's death. Why do you ask?"

"Is he more considerate of your feelings, your preferences than was your father?"

Ealdgyth was puzzled by this line of questioning. "Yes, I would say so. He and I were extremely close. He tried to convince Father I was too young for marriage, too young to be sent to wed Gruffydd. He argued with Father on my behalf, but of course, he ultimately failed to win him over. Why? Why do you ask?"

Margaret turned to look deeply into Ealdgyth's eyes. "We must get you and your child back to Edwin, back to Mercia." She seized Ealdgyth's elbow urging her to stand. "Perhaps Edwin can protect you from Harold. He could secure another suitor for you or let you live on your own terms in the land he governs. Mother Mary has shown me what you must do. You must run away. And I shall help you."

Ealdgyth laughed at the folly of such a plan. How could this simple girl be anyone's savior? But . . . then again, what other options did she have? Margaret's idea was better than any she herself had envisioned. It was certainly better than wasting away the hours and days until she was passed on to another man who would take her without her consent. Take her without even knowing or loving her. An outrageous plan it may be, and yet the girl beside her seemed to be lit from within, glowing with a strength that seemed to originate from some supernatural force. *Perhaps this is what true faith looks like,* Ealdgyth thought to herself.

With nothing left to lose, Gruffydd's widow surrendered her skepticism and offered her hands palms up toward Margaret. "I place my fate and that of my child in Mary's hands. What does she say I must do?"

*　　*　　*　　*　　*

Since it was well after Lauds, Margaret knew she would find him in the garden, cultivating the roots and raw herbs that would assist in healing. Just stepping into the greenery instilled a sense of tranquility in her, a calm that loosened the strings of tension tugging at her heart. Everything was so neat, so orderly. Its circular layout mirrored the infinite world of the sacred while the interior four squares reflected the concerns of the earth—the four seasons, the four elements, the four humours. There she found Brother Tobias on his knees, head bowed, hands delicately touching the leaves of sage. With his thumb and forefinger, he pinched the main stem just below the top whorl of leaves and added the bunch to the pail that rested on the ground next to him. As she drew closer, she could hear him humming "*Sancti venite*" while he worked.

Sensing her approach without even looking up, he calmly welcomed her. "Good day, Lady Margaret. No journey for you today? Not heading back to Wilton?"

He still kept his head down, focused on the leaves. "I saw you earlier at prayer but could not stop to bid you good morning. With some of the brothers ill, we have had to double our responsibilities." Satisfied with the size of the pile he had accumulated, he pulled his head away from the plant and sat cross-legged on the ground. He tapped the soil next to him in invitation.

When it came to conversation, Margaret practiced no form of artifice. She had no skill at circling around topics in order to win people over first before later getting to the point at hand. "I must tell you something, Brother. The Blessed Mother told me I could confide in you."

She joined him on the ground, lowering her voice to a whisper. "It has to do with the Welsh campaign. I am sure you heard all the excitement over the victory. But there is also a dark side to such triumph. So many women and children have been captured and brought here as slaves. Did you see the arrival of King Gruffyd's widow? Chained in a cart like a common criminal? She is a prisoner too and will remain so until Earl Harold takes her as his wife."

Tobias dusted the dirt from his hands as if to dismiss the possibility. "Well, that union cannot take place for quite some time. It would be irreverent to force a widow to wed before the year of mourning has run its course. Even Earl Harold would not violate such a law and risk his good standing with the church. And much can happen in a year's time."

She shook her head in disagreement. "Forgive me, Brother, but I am not so sure he cares about heaven, certainly not as much as he cares for the crown. And marrying Ealdgyth gives him more earthly power than ever before. With her, he wins control of every region.

And even if he does wait out the year, what kind of existence would that be for her? For her daughter? It would be like standing in rising water, knowing you could do nothing but wait helplessly until you were completely submerged."

"A daughter? How old is the child?"

"Just a babe, and an angelic one at that."

"Hmmm. What choice does the widow have?" He noticed Margaret's head tilt slightly as if carried away by thought. "What are you contemplating? Have you prayed on this? Have you turned the matter over to Jesus? What of the Black Rood? Has it spoken to you?"

Margaret's lashes fluttered, their thickness settled and rested upon her cheek, curtaining her gaze from him. "When I empty my mind to contemplate the crucifix, all I see is Our Lady. Her image stands at the foot of the cross as she did during her son's final hours. She beckons me and tells me to help Ealdgyth. She infuses me with a strength that makes me believe I can help her, help her and her child. Save them from Harold and such a fate."

She looked at him for reassurance. "I know, I know. It sounds crazy. A girl like me taking on a man nearly as powerful as the King. But Our Lady is calling me to act. How can I deny that call?"

Tobias unfolded his legs and reached out his hand to Margaret. "Come." He walked with her to the next set of four squares where wood betony grew. "Let me resume my work before anyone overhears me agreeing to undertake more."

Handling the clipper as if it were a sacred tool from the altar, he maneuvered it in and out of the matted clumps of tall purple flowers. "How can they be saved? Have you asked Mother Mary this question? Does the widow have friends in the region? They will need to be very influential friends indeed if they are to halt Harold's advances. I am afraid I do not know much about these things. I have never been the kind of priest who gains satisfaction by dabbling in politics and affairs of state. So forgive me if I do not know the answer to such questions. Who can petition for Ealdgyth's release?"

Margaret went down upon one knee and began straightening out the fresh clippings he had placed next to her. She laid out a tentative plan. "She must get away from here. We have to help her escape. Her brother is the Earl of Mercia. Once home, she will be surrounded by family and friends who can shield her from Harold."

"So you want me to bring her to Mercia then?"

"Oh, Brother, that would be too much to ask of you, surely." She reconsidered. "But . . . could you do it?" Her voice rang with desperation.

He tapped the tool upon the ground as he considered the feasibility of such a plan. "It is unlikely that I would be given permission by the abbot to be gone for the duration of such a journey. But, I could get her to Abingdon Abbey, and from there, someone could bring her to Leicester and then on to Lichfield, and then home to Chester. It would involve a network of guides and extraordinary coordination amongst us, but it could be done."

He then hesitated. "Even if all that works out, who's to say that her brother will heed her wishes and reject Harold's proposal? We may still fail in the long run." He looked grave.

His words did not discourage her. "No doubt, you are right about that. We may very well fail. But the outcome is not ours to determine, is it? All one can do in this earthly realm is be an instrument that promotes life, and helping Ealdgyth now will do just that. At the very least, it will grant her more time to live on her own terms. Surely there is victory in that."

Tobias sniffed the green leaves of wood betony that hung from the stem he was about to cut. In a few days, these nondescript fronds would become a most powerful remedy against all sorts of ailments. Margaret was right. It is true that one cannot always see how things will turn out in the future. One can only do what is good for that day alone.

"I will speak to Boniface after Vespers tonight and ask permission to visit Father Timothy. I was told he never made it back to Glastonbury, choosing instead to remain in Northamptonshire at Abingdon. If the Blessed Mother is on our side, I will have an answer for you at Lauds, and Gruffydd's widow will ride out with me tomorrow eve."

He slid over to reach into the pile of clippings. "Here, take some of these. Place them in a jar and give them to the girl. Tell her to carry them along with her belongings. When they dry out, she shall make tea with them. It will protect her on her journey once we have parted ways."

Margaret found it difficult to contain her joy. "Brother Tobias, how can I ever thank you? How can I repay you for this?"

He rose to a standing position, resting his hand upon her head while she remained on one knee. "Thank me? It is I who live to serve you. To me, you are everything that is good in this world. And although it is true we cannot see the future until it becomes the present, there are some among us, like Father Timothy, who grant us glimpses of what tomorrow may be. And I shall be even happier than I am today, my lady, if his words are true, and that the world will, one day, be governed by a noble heart such as yours. Until then, we continue to preserve and promote life, one encounter at a time."

Smiling, he made the sign of the cross upon her head and walked away to continue gardening. When he came upon the sprigs of rosemary, he stopped to recall its appearance in the story of Mary and Joseph's flight to Egypt. Carried away by the legend, he inhaled its sweet scent, remembering how Mary had changed the white-blossomed bush to blue after draping her cloak over it. Tobias then reached into the pail for his clippers and snipped a few stems to bring with them on their upcoming journey, a reminder they were not traveling alone.

*   *   *   *   *

"Hello again, my lady," the burly guard bowed at the waist in a show of respect. "Two visits today? I see you have come again to break bread with the widow." He motioned with his head toward the basket and flagon she had brought with her.

"Actually," Margaret said sweetly, "the Queen said I could bring Ealdgyth to Compline tonight in the chapel since mid-day prayer had given her so much comfort. Her Majesty said it would do Ealdgyth good to find some peace in her heart while things continue to sort themselves out." She then lifted up the basket in his direction. "So, in truth, the food and wine are for you to enjoy. It is but a small token of gratitude for how kind you have been to me and for how gentle you have been to her."

He smiled authentically, making his physical presence less threatening. "Well, that is quite generous of you, Lady Margaret, but I have done nothing other than perform my duty—nothing more, nothing less. Still, I thank you for this." He reached for the basket and the bottle and took them from her hands. Placing them on the ground beside him, he said, "This will help me pass the time while you two are at chapel." He stepped aside to make room for Margaret to get to the door.

Margaret followed the same routine every time she visited Gruffydd's widow. She knocked lightly, pulled the latch, and called out before fully stepping into the room. "Ealdgyth? May I come in? The Queen said we could pray once more before retiring to sleep . . ." Margaret could see only the babe sleeping on the bed, her arms raised and bent at the elbows, legs bowed. Were it not for her tender age and the look of contentment on her face, Nest resembled an unfortunate traveler in the process of surrendering to highwaymen. From behind the door, Ealdgyth's single hand reached out and seized Margaret's wrist, pulling her aggressively into the room. The widow was about to start talking immediately, but Margaret raised a finger to her lips to demand quiet. Only after the door was firmly closed did Margaret signal it safe to speak.

Ealdgyth was in distress. "This is all so frightening. How will we ever get out of here without being caught?" In the candlelight, her dark eyes glistened with panic. "What about the guard? We cannot leave the room with him out there like that! How can this even work?" Ealdgyth's grip on Margaret's wrist was so intense that Margaret could do nothing to break the connection.

"Do not be afraid, Ealdgyth," Margaret reassured her with a confidence that came from complete faith. "Everything is already in place. The guard knows you are going to chapel with me. And once we are gone, he will eat and drink what I have brought. The wine has a little extra something in it—thanks to Brother Tobias."

Margaret slowly peeled away Ealdgyth's fingers one by one to loosen the girl's grip on her arm. "When the guard awakens, he will see the closed door and think you have already returned. We just have to make sure that we close it now upon our leaving. It will appear all the same to him. Your escape will not be known until they come to deliver your meal in the morning. By then, you and Tobias will have put many miles between yourselves and Westminster."

Putting her arm around Ealdgyth, she guided her over toward the bed. They sat down gently, careful not to disturb the sleeping child whose arms and legs were still extended. "Breathe deeply. In and out. Cast your worries aside. Everything will be fine. How can it not be when Our Lady is watching over you?"

Ealdgyth leaned forward and tilted her head to face Margaret. She studied her carefully as if searching a book for an answer. "Oh, dearest Margaret! I cannot pretend to understand why you are doing this for me, why you have chosen to help me and my child. I myself would never have done for someone else what you are doing for me. Most people would not. As they said about Christ, you are 'in this world but not of it.'"

Margaret blushed but deflected the praise. "Come now. You know that is not true. If our roles had been reversed, I know you would have come to my aid."

"Ah, you give me too much credit, my dear Margaret. With bitterness as my constant companion, I cannot see beyond my own pain to alleviate anyone else's. You alone are the remarkable one. The rest of us are cowards in comparison." Ealdgyth placed her hands on Margaret's shoulders and fixed her dark eyes upon Margaret's face. "But someday in the future I do hope to be of service to you. I *will* be of service to you. Whatever form that may take. I will never forget the debt I owe to you. Call on me for anything, at any time, and I will answer that call." She drew Margaret to her in a tight embrace, marking the intensity of her promise.

They remained there locked together for a minute or two longer, sealing their pledge. Margaret pulled away first. "You have no belongings to speak of, so you need only take the child and walk out the door. Tobias has a cloak for you and a blanket for Nest. Just remember, if we are supposedly going to chapel, then our minds should be devoid of all worry or concern. Try to appear relaxed."

Margaret maintained contact with Ealdgyth by keeping her arm around the widow's shoulder. She helped the girl to stand. "Grab the sling for the little one, and let us walk out of here as if this were the most natural thing in the world to do. We are simply visiting church to place our intentions before God." When Ealdgyth's eyes flashed in defiance, Margaret corrected herself. "...before the Blessed Mother, I mean."

After retrieving the cloth, Ealdgyth kissed the top of Margaret's head and then turned toward Nest. Tenderly, she slipped her hand beneath the child's body and placed the little one on top of the outstretched cloth. Lifting the babe to rest upon her chest, she watched Margaret step around them both to fasten the knot on her shoulder to form the sling. Once it was secure, they smiled at one another for encouragement, nodding in agreement that it was time. They started to walk toward the door, but Margaret stopped mid-stride and turned back to take care of one last detail. Quickly rearranging the blankets on the bed to leave them in disarray, she then returned to Ealdgyth's outstretched hand and wrapped it firmly in her own. The two women crossed the threshold together, each praying intensely though no church was yet in sight.

*   *   *   *   *

Miracles and marvels. That is all that Margaret could think of as she ran swiftly away from the stables. She pushed aside her guilt, relegating it to the most remote corner of her mind; she did not want to think about that now. She knew there would be time for her to make reparation for lying about attending Compline. She knew there would be time for her to fast and pray fervently for forgiveness. But in this moment, right now, all she wanted to do was revel in the bliss of having accomplished their goal.

Ealdgyth and little Nest were on their way home, a long journey though it may be. God bless Brother Tobias. As reliable as the North Star, he shone through the darkness—steadfast and constant. He was there, awaiting them on the hill past the stables, mounted on the finest steed the abbey owned. No doubt Father Boniface looked upon Tobias with great affection and respect.

Yes, miracles and marvels. Amazing that little Nest never stirred, despite the shuffling and running and fear in the air. *This is what happens when divine intervention is at work,* Margaret thought. Just like fish who swim with the current, all they had to do that night was surrender to the flow of events Margaret had been shown in her vision.

Would Ealdgyth make it safely to Mercia? Of that, Margaret had no doubt. Ealdgyth would be in the hands of the Blessed Mother, traveling from abbey to abbey, offering prayers and petitions along the way. Margaret had total faith that the young widow and daughter would arrive home safely.

Would Ealdgyth's brother Edwin protect her from Harold? Would he honor her wishes? Of that, Margaret was not so sure, for this involved decisions made by men, men who were motivated by earthly not heavenly treasure.

Like the sin that lurked in the recesses of her mind, Margaret set aside her worry over Edwin's decisions and instead focused on the miracles and marvels that made such an escape happen. At sunrise, she would be heading back to the convent at Wilton long before Ealdgyth's absence was discovered. For tonight, that would be enough.

*   *   *   *   *

The serving maid wiped her runny nose with her forearm before placing the bowl of oatmeal and pitcher of milk on the stone floor outside the door. When she saw the sleeping sentinel and the empty wine bottle, she shook her head in disappointment and scowled at the large body stretched upon the ground in front of her.

"Tsk, tsk. You lads that cannot hold your cups. Shameful."

She wiped her nose again, this time with the back of her hand, as her words went unheeded. The guard snored loudly without interruption. She continued to click her tongue at the sight of him, wondering what to do next. She would have to roll him away from the door. With both hands planted on his back, she pushed hard against his body to create space. Breathing heavily through her mouth, she struggled with his weight.

After freeing up enough of a gap between him and the entranceway, she sidestepped carefully into the open area to reach for the latch and enter the room. She figured she would first open wide the door and then come back to retrieve the provisions she had brought for the woman and her child.

But when she looked into the room, she found no one there. Her hand still suspended in mid-air, she froze. Facing forward and not changing position, she turned her head very slowly to the side. Although the bed did show signs of having been slept in, mother and child were most certainly gone. Her hand went to her throat as if to hold back what she saw, but the truth of it burst through.

"Guard!" she screamed. "Guard! Wake up! Where are they? Get up, now! Where have they gone?" She was even more aggressive with him this time, using her foot to kick against his broad back.

"Get up, you dumb ox! Get up!" She became frantic when he still lay immovable. "Are you dead or something?" Grabbing the pitcher, she doused his face with the milk. "Wake up, you clod, or we will both be done for!"

He sputtered on his next breath as the liquid went up into his nose. "Wha—? Wha—? Huh?"

Using one arm to raise part of his chest off the floor, he turned his head to confront her. "What? What is going on?" He shook his hair to the side in order to see through the white droplets.

"Gone, I say! The two of them are gone!" She squeezed his elbow to make him stand up. "Look, you idiot. Nothing. Not a trace of them."

The maid gestured toward the bed. "They must have awakened and slipped out right past you whilst you were dead in your drink." Her eyes grew wide with fear. "Now what is going to happen to us?"

She thought better. "What is going to happen to *you*, that is, since I have naught to do with any of this. My job is to bring food and drink and then take it away. 'Twas your job to oversee them, not mine. It is your hide that'll be skinned for not keeping proper watch." She extended her arms toward the bed and almost started to neaten the blanket but stopped when she remembered to stay uninvolved.

The once formidable soldier quaked like a fearful child. He said nothing. He knew she was right. He could not even look at her. Wiping away the milk that had dampened his eyes and face, he saw clearly what his negligence had caused. With dread, he imagined what punishment awaited him.

The maid servant wanted to distance herself from him as soon as possible. She snatched up the bowl and empty pitcher and scurried away so quickly that her feet kept pace with the mucus running from her nose.

*   *   *   *   *

Harold and the guard marched up the narrow stairway together. The Earl followed him closely, condemning the man for his ignorance, poor judgment, and overall incompetence. Harold's words were meant as a prelude to the physical damage he would inflict upon the man later. Trailing behind the two of them at a much slower pace was Father Thurstan who injected his own criticism whenever Harold paused.

As they entered the chamber, the remorseful soldier tried to explain. "Please, my lord. Come. look here. This is exactly how I found it earlier this morning when the servant came with breakfast. The bed has been slept in, so they could not have gone very far . . ." His voice lilted with hope.

"The question is not how far on the road they have gone. The question is how they got past you in the first place, you worthless sot!"

Harold stepped closer to the man, thrusting his chest against him so that the guard had to back up further and further away. Spit congealed on the edges of Harold's lips, and his eyes were clouded with disgust. "You say morning, but when did you last see them?"

The guard rubbed the coiled whiskers on his jaw. "I spoke with her in the evening, before she went with her pious friend to pray at chapel."

"And at what hour did she return?"

Sweat began to form on the man's brow. "I am afraid, my lord, I do not know exactly when they came back..."

In a flash of movement, Harold fastened his hand on the guard's throat, his thick, wide fingers encircling his neck. "It was your job to keep watch." His grip tightened. "Was that so hard to do?"

The man's head dropped back as he struggled to maintain his breath. His eyelids began to close as he focused only on Harold's moving lips.

"A weak woman and a helpless infant. That was all you had to contain." He squeezed even tighter. "You did not have to restrain an outlaw. You were not guarding over an enemy soldier. Just a frail girl and a helpless child, and you could not even do that! You failed even at that!"

The soldier's eyes bulged from lack of air. In panic, he raised his arms to tear away Harold's hands. But Harold let go of his own volition and shoved the man across the room until he crashed against the opposite wall of stone.

Not yet satisfied, Harold marched toward the crumpled body and knelt down to pin him against the wall. He brandished the cold steel of his dagger horizontally in front of the man's eyes.

"Since these are useless anyway," he pointed the tip at each eye socket, "perhaps it would be best to display your ineptitude to the whole world!" Harold pressed the edge of the dagger into the delicate flesh of the man's eyelid and pricked the skin deep enough to draw blood.

"No! Please, my lord, have mercy on me. Let me make amends!" Harold's blade penetrated deeper. "Please, please. Let me give chase. I can track them. I will find them for you and bring them back. Please, my lord. Do not do this!"

The guard felt a trickle of blood wet his lashes and, from his other eye, saw another hand extend from a large black sleeve to rest upon Harold's own. The arm tugged against the Earl's will.

"Come, my son. There may be a time for that in the future, but for now, let him go." With those words, the priest broke Harold's intent.

The Earl stopped glaring at the soldier and slowly arose from his kneeling position. He looked only at the priest.

Father Thurstan spoke again. "Come. Let him be for now. Send him out after them. Let him track them to discover their whereabouts."

As Harold considered the idea, the priest jumped into that gap of hesitation to present his case. "My lord, be reasonable. Think of how it would look if people found out your prisoner had escaped? You know what they would say. What kind of leader allows for such a thing to happen?"

Now that Father Thurstan had Harold's attention, he winked once conspiratorially at the Earl before motioning with his finger toward the guard, telling him to stand up. The man scrambled to his feet, grateful for having retained his sight and his life. Father Thurstan addressed the guard directly.

"You see, what happened here is just one big misunderstanding. Earl Harold *willingly* permitted Lady Ealdgyth and her child to depart from the castle at dawn, and they happily did so while you were sprawled out drunk at their doorway. The problem is, no one informed you about this change of plan. She has a year of mourning ahead of her before she can consider marriage, and the Earl knew that she would prefer spending that time in Mercia, of course, amongst friends and family. But, to make certain, you will confirm this to be true, yes? You will make sure that she is, in fact, on her way to Mercia?"

Relieved, the guard nodded enthusiastically, his arms held firmly at his sides.

Father Thurstan turned next to Harold. "I will explain the mix up to the serving wench and let her know that Ealdgyth's release was decreed by you. That will put an end to these nasty rumors that she somehow escaped and ran away.'"

Harold had not yet put away his knife. He spoke to the priest without taking his eyes off the guard. "Agreed. 'Tis best to present it this way."

Raising the dagger once more to point at the guard's eyes, he threatened him again. "Leave here immediately. Find them and report their location back to me. If you fail me in this, you will lose more than just your ability to 'watch.'"

The soldier nodded in relief and scampered away.

Harold and Father Thurstan stood together in silence. They stared into the vacant room, each wondering how two helpless females could have seemingly vanished into the morning mist without anyone's knowledge. Harold examined the traces of blood on the blade of his dagger.

Wiping the steel on the bottom of his tunic, Harold pondered over something the guard had said. "Pious friend?" Then wiping the back of it, he considered the identity behind that description.

"I must pay a visit to this 'pious friend' to discover just what kind of pilgrimage she convinced Ealdgyth to take."

*   *   *   *   *

Margaret sat outside the stables, biting the nail on her smallest finger until it bled. She tasted the bitter flavor in her mouth and withdrew the finger from her lips to examine it more carefully. Good. Now its rawness matched all her other fingernails. And that gave her satisfaction. Inflicting pain upon herself made her feel better, which was also why she had laced up the hairshirt that morning to wear beneath her dress.

The coarse strands of goat hair rubbed and scratched against her bare skin. She endured it as an act of penitence. She had lied about her whereabouts, she had lied about her intentions, she had lied about her actions. In order to avoid further duplicity, she would escape to Wilton. She had hoped to already be on her way and should have been at the first sign of dawn, but her departure was delayed. One of the mares was having trouble foaling and the stable master—the man she was to travel with—was the only one who could help.

Earlier when Margaret had arrived with her travel bag in hand, she found him on his knees in the hay-covered stall with the mare writhing back and forth on her side.

"I am sorry, my lady, but I must see to this first. Something's gone wrong. Only one front leg is showing." He spoke to her over his shoulder, his concentration fixed on the animal.

He leaned his weight onto one arm and reached with the other into the birth canal. "Yes, there it is. One foot's turned back. Matthew?" He called out loudly to the young stablehand, then rose to his feet.

When the gangly boy rushed over, John pointed at the struggling mare. "Come, let us get her up on her feet. I am going to push the leg back in a bit and pull on the missing one. You need to hold fast to her."

Then, he remembered his visitor. "I am not sure how long this will take. Perhaps you would rather return to your chamber, and I will send for you once we are done here?"

Knowing what would be awaiting her inside the castle, she told the head groom she would be fine waiting at the stables, and so she had passed the time by gnawing away at her fingers and praying for both the creature's deliverance and her own.

As morning deepened, shafts of sunlight peeked through the trees and shone through the large open door of the barn. Little specks of dust became visible in the air and began to dance before her as she paced from one edge of the doorway to the other. Her breath was fast and shallow when she imagined what would be taking place once Ealdgyth had been discovered missing. Harold would piece it together and would come for her. *Please let this foal make its arrival so that I can be on my way,* she thought to herself.

From within the folds of her skirt, she pulled out the black crucifix with Christ's ivory body upon it and held it close to her breast as she tried to quiet her heart. When she heard shouts of elation coming from the rear stall, she turned her back to the entrance way and dropped her hands to her sides in relief. It was done then. They could now begin the journey to Wilton.

She did not hear him approach.

Her wrist was seized and her body flung around before her mind registered what was happening. Hoisting her sideways upon his hip, Harold used his free hand to cover her mouth and nose as he dragged her to an isolated spot away from other eyes. Down the embankment he carried her, his rage crushing her ribs as if he were squeezing all the breath out of her. He kept his other hand fastened upon her mouth just in case she dared to call out for help.

When he felt he had reached a safe distance, he released his grip on her body and dropped her feet to the ground. The hand he had used to cover her mouth now grabbed hold of her braid. He pulled on it as if it were a rope and she the mule tethered to it. To keep up with his long strides, she was forced to take mincing steps over the rocks and pebbles that were still mossy and wet from the ebbing tide. The pain of having her hair wrenched from her skull made it nearly impossible for her to think of anything else, but she kept her eyes fixed on the ground, knowing that one misstep could mean disaster.

Eventually, he let go of her hair and turned to face her. Grabbing her shoulders, he pushed her in front of him and then shoved her toward his right where a formation of large boulders had created a small enclosure hidden from view. He thrust her through the opening.

She crashed onto the rocky floor of the cave, her cheek scraped against the jagged edge of a stone that protruded from the ground. When she lifted her head, a small globe of blood had formed on the rock's surface. The palm of her open hand was scuffed and bruised, the knuckles on the other scratched and bleeding because of her refusal to let go of the cross.

The enclosure was too small for Harold to stand fully, so he bent at his waist and hung his head lower to loom over her. "Thought you would be gone by now, did you not? Ruin all my plans, and then scurry off to the safety of the convent before anyone found out, right?"

Margaret saw a reddish hue wash over his face and felt weakened as the intensity of his eyes bore into her. Very slowly, without ceasing to look away from him, she inched away until her back hit up against the wall of rock.

"Where is she? Where is the Welsh bitch and her whelp?"

No words came from her mouth. She would reveal nothing. She grasped the relic tighter when he advanced toward her, smothering her with his hot breath.

"Not going to talk, eh? Not going to tell me how you did it, are you? I would have thought you would welcome a union between Ealdgyth and me because it would have kept you safer. But I guess you did not see it that way, did you? Well, your heroics may have saved her for the time being, but it has damned you forever, hasn't it?" He was close enough now to reach out and grab her hair again.

"And I am not just talking about eternal damnation but earthly damnation as well. I know you—saint that you are—you would only concern yourself with the condition of your soul, but you should have considered the preservation of your body even more." He pulled down hard on her braid, exposing her neck. Nuzzling in against it, he ran his lips up and down her throat, moaning with a combination of hatred and desire. She struggled to shove him away but had not the strength to dislodge his hold on her. She was sickened by the sensation of his bristly beard rubbing up against her neck, but even more so by her own helplessness.

"Get off me!" she yelled. "Get away!" But she was pinned between him and the rock.

He latched one leg around her body and thrust his hips against hers, mimicking the act of deflowering her. "I will have you one day. You know it to be true." He panted with yearning and excitement because of the power he wielded over her. "Whether it is properly sanctioned or not, I will take you—over and over again." He leaned in closer to her ear and let his lips contact the soft flesh there. His warm breath made her body shudder. "And one day you will cry out in ecstasy for me, and when you do, I shall then abandon you for being the scheming wench I have always known you to be."

Leaning hard against her, he freed his arm to pull down her blouse. He raised his head in surprise after seeing the hairshirt beneath. "Aah, see? You know yourself that you are a sinner. Here is proof of it. Well, let me leave my imprint on you as well—a reminder that you will never be safe from me—never. Not even the convent can protect you. We Godwinsons have been known to abduct a prioress or two in our day, I daresay."

He relished her fear. "With Ealdgyth gone, I may have lost out on a Welsh queen, but a Saxon whore would do me well for a bit of sport now and then." He moved his head down her body until it rested on the coarse texture of the sackcloth. Using both hands, he ripped a seam down the front and felt his blood surge when he saw the outlined curves of her breasts—light pink with youth and shaped like teardrops. He fastened his lips upon one mound and sucked hard, tantalized even more by her legs thrashing beneath him. After some time, he looked up and surveyed his work with pride before burying his face into her other breast to leave his mark on her there as well.

Margaret's tears fell unchecked, her cries were unheard. The blows she delivered on his back made no impact.

Satisfied with his message, he returned to his feet. With the top of his head touching up against the ceiling of the cave, he remained hunched over, surveying the girl who struggled to cover her nakedness from his hungry eyes.

"I was not going to marry her right away anyway, you know. She had a year of mourning ahead of her before I could do anything. For you though? You are not as lucky. Time is not on your side. Our union does not require legitimacy. Unless of course your maidenhead comes with a crown." Harold pressed down his hand against his tunic to subdue his masculinity.

"Keep watch. No one is safe. Even the former abbess of your convent would agree. For nothing can stand in the way of a man's desire. Know it well, innocent novice. Think of me when you undress each night, and be assured that one of those nights I shall come to mark you more permanently."

When Harold turned to make his way out of the cave, his body blocked the light that came from the world outside, and she was glad for it. Glad for his departure and glad for the darkness. She wished she could hide in the shadows forever and bury her shame inside it. Hugging her arms tightly against her body, she closed her eyes and rocked back and forth, letting the tears run freely down her face. Her sobs choked her breath as she cried over the way he had touched her in places that should have belonged only to herself. He was now more of an enemy to her than ever before, and this encounter proved she could never defeat him alone. She had not the strength to overcome him. She remained like that until no more tears came forth.

When her breath evened out, she opened her eyes and saw a thin ray of light streaming in from the opening of the cave. She had to pull herself together. By now, the groom was probably wondering what had happened to her. He was probably getting impatient over having to wait for her. Freeing her arms from encircling her knees, she tried to salvage the hairshirt by tucking in each side and then lacing up her bodice tight enough so that it would keep the ripped piece in place. She would mend it when she returned to the abbey. But how would she mend herself? After shakily braiding her hair again, her scalp still sensitive and sore, she stood up and readied herself to leave. Her eye was drawn to a flash of white that shimmered in the gloom. Near the rocky wall a small object glowed, illuminated by the single beam of light that had penetrated the cave. The black rood bearing the ivory body of Christ. It had slipped from her hand during the assault. Its gleam, though faint, was enough to guide her way.

IN HALLOWED HALLS

WILTON ABBEY - FALL 1064

Even before the tinkling of the bell, Margaret was awake and alert. Her sister Cristina, who lay beside her, had stolen most of their shared blanket and was still wrapped up in slumber. Past midnight yet before Matins, everyone in the dormitory was existing in a separate world of their own making, a private reflection of their individual thoughts, hopes, and fears.

Harold's threat never completely vanished from her mind, but she did feel some degree of relief once she had learned he left the region. When the news came—that Harold had set out for the continent—a bit of her fear sailed away with him and peace soon settled in her heart. Until there came another disturbance.

Whoosh, thwap. Whoosh, thwap. Again and again the noise sliced through the evening air. Going back to sleep was no longer a possibility. Not with that sound repeating in her ears. It had to be Sister Clara.

Margaret got up from the mat, leaving Cristina in full possession of bed and blanket. As she tiptoed softly down the row of sleepers, the noise grew louder while she walked toward the door at the back of the dormitory. After each thwap came a muffled groan of pain. Such was the penance Clara assigned to herself.

In a dark corner beside the night stairs that led up to the chapel, Clara stood, hunched over at the waist with her shift hoisted to the upper portion of her back. Her right hand clenched the thick handle of a rope made of seven cords, each with a huge knot at its end. Clara picked up momentum by swinging the whip from the front of her body to thrash her exposed lower back, buttocks, and legs. Margaret could not see the welts upon Clara's skin, but she knew, come first light, they would be there.

"Clara, please! Stop doing this! There are other less painful ways to make reparation." Margaret whispered to her with urgency, trying to intercept the next blow by placing her hand on Clara's forearm.

But Clara would not be deterred. "Do not touch me, Margaret. My body is tainted with sin. Leave me to my penance unless . . . you would oblige me by taking over. Strike me with your own hand. Make it even more severe."

"No! Your sins cannot merit such torture. Our Lord demands humility, obedience, and purity of heart, but when we fall short in those precepts, His sentence involves correction not condemnation. Surely there are less intense ways to feel His justice. Your prior wounds have barely healed!"

"Such is the depth of my depravity." Clara let down her gown and stood upright. She grabbed Margaret's hand in desperation and drew her closer. "I dreamt of him again." She let go of Margaret and covered her face with both hands, the whip still grasped tightly. The cords dangled freely across the front of her body, pulsing up and down with her sobs.

"I was in his arms again. My body melted into his. He touched me in places I am ashamed to speak of now, but I felt no shame in my dream—only overwhelming joy, bubbling over and rippling through my body. The intensity of that pleasure must be countered by an equal measure of pain."

Margaret was ignorant of such sweet surrender but a dim memory surfaced that offered a touch of that feeling. She remembered the internal heat she had felt when a powerful warrior dropped the pebbles from his hand to brush his callused fingers upon her face. She buried that forbidden sensation under layers of responsibility, duty, and routine. In a very small way, she understood Clara's meaning.

Margaret wrapped her arms around the girl, careful not to make contact with her fresh wounds. "Being separated from the one you love is penance enough, do you not think? Time will heal your sorrow. Soon these visions will disappear forever. Doing this to yourself will only rip your heart anew and keep the pain of separation alive."

Clara dropped her head onto Margaret's shoulder, her arms remained fixed in place. "But will I ever stop loving him? Stop wanting him? I did not care that he was a mere carpenter. I would cast aside my name and my title for the richness of his love."

"Oh, Clara. You keep dreaming of him because you believe you can make the world fit your vision. But your fight is a futile one. Your father sent you to Wilton, and he is the only one who can bring about your release. Understand that you are powerless to exchange the real world for your imaginary one. The longer we persist in believing we can alter circumstances to match our desires, the more miserable we become when we learn the truth. When you finally accept that everything resides in God's hands, the sooner you will relinquish your desire to control outcomes and the sooner you will find peace."

Clara raised her head. With her eyes closed, she nodded at Margaret in understanding.

"Here, come. Let me take possession of this." Margaret unfolded Clara's fingers to gently remove the whip from her hand. "When next you wish to resort to this, reach out instead to me. Together we shall pray for humility to accept God's will. If you need to feel the physical pain of penitence, do as I. Wear sackcloth, fast, keep a pebble in your shoe. But know that the Lord takes no pleasure in the mutilation of the body."

To lighten the moment, she added, "Nor does He advocate for the absence of washing—as Sister Norbert firmly believes. The only ones who suffer the pain of that penance are those who are forced to sit next to her at prayer!"

After getting Clara to smile, Margaret guided her toward the kitchen where a water basin was stored. "It will soon be time for Matins. Let me first bathe your wounds, and then we can ready ourselves for devotion."

Clara stopped one last time to face Margaret. "But how do I rid myself of such yearning? How do I stop thinking of him?"

Margaret thought carefully about Clara's question. She considered her own inability to completely erase Malcolm's touch from memory. "I do not think it ever fully goes away. But you can soften the recollection by framing it with fondness instead of desire."

Arm in arm, the two women walked down the hall together hoping to find in prayer the salve for their broken dreams.

*   *   *   *   *

The next few hours between the service of Prime and Terce were devoted to work, but before Margaret could report to her duty in the scriptorium, she had to wait her turn to leave the chapel. Sitting in the final pew at the back of the church, she had full view of her religious companions.

All of the women, in various stages of their own faith journey, patiently followed the pattern for dismissal. From a distance, they all looked the same: long black gowns over which hung a white scapula. From each neck dangled a wooden cross that was raised to the lips and kissed at the exact moment the knee lifted from the ground after genuflection. Protocol and clothing aside, there was a noticeable difference with regard to hair coverings and personality. Consecrated sisters wore the full wimple, tight around the face and completely covering the neck, while oblates and novices like Margaret, her sister, and Clara—donned a short white veil that was much less severe.

When it came to dispositions though, the twenty or so women mirrored a cross-section of the personalities one would find in the secular world. From lively to irascible, loving to cold-hearted, easy going to strict—all types could be found inside the abbey. There were leaders and followers, visionaries and pragmatists, angels and hypocrites. And their ages spanned a vast range as well, going from the wide-eyed innocence of seven-year-old Eve to the cynical wisdom of seventy-year-old Sister Eleanor. Regardless of the differences within the population, Margaret and Cristina were accepted by them all, Cristina garnering much praise for her skill at needlework and Margaret for her precision at illuminating and copying texts.

Margaret and Cristina waited for the line to file out, knowing that they would go in separate directions for their work detail. Later all would reconvene in three hours time for Terce and the reading of the psalms. Most often silence prevailed over their interactions, so they learned to communicate through facial expression and body movement. Clara, who was one row in front, looked back at Margaret to send a quick nod of appreciation her way.

As daughter of a nobleman, Clara had originally been granted a position working in the scriptorium with Margaret, but she soon requested a new assignment when she could not stop herself from thinking of her former lover. Now she tended to the fields, orchards, and gardens which kept her too busy for her mind to wander. It pleased her to think of her father's dismay when he would visit the abbey and see the damage done to her once pampered hands. Freckled and wrinkled by the sun, dry and cracked from working in the dirt, her hands were now a great source of joy because they leveled her status to that of a laborer, one more aptly suited to wed a carpenter. She may have been too busy to think of him on an hourly basis, but each night before going to sleep, she would imagine a future with him in it.

Finally, it was their turn to leave. Cristina led the way, next came Eve. Margaret placed her hands on the child's narrow shoulders to point her in the right direction, but the little one jumped, startled by the touch. She even sped up to avoid further contact. Margaret pitied the child. Eve needed the warmth of companionship, but in the fortnight that she had been in the convent, the little girl reached out to no one. Her solace came from being alone.

At the front of the chapel, the priest reappeared. He came out from the sacristy after removing his vestments and was now wearing his black habit and cowl when Cristina, Eve, and Margaret were on their way out. His spectacles hung from the neck fold of his habit, and he moved with a swiftness of one who was late for an event and needed to make up time. His tonsure formed a perfect circle upon his head, smooth and shiny from its baldness. Beneath that blank spot fell strands of reddish-brown hair that matched the color of his beard and mustache.

"Sisters, I bid you good morning." His eyes flashed with delight. "We have a great day in store for us, do we not?"

Eve, who rarely engaged with anyone, always seemed to perk up when she was with Father Goscelin. The questions she posed to him far exceeded those expected from a child, and Goscelin looked upon her as a person with a true calling.

"What shall we be examining today, good Father?" Eve's voice was barely above a whisper, making her seem more elf than a human. Her gown, much too large for her body, dragged upon the ground leaving its edges frayed and tattered. Once or twice she even stumbled when her front foot stepped on the hem, causing her to nearly topple over.

Cristina waved and went off to join the sisters in the sewing room while Eve and Father Goscelin walked together with Margaret following. No one spoke as they walked down the narrow passageway to their destination. The scriptorium contained seven writing stations, one for Goscelin and six for his assistants. Each station consisted of a wooden chair and desk whose surface was large enough to accommodate two opened texts, lying side-by-side. Behind the work area was an arched opening that led directly to the library where gospels, psalters, and books about saints' lives were shelved.

That day they had the room to themselves as two sisters were in the infirmary and the other two had gone there to care for them. Because of that privacy, Father Goscelin felt free to share his discovery with Margaret and Eve. He gestured to them to join him at his desk which stood centered at the front of the room. On it lay the notes he had recorded. "Look here. I have unearthed some very exciting information that I can now add to my project, *Vita Edithe*."

"Let me see." Margaret moved in closer to study the parchment.

Goscelin lifted the spectacles that were hanging on his robe and fixed them upon his nose. "Right here. Evidence of another miracle!" He pointed to a particular section of the paper.

Margaret read aloud. " . . . when a candle accidently fell into her chest of clothes, the container showed signs of damage but all her clothes were left intact. Nothing was affected."

Eve raised up to her toes to silently read along, while Margaret considered the rarity of such an occurrence. "Did the convent preserve the clothing as proof?"

"No, I am afraid not. Some clothes from her childhood are still here, but no one pays them any mind. The pieces of interest, the ones involved in the miracle, have not been found." After voicing his regret, Goscelin then rubbed his palms together with enthusiasm. "We may not have the clothes, but—" His robes swung freely as he rushed into the library and then returned, dragging an object across the floor.

Margaret recognized the object right away. "You found the chest?" She walked around it in a full circle, reaching out to touch the areas that were scorched.

"Yes, I did!"

"Where was it? How did you know where to look?" Margaret was now joined by Eve in examining the chest.

Goscelin smiled broadly, and when he did, his face scrunched up so tightly that his eyes were no longer visible. "Sister Eleanor. She has been an incredible resource for me. Not only is she responsible for recounting most of the stories in here," he motioned to the book on his podium, "but she also made sure to preserve certain pieces of evidence—like this chest. She told me she had stored it away in the cellar, so I went down, found it there, and then carried it here."

He went down upon his knees to poke his head into the interior of the box. "I am aware that some people found fault with Edith and called her vain for her fine clothing and such, but her impressive style and courtly manners did secure the patronage of many a wealthy lord and lady. Wilton would not be as prosperous as it is today were it not for our well-dressed, dignified saint."

Goscelin closed the lid of the chest and tapped it gently. "But there is still a great deal to learn about her, so Margaret, when you go to your desk, you will find Edith's manual of prayers. I would like you to make a second copy of that, all right? And Eve, continue painting the marginal figures you started yesterday for *Vita St. Denis*. The angels accompanying him are just exquisite."

Eve fluttered her eyes, embarrassed by the compliment. Dropping her chin to her chest, she murmured a barely audible, "Thank you." As she walked over to her station, she said, "I must add a bit more color to their wings. But after that—" She looked over at him with eyes rounded with worry, begging a silent favor.

Guessing the reason for her hesitation, he offered comfort. "Yes, and after that, I will take over and insert his decapitated head. You need not worry about completing that aspect of the picture, gentle lamb."

Eve smiled with relief. "If you do not mind doing that for me, then I will do something for you as well. When you get to that part in your book about Saint Edith's pet menagerie, I can help with the animal images." Too short to reach the desk from a seated position, Eve raised up to her knees in order to be high enough to complete her work. Before settling in, she added, "I would much prefer drawing a monkey or even a ferret than sketching a severed head."

*   *   *   *   *

With each scribe immersed in their work, the hours passed quickly. The crinkling of the parchment was the one sound that united them. Otherwise, they were journeying along on separate roads, focused on different destinations. Eve was up in the heavens with her cherubs, Goscelin was reliving miracles, and Margaret was copying gospel passages and prayers that were among Edith's favorites.

When Margaret turned the page to begin the next section, her hand and heart froze. The intervening years disappeared faster than candlelight in a gust of wind. She was back again in Baranya. The words she was about to copy from John's gospel hearkened back to the day when her carefree existence was snuffed out: "*Let not your heart be troubled . . .*"

Oh, Gerhard! She had not allowed herself to think of him since he passed away. *Oh, how my heart was troubled that day and has remained so ever since!*

At home by the fireside, she had copied that verse while her brother slept innocently nearby. It was a text meant to soothe Gerhard's agitation, but he was not the only one suffering back then. Those same pangs of worry and doubt had rankled her as well. She returned to her desk in the scriptorium and looked around. Neither Goscelin nor Eve noticed she had stopped working. Resting her cheek upon her hand, she stared at the stained glass window on the distant wall and did not fight against the swell of memory.

They had lost so much—peace of mind, security, trusted friends and neighbors—all things safe and familiar had been replaced with uncertainty and suspicion. *Oh, Gerhard, you knew, did you not? You knew that we were moving headlong into danger. But we did not heed the signs, we did not sense the trouble ahead. You could not forgive yourself for Father's death even though another man's evil was to blame. You carried that burden of guilt until the heaviness of it crushed your will to live.*

But your words did have an impact on me, and your counsel remains alive in my soul. Once again, I am blessed to be under the care of a good and holy man. And I am wise enough now to seek fulfillment inside these hallowed halls of prayer. For it is indeed true as Jesus once said, "In my Father's house there are many mansions," and I believe this place is the one He has prepared for me.

As Margaret was lost thoughts of the past and future, a knock upon the door intruded into the present. All three writers looked up to discover the source of the disturbance. Sister Clara pushed open the heavy wooden door, and after taking one step inside, she looked behind her and said, "Yes, they are still here. Come in."

Clara ushered in her two guests, one a priest and the other a novitiate. The priest was a young fellow, a bit untidy and soiled from travel, but energized from within. His rosy cheeks and friendly grin warmed the room, but the girl remained distant and cold. She seemed to be an older version of Eve, timid and clinging to the shadows. Restrained by her own apprehension, she held back from fully entering the room. Both hands she had clasped tightly together in front of her body, her fingers digging into one another from nervousness.

Margaret put down her pen, and Eve sat back on her haunches, watching the strangers as Goscelin went to the door to receive them. Springing from behind his desk, he approached the pair with warmth. "Good day to you both. I am Father Goscelin. This is Margaret, and this is Eve. What can we do for you today?" He stretched out his hand to welcome the jolly young man, but when he turned to the girl, she refused to come forward and only bowed her head toward him instead.

Clara stayed close to the door. "I know it is nearly time for prayer, but the Abbess said I should bring them here and introduce them to you before chapel begins. They are from Normandy." She scowled when announcing their origins. Despite King Edward's affinity for the place, anti-Norman sentiment was escalating—even in a convent like Wilton. "This is Father Joseph."

The young man bowed to all three members of his audience, but none were impressed by his showy display. Clara hid her dislike of him by speaking of practicalities. "The Abbess said he is here to study under your tutelage, Father Goscelin. He wishes to learn your methods of research as he will be compiling stories of saints' lives himself when he returns to Rouen."

Father Joseph picked up the thread, speaking with only the slightest of accents. "I have heard, Father, that you have discovered ways to verify miracles by documenting firsthand experiences of the residents here. I would like to do the same back home in Rouen. You must teach me how to get the silent to speak—ha, ha!" His white teeth sparkled as he laughed at his own joke.

Clara returned toward the doorway to retrieve the other traveler. "You can not hang back there all day." Clara physically moved the nun deeper into the room. Holding fast to the top of her shoulder, Clara directed the girl to stand before Goscelin. "And this is Celia. She is a distant relative of the Duchess of Normandy." The girl kept looking at the floor, her head lowered in deference. "She too has come to study with you, Father Goscelin. Duchess Matilda's letter stated that Celia will one day be in charge of the abbey at Caen." Moving closer to whisper into Goscelin's ear, Clara added, "According to the Abbess, the Duchess sent along lavish gifts for Wilton to ensure these requests be fulfilled."

Margaret studied the two visitors. On the surface, Father Joseph seemed already at home, looking over Goscelin's work and complimenting Eve on her drawings. He was even able to get the child to talk when he asked her about her intricate criss-crossing patterns in the margins. But the Norman girl? She appeared on edge, fearful and worried—as Margaret had once been when she had first come to this new land. Like Ealdgyth had been as well. Although their reasons for coming to England differed, each woman had needed someone to trust. Margaret placed her trust in God, and from that foundation, she became Ealdgyth's confidante. Perhaps she could do the same for this newcomer.

Clara was about to walk out the door, but then remembered one more thing. "Margaret, your brother also made the trip with Father Joseph and Sister Celia from Westminster to here. He said he would speak with you after the next service, as he does not wish to disturb your prayer." She did not include the two new arrivals in her final farewell. "I shall see you at Terce then."

The news of Edgar's arrival brought a swell of joy to Margaret's heart. The last time she had seen him was a full year ago after the defeat of the Welsh. She was certain Edgar would have news of both Harold's whereabouts and the happenings at court. In the meantime, she would comfort this Norman stranger.

Moving away from her desk, Margaret approached Celia purposefully, stretching out both hands to join with the girl's. "Come over and see what I have just copied out from Saint Edith's prayer manual. This gospel text was one of her favorites. It was one that helped me long ago. Perhaps it will help you too."

Celia hesitated, but Margaret tugged on her hand until they came to the place where Celia could easily view the open text. After a moment or two of silence, the Norman visitor looked over the work and then lifted her eyes toward Margaret. *Crystal blue, like the sea,* thought Margaret. *So pure you could gaze right to the bottom and see every shell, fish, and sea plant below.* Margaret dared to hope that she had found in Celia a kindred spirit, one who believed in the power of faith and had the innocence to embrace it without cynicism.

The shy stranger finally spoke. "You are Margaret, yes?" When Margaret nodded, she continued in a voice that was both soft from modesty and firm with knowledge. "The words are from John's gospel, are they not? I know it well from my studies at Caen."

"That is right. And so we are all linked together then! You and I and Edith. For we were all drawn to the same text." Margaret clasped her hands together and brought them to her chest in happiness. "Clearly, this is the place that the Lord has prepared for you, Celia. And He has chosen me to help ease your way."

Celia dropped her eyes again at Margaret's last comment, knowing that the Saxon girl had it wrong. She had foolishly inverted their roles. Celia knew that it was she herself—not Margaret—whom God had chosen to do the leading.

PART FOUR

LUSTER BORNE OF SORROW

Fall 1064 – Winter 1068

CELIA & MARGARET

UNDER SCRUTINY

WILTON ABBEY – FALL 1064

"Are you happy here at Wilton, Margaret?"

Edgar carried a pail in each hand as he walked with Margaret on their way back from the gristmill to the convent. She carried a single bucket and, as one arm tired, switched it to the other.

"I am, brother. I am. I believe it is the place for me."

They had just reached the crest of the hill in a densely forested area. Although there was no formal road to speak of, a walking path wound its way in and among the trees. Off to the side was a dilapidated cottage whose rear section had sunk into the ground, crushed by the weight of a fallen ash tree. The prior owner of the cottage had taken great care to create a small clearing near the front of the structure, but no such attention had he given to the back of the house. On one stormy night, he paid the price for his negligence.

She put the container on the ground and sat down in the open area, patting the space beside her. "Let us rest." Edgar put down his two buckets and joined her.

She pulled two shiny red apples from the pouch that hung sideways across her habit and offered him one. "Sister Eleanor passed these to me on the way out. She must have known the tedium of the journey, having completed it so often herself in her younger days."

He bit into the fruit, savoring the sweet juices that filled his mouth while waiting for her to answer his question.

"You know," she stopped to chew and then resumed talking, "there was a time when I thought I might better serve the Lord by walking amongst His people rather than be isolated from them. And it was not very long ago when I thought that performing His works in the temporal world would be the most impactful thing I could do. But I soon discovered that I am no match for the evil that pervades this world. I am too weak to defeat it. I could not even make a difference within my own limited circle of people."

"You are thinking of Harold and Father Thurstan, are you not?"

"I am." She lowered the apple down to her lap and took a deep breath, preparing for a confession of sorts. "I never told you this, but…" She stopped to choose the right words. "He attacked me. Harold. After Ealdgyth disappeared. I never told you because I ran away that same morning. And I never wrote to you about it because I did not want to put you in harm's way. You are too young to take him on, and you would have done so regardless. So I tell you about it now because he is no longer in England, and that distance keeps you safe from peril."

The sun, a watery yellow too feeble to generate any real warmth, could do nothing to soften the chill in the air. For Margaret, the air grew even colder once the conversation shifted to Harold. Edgar struggled with his decision to speak the next three words, but truth overcame his hesitation.

"He is back."

Instinctively, she pulled her shawl tighter around her body, remembering the day he had thrown her to the ground and marked her body with his vengeance. "When?"

"The two Normans visitors who came to the convent today? They were on his vessel. They all arrived together."

The wind whistled in and out of the empty holes in the abandoned house as Edgar continued the story. "And Harold's return ruins everything for me as well. While you have been at Wilton, I have grown closer to the King. My relationship with him has deepened. I have earned his favor. When Brother Aelfwig asked for a series of names the monks could pray for, King Edward entered mine next to his and the Queen's, just as if we were a real family. He even refers to me now in public as the Aetheling, the title given to a ruler's son.

"Not only that, I have accompanied them on grand occasions and was granted the promise of a royal estate. Without Thurstan there to poison the King's mind, I am finally being accepted as his successor. If circumstances could only continue that way, I am certain the Witan would vote in my favor. But now with Harold and his priest back at court, everything I have come to enjoy will be snatched away from me yet again."

Margaret slid closer to Edgar and wrapped her arm around his shoulder. He turned to embrace her fully as they reverted back to their former roles when she, the older and wiser sibling, would console him and help him overcome his troubles. But he broke their bond abruptly.

"Aarrgh. I am just so frustrated. Can you understand that, sister?" He withdrew his arm and evaluated his eaten apple, throwing the sliver of the core deep into the brush.

"Yes, I do. But what does the King think about the Earl's return? Perhaps the King is displeased with him? After all, he did take that journey without Edward's permission, did he not? Maybe King Edward will relegate him to a position of less power?"

Restless, Edgar rose to his feet. "You are right that Edward still hasn't forgiven Harold and Thurstan for sailing to the continent—

although he was pleased to see that they had secured Hakon's freedom." He kicked aside some of the leaves that had piled up in front of him. "Everything was going so well these past few months. The King was definitely preparing me to fulfill the plan he had laid out for Father. He spoke to me of forming an alliance with Malcolm of Scotland in order to strengthen my support."

Edgar knew he had to tread carefully with the next bit of information, so he tried to sound as casual as possible. "He even suggested offering Lothian as your dowry."

Margaret swung her head around to confront her brother. "My dowry? What is that you say?"

"Remain calm, sister." He squatted beside her, his knees to his chest. "Have you not listened to anything I have said? With Harold's return, the King's plans for me and for you are over and done with. Stomped down and crushed under the forward march of Harold's ambition. There will be no marriage for you, just as there will be no crown for me—so do not fret. Return to your state of oblivion and contentment. But know that I cannot follow you to such a place."

Edgar assessed the fading light in the sky and then scanned the valley at the bottom of the hill. "I suppose we should be heading back now." He looked over at the three pails they had left on the ground.

"Wait, brother. You are wrong if you think my contentment is derived from your disappointment. My relief comes from being left alone, safe from court with its hidden manipulations and obsession with power. My only wish is to pursue a contemplative life devoted to God." She saved the rest of her apple for later, placing it inside her pouch. "Perhaps the future will still unfold according to your wishes. If you believe the throne is rightfully yours to occupy, then ask the Lord to help make it so."

As she started walking toward the buckets, Edgar seized her arm and pulled her back to face him. Her faith annoyed him. "You just do not get it, do you? It is not God's will but man's will that forces things to shift into position. People can not wait for some hand from heaven to speed things up or slow things down. The responsibility is our own. Man must quicken the pace of the action or impede its progress."

Margaret stared at the redness forming below her wrist but did not try to break Edgar's grip. Soon his eyes followed hers, and he realized what he had done. He relinquished his hold but still remained impassioned. With his finger, he pointed to the earth. "This is what I fight for. I am not concerned with eternal homes or divine kingdoms. It is about what is here, and what is now, and what is just. Look at the King of Scotland. If he waited for heavenly intervention, he would still be without a country to rule, wallowing in the background while his father's murderer wore the crown that was rightly his. But Malcolm did not do that. He took action, slaughtering Macbeth and Macbeth's son. His sword invoked justice, and he regained his birthright. A fatherless exile like me, he has promised his support when the time comes. I have letters from him stating so."

Edgar could see that his words had upset her. Placing his palm upon her shoulder, he spoke softly. "Each person must follow the dictates of his heart. You must walk the path you believe to be true, and so must I. Do not judge me, Margaret, as I hope not to judge you either. I will speak no further of these things since they disturb you so deeply. But there are very few people I can trust, and that is why I turned to you and confided in you. Pray for me, if you will, dear sister. That is all I ask. I do not ask you to understand me or to justify my motives. I do not ask you to marry against your will. I do not ask you to plot or plan with me so that I may remain in the King's good graces. I ask only that you pray for this sinner before you, and forgive me for believing more in this world than in the one to come."

Edgar bowed before her, but Margaret quickly pulled him upright. "Brother, do not look upon me as some kind of saint. I am not here to judge you. It is true that I cannot understand your desire to rule a land that is so foreign to both of us, but even so, I will try to focus only on what is right and proper with regard to the succession. If the King looks upon you as his son and the Witan agrees that you shall rule after him, then you shall have all that you wished for, and I shall be happy for you. But I will experience even greater joy if you promise to act only according to what is good and righteous in pursuit of that goal. For fear of angering you again, I will not say let God's will be done. Instead, I will just encourage you to perform all of your actions with a heart that is pure and a code that is honorable."

"Thank you, Margaret. Your prayers are worth more than gold." Edgar smiled at her with sincerity. He bent down to pick up the containers, but then remembered something and left them resting there a bit longer.

"Here," he reached into the lining of his cloak. "This is for you. I almost forgot. Malcolm sent a message for you as well. Obviously, he did not know of Harold's return when it was written, so it may only speak of King Edward's plan for the alliance between our two families. The plan for you to be given to Malcolm along with Lothian."

She was too afraid to take the note from him.

"What is wrong, sister? Do not be frightened. Malcolm's words do not really matter now, right? For God's will be done, is that not what you said? And if God wants you in a wedding veil rather than this one," Edgar gestured to her hair covering, "then so be it. But I shall be his kinsmen either way."

Margaret took the letter from his outstretched hand as carefully as if she were removing a splinter from a finger. Just as she was placing it into her purse, they heard voices and the sound of horses.

"I always thought it was Charles Martel that wanted to marry her?"

"No, it was Charlemagne."

"Well, one of them broke her arm trying to get her to renounce her vow to remain a virgin."

"Yes, that was Charlemagne, but he could not carry her away, and then he became gravely ill. But Amalberga forgave him and prayed to God for his healing. And thus he recovered."

"Did not she cross the river Scheldt mounted on a giant fish or something—oh, hello?" Father Joseph noticed Margaret and Edgar, his eyes alight with welcome and cheer. He dismounted to greet them warmly.

"Margaret, Edgar. So soon we meet again, my friend," Father Joseph patted Edgar's shoulder in fellowship.

Goscelin then pulled up alongside them, his chestnut horse dragging a canvas that already had a pile of chopped wood on its surface.

"We were just heading back with the flour from the gristmill," Margaret raised the bucket in her hand.

Goscelin turned to his partner. "There are a few fallen trunks here already, Father, which will take me no time to chop. Why do you not clip the flour buckets to the sides of your saddle and accompany them back to the convent. I will not be long here."

But Edgar protested. "Thank you, but that is not necessary, Father. Do not worry about us. These aren't heavy at all. We are fine. Do not let us stop you from doing what you set out to do."

Father Joseph stole a quick look at the fallen tree that balanced on top of the cottage and almost spoke out loud when he detected the slight movement of something larger than a forest creature darting past the collapsed window. He looked at the pair of siblings and considered how they had taken on this errand without bringing anyone else along for accompaniment. He guessed then at the identity of the hidden figure.

Trying to sound as if there were no connection between his discovery and his desire to stay longer, Father Joseph proposed another solution. "Father Goscelin, why do you not head back with them and let me cut up the wood?"

"And leave you to navigate your way home alone in a region unknown to you, when night is falling and the path barely visible? No, let Margaret guide you both back, and I shall join you later at supper."

Thwarted, Father Joseph cleverly hid his disappointment by turning back to Edgar. "I am afraid you have heard all my stories on the way from Westminster here, but Sister Margaret has not. And so I beg your patience if I regale her with ones that have already passed through your ears. Actually, I must amend one of them that I erroneously recounted involving Charles Martel and Saint Amalberga of Flanders." Father Joseph had already clipped the containers to dangle over the horse's side. He then moved around to the front of the animal to grab the reins and follow Margaret and Edgar down the hill.

As Goscelin watched the three of them departing, he stood for a moment smiling to himself at the lively personality of his new acolyte. Practicing silence was sure to be Father Joseph's greatest challenge, Goscelin thought, as he lifted the axe from its holder and walked around to the back of the cottage where the tree had fallen.

He examined the enormous mound that housed the roots and knew it would be best to begin chopping about five feet from that spot. Then when that part was severed, he would cut away at the section right before the roots. The trunk was thick and wide, its dark ridges already bleached by the sun to a lighter color and whitened even further because of its deadness. He raised the axe behind his head and swung down into the wood. With each contact, the slice grew deeper and larger. Despite the cold, his body heated up with sweat.

Taking a moment to wipe his brow, he stopped his hand at the mid-point of his forehead. He heard something. It came from inside the cottage. A squirrel or rabbit, he thought, and finished the sweep across his head. He then wiped his moistened hand on his robe but stopped once more. He heard the noise again. The hair on the back of his neck rose. His skin turned prickly. Was someone watching him?

He did not fear creatures of the forest—or animals of any kind—for were they not all God's own? Then why did he feel so tense? Something was amiss, but he could not quite label what it was. He left the axe wedged in the tree and began moving closer to the house, careful not to step on any twigs or make known his footfall. His actions felt unnatural. He was not a hunter and had no desire to ever be one, so he was untrained in how to make a stealthy approach. Nevertheless, he kept advancing until his foot got caught under a lengthy vine. The ropelike cord truncated his next step, and he faltered. The sound alerted whatever or whoever was inside the cottage. The creature sprang up and darted out the front entrance. Its two legs, restrained by a long dress, raced vigorously down the hill.

No longer needing to conceal himself, Goscelin also ran. When he arrived at the front of the structure, he caught a quick glimpse of the escaping intruder. Beneath the white veil that rippled in the wind was a long, black braid that bounced up and down with each stride. Although she never looked back to face him, Goscelin knew who it was.

He had always prided himself on being a good judge of character, and his discernment in this case did not disappoint. Just as sweet foods can be appealing at first but later cause great damage, so too are people. He had thought her a bit too obsequious. A bit too servile. As he turned from the path to resume his work, he vowed to keep a closer eye on that Norman girl, Celia.

*   *   *   *   *

They spoke only in French.

"I think Goscelin saw me—actually, I know he did." She was nervous.

It took all of his will power to remain calm. He breathed hard through his nose as he gently led the horse back into the stable. He cleared his throat. "You are a fool." Dropping some extra hay onto the floor of the stall, he persisted. "Why could you not have just waited until he was done? It would not have taken him that long."

He headed back outside. Celia trailed behind.

"I was afraid I would not be able to find my way back in the dark. I had not paid enough attention to the path we took when I followed them earlier to the mill."

They had passed the water trough and were now approaching the fresh spring well. Father Joseph was too agitated to sit, even though large stone benches formed a semicircle enclosing the bubbling water. Instead he continued along the walk, a circular path commemorating the spot where Saint Fremund touched the ground with his sword and a spring of water gushed forth.

When they were far enough away from the torch lights outside the barn, the darkness cloaked them in secrecy. He deliberated over what punishment to inflict. It could not be visible or stir gossip. Joseph stopped walking and turned abruptly to face Celia. Sensing the outline of her body, he bent his leg and plunged his knee into her stomach. The force of the blow lifted her off her feet and sent her backwards onto the ground. She wrapped her arms around her body and struggled for breath.

"You had better start paying attention, woman, or our mission is doomed." He offered no assistance or compassion.

Before she could restrain it, a tangy liquid rose up her throat and came out through her nose and mouth as she vomited on the dirt. A slight turn of her head at the last second prevented it from soiling her dress.

"If such incompetence affected only you, then I would not care at all, and your singular life would pay the devil his due. But we are tied together in this. Your mishaps and failures drag me down with you. And I will not suffer the consequences for someone else's blunders."

He stood over her with his arms folded and his body rigid. The whiteness of his bared teeth was the only light in the dark courtyard.

"Now Goscelin will be suspicious of you, suspicious of me. We will have to think of a reason to explain why you were in that abandoned cottage. That is if he asks. But he probably won't ask. He is too smart to show his hand. And that is even worse. Because then he will be looking for more things to make his doubts grow."

With her head still down, she continued to cough, finding it difficult to clear all of the particles from her mouth. This angered him even further.

"Oh, come on. Stop it. Get up!" He pushed his foot under her leg and lifted it upward as if to raise her himself.

Celia whipped her head up so quickly her veil flew off her hair and landed in the puddle of bile. "Do not touch me. Do not ever touch me again." She placed her hands on the ground behind her and lifted herself up to stand in his space.

"Now get this straight. I do not want to be here and never *would* be here if I were not forced into this. And what hangs in the balance is so valuable to me that I had rather die than fail in this mission." She spit a few chunks of undigested food upon the ground right next to his feet, forcing him to take a step backwards. "You say we are in this together, but I say you mean nothing to me. Nothing. I will do all my work alone. The only thing I need *you* for is to report my information back to Normandy. That is the only reason why you matter to me." She lifted the hem of her gown and reached into the lining she had sewn into her habit. From it, she pulled a small knife. "Otherwise, I would slit your throat right now."

The moonlight reflecting off the blade momentarily outshone Father Joseph's teeth. Celia kept holding it straight up in front of her face so that he could read the determination in her eyes.

"I may have made an error by being seen by Goscelin, but my presence in that house was worth something. Here is what you can report to the Duke. Before Earl Harold returned, King Edward had practically named Edgar his successor. The boy was being referred to as the aetheling, he had been presented as such at ceremonies, and had even been promised a royal estate."

Still holding the knife, she wiped the spittle from her lips with the back of her hand and continued. "Betrothal papers have been sent to the King of Scotland regarding Margaret's hand in marriage, and King Edward has offered all of Lothian as her dowry. Whether these events come to pass or not remains to be seen. Much depends on how well the English king can control Harold's ambition."

Before her eyes, Father Joseph transformed from vicious beast guarding his territory to contented hound after a full meal. "Well, well, well." He smiled with satisfaction. "Good work, *ma moitie*. Very good work, indeed."

Celia uttered a curse under her breath and left him standing there in his smugness while she retrieved her veil from the sticky liquid. She moved gingerly, her mid-section still throbbing from his assault.

"Save your compliments for someone else. Just make sure the information gets back home. And as far as paying closer attention, you are the one who needs to listen. Pay attention to this. I will come to you when I have something to share. Otherwise, stay away from me."

Father Joseph had already shifted into his alternate persona—jolly, receptive, lighthearted. "Aaah, Celia. We both wish for the same things. We are more alike than you realize." His eyes softened. "Tsk, tsk, tsk. I am sorry I struck you. I thought I had been partnered with a dumb ox. But now I know that I have been paired with a fellow wolf."

She snickered at his attempt to restore their friendship. "I am not looking for a mate. You will serve your function of course, but I hunt alone."

She left him standing there on the path as she made her way back to the fresh spring. Placing her veil into the churning water, she rinsed out the remnants of her interaction with him. Pulling it out from the froth, she admired it for its purity, her singleness of purpose unshaken.

*   *   *   *   *

After the incident at the cottage, Celia kept her head down and her thoughts private. Father Goscelin, as Joseph predicted, never confronted her about her presence at the cottage. The topic hung in the air over Celia like a heavy cloud waiting for the right moment to belch its rain.

But no trouble ever came, and the days and weeks fell into a steady routine. Interspersed with their prayer services, she spent her working hours in the scriptorium where stillness and silence prevailed. Eve continued designing her colorful margins, Goselin kept researching additional miracles, and Margaret focused on copying Saint Edith's favorite prayers. For the last few days, Celia was doing

351

no transcribing; instead, she was rereading Goscelin's history of Saint Eadwold, a former prince turned hermit whose staff converted a piece of dead wood into a living tree. Unlike the saint, she had no magic wand that could transform the tedium to excitement, so she found herself driven mad by the monotony of it all. She strove hard not to get totally sucked into the boredom by reminding herself that such repetition was necessary to endear herself to Margaret. Celia's ability to convince Margaret to remain in the abbey meant the difference between life and death for both herself and her sister. In that way, Celia, like Eadwold, did wield the power to resurrect.

After Edgar's departure, there was no further news for Celia to report and therefore no need for her to deal with Father Joseph. In front of everyone else, he remained cheerful and carefree, but Celia knew how easily that mask could be cast aside, especially when it was just the two of them and he no longer needed to pretend. Each of them knew what the other was about. She tolerated his presence and was grateful that he was not working right next to her. Off toward the other side of the room, he busied himself with cataloging all of the books in the Wilton library.

When the church bell sounded, Margaret scrunched up her eyes and rubbed her thumb and forefinger against them. "Oh, Goscelin, I am sorely in need of a break. My sight is blurry from too much concentration."

Little Eve offered nothing in response except a smile, but Goscelin agreed with Margaret. "That is true." He stretched his lean body, reaching both of his arms high into the air. "Examining these documents for hours at a time can take its toll. But the good news is that it is Friday, and you will have the opportunity to escape this chamber for a while. Exercise the body, not the mind for a change."

"Yes, it is good to be of service in a different way, do you not think?" Margaret asked Celia. She closed her text and stored the book into the lower compartment of her desk.

Celia was happy about not having to lie, "I do enjoy helping the children." She could never speak to anyone of Vivienne, so these Friday afternoons spent with the young ones helped Celia keep her sister's memory alive.

Goscelin left his podium to inspect Eve's drawings. "Ah, well done. Very well done." He patted her on the crown of her head. "Will you be joining the other sisters in their ministry?"

Eve whispered quietly. "No, thank you though. The children are too loud, too noisy for me. After noonday prayer, I shall remain in the chapel."

Father Joseph, sitting on the ground amidst two towers of books he had pulled from the shelves, stretched his head around to peer into the outer room. "Perhaps a romp in the countryside might do you good. You seem more hermit than child, Eve."

Eve answered without turning to look at the priest in the library. Instead, her eyes went up toward heaven. "God willing, I shall be." She put down her pen and shuffled quickly to be the first one out the door in order to avoid any further communication.

*   *   *   *   *

Their arms were full.

While the four children sat on a blanket eating their lunch of bread and herring, Margaret and Celia carried out the donated winter coats from which the orphans could choose. Margaret, her face nearly buried under all of the clothes, called out cheerily to Celia.

"And did I tell you the best part? Sister Clara said that they are sectioning off a part of the hospital. The Abbess apparently asked the

353

wood builder to partition the infirmary so that the children would have a place to stay this winter."

Celia had to twist her head around her pile in order to see where she was stepping. "But I thought Clara said every bed was filled with the sick and aged?" The decline from the abbey to the meadow was steep, so her short brisk steps made the cloaks bob up and down.

"They are. But they are going to use part of the travelers' area for the orphans. It will be just for them." Margaret was doubly excited at both the news and the fact that she could drop her cargo.

Bending down to her knees, she began laying out each of the coats side by side, arranging them from small to large.

A frail child trundled over, her hand still grasping a mound of bread. Her cheeks were rosy from the cold, but over the pink were smudges of dirt from rough outdoor living. Wisps of blonde hair, too thin to fight against the wind, escaped from beneath her cap. The strands swirled about her face in a kind of manic dance. She had to use her other hand to anchor them down.

"Sister Margaret, are all these for us?" Not letting go of the bread, she motioned with her arm across the display in front of her.

All four children were in dire need of heavier clothes, especially since the weather was turning colder. Little Clainnis' dress—given to her by a kind stranger—was far too big for her diminutive size. It continually fell off one shoulder and then the other. The three boys had the opposite problem. They had outgrown their threadbare tunics so that the fabric did not even reach their knees. They had no breeches or tights, and the shoes on their feet, made of cloth not leather, were held together with a single strand of twine.

Still tidying things up, Margaret answered from her position on the ground. "Well, not all of them. You can count, can not you,

Clainnis? Let us count together. See there are four of you and eight of these. So each of you can choose any one of the eight you like best."

Celia could not stop herself from placing her hands on either side of Clainnis' cap and kissing the waif upon the head. "And I think I see one that is absolutely perfect for you,"

A grimy hand thrust itself at Celia's elbow. "And what about me?" Charles, the biggest of the four children, pushed his way forward. He was the only outsider in the group. The other three were siblings.

Margaret, ever patient and kind, answered him. "Charles, each of you will have a turn, and there is plenty to choose from. Whichever ones remain will be returned to the convent."

"But I want to choose now!" Charles was about to use his shoulder to push Clainnis off to the side when another boy tugged on his arm and dragged him back.

"She said we'd all have a turn. And, it is not your turn right now. It is Clainnis'." Although this other boy was smaller in size than Charles, he put his shoulders back and stood his ground. His nose reddened, and his eyes glared with challenge.

Charles closed his hand into a fist, but then reconsidered. "Eh, who cares anyway?" He shoved Clainnis' brother and started to walk back toward the blanket. "I do not need anything from anyone."

Before Charles could get very far, Margaret intercepted him. "You will go next after Clainnis. Not because of your boldness but because of your age. There are three boys here, and you, Charles, are the oldest. Then comes Will and then Jack. So that is how the choosing will go."

"Fine." Charles pretended to be indifferent, but Celia caught him smirking at Will, gloating over having gotten his way. Frustration rose inside her from pent up anger. These were the times she felt it most difficult to be kind and merciful. The impulse to smack the grin off his face was nearly overwhelming.

Celia ushered the little girl forward. Chomping on the bread and savoring every crumb, Clainnis looked at the two smallest coats. "Hmmm. How about this one? May I have this one?" She pointed to a child's cloak, maroon in color with a fur-lined hood.

"What a marvelous choice!" said Celia. "The perfect outfit for a princess like you." Celia lifted it from the ground and guided Clainnis' arms through the sleeves. "I bet you did not know that this once belonged to the daughter of a king, did you?" With a yearning for her faraway sister, Celia hugged the child in close. Extending her arms to get a good look at the newly robed princess, she added, "Yes, indeed! What a fine lady you are and shall be, my love!"

Clainnis glowed with excitement, moving her tiny hands up to the collar to cinch it up tighter. "Do you think so, Sister Celia? Do you really think so?" The child kept looking at the cloak in awe. Then she spun in a circle with joy.

Margaret removed the unchosen female coat from the row. "Yes, and that princess lived right here, in this very abbey. And later she performed such miracles that she was named a saint!"

Ugh. Leave it to that one to ruin the story. What kind of princess chooses to be stuck in a convent? Only the dying and the near dead care about saints. Let the child think she is royal. Give her a chance to believe that dreams can come true. Right after thinking this, though, Celia realized the true impact of Margaret's words. What Margaret had just described—Edith's decision to retreat from the secular world into the safety of the religious one—was exactly what Celia needed Margaret to do. And judging from the excitement in Margaret's voice regarding Edith's decision, maybe Celia's underlying mission would not be that difficult.

Clainnis was still carried away by the beauty of the garment. She clapped her hands, and asked the two women, "And if I wear her clothes then maybe I can make miracles too? Do you think so, Sister Margaret? Do you think so, Sister Celia?" Her eyes rested upon Celia for reassurance. "You know what my first miracle would be? For Mother to escape the fire, the way she made sure the rest of us did. And my second miracle would be for Father to return home safely from battle."

Charles broke into Clainnis' vision. "It is just a coat." He snatched the largest one from the assortment and put it on without further comment.

Before Will went to choose, he bent down toward his sister and whispered tenderly to her. "Mother and Father may be gone, but you will always have me and Jack. We will never leave you."

Celia witnessed the touching exchange and thought of the promises one makes with the best of intentions and how the world often shatters those vows. She remembered once upon a time making the same oath to Vivienne, and yet she was forced to abandon her. Life's twists and turns sometimes destroy the words that are intended to be steadfast and true.

Will made his choice and motioned over to Jack, the last one in the group to go. The middle child in their family, Jack should have been taller than Clainnis but was not. The two of them appeared to be identical twins. His quickness made up for his lack of size as it was he who often was fast enough and smart enough to secure food for them all. With a sharpened stick, he could spear a trout. With his tattered shirt, he could trap a heron. And with his nimble legs, he could climb to get the finest apples.

Jack's face was sprinkled with freckles, and his eyelashes were like red brushes that matched the color of his hair. Despite his colorful appearance, most people (and animals too) barely knew he was there, so few words he spoke and so silently he moved.

Indeed, Celia and Margaret had never heard Jack's voice, thinking perhaps he was mute. But Will told them that was not the case. Jack could talk, he simply chose not to. After their parents died, Jack turned solemn and refused to engage with anyone other than his siblings. Perhaps he thought it was safer not to extend himself and make himself more vulnerable. That way he could limit the potential for future suffering and loss. He nodded in gratitude at the two nuns and chose the smallest coat that remained which, when he put it on, still hung loosely over his narrow frame.

Margaret piled up the jackets that were left over and gave half to Celia. Warm and snug, the children sat on the blanket finishing their food while the two women walked over to the bench outside the abbey where they would drop the remaining coats and return them later to the storage place inside.

"It is just so awful about their parents, is it not?" Celia walked alongside Margaret. "I mean, a father who goes to war to protect his family and a mother who essentially does the same. I wonder if she knew she was going to die. I wonder if she knew as she pushed the last child to safety that it was too late for her. That the roof would collapse, and she would perish in the flames."

"'Greater love hath no man than this, that he lay down his life for another…' Is that not what Jesus said?"

Celia kept thinking about the mother. "You and I shall never bear children. I wonder what a love like that feels like..." Celia let the words dangle in the air, watching carefully as Margaret seemed lost in thought. She pushed further. "Have you ever thought of a life outside the convent? With a husband by your side and a child in your arms?"

Margaret still appeared to be distracted. "Not really." She spoke dreamily. "Well," she tilted her head back as if considering the question more carefully. "Maybe once."

After placing their load down on the bench, they started on their way back to the children. Margaret's pace was slow. She stopped to pull a small branch off one of the holly bushes that lined the stone walk. "It was the timing of it all." She began sharing the memory with Celia. "I had just lost my father. And my teacher, the only other friend I had, was dying. And then, it seemed almost as if the Lord was sending me another protector, a kind of earthly savior who would be able to console me and watch over me. Keep me and my family from harm." Her eyes warmed, her face flushed pink with emotion, and she smiled. "To everyone else, he appeared rough and untamed, but to me, he was kind and tender. His touch was like a fresh rose petal brushing up against your skin—which made no sense because his hands were battle-scarred and callused." Margaret laughed at the incongruity.

Celia needed to pry deeper. "Do you ever hear from him?"

"I did receive a letter once. A few weeks ago." She jumped when she pricked her finger on the sharp edge of the holly leaf.

Celia was afraid that the sudden jolt would disrupt Margaret's reverie, but Margaret only stared at the small droplet of blood forming on her finger as if it were not even real.

"He spoke only of my visiting him. In his kingdom. He wrote nothing of marriage or parenting or children." She looked at Celia as if she was thinking something for the first time. "He hasn't mastered his letters so he lacks the ability to write. I am guessing he dictated his thoughts to a scribe. Maybe that is what stopped him from being more personal . . ." Something caused her thoughts to change direction. She flung aside the holly branch and wiped her finger on her dress. "But, what does it matter? I did not write back nor do I plan to. My place is here."

Celia felt great comfort over Margaret's final words. "As is mine."

As they stepped down the hill, they could see the four orphans had finished lunch and were growing restless. At the sight of them, Celia felt life's cruelty all over again. She could not imagine the pain that woman endured—the horror of losing the man she loved and the agony of leaving her children behind.

But Celia then realized that she did not have to imagine it all; she had lived it herself.

*　　*　　*　　*　　*

While Celia and Margaret made their way back, the four children were busy in their own imaginary worlds. Clainnis, waving a stick she believed to be her scepter, commanded Jack to be her nimble jester. He did so by twisting his body all sorts of ways, performing somersaults on the ground and flips in the air. Will, meanwhile, folded the corner of the blanket, trying to figure out how to fashion a decent hand puppet, and Charles was using his finger to squash a colony of ants one by one.

Watching the children at play reminded Celia of Rowena and all the creative activities she undertook with her little ones. Her mind clicked after remembering one particular project, so she made a quick detour to the garden, grabbed a shovel, and handed it off to Margaret, promising to explain its purpose later. She then ran toward the blanket and pounced onto it like a puppy. With her hands and knees on the ground, she said to them, "I have got a plan for something fun we could do! How about we go down to the river and find some treasure!"

Clainniss immediately dropped her stick and began clapping with joy, but Charles did not even bother to look up.

"There is no treasure in that river." Now he was using a rock to crush each bug.

Celia rolled her eyes at Margaret. She wanted to tell the boy to stay behind—nobody wanted him there anyway, she would have added—but she knew sweet Sister Margaret would be horrified by such a brutal comment, so Celia kept her tongue and played along. Faking a cheery tone, she challenged him. "Oh, yes. There is treasure, but only those who have really sharp eyes can find it."

"I have good eyes," shouted Clannis. Jack nodded in agreement with regard to himself, and the two scooted next to Celia.

"Me too!" Will's puppet collapsed as he dropped the corner of the blanket and joined their group.

"Well then, you have a very good chance of finding something special!" Celia opened up her arms as if to gather the three children together and began walking toward the gravel path that would take them over the bridge to the opposite side of the river.

"Come along, Charles. You do not want to miss out on the fun." Margaret leaned her arms on the top of the shovel and waited for him to join her, but he refused to budge.

He scrunched his face into a scowl. "I told you there is no treasure there. Otherwise, there'd be pirates." He continued his small-scale killing spree.

"Just leave him," Clainnis whispered loud enough for him to hear. "He is always causing trouble. Even the crazy house did not want him."

"Hush, child," Margaret tapped Clainnis' hand in reproach, hoping Charles had been too preoccupied with his bugs to hear what the young girl said. But Margaret was mistaken.

Right after Clainnis' comment, Charles jumped to his feet. "Fine. I will come." He threw the rock onto the ground with force, hoping to destroy a few more victims just for good measure.

Margaret tried to walk alongside the young boy to soothe his temper, but he remained one step ahead of her and directly behind Celia and the others. When they all reached the top of the bridge, Celia stopped to point down at the riverbank. Each of them held fast to the stone edge while they peered down below them.

"When we get down there, we are going to look for mussels. Look for the ones that are dark brown or black. We will find them fixed in the sand. Some are buried halfway in. They try to look like soldiers, but they're a little too wobbly to be prim and proper. The buried ones will be harder to find of course, but you can use the shovel and sift through the sand to get them too. And if we are really lucky, when we open them, we might find treasure inside!"

"What kind of treasure?" Will asked with interest.

"Well," Celia bent down lower to meet the group at eye level, "if you are lucky, you just might find a pearl—pink or tan or brown or white." She touched her finger upon each of their noses after saying "just might find."

"Oh, Sister Celia! I bet that is what a princess would wear," Clannis looked at Celia with eyes round with hope. "A necklace made of all those colors."

"But how are we going to open them? What if they do not want to open? Do we have something we could stick inside them to make them open?" Will's questions tumbled out fast while Jack looked down at the river with fascination.

From this position on the bridge, they could see the water about twenty feet below running fast over the boulders by the left and right side of the bank. Directly in the middle, it seemed steady and still.

Charles tried to assert his power. "We do not need any special tool to open them up." His interruption distracted Margaret long enough for Celia to quickly remove her knife from its hiding place. She did not want Margaret to know she carried a weapon on her person, so she kept the blade hidden in her hand until Charles was done talking.

"I can just smash them and then you will all see that they're just filled with slimy goo and nothing more."

"Charles!" Margaret frowned at him in disappointment.

"Why do you always want to break things?" That was the second time Clainnis had insulted him, and Charles' face turned crimson with anger. Sensing the intensity coming off him, the girl shuffled closer to Celia for protection.

Celia kept drawing their attention toward the bank. "Can everybody see where we are going to be looking? Once we pull enough of them from the water, Sister Margaret or I will use this knife I took from the convent kitchen to pry open the shell."

Will raised his hand immediately. "Jack can do the searching in the water. He does not mind the cold—do you, Jack?—and he is really good at catching things, moving things. So shells that do not even move should be a cinch for him." His voice overflowed with anticipation. "And I can do the opening. I am strong enough. Father showed me how to skin animals pretty well, and I have been doing that all along since we have been on our own. So opening up a shell is nothing at all!"

Celia was swept away by their enthusiasm. "That would be terrific. And then Sister Margaret and I can do the initial scouring. And if we look inside and see there is something worthwhile inside, then Clainnis can pull out the jewel!"

"So wait a minute. We are not going be crushing or breaking anything? None of that?" Charles grew more agitated.

Clainnis tugged on Margaret's gown. "See what I mean? That is all he cares about," she gestured her thumb in his direction. "That is probably why his father put him away, had him locked up. He is always wrecking something. He even broke his mother when he was born."

Those were the last words Clainnis uttered. Charles flew at her from behind, and as he yelled, "Shut up!" he thrust both of his hands into her narrow back. Her body flipped over the edge of the bridge and, with nothing left to hold on to, she tumbled over into the water below.

Clainnis' scream pierced the air as her limbs flailed in a kind of grotesque dance. For a split second, everyone froze in fear as they watched the child fall helplessly into the rushing river. After the splash, Margaret screamed too, dropping the shovel and drawing her hands to her face in shock. Will took off across the bridge and down the embankment, yelling loudly, "She can not swim! My sister can not swim!" Celia jumped.

Without stopping to think, Celia launched herself from the bridge. Her tunic and scapular blew upwards, billowing open as she crashed into the current. The water was shockingly cold, pricking her face and arms like sharp icicles, and it was a struggle to return to the surface. When her head did pop up again, she gasped for breath because of the jarring sensation. Even though the water had once been clear, the crash of the two jumpers disturbed the sediment so that particles were swirling and visibility muddied. Celia knew she could not wait for the silt to settle though. She must start searching immediately for the little girl.

She dropped her face into the water and forced her eyes open. From her position, she could perceive the bottom to be about eight feet below where she was now. Moving her arms gently but firmly, she drove herself deeper. Nothing. She returned back to the surface to take another gulp of air and then went down again. Her mind clicked when she saw a reddish color staining the river floor. Was it blood? Was she too late?

Knowing her air intake was limited, she had to force herself to calm down and not think such thoughts. Of course it was not blood, how could it be under the water? Perhaps it was Clainnis' maroon cloak? Yes, that is exactly what it was, for she could see the wisps of yellow hair floating like reeds back and forth in the current. Reaffirmed in purpose, she pulled her arms faster and stronger toward the bottom until she fastened her grip around the child's waist. Kicking ferociously, she darted up toward the surface with the limp creature fastened firmly to her side.

When Celia broke through the water, she inhaled deep breaths of air and lifted Clainnis higher than her shoulder to encourage the child to do the same for herself. "God, no. Oh, my God, no!" The weight in Celia's arms came only from the heaviness of the child's coat, her body limp and lifeless. Despite her doubts, Celia believed she could still save her. She swam hard with one arm in order to get to the shallow water where she could stand.

By this point, Margaret had run into the water and was standing in it up to her waist. She drove her legs hard, the weight of her habit impeding her forward progress. Will too was in the water as he tried to match Margaret's location, but the water level would have enveloped most of his small body, so he waited a few steps further back. Margaret dragged and pulled herself forward into Celia's path and then opened her arms to receive the child. Exhausted, Celia handed her over.

Trying to run but mostly just trudging forward, Margaret reached the bank and carefully laid Clainnis down upon the softened grass. The little girl's lips were blue and her face gray and chalky, like the underbelly of a fish. The cloak she once believed would elevate her to royalty had anchored her instead to a much different fate. Sodden with water, it chained her to her own mortality.

Celia could not take a further step. She dropped to her knees, the shallow water now level with her waist. She cried inside as she watched the scene before her. It seemed as if time had slowed to a point where even the simplest movement took hours to perform. She saw Margaret make the sign of the cross ever so deliberately over the body. She watched Will pound his fists into the earth, moaning over his inability to save his own sister. And she noticed Charles, hiding behind a tree, either ashamed of what he had done or gloating over having had the last word. She had to shake herself from this state of helplessness. She had to do something.

A long time ago, she had nearly given up on a different child, ready to surrender the little one to the angels. But God saw fit to resurrect that baby, placing her into Celia's arms. Dare she pray for His intervention one more time? She rose to her feet and fought against the current to get to the shore.

In his devastation, Will stopped punching the ground and instead pounded against his sister's chest. Both his hands struck together upon her body—once, twice, a third time, and then a sound. A gurgle emerged from the dead girl's lips. He froze for a moment in disbelief. Then he pushed even harder on her chest. Margaret opened her eyes but never ceased praying as she assisted Will's efforts by placing her hand under Clainnis' neck to help her get air. Another gurgle, and then a rush of water streamed from her mouth.

Celia ran faster. She collapsed again—on the grass this time—to witness Will and Margaret bringing life back to the dead. Like angels, they were. The kind that held the key to heaven's gate behind their back in one hand, while offering life-giving force with the other. Celia watched as Clainnis' face went from gray to light pink. The child's lips were still blue, but they soon began to quiver in search of air. A few more coughs, and then her eyes flashed open and her head lifted up on its own from the ground.

When he saw his sister coming back, Will's broken sobs turned to hiccups of laughter. Margaret recited the *Pater Noster* even louder as she hugged Clainnis' body to her heart, her tears mixing in with the child's dampened hair.

And Charles watched it all from his hiding place.

That is, until, the angel of death called him home.

*   *   *   *   *

At first, Celia was the only one who noticed Charles. She saw him behind the tree. Then she saw him fall.

Will and Margaret were too busy reviving Clainnis to be concerned with anything else. The two of them had their arms wrapped around the little girl, squeezing hard to reassure themselves that she was real and not a spirit. Celia was there too, engaged in her own internal battle over whether she should stay and relish Clainnis' recovery or go and tend to Charles. She chose to remain with the others in celebration.

In the past, Margaret had counseled Celia to show the boy mercy, but Celia felt that at some point excuses should no longer be made for Charles' horrid behavior. While she could agree that circumstances did dictate many things in life, she also knew that what a person does with those circumstances determines his fate. There are virtuous blacksmiths and evil ones, just as there are benevolent princes and villainous ones. It is not heritage or status that controls the substance in one's soul. It is the choices one makes that determines the content. The three siblings barely had shoes on their feet, but they carried themselves honorably. Charles' soul, on the other hand, was blacker than a moonless night. He chose to remain in the darkness and shun the rays of light that offered him the chance to change.

Charles never knew his mother. She died while giving birth to him, and his father never forgave him for his fatal arrival. When he looked at his son, he saw only a life-snatching devil, not a fragile little boy. Because of that, Charles shed his vulnerability faster than the whip that slashed his back. Any softness in his heart was swallowed up by the coldness that settled upon his heart. Before long, his temper matched his father's, and one day after returning the old man's punch with one of his own, Charles was sent to the monastery at Sherborne. The monks had a special dormitory for wayward boys whom they believed suffered from some type of mental imbalance. That was where Charles was placed.

He railed at his captors. When they tried to cut his hair, he punctured the barber's arm with the man's own shears. When they strapped him to his bed, he cursed and spat in the faces of those who came to feed him. Not sure what to do with him and starting to believe he was beyond saving, the monks removed his bindings and brought him to the chapel to cast out any unclean spirits. Before the priest could begin his opening prayer, Charles grabbed the vial of salt and water and flung its contents into the man's face. He smashed the bottle against the marble altar, dashed down the aisle, and ran out the door to freedom.

For a time, he wandered alone, pilfering food when he could, sleeping in barns when no one was watching. As the weather turned colder, he sought shelter, eventually stumbling into the cave where Clainnis and her brothers lived. Charles promptly set himself up as their leader—although none of them cared for him or wanted him to stay.

A few weeks ago when Celia first visited the orphans, Margaret had told her Charles' sorry history, and it was true that, initially, Celia pitied the boy. It certainly was not his fault that his mother died and that his father was a lout. But, in Celia's opinion, when given the chance to receive acceptance and friendship, Charles rejected both. He mocked the children for their kindness and kept them in fear by threatening and belittling them. For Celia, today's incident proved he was beyond redemption. He wanted Clainnis dead. He pushed her off that bridge and wanted her to die. Celia did not care that Clainnis' words cut him deeply. One cannot die from words. His response proved he was irredeemable. Celia had been right about him the whole time.

Clainnis was sitting up now. Her tiny hand, shivering with cold, swept her wet hair off her face. Will had run to get the picnic blanket to wrap around his sister's body, and Margaret was busy wringing out the girl's cloth shoes. Celia slid her knees over towards Margaret, one shuffle at a time, until she was close enough to tap her on the shoulder. Blocking Clainnis' view, Celia pointed over to the body that lay face down next to the tree.

Margaret gasped and locked eyes with Celia. Unspoken fear passed between them.

"Sweet child," Margaret cooed softly, "let us turn your face from the wind. I will help you spin around. Sister Celia, can you get that rock over there for her to lean on?"

Once Clainnis was comfortable, the two of them sped over to where Charles lay. As they drew closer, they knelt down on either side of the boy. Margaret's hand hovered over the back of his head, trembling as she reached out to caress the raised bump that appeared behind his left ear. The bruised area extended to the ear itself. The curved portion at the top looked purple and enlarged. A trail of blood streamed down from there along his cheek and jaw. Gazing at the frailty of the body, Celia felt sorrow wash over her.

Margaret gestured her head toward the shovel that was discarded behind the tree, imploring Celia to take a look. They both surmised the truth. Margaret confirmed it with a single word, "Jack." Celia nodded.

Neither woman had seen the child since Clainnis' fall, but it was easy to figure out what he had done to rectify the situation. It was an act of revenge. A life for a life. In the young boy's mind—and in many a man's—such an action was more than justified. But Celia wondered if Margaret would see it as such. She doubted whether Margaret had the ability to appreciate the difference between what was right as stated by law and what was right inherently. It was easy for Celia to make that distinction. The Lord's Commandment listed murder as a most grievous sin, but could it ever be considered justified? With the consequences displayed before their eyes, would Margaret be focused only on Jack's decision to kill or would she be able to examine the circumstances that compelled the boy to make that decision?

It did not help that when Celia rolled Charles' body over she could see the tracks of tears along his cheeks. A clear sign of his remorse. She secretly tried to wipe the moisture away, but she was not fast enough. Margaret seized her wrist and said. "At least he acknowledged his sin. 'Twas a good death."

Celia tilted her head, stunned that the pious nun could grasp the larger context of what had occurred.

Will, blanket in hand, sprinted down from the bridge toward his sister but slowed his pace when he saw the two nuns leaning over a crumpled mound. Starting to put the pieces together in his mind, he looked at the shovel and Charles' body. Tiptoeing closer with caution, he whispered, "Jack?"

Neither woman answered what Will knew to be the truth. A critical moment hung in the balance before them. The next action taken would be irreversible. Celia wanted to be the one to make the decision because she knew she would let Charles' life be the debt paid for the survival of the other two—Clainnis and Jack. And she was about to step forward and make that decision when Margaret shocked her once again.

Removing her cloak, Margaret stood up and handed the garment to Will. "Give this to Clainnis. Take off her wet cloak and wrap her in this. Bring it back when you return to see us next week." She nodded solemnly like a priestess in a temple.

Relieved, Will at first did not know what to say. His eyebrows drifted downwards with worry. "But what about—?"

Celia did not wait for the boy to finish. Whether Will was referring to his brother or the body made no difference. A decision had been made. "No need to worry about anything further. Just gather up Clainnis and be on your way, love."

Margaret stepped closer to the boy and placed her hands on his face, hoping to ease his troubled mind. Watching his bottom lip buckle in sorrow, she soothed him. "Seventy times seven. Do you remember? Jesus calls us to forgive not just seven times, but beyond measure. The grace we extend to another is abundant, overflowing, and limitless. And we shower that grace upon your brother who remains among us and upon Charles who rests now in the arms of the angels."

He looked up at Margaret, his eyes welling with tears. When he nodded, they started to spill over.

With a soft kiss upon his head, Margaret dismissed the child, and the two women watched him help Clainnis out of one coat and into the other. Cradling her in close, he kept her back to them and led her into the woods to return to their hovel. From the top of the bridge, a reddish sprite vanished like mist upon a strong wind.

In silence, Celia studied her partner, touched by the way Margaret's heart seemed to follow the orphans homeward. She admired the way Margaret had framed the tragedy, astonished by Margaret's understanding of justice. Perhaps the two of them were more alike than Celia had ever thought.

When Margaret's eyes finished staring in the direction of the children, she looked with deep sadness upon the boy whose limbs were cold and stiff. Dropping her bravery, she turned to Celia with a plea for help. "What are we to do now? Should we go tell Goscelin or the Abbess? I guess we just leave him here until we can bring someone back with us. But how shall we explain what happened?" Margaret covered her mouth with her hand and closed her eyes. She shook her head from side-to-side, feeling the implications of their predicament.

Now it was Celia's turn to make decisions, and she was more than ready to take charge. Without speaking, she marched over to the discarded shovel and grasped its handle firmly. She returned to where Margaret was standing and answered her question.

"What we do now is pray, both in word and deed. Your voice shall lift toward heaven. My toil will penetrate the earth. And for some reason, I believe God will appreciate that we can only do what we are best suited to do."

Digging a grave was something Celia knew all too well. She picked a space in between three trees to carve out Charles' final resting place where he would no longer feel alone, a place where he could sleep eternally amidst the companionship of the natural world. While Celia prepared the trench, Margaret remained with the body, doing what she did best. She placed her hand upon the boy's quieted heart and prayed intensely for the salvation of his soul, content in knowing that he had renounced his actions before he took his final breath.

In that way, each woman glorified God and came to a greater appreciation of the other. And both begged Christ for forgiveness.

CHANGES IN THE AIR

WINTER 1065 – SPRING 1066

The faint glow of the candle illuminated the displeasure on his face.

"She is going back? Are you joking?" Father Joseph wrinkled his nose as if he had smelled rancid cheese. "Oh, no. That won't do. She must not go back to Westminster. You have to convince her to stay here."

Celia waited before answering him. A trickle of water dripped on the wall behind her, landing on the cellar floor with a repeated plink. She carried no light herself, so his countenance was the only visible thing in the room. Darkness enveloped the casks of wine that rested against the stone walls, and when she placed her palm on the side of one, she flinched from the stickiness of the cobweb that clung to it.

"Well, I can not very well chain her here, can I? Plus, she has been summoned. Both her brother and mother want her there. You should be pleased I was able to manipulate her into asking me to join her. Give me the food."

He dropped the satchel on top of the wine barrel and watched as she rushed to take out its contents, a wedge of cheese and a handful of nuts. Swiftly, she broke off a corner of the cheese and shoved it into her mouth. He observed her critically. "Clearly, fasting is not one of your strengths."

She stopped chewing to stare him down. "That was not part of the bargain—matching her self-denial—but I am doing it anyway, am I not?" She poured a stream of nuts into her mouth and with her open hand wiped the crumbs from her lips. "The girl starves herself. And if she does partake of anything, she pecks and nibbles at it like a bird. It is a wonder she does not waste away."

"Just keep pace with her and let her starve herself deeper into her vocation or into the grave. As long as she remains out of Malcolm's reach and away from the crown, we have succeeded at our job."

"Look, I am doing everything I can to convince her of that, but I can not stop her from returning to Westminster. Not when she has been summoned like that. But . . . her brother's letter contained much that would interest you, much that would interest the Duke." She tore off another piece of cheese and plopped it into her mouth. She talked and chewed simultaneously.

"The King is ill. Very ill. Seems he has retreated from everything, save going to chapel. The fallout between Harold and the brother Tostig makes the King despondent. He feels the country is on the brink of civil war and does not want to witness such a calamity in his own lifetime." Father Joseph offered no comment, remaining quiet while she spoke. "And apparently, Harold seems not to care that the Godwin family lost Northumbria because the region landed right back in Harold's hands again—indirectly through marriage. The earldom was given to his wife's brother."

Celia looked at the containers of wine that surrounded her. "I am thirsty. What did you bring me to drink?"

Now his temper flared. "I brought you nothing. Are you not able to fend for yourself in some regard? What am I caring for? An infant?"

She stepped in closer to him and spoke through gritted teeth. "Listen, I am the one doing all the work here. If I were not supplying you with information, you would be of no use. You would have nothing to report to the Duke other than the number of biographies in the Wilton library."

"Oh, stop complaining and get on with it. Why did they send for Margaret?"

She moved away and turned her back to him, examining the last piece of food before picking it up. "That is when she became very sad. Her eyes turned misty when she read the part about Harold's new wife..." After wondering over the mystery behind Margaret's reaction, Celia ate the final morsel. "In any case, Agatha, her mother, wants them all together in one place—Edgar, Cristina, and Margaret—because there is danger all around. Edgar writes of gloom and suspicion—saints' predictions about the end of the Saxon line, rumors of invasions. That is why the two girls must return. And she wants me to go with her."

Father Joseph started biting the nail on his thumb as he pondered what this separation would mean to the flow of information between them.

"Relax," Celia patted his arm as if she were soothing a child. "I managed to convince her that we needed more than the beardless courier to protect us. You will serve as our escort."

Celia rubbed her hands together to show she was finished both with her meal and with him. "Now who is caring for whom, eh? We leave at dawn."

Before departing, she noticed how the light of the candle shone upon the leather strap that hung across his shoulder. Curious, she walked nearer to inspect it. Lifting the strap up and over his head, she saw a flask dangling from its end. She winked mischievously at him, raised it to her lips, and took a long draught. After draining it dry, she flung it aside until it tumbled into a dark corner of the cellar.

"Oh, what a shame! Looks like you may have to do some crawling around to find it. Who's the infant now? I do hope you are not afraid of the dark." Inhaling quickly, she blew out the candle and left him to the shadows.

*   *   *   *   *

Their progress was slow. Three horses trudged along in single file, the freezing rain and layer of ice on the ground made every step a challenge. Tyler, the courier, led the way with Margaret and Cristina seated together on the next horse, and then Celia and Father Joseph on the third. Because of the slippery terrain, they kept a good distance from each other to allow space for missteps.

The driving wind pressed against their faces as they made their way uphill on a narrow, rocky path. Tyler kept looking back over his shoulder to check on his companions, hoping they were managing all right. Margaret and Cristina were not. Cristina rode inside Margaret's arms, but Margaret's knuckles and face were blanched white and her eyes enlarged with worry. She bit her bottom lip in concentration, praying that she could simply copy the forward pattern of the beast in front. She was not an experienced rider and conditions made it even more evident. It was not easy for Tyler either. When the click-clack of his horse's hooves slid off the edge of a large stone, he decided it would be best to stop checking behind him and instead keep his eyes fixed in front—unless he wanted his horse to topple sideways and himself to be crushed beneath it.

Celia was frustrated. "This makes no sense." She turned her head to the right and spoke to Father Joseph loud enough to penetrate through both the rain and the cloth of her hood. "She does not know how to command a horse at all. You should take Cristina, and I should ride with Margaret. We should switch."

376

"Not a bad idea. The messenger said we had at least a three hour ride before our overnight rest stop." He stretched his neck higher to see over Celia's head. "We still have quite far to go before we get to the summit, so we can not do anything about it right now."

The unceasing rain continued to weigh them down, drenching their cloaks and sinking their spirits. Celia's thoughts were saturated with bitterness. She envied Margaret for not having to endure ordeals like this alone. She had her sister with her. Someone she could confide in, someone she could trust, someone she could be herself around. Celia did not have that. She suffered, and suffered alone.

Celia did not even know who she really was anymore. Around Margaret, she was a hypocrite. With Father Joseph, she was a conspirator. With Matilda, she was a fawning servant. What had happened to the person she once was? Was there any goodness left in her any more? Could virtue regenerate like dried moss that springs to life again after a sprinkle of fresh water? She scowled at the inaccuracy of the analogy. Despite the rain that pelted her face, she felt nothing but dead inside.

*   *   *   *   *

Two men conferred together at the bottom of the incline, their hoods down far past their heads so that only their mouths could be seen. The taller of the two had an unruly reddish beard speckled with gray while the shorter one had the beginnings of a faint mustache that bespoke his youth. Still mounted on horses, they paused in this location to reconfirm their purpose.

One whispered in hushed tones. "I tell you, they're up to no good. Two of them spoke French. They could be agents sent by that bastard from Normandy. I feel it to be so."

The older man remained doubtful. "But four of them are clergy. They could just be scholars able to speak in a foreign tongue."

"Aye, but why are they traveling with a lead man who wears the colors of the King? They're not just regular clergy then. Who is to say this priest is not another one of those Norman monks come to undermine the Godwins as Archbishop Robert did to Harold's father? Wheedled his way into King Edward's favor and had the whole Godwin family exiled? We need to capture them and bring them to the Earl."

The bearded fellow took this into consideration. He looked up at the group that was making its way up to the top of the hill and then looked back at his companion. But still, he remained uncommitted.

The boy rushed on. "Are we to stand by and let these foreigners infiltrate our shores? You have heard the talk? About an upcoming invasion? We detain the two French ones—the priest and the girl with him—and question their true purpose. The others are of no concern to us." His whispering grew more intense. "Imagine the reward if I am right, and we turn them over to Harold! We'd not need to be out in this foul weather any more, hoping to secure food and drink by waylaying travelers."

The idea was appealing—being indoors beside a warm fire with a full belly and a flagon of ale—yes, it was certainly appealing. The older man was slowly coming around to see the value of taking action. "And if you are wrong in your guess about them, then what?"

"Then, we just rob them as we normally would and disappear into the woods. Judging from their mounts and the presence of the King's messenger, surely there will be something of value on them. It would be foolish to let them pass by untouched."

With a slight nod of his head, the leader agreed. "We will overtake them then at the top of the hill. You grab the girl and I will nab the priest. And we have to make sure the other three do not follow us."

The two men remained silent and still at the bottom of the incline, allowing more time for their victims to make their way upward. As the sleet continued to pelt against their heads, their minds held fast to the thought that by eveningtide they would be dry and warm.

*   *   *   *   *

Nearing the crest, Father Joseph shouted loud enough to be heard at the front. "Tyler, when you get to flatter land, we need to stop."

A deep gully had formed in the path directly in front of Tyler's horse, so the courier could only acknowledge Father Joseph's request with a wave of his arm. In resistance, the animal pulled its head up against the reins, and Tyler was sensitive to its hesitation. Very gently, he guided it around the ditch, leaving the sheen of ice that stretched across it intact and the depth of water beneath a mystery.

Because Margaret's eyes were fixed upon the area right in front of her horse's snout, she did not notice Tyler's detour. Instead, she kept riding forward until her horse froze in panic. Even with her lack of experience, she could sense a shift beneath her as the horse's weight moved towards its hindquarters making the front end lighter. Margaret started to call out to Tyler when the animal took two steps backward and then reared, its forelegs off the ground, its body nearly upright.

Celia screamed out to her, "Lean forward! Lean forward! Grab his neck!" But Margaret heard nothing. She slid straight down the back of the horse and landed with a thud as her lower back slammed into a rock and her body fell limp like a doll.

Cristina, out of fear, clasped onto the horse's neck and managed not only to stay on its back but also unknowingly encourage it to land. Still spooked, the animal galloped away with Cristina as its hostage.

Tyler spurred his own horse into action, calling out to them, "See to Margaret," before jetting away in pursuit.

379

Celia and Father Joseph quickly dismounted, and Celia dashed over toward the fallen girl. Before reaching her, someone seized her waist and started pulling her in the opposite direction. "What are you doing? Let me go," she yelled, thinking that Father Joseph was trying to prevent her from saving Margaret. In a sinister way, perhaps he thought Margaret's death would effectively eliminate one threat to the Duke's claim for the crown. With his betrothed in a sepulcher, Malcolm's hopes for a union between England and Scotland would be buried as well.

When she turned around though, she saw Father Joseph on the ground, wrestling with a large, hooded figure. And if he was not the one pulling her away from Margaret, then who was? Her question was immediately answered when the man yanking her arm spun her about to face him.

"Norman bitch!" He spit at her as his lips formed the second word. She felt his saliva spray her face. "Who sent you and why are you going to the King?" She tried to wrench her arm free, but his grip was too intense. She could feel a throbbing sensation above her elbow and started twisting her shoulder to create better leverage.

"Stop squirming," he slapped her face hard and then started dragging her toward his mount. Her cheek stung from the blow, and her legs soon gave way. Because her gown shifted upwards, her skin was exposed, and she could feel the icy rocks and frozen twigs cutting up against her knees and lower body.

He called out to his partner. "I have got her. I am heading out. Bring him there too." But Father Joseph and the other man were still locked up together, exchanging punches and rolling in one direction then another in a quest for dominance.

Celia and her assailant arrived at his horse. Still holding fast to her arm, he readied himself to hoist her up onto the animal's back. As he reached with his other arm to encircle her waist, he bent his head down, leaving his head and neck open to her. Frantic over what he might do to her, Celia noticed the soft cuff of his ear. Like a mastiff, she opened her mouth wide and bit down, tearing away at his flesh until a piece of it landed upon her tongue. Triumphantly, she spit it out.

The man shrieked in agony and rushed both of his hands to his wounded ear. Blood trickled through the gaps between his fingers as he stood horrified over the injury to his body and the audacity of the wench. Now freed of his grasp, she lifted her bruised and scratched leg and thrust it with all her might into the man's groin. Another scream and he fell to his knees, his crimson hands smothering his crotch. With his head bowed, a rose-colored puddle formed as the blood from his ear mingled with the icy ground.

But Celia knew he was not done away with yet. She searched her surroundings with her eyes to find some kind of weapon to rid herself of him permanently. But her inspection ended almost immediately when a huge rock skated off his head and his body fell forward. He crumpled lifelessly to the ground.

Behind him stood Margaret, wide-eyed with shock and guilt.

She raised her arms in disbelief. "I . . . I . . . I did not know how to make him stop."

Celia cautiously bent down over the body to check and see if he was really dead. Margaret covered her face with her hands and tried to explain herself. "I remember . . . falling off the horse, and then I remember . . . waking up and . . . seeing him hit you, but I did not think I could get myself up. But when I . . . saw him dragging you, I started shaking out my feet, then my legs, then my arms to make sure they would work. All the while, I was imagining the depraved things he could do to you . . . The rock was all I could think of."

Celia stepped around the dead body and hugged her reluctant hero. The two women trembled with fright, gratitude, and relief. She broke their embrace when she remembered the second villain. Thinking they could use the same strategy twice, Celia ran to pick up the weapon of stone. She commanded Margaret, "You stay. I will go this time. Pray that my aim is as sharp as yours."

"It will be. And we shall both do penance together afterwards." Margaret pressed her hands together in prayer. "There is comfort in that," she whispered that final part to herself.

Celia darted into the woods expecting to see the two men battling, but she saw and heard nothing. She went further down the hill, but found only the remnants of a fight—a broken strap, a discarded hood, some fallen branches and twigs. Maybe Father Joseph was taken hostage? Much as she would like to be rid of him forever, she still needed him until she could be reunited with Vivienne. She continued to scour the area but did not find a trace of either man. Holding fast to her weapon, she climbed back carefully to where she had left Margaret.

Celia found the girl leading the horse by its reins, moving away from the area marked by death. Celia called out to her, "Father Joseph is gone. I fear he has been taken."

Margaret stopped and turned back to acknowledge Celia, but her stare was blank as if the words had not registered in her mind. Then she dropped her chin to her chest and raised her shoulders, shifting her eyes back and forth in fear of the unknown. From above them came the cracking of ice and the rhythmic clomping of a horse.

Celia dropped the rock and sprinted toward Margaret. Placing her hands on the animal's back, she bounced once upon the ground and sprang into the air, hooking one leg over the top. Once mounted, she reached down to Margaret with the offer of her hand. "Hurry up, get on!"

Margaret followed her command and planted herself in front of Celia. She gripped the horse's mane for stability as Celia drove the animal up the incline. Slapping its flanks, Celia willed it to overcome its own caution to obey her command.

There at the top of the hill were the other two horses. Tyler had a sobbing Cristina tucked under one arm and in the other he held both sets of reins. "Your sister has had a bit of a scare, but she is doing all right. It would be best though if she rides with me until we get to the abbey." He looked with approval at the arrangement of the other two. "And I think that is best as well. You seem more comfortable managing a horse, Celia. And Margaret, that was a bit of a tumble, are you well enough for us to carry on? We still have quite a few miles to travel before settling in for the night." Eager to be done with this assignment, Tyler did not wait to hear any protests. The girl could sit upright and that was good enough for him.

"The ground will be more even from here on out. We should be able to pick up the pace once we are on our way." Then he noticed something missing.

"Wait. Where is the priest?"

Both women did not know how to answer his logical question that demanded a response. They would have to tell him about the encounter, but would they need to tell him everything?

Tyler brought his horse to the edge of the precipice and looked down. "Did you leave him down there?"

"I am right here." Father Joseph stepped out from the brush behind Tyler and Cristina as if he had run ahead of them on the journey. His black hair stood up like frozen spikes jutting from his head, and his nose was swollen and red. "Got cut short, then lost my way. Took a few nasty falls along the way," he said with a laugh. "Next time I won't venture so far when I need the privy!"

His priestly habit was in disarray. The gown hung unbelted and fell down so far past his feet that the hem dragged on the ground. In his hand was the rope he normally corded around his waist. Snapping it taut, he communicated to Celia without words how he had disposed of his assailant.

Tyler pointed his horse eastward and tossed the reins to the other horse to Father Joseph. "Pull yourself together, Father, and let us be on our way."

Celia agreed that the courier's words meant a good deal more to all of them than he could ever know.

THE PALACE AT WESTMINSTER

DECEMBER 1065

The Advent period of fasting was over—but try telling that to Margaret, Celia thought. Sometimes the frustration of being her companion was too much for Celia to bear. That is why she liked being put to work. Staying busy was good for her mind, otherwise she would dwell only on the foolishness of her friend's piety.

Celia had just placed ivy clippings all around the top of the mantelpiece above the fireplace and would next weave in sprigs of holly to make the room feel festive. With her back to the entranceway, she did not hear Margaret enter.

"Would you like some help?" Margaret delicately fingered the prickly green boughs that lay on the table, hoping she could do something other than worry about the King's sickness.

Celia looked at the girl's green eyes and felt sorry that Margaret took everything so hard. Since both incidents—the one by the river and the one in the forest—Margaret had followed a strict regimen of contrition, denying herself the comfort of food or the diversion of Christmas celebrations. She even went so far as to cut off most of her hair. Beneath her veil, all that remained were short sticks of yellow straw that barely touched the cheekbones on her face.

Celia smiled with welcome. "Of course. I would love the company and the help. Mistress Winafred gave me permission to add a little decoration to the room to brighten things up a bit."

"And it does brighten the room, you are right. Strange, do you not think, how it does not even seem like Yuletide at all, what with the condition of the King and all. Everyone is so edgy and irritable. No one wants to make merry."

Celia giggled. "Ha, ha. I never thought you were one to care about making merry!"

"Not me, no," Margaret blushed, "but everyone else. They're all suspended like scales on a balance, waiting to see in whose favor the power tilts."

"Have you been allowed to see him?"

"No, the Queen mostly tends to him. And the physician, of course. Although her brother sometimes goes in there too."

Accepted amongst the laborers in the castle, Celia had heard the rumors. "But servants talk, you know? That is until Her Majesty silences them for speaking out of turn." Her words made Margaret stop arranging the greenery. "They said one side of his face is frozen. His eye and mouth are droopy. And he can no longer use his arms. Queen Edith has to feed him like a baby."

Margaret covered her mouth in horror and closed her eyes, shaking her head from side to side. She whispered through her fingers, "It is just dreadful. Based on the Queen's behavior, I fear it cannot be reversed." She handed some of the boughs to Celia who went back to entwining them with the ivy. "He cannot even attend the consecration of St. Peter's on the Feast of the Holy Innocents. The church he strove so hard to build."

Celia could certainly think of more exciting things to regret missing than the dedication of an abbey, but when she remembered who was recounting the story, she understood the magnitude of the claim.

"Does that not look festive?" Celia stood back to admire one side of the mantel. "Bring over some more, would you?"

Margaret, frail from self-sacrifice, moved from the hearth to the table and back again with the lightness of a ghost. "It is more than just visual beauty, Celia. The sharp leaves are like the crown of thorns and the berries are the droplets of blood Christ shed for us. The ivy too represents something, the purity of the Virgin Mary." She carried more sprigs over to Celia and admired the work her friend had already done. "That makes it even more beautiful, do you not think?"

Celia accepted the greenery and turned her face toward the hearth. She breathed in deeply and closed her eyes in exasperation. *Why does everything have to come back to religion with that one?* Celia nodded her head at Margaret's comment, but in truth, when she looked at the decoration, all Celia saw was Nature's charm.

"You know what? Let us go outdoors and gather some more boughs and vines. We could drape it around every fireplace in the palace."

"Yes, that is a fine idea. I will come with you. And maybe we can stop by and see Brother Tobias. There is much we can talk to him about." Margaret had more than plants in mind when she mentioned Tobias. She hoped to have the chance to ask him about the secret journey he had undertaken at her request.

Celia grabbed two baskets from the table by the door and handed one to Margaret. But as they turned to leave the room, they collided with a thick, burly man who seemed to be in a great hurry. Harold. His black eyes glistened at his good fortune.

"Well, well. What have we here?" He looked at Celia briefly, but concentrated on Margaret with much more intensity. Celia noticed how her friend cowered beneath his scrutiny. The girl drew her basket closer in toward her body and turned her face away from his leer. If her hair covering were longer, she would have hidden completely under it.

Celia knew he recognized her as Duke William's agent; they had sailed together in the boat from Normandy. But Margaret would have known that fact as well, so there was no need for secrecy regarding their familiarity. There was something quite disturbing though about what she was witnessing between Harold and Margaret. She wondered what sort of history existed between the two.

Amused by Margaret's discomfort, Harold toyed with her even further. Aggressively stepping toward her, he placed his hands on his hips and leaned in. "My new wife is arriving here tomorrow." Beneath his lengthy red mustache, his lips curled in a menacing smile. "Does that surprise you at all? Being sequestered away in the convent as you have been, I suppose you have not heard of our recent nuptials." Margaret continued to stare at the empty basket she held in her hands, wishing she had the power to make him vanish.

"I am sure you and my wife will have much to talk about," he added smugly. Raising his arm toward Margaret's face, he extended his short, stubby fingers to move aside her hair covering. "I see the convent has left its mark on you," he squeezed a butchered strand between his thumb and forefinger. "Though I much prefer the one I made to theirs."

Margaret jerked her head away from him, nearly losing her balance from the sudden movement. Her fear amused him, and he was pleased to have an audience to perform for. He glanced over at Celia with arrogance. "The abbey may be the best sanctuary for both of you in the weeks and months to come. I daresay there is no place for either of you here."

If Celia had not disliked the man enough before, now she utterly despised him, especially at the way he stomped upon an innocent soul like Margaret's. In principle, Celia refused to scamper away in fright.

She made a commitment in her mind that she would not be bullied by him. She would not leave the room before he did, and her stubbornness forced Margaret to wait as well. Harold, unaware of her private pledge, read nothing into Celia's stance. He departed when he was ready to do so, and that decision was made when he remembered there were more important people to see than these little church mice.

When his heavy football echoed away down the hall, the two women felt a sense of release. Celia broke the tension. "Are you all right?" Margaret only nodded. "I feel sorry for whoever is his wife."

Just above a whisper, Margaret struggled to find her voice. "And I too." Thinking back to the night when she freed Ealdgyth and her baby from captivity, she added, "It is a shame the convent could not protect her." She revisited her earlier idea. "Let us go find Brother Tobias. We both have questions to ask him about where to find certain things."

Celia picked up her cloak from the window seat and wrapped it around her body, still distracted by what had just happened between her friend and the Earl. While Margaret went down the hall to her chamber to retrieve her coat, Celia waited alone in the room and decided that she would save her more complicated questions not for Brother Tobias but for Margaret herself.

*   *   *   *   *

The twelve day celebration was drawing to a close, and no amount of festive trimming or cheer could lift the pall that enveloped the court. The King teetered between life and death, but the real tension in the room stemmed not from questions surrounding his mortality—everyone knew his departure from this world was imminent. No, it was the uncertainty of what would happen next in his kingdom that made everyone short-tempered and on edge.

Everyone of importance assembled in the Great Hall, seemingly divided into three camps: those who favored Margaret's brother, Edgar the aetheling, those of Norman background who pushed for William, and those who supported the Godwinsons and Harold. Because access to the King was so limited, none of them rightly knew what his final wishes would be, yet each believed unquestionably in his respective leader's right to succeed. Fear and suspicion reigned as they wondered what was taking place in Edward's private chamber. Harold's family clearly had the advantage as it was known that both the Earl and of course his sister, the Queen, were behind those closed doors.

"The Witan wants *me*," Edgar whispered from behind his hand to his sisters and his mother. "They have told me so." His eyes shifted from their faces toward the open entryway. "All I need to do is get into that room and hear the King confirm their decree."

The three women pretended to be calm and detached by focusing on their sewing, but the beads of sweat on Agatha's forehead betrayed the worry she felt for her only son. Her preoccupation with his status resulted in imprecise stitches that needed constant correcting. "The only thing we can do, son, is wait—"

Margaret jumped in, "And pray."

She took the opportunity to examine Cristina's work and patted her hand in approval when she saw the outline of the lion beginning to emerge. "But, brother, why do you care so much? These are dangerous times, and you are so young to wear the mantle of a king. Can you only feel happiness in your heart if a crown rests upon your head? We must prepare ourselves for the real possibility that you may be passed over. Is there not some other well to tap into for fulfillment and joy?"

Edgar sidled up closer to Margaret, angry at her for not recognizing the injustice of such a decision. His face flushed red, and his words came out faster but still in whispered tones. "How could you even ask me 'why do you care'? The only reason why we are here in the first place is because of Father. And I 'care' that he was murdered when he should be here with us right now. There would be no question of succession then, would there?" At the mention of their father's name, Margaret and Cristina felt their loneliness swell. Agatha stiffened to hide her emotions.

Edgar continued. "The King would not have asked him to come to these foreign shores if he did not have a plan in mind. Despite all the twists and turns over these last eight years, I believe King Edward's resolve has not changed. He wants the kingdom to be ruled by someone who shares his blood. There is no other candidate but I who has that distinction. It is up to me to ensure that the King's command is carried out."

Edgar stirred himself up so much that he could no longer remain seated. His quick movement drew attention from the Norman contingent as well as Harold's allies. Both eyed him with suspicion. They studied the young man carefully as he paced back and forth in front of his family.

Agatha reached her plump arm toward him and grabbed the fabric of his sleeve. Intercepting his next step, she spoke sternly. "Sit down."

Sounding more like a child than a king, he whined, "But I must gain entry into his room. I need to hear what he says—if he can even say anything at all. Only then will I know for sure where I stand, and if his wishes are being carried out."

Cristina raised her eyebrows and corrected him. "Where *we* stand." She then resumed threading her needle.

"If he cannot or does not speak, then the Witan will determine the successor. And even if the King does voice a selection other than me, it still comes down to his advisors, and I know they favor me. But I should be in there. I should be present for that moment. Save that the Queen refuses to allow anyone else in the room other than the physician, her brother and the Archbishop, and one or two of Edward's kinsmen. Why was I not included?"

Agatha said more firmly, "Be still. You will know soon enough whether or not there is a future for us here." Duly reprimanded, Edgar threw himself with a huff back into his chair. He stared up at the ceiling while the women went back to their sewing.

On one of the long benches that leaned up against the stone wall, Celia sat with Father Joseph at the end farthest from the door. She raised her prayer book up to her chin so that her eyes could scan the room while she appeared to be reading. Across from her above the hearth, the holly and ivy had started to droop, losing its luster after having been plucked so many days ago. But to the right of that fireplace stood a woman whose vitality was palpable. She outshone everything and everyone in the room. Her lips were deep red, richer in color than the berries that once cheerily adorned the walls. Her ebony hair accentuated her marble skin, which bore no blemish or wrinkle. If Celia's imagination had to conjure the likeness of a princess, this woman was the perfect model.

The mole-like priest, Father Thurstan, had attached himself to that princess, behaving more like captor than companion. Any time she moved, he trailed her. Wherever her eyes went, his followed soon after. Celia recognized him as the Earl's friend, the man she had overheard in the church, the one who plotted with Harold to remove any rival who threatened the Earl's power. Behind Father Thurstan was a group of Saxon men who wore long sleeved, knee length tunics of brown and gray, pouched at the waist over a belt. On their legs were tight fitting hose with criss-crossed binding, but it was the woman who intrigued her most.

She elbowed Father Joseph to get his attention, not realizing that because of her raised hand she had poked him in his face.

"Ouch! What did you do that for?" He dropped his psalter onto his lap to rub the side of his temple.

"I did not mean to do that. It is a pity you are just so short." She gazed down upon him with distaste. He glared back at her and pursed his lips in rebuke, but said nothing. "Is that woman Harold's wife?"

Again remaining silent, he used only his eyes to communicate that the answer was obvious.

"I thought so. She is quite stunning. Margaret said she was once Queen of Wales."

Father Joseph shook his head to rid himself of the sting from Celia's point elbow. "And if Harold is chosen, she may be a Queen again. Who knows?" He lifted his book and pretended to read. From behind the pages, he spoke from the side of his mouth. "Remember though, it is not Harold's title to claim. You were there. You witnessed it, as did I. The man swore an oath to Duke William to defer to him, to pay him homage. We all witnessed it."

"But most of the people in this room did not witness anything. Only ourselves and those fellows over there—see them?" She gestured to the group of Normans who stood against the other wall with their backs to the door. "Only they can attest to hearing the oath."

"Indeed. King Edward's Norman friends. They may not be quite ready yet to lift their swords in defense of the Duke, but I trust a day will come when they will do so. Woe to the man who is falsely named the next ruler of England."

Celia examined the men from her native land. None wore beards, and as tradition decreed, each had the back of his head shaven to commemorate his first kill on the battlefield. From time to time, they measured up the individuals on Harold's side of the room and smiled contentedly at their own superiority. One of her countrymen was facing sideways and she could not see his whole face, but there was something about his carriage that seemed familiar. Was it that he reminded her of Philippe? No, Philippe was much more slender. This man's chest was round and thick. His torso narrowed considerably at his waist so that his shoulders appeared broad and sturdy. In height, he stood almost a full head taller than the two other men with whom he was conversing, but it was his hands that captured her attention most intently. She tilted her head as she studied them, freckled and weather beaten yet capped off by long tapered fingers that seemed equally skilled at both launching an arrow or strumming a lute.

As he spoke, he gestured with those hands, freely and emphatically, and she followed their movement with her eyes. All at once she felt her nose tingle with the scent of low tide and could hear the sound of rushing water. The tangy taste of salt lilted upon her tongue, and enchantment transformed the empty air in front of his hands to an unweighted willow trap.

But this could not be.

Simon was dead and buried. Philippe had told her so.

When an emissary came into the room, that same Norman soldier turned to hear his news. Now she had full view of his countenance. Those eyes, the softest brown, a few shades lighter than the hair upon his head and turned down at the edges to give an impression of perpetual tenderness. The nose, straight and long, situated between cheekbones that rose high upon his face. And then, there it was—the scar that ran from beneath his eye to his jaw.

She gasped. The prayer book slipped from her hands to the floor, but no one noticed. All eyes were fixed on the messenger. Seated persons rose immediately. Everyone leaned forward in anticipation.

Edgar kneaded his hands together. Margaret made the sign of the cross. Agatha hugged Cristina to her bosom. Ealdgyth backed away to lean against the wall. Father Thurstan licked his lips with hunger. And the Norman warrior drew back his shoulders to greet the announcement stoically.

Celia, existing in another place and time, saw nothing but Simon. Her heart fled across the room. She delivered it willingly into his hands. Unaware of her presence as yet, he—like everyone else—awaited the man's proclamation.

The messenger cleared his throat and lifted his head to speak. In a loud, clear voice, he addressed the crowd, but did not make eye contact with anyone. He spoke with his chin pointed toward the ceiling as if he were speaking to someone suspended at the highest point on the wall.

"Aethelred's son—he who ruled the Welsh, the Scots, the Britons, the Angles, and Saxons alike—King Edward offered his righteous soul unto Christ on this day, the fifth of January in the year of 1066.

The King is dead, long live King Harold."

A rumbling mixture of celebration and defiance erupted as the emissary turned on his heel and raced from the room to escape the consequences. Father Thurstan shot a look of triumph at Edgar, as the boy turned to Margaret in disbelief and whispered, "It is not official yet. It cannot be official. There is still time. Until the Witan makes a formal announcement, there still is time!"

Margaret heard the desperation in his voice and pitied him. She knew it would be nearly impossible to shift the balance of power from the Godwin family to their own. The sooner she convinced her brother of that, the better it would be for all of them. She was not being pessimistic; she was just acknowledging the truth.

More people then filtered into the room, including those who were present in the King's chamber at the time of his death. A short, bespectacled doctor searched the room for Ealdgyth, but his lack of height made it difficult for him to find her. When he did, he described Edward's final farewell in a voice loud enough for all to hear. "The Queen made His Majesty comfortable, remaining at his side, warming his feet in her lap, but he seemed already beyond this world. In a last moment of clarity, he nominated your husband as his successor—"

Just then a thick-set Norman jostled the doctor from behind. He pushed against the small man's frame, forcing the physician to take a few steps backward. "You lie. I was in that room too." He shouted to assembly of people. "I was one of the King's closest friends, and I was in there too. King Edward never said successor. He told Harold to look after the Queen and this land until God decides what is to be done. What you are promoting is false!"

The man then turned to his companions who had not known that he had gained entry into the King's private chamber. "Yes, I was in that room to prevent such lies as this. Besides, the sole wish of a ruler does not guarantee succession in this kingdom. It is up to the Witan to decide. No announcement should have been made by that traitorous courier. And you, doctor, keep to your remedies and ointments, and let the Witan inform the people of their future leader."

The physician cast an icy look at the Norman lord but chose not to challenge his claim. And as for the messenger, fortunately he had left the room and thereby avoided blame for the hasty declaration. Those who supported Edgar or the Duke could now temper their initial anger with hope. Nothing was yet official. There was still a chance that the outcome could swing in their favor. All was not lost.

Wearing his purple cassock and a long, narrow stole draped around his neck, the Archbishop of Canterbury entered the Great Hall and demanded silence. Pleased to see someone with authority taking charge, the crowd quieted. Before speaking, he let his eyes rest upon every corner of the room, staring down into the faces of all who gathered there. "The bishops and the royal advisors will convene to discuss the succession. Be assured we are aware of the gravity of our decision. The future King of England must be one who can stave off threats from all outsiders, especially those who may try to invade our shores from every direction: south, north, east, or west. We shall reach a decision before the burial mass tomorrow morning, the feast of the Epiphany. Go home to your respective residences, all of you. Nothing further can or will be decided tonight."

Archbishop Stigand left the hall to gather together the King's council, and almost immediately, private conversations broke out once again.

Father Joseph had been too engrossed to pay Celia any mind, but now that the show was over, he noticed her detachment. Close to her ear, he slapped shut his prayer book to break her trance. "Hello? I must make way and send out this information to Duke William as quickly as possible." Celia did a double take as if seeing Father Joseph for the first time. Her face conveyed no feeling. "Did you hear me? Have you listened to anything at all?" He traced the line of her vision until it found the object of her interest. "What?" He grabbed her wrist. "Who is that?"

Celia shook away his hand and left him behind, starting to gently maneuver her way through the crowd. Her body bounced off others', and at times, she was nearly spun about, but she kept her head steady and her eyes fixed on the man who represented home. When she was close enough, she extended her trembling hand to touch his shoulder, but before she could make contact, it was as if he magically felt the pull of her desire. He turned around. At first, he was confused by the figure in the long, black gown with the veil pulled tightly over her hair. Who was this nun who seemed compelled to speak with him?

With stumbling words, he murmured, "Yes, Sister?" giving her a casual glance. But then he paused to look more deeply. He studied her face. The deep blue eyes like limpid pools. The delicate little nose. The lips of raspberry. The glistening smile that dazzled him at the moment he truly started to "see" her. Waves of emotion rushed over him. He felt a rippling sensation of unadulterated joy coursing throughout his body.

The words came out softly. "Celia?" He squeezed her shoulders in ecstasy, but then pulled back his hands as if scorched by fire. He recoiled at the habit and veil and begged forgiveness. "I am sorry to have done that. You have taken vows? I should not have touched you so. Why did you not wait for me, Celia? Oh, why did you give up on me? Again, I am too late." His heart began to splinter, taking with it his powerful and commanding presence. His inner resolve shriveled in size, and he became as vulnerable as an unprotected child.

Celia was just about to correct him, to shout out loud that she was free—free to love him, free to be his. The garment was a facade, her passion for him and for life itself still burned within. She would be his and only his forever. The confession was readied on her tongue, but as she prepared to make this declaration, Margaret materialized right beside her.

"Is everything all right, Celia?" Margaret waved her head back and forth between her friend and the stranger, wondering what palpable connection joined them. "Do you two know each other?"

Simon opened his mouth to answer the sweet and gentle nun, but Celia cut him off by speaking first. "Yes, yes, of course. We know each other from back home. But you know, that was a long time ago." She forced herself to shift her gaze. Instead of looking at his face with longing, she stared at the ground with resignation. Recalling a conversation she had shared with Margaret some time ago, she used Margaret's own words. "It was the timing of it all. My mother and father had died, and my brother had just left home. Simon was a good friend to me during those days of despair."

It hurt her to lie about this next part, and she prayed that she would be able to explain herself later to Simon when the two of them were alone. "But those days have passed. My place is now with you at Wilton." With her eyes still downcast, she smiled in capitulation. When Margaret turned aside, Celia lifted her head ever so slightly to beg Simon for his understanding. Her words said one thing, but she hoped her eyes would convey another. He had not lost her. He was not too late. It did matter that he had come back. It changed everything for her, for both of them.

She wished he would look at her, but he did not. He just stared at his scarred hands, disconnecting from her and returning to the harsh truth of his existence. He was meant to be alone. Loss cast a shadow upon his face as his shoulders lowered in defeat. If only he would look up! She could send him some signal, some hint that there was more that she needed to say and that what she would say would be good.

But no further communication ensued. Unaware of the unspoken words between the two, Margaret innocently put an end to the conversation by gently taking hold of Celia's elbow and leading her away, back to their rightful place in the world.

It cannot end this way, thought Celia. She stole one last glance over her shoulder. At that very moment, Simon raised his head as if to brace himself for a desolate future. Fortunately, his eyes met hers. Her heart fluttered. She winked at him with promise. He raised his eyebrows in confusion. Her sly grin left him with a measure of hope, a hint that perhaps all was not lost.

Margaret meanwhile was buried in her own thoughts, empathizing with her friend's plight. Margaret knew too well what it was like to walk away from a man one could love. If Celia's feelings for this stranger were as strong as hers once were for Malcolm, tonight would be a sleepless one, regardless of the day's earlier problems involving politics and power. For women like them, heartache had little to do with thrones and crowns. Unfulfilled love was to blame.

*   *   *   *   *

Under the hush of darkness, Celia slowly pushed aside the blanket and reached beside the pillow for her veil and under the bed for her cloak. To make for a quicker exit, she had slept fully dressed and kept her outer coverings resting now in the crook of her arm until she was safely out of the common room and at the upper staircase. With the help of a scullery maid, she had been able to get a message to Simon asking him to meet her after midnight on the wall walk. The hour had come.

She affixed the veil to her head as she walked briskly from her room to the end of the corridor. Once there, the stairs leading upward were thick and steep. She had to take care not to trip, lifting her feet high enough to meet the step without getting entangled in the cloak she was trying to put on. From the partially opened door at the top, a draught streamed down the narrow enclosure, blowing back her veil and sending a tingling chill upon her face. There were no wall sconces, and she carried no light—the wind would have extinguished them anyway—so she placed her hands on either side of the stone wall for balance. Nearing the top, she passed a pile of stones and two quivers full of arrows that could be showered down upon would-be attackers below.

Simon had arrived before her, and when he heard the sound of her approach, he met her at the door. Extending his hands from above, he reached out for her as she came to the top step. She felt his powerful grip envelop her cold, brittle fingers and immediately found comfort in their rough warmth.

Without speaking, he led her forward along the elevated platform that was edged on each side by walls of gray. Points of silver light dotted the sky above, their glow illuminating the way past the openings in the stone where sentries would keep watch. Holding her hand and walking toward the end where the corners connected, Simon then stopped and sat down against the ledge, lowering himself to her level.

His brown eyes traveled back and forth across her face while he searched for meaning. "Tell me your summons tonight was not intended to be a final farewell?" He had not relinquished his hold on her hand, and now he sought the other. She met him willingly and pulled on his arms to draw him in closer.

Her answer fell upon his lips when she kissed him deeply. She felt the coldness of his skin upon her face and drank deep beyond the chill into the power and virility that smoldered beneath its surface. While their lips remained together, she guided his arms about her waist and onto the lower part of her back so that their bodies would touch. Once anchored there, she moved her hands to his face, caressing him gently as she pulled away softly. Like blue crystals, her eyes sparkled and rested upon him with contentment. "Not a farewell, Simon, but a beginning. I cannot bear to be without you." She lowered her head again to seal her words with intention, savoring the taste and smell of the soldier who had come back from the world of the dead.

When she drew back a second time, his eyes were still closed as if he were dreaming and afraid to have the vision dissolve. But open them he did and spoke hesitantly. "A beginning for us? Would you still have me . . . even after this?" His eyes gestured to her clothing and veil, his hands shifted to join hers which still rested upon his face.

Demurely, she dropped her gaze so that all he could see were her long lashes fluttering in the starlight. Her voice cracked with emotion. "I thought you were dead, Simon. Philippe came to Rouen and told me so. Without you, my thoughts turned so dark. I could not see any way out of my misery. I was forced to take on this role of informer. To spy on Edgar's sister and prevent her from making an alliance that would strengthen Edgar's claim to the throne." Here, she motioned to her clerical garments. "I had to. I had to do this in order to keep my sister alive. I have no true vocation. I care nothing for the abbey and have no use for such an existence. My one and only sacred vow is to protect Vivienne. Any prayers I utter are only with her safety in mind."

"*Mon tresor*," he brushed his thumb beneath her lashes to trace the contours of her face. "Then let me give you good news. I was in Caen before sailing here, and the little one thrives. She is with Rowena and speaks of you as if you are separated only by a night's slumber. There is still a lightness in her step and a smile in her heart. Remember, that to a child, time is fluid. When you rejoin her, she will behave as if you had missed but one sunrise together."

His thick fingers turned gentle as he removed her veil and let it flutter to the ground. Delicately, he lifted her long hair from in front of her shoulder so that it rested behind her neck. Then he cupped the base of her head and kissed her more passionately. He felt himself grow in desire as his tongue sought hers, pulling her tighter against his body. When he sensed her surrender, his earlier tenderness melted away as he began to drown beneath the waves of unrestrained longing.

Celia too felt this surge of passion but pulled away from him in guilt—not because of her unbridled desire but because she knew he was in love with a woman who no longer existed. She stared upon the ground, shaking her head back and forth. "But, Simon, I have done so many things you have no knowledge of. Things I am ashamed of. You could not possibly want me if you knew the whole of it. You still think I am an innocent maiden wronged by the world, but I have committed offenses of my own. I have lied, I have enacted vengeance, I have killed and been glad doing it. I am not the same girl you taught by the riverside all those years ago."

Placing his hand beneath her chin, he forced her to look up at him. "Then I suppose that puts us on even ground, does it not? For I am no angel either. And never was. I will not frighten you of the details of my recent past. Just accept that although we are not fit right now for heaven, neither are we devils. Our sole crime is wanting to survive, and should we feel guilty for wanting to live? We may have been forced to do things that are best cloaked in darkness, but the sun does shine in the morn, and we are blessed to be among those who get to witness another day. Say a private prayer of penance and be done with it. The Lord can see the goodness in our hearts even if we ourselves cannot."

He spun her about in his arms so that he could rest her back against his chest. They stood together in the stillness of the night with only the yearning of their hearts breaking the silence. Gathering up her hair into his hands, he breathed in the scent of her. Upon her bare neck, he brushed his lips, forming gentle kisses as he went. She opened herself more freely to him by tilting her head sideways to gaze up at the sky.

"After tonight's proclamation," she spoke softly, her words tinged with hope, "my mission here should be over. The Duke will have no further need to monitor Edgar or his family since, most likely, Harold shall be named King." She studied the points of light above, mesmerized by a single star that stood out from all the rest. It flashed and flickered making the others look dull. "I only know that I cannot continue to play this role any longer."

He held fast to her, her back pressed up against him while he traced the path from her neck along her shoulder. "You may not have to pretend anymore. Things are moving quickly, more quickly than anyone had even imagined. Alliances are forming as we speak. If Harold's memory should fail him, my companions and I are here to remind him of the oath he pledged to the Duke. Because of that pledge, the Earl has as much right to the crown as I. If, on the morrow, Harold should make the mistake of accepting the kingship, I fear he will pay a heavy price for his treachery, a price exacted not just upon himself but upon all of his people."

He wrapped his arms around her and held her even more tightly. "I promise you, Celia, I will secure Vivienne's safety when I return to Normandy to deliver news of King Edward's successor. You will be free then to make whatever decisions you wish without worrying about putting her life in jeopardy. You can walk away from this charade because I will come back for you either way—in peace if William is given his rightful title of King or in war if Harold betrays the Duke and steals the crown for himself. Either way, I promise I will bring you home."

He pulled upon her shoulders to summon her to turn back and face him. Her half-hearted smile conveyed doubt. "You do not believe me, Celia, do you? But you must have faith. I have endured more suffering and overcome more challenges than most men face in ten lifetimes. What I hope to do now are but simple tasks to perform: secure Vivienne's safety and get you back to her." He lifted his eyes to study the starlit sky, placing his hand against the back of her head so that her cheek rested against his chest. "We may be apart, but the stars unite us. Whether I be at sea, on Norman soil, or on some battlefield in this country, it will take but a moment for you to feel the bond between our hearts. Just raise your eyes to the heavens and think of me doing the same. And despite the distance that separates us physically, we shall bridge that gap with shared thoughts of love."

When he went to kiss the top of her head to seal his promise, a shout from the doorway startled them both. "Unhand her, you filthy Norman swine!"

Bounding toward them was one of Harold's huscarls, helmeted and brandishing a spear as he ran. Rapidly closing the distance between them, he yelled again at Simon, gesturing to the veil that lay discarded on the ground. "How dare you defile an innocent maiden, a virgin betrothed to the Lord, no less!" Inspired by his own righteousness, the warrior spit out his words with fury.

Simon pushed Celia in the opposite direction from the guard. "Go! Head that way! Hurry! Turn the corner and take the other staircase! Now!" His brown eyes flashed and then narrowed as he prepared for the confrontation.

Celia started to follow Simon's command but stopped when she heard the scuffle behind her. How could she leave him? Simon had no shield, no weapon, only his bare hands while the guard was fully armed. She stopped running to watch. The spear the man wielded rendered Simon's fists useless, the gap between them too large for Simon to strike a blow. Simon kicked out his left leg as a distraction, while lunging with his left hand for the spear. Grabbing hold of the shaft directly below the blade, Simon pulled his attacker closer to him and kicked him in the gut.

The soldier winced in pain, bending down at his waist, but the strike was not enough to overcome him. He never dropped the weapon. Instead, his determination doubled.

Celia looked frantically about her for some way to tip the balance in Simon's favor.

The soldier struck back with unchecked desperation, wresting the spear from Simon's grip. In a sudden maneuver, he twisted the blade upward to slash the skin of Simon's throat right beneath his chin.

Blood gushed freely from the sliced wound. Celia's hands went to her own throat in horror.

In the moment it took for Simon to reach his hand up to stanch the blood, the soldier turned the spear sideways and pushed down upon him until Simon's back lay across the aperture in the rock. With the shaft pressing down further upon Simon's throat, the Saxon seethed with contempt. "We will soon be rid of the lot of you—all of you Normans—in the days and weeks to come. Let you be the first to lead the way to hell."

Celia saw Simon struggling for breath, reaching with one arm to try and lift the spear from his neck while the other fought hard to anchor himself to the wall. Watching the futility of his efforts made her feel like a cornered animal. Unknowingly, she emitted a low growl before springing into action. Darting past the two figures locked in a fatal embrace, she returned to the doorway to find the stored weaponry. Seizing three arrows, she sprinted back to the spot, positioning one barb in her right hand. Sneaking up on the soldier from behind, she raised the arrow by her head and plunged it into the side of his neck. Instantly, the guard let go of the spear and sent both of his hands to tug at the embedded dart.

Despite his frenzy, the arrow would not budge. He soon fell backwards onto the ground, his eyes rolling white before breathing his last. Stunned, Celia dropped the other two weapons. They rattled when they fell upon the cold stone.

A gurgling sound like water jolted her from shock over what she had done. The noise was coming from Simon. She put aside thoughts of the dead soldier and turned to her lover. "Oh, Simon, no! Simon! You must not die. You must not leave me!" Her hands clung to the edges of his coat whose collar was now stained red.

His eyes registered life, but his body remained motionless, save for the one hand fastened to his throat. Lodged between the edges of the stone wall, he lay there suspended. Celia kept hold of his clothing as she went to her knees, pulling him away from the edge and down to the floor with her. She was too afraid to examine his wound for fear it was fatal. When she eventually found the courage to cast her eyes upon it, she felt a small sense of relief once she noticed that the flow of blood had stopped.

Gingerly, he reached out for her with his other hand and brought her arm closer to him. They remained silently connected for a few moments until she whispered. "Speak to me, *mon amour*. Tell me you will recover, tell me this is not the end."

He nestled in closer to her. "I will, the wound is not deep." He moved away the hand that had been clutching his neck and saw that there were no new stains of fresh blood upon it. "The gash will heal, but my heart will not if you are kept away from me. I must go into hiding and then hasten my departure for Normandy. But I shall be back." He brought her closer to rest upon his chest once more and breathed in her scent, letting it serve as a remedy for his pain. He spoke to her softly to seal their dream. "I am there for you. Always. Find the brightest, most steadfast light in the night sky. And know that I am with you."

Not wanting to look up to the heavens for fear that the earlier star had faded, she buried her face into him with an intensity she hoped would make his pledge come true.

*   *   *   *   *

Celia was still trembling when she dipped her hands into the water trough outside the stables. Little ripples skirted through the water, carrying with them clots of red until they broke apart and dissolved into threads of pink. What had she done? She must not allow her mind to go there. Like a shutter on a window, she closed down those thoughts and dwelt instead on the fact that she had saved Simon from sure death. Faced with no choice, she did what she had to do in order

407

to rescue him. How could she be wrong for that? Despite her supposed resolve in believing this to be so, she was still so jittery that when there was a rustling behind her, she gasped and spun about guiltily.

It was the stunning woman from earlier that evening, accompanied by a man and two female servants. Her hood of dark velvet covered her hair, making her alabaster skin glow with a beauty that matched the starlight above.

"You!" she stepped closer to Celia so that their heads nearly touched. "Are you not the one who was with Margaret tonight?"

Celia kept her hands behind her back, only nodding in response. It was clear to see that Ealdgyth's bearing was that of a queen, regardless of the status of her husband. Her chin raised slightly, her shoulders were pulled back in a position of authority. With the slightest glance at the water trough where a pink thread of liquid still swirled, she took note of Celia's hidden hands. "I suppose every woman has her secrets, hmm?" Ealdgyth's eyes travelled across Celia's face, evaluating whether or not the girl could be trusted. The quiet lasted a few moments before the woman leaned in closer and whispered, "Well, you tell Margaret that in light of tomorrow's announcement, she and her family can find sanctuary with me if need be. One kindness deserves another."

By this time, Ealdgyth's group had already reached the front of the stable, and the man motioned with his hand for her to hurry. Ealdgyth's eyelashes fluttered at his command, realizing that she must be on her way. She grabbed Celia's shoulders and squeezed them with intensity. "I have to go. You tell her what I said. Laughton. South Yorkshire. She can find me there." Having delivered her message, Ealdgyth quickened her pace to catch up with her traveling companions. Celia was left with even more thoughts to muddle her already tortured mind.

Would Margaret and her family need to take to the road after tomorrow's declaration? If Harold was named King, would they all be in danger, or would he allow them to remain at court? What need would he have of them though? Unlike King Edward who was bonded to Margaret's family by blood, Harold owed them nothing, except for the suspicion that one day Edgar would likely contend for Harold's crown. Such questions about the future needled her like the cold that pricked her exposed skin.

Oh, why should she even care about Margaret or the girl's family? Her job with them would be over once Harold was named King. Was this not the best outcome for Celia herself? Duke William could then focus on Harold and the Godwinson clan and toss the rest of them— Margaret and Malcolm and Edgar—aside. Indeed, the morning's announcement could mean liberation for her if things played out in that way. And what would she do with herself in the interim—the time between the announcement and Simon's return? She would have to remain by Margaret's side, no doubt, so that Simon could find her.

To be honest, Margaret and her plight had touched Celia, though she did not want to admit it. The guileless novice possessed more strength than Celia had imagined. In many ways, they were more alike than different, fighting against restrictions placed upon them both.

Through it all, her mind kept coming back to Simon. In him, she found someone and something she could trust. He would ensure Vivienne's safety and come back to England for her. Whether he would come in celebration or in battle depended on tomorrow. Either way, as he had told her, he would return.

*   *   *   *   *

A throng of people amassed outside the abbey at Westminster. This was the closest they could get to the double ceremony about to take place that day. An ending and a beginning. The burial of one king and the coronation of another. Servants and tradesmen, London families and out of towners—all were assembled to witness the changes in the air that mixed with the pungent smell of skewered sausage hawked by street vendors outside the church looking to turn a profit.

Inside, Margaret, her mother, her sister, and Celia sat five pews from the front while Edgar found himself squeezed between Father Thurstan and Father Joseph in the second, directly behind the Godwinson brothers, Leofwine, Gyrth, and Harold. At the altar, Bishop Ealdred awaited the arrival of the former king.

With crisp, clear voices, the boys' choir lifted the congregation toward heaven as they chanted the words of Psalm 27, *"Dominus illuminatio mea et salus mea; quem timebo?"* Celia's heart rose with each note they sang, and when her nose began to tingle from the sweet smell of incense, she breathed in and surrendered to its aroma. Such pageantry was all new to her, her hometown village far removed from ceremonial displays as this. Three young acolytes processed up the aisle, each clinking his censor and leaving a thin trace of smoke behind him as he walked. Celia craned her neck to the side so that she could get a glimpse of King Edward's bier carried by four priests she did not recognize. The King's body was cloaked in purple—the color of royalty—his face as pale and colorless as it was in life.

Nearing the altar, the four priests came to a halt right before the steps and began lowering the casket into the deep hole that laborers had dug feverishly the night before. Using ropes fastened at each of the four corners, they settled the coffin into its final resting place and timed its completion with the final words of the Psalm. Ealdred, the Bishop of York, stood on the raised platform of the altar. As the official celebrant of the service, he was in full command, revealing the proper time for his audience to sit, kneel, or stand. At the conclusion of the ceremony, Celia watched with curiosity as the stone lid was returned and the flagstones put back into place. Absent of any deep feeling, Celia was rather surprised to see that was not the case for Margaret. True, the old King had been kind to Margaret and her family, and there was some history between them, but surely, the man seemed too quirky and too aloof to foster such deep feelings.

After watching a few tears make their way down Margaret's cheeks, Celia whispered, "What troubles you, Sister?" She clutched Margaret's elbow with concern.

Margaret's green eyes gazed at some far away vista, her voice rather faint as she spoke distractedly, "Alas, he never saw his vision for this abbey come true . . ."

Celia thought it strange that this—and not what was going to take place next in the church—was what disturbed Margaret most, for earlier that morning, Father Joseph told Celia of the Witan's decision. With the rising of the sun, they had declared Harold Godwinson the new King of England, relegating Edgar and Margaret's family to the shadows. Celia could see that such haste regarding the coronation bespoke of the country's tenuous situation. Clearly, there was danger all around, coming from every direction. And yet, this simple girl beside her gave little thought to such threats. All Margaret could cry about was the sentimental vision of a dead king and not the sinister plans of the next. The girl needed to get her head out of the clouds.

*   *   *   *   *

The somber mood of the funeral then shifted to one of smoldering excitement as the congregation began to chatter quietly about the coronation. Their enthusiasm was tempered by fear when Harold's huscarls burst through the church doors and proceeded to forcefully usher out anyone of Norman descent who had been foolish enough to linger after the funeral earlier that morning. Throughout the night, the wiser ones—to protect their fortunes and their lives—had made their way to the coast to board ships and sail for home. The shift in

411

sentiment affected Celia as she felt suspicious eyes turn toward her. She marveled at how casual Father Joseph seemed to appear and wondered how he could remain so detached from the hostility that swirled around them. Sensing Celia's apprehension, Margaret reached for her hand, interlacing her fingers with Celia's to form a unified bond.

As bodies were jostled and pulled from the pews, even the people who remained felt disturbed by the raw cold wind that rushed in through the opened doors. When the last foreigner was thrust outside and the ice upon the church steps crackled for a final time with that person's expulsion, the massive portal was shut and a new noise arose. A lusty shout of "*Vivat Rex*" from two warriors stationed at the back shut one chapter of history and welcomed another.

Celia's palm grew moist, but she refused to break contact with her Saxon friend. They needed each other for different reasons. She appreciated Margaret's protection and offered sympathy to her as repayment. Although Celia was unaware of the depth of Margaret's interaction with Harold, she knew it involved something dreadful, something that made Margaret quake with either fear or rage. Celia was not sure which emotion dominated Margaret more. Panic over what Harold could do to her, or anger over what he had already done? Perhaps it had something to do with the loss of her father all those years ago? Whatever the case, Celia saw Margaret's chin drop to her chest, her eyes close with apprehension. She watched the girl's lips move in silent prayer while Bishop Ealdred, from the front of the altar, delivered his petitions out loud.

Psalms were recited, hymns were sung, and Harold was called from his seat to come forward. His long, wavy hair fell to his shoulders. Parted down the center, it had been combed vigorously until its auburn color shone bright under the candlelight. His blue tunic was fresh and clean. His thick, muscular arms hung rigid on either side of his body. Facing the audience, he remained expressionless, his dark eyes focused at a point above everyone's head. A steely determination, absent of any sense of joy or triumph, was his unspoken proclamation. At the Bishop's request, he turned his back to the congregation and assumed a kneeling position, raising his head to face the prelate.

With his thumb, the Bishop swept his finger across the brow of the new king of England, anointing him with oil of chrism. The four priests who had earlier served to carry and inter King Edward's body now provided Ealdred with the symbols of earthly power the bishop would bestow upon Harold: crown, ring, sword, and scepter. When the crown was placed upon Harold's head, the new monarch rose to accept the other items. Once in possession of these emblems of power, Harold Godwinson turned to face his people. Resounding applause and continued shouts of *"Vivat Rex"* accompanied him as he walked down the aisle followed by the Bishop, priests, acolytes, and his two brothers. When the guards opened the doors to the outside world and to Harold's kingdom, the freezing rain did nothing to dampen the spirits of his subjects. They cheered him on, calling out his name and waving their arms in support of the man who would lead and protect them from harm.

Throughout the coronation, the two young women had not broken their shared clasp. It was fitting that they did not do so even after the ceremony, for neither felt the need to applaud or celebrate what was about to come.

THE CONVENT AT WILTON

SPRING 1066

How many nights have you seen this?" Margaret gazed up at the night sky in wonder.

Father Goscelin was seated on a stone bench in the cloister of Wilton with Margaret on one side and Celia on the other. With his head tilted upward, he spoke sparingly. "Three nights in a row, I daresay. Yes, three, that is right." After a few moments, he dropped his head to his chest to release the strain in his neck. "I was unsure if it were just a random occurrence, but when it came back a second and third time, I felt I had to give you both the chance to witness it too."

Winter still clung to the earth even though Easter had been celebrated two days prior. Celia wrapped her cloak more tightly around her body and shook her dangling feet back and forth to generate warmth. "What should we be looking for?"

"Trust me, you will not have to look for anything, really. It will find us, I am certain." Goscelin sat quietly with his hands in his lap, looking perfectly content doing nothing.

"What does it mean though?" Margaret hoped to attach some kind of significance to this special event.

"Does it have to mean anything? Can it not just be a display of the Lord's power? An experience in humility for us all?" Goscelin answered without taking his eyes from the sky.

"Well," Margaret pondered his words and proceeded politely, "Did not the star of Bethlehem point to something deeper? It too was a display of God's power and the beauty of His creation, but it meant something beyond that, of course."

"Portents, auguries, omens—one must be careful not to shift too far into pagan superstitions. But, yes, we all know you are right about the deeper meaning of the Bethlehem star. There has been no greater event than the coming of Christ into the world."

Just then, Celia gasped and pulled on Goscelin's arm. "Look! I see it! It is coming closer. Look over there, by the east wall of the convent. See the ball of fire?"

"Oh, my! I never saw a round star before!" Margaret pointed to the heavens. "Wait! There is more. It has tendrils coming off it!"

"Like fiery strands of hair!" Celia chimed in. The young girls sat in awe as the star traveled slowly across the sky above the open courtyard. Silence ensued as all three were captivated by the awesome display. It took several minutes for the star to move beyond their line of vision, and even after its disappearance, none of them felt right about breaking the enchantment by speaking.

In the stillness, each offered a quiet prayer of thanksgiving for its beauty as well as a petition for deliverance from possible ill-will. Despite the cold, they were warmed by the shared experience that linked them together. Their reverie was interrupted though when the door to the courtyard creaked open and through it walked Father Joseph, his hands swinging by his sides with unspoken cheerfulness.

"I was told I could find you here." He motioned to Celia, but Margaret answered him first.

"Father, we have just witnessed the most amazing sight! Did you see it yourself? A star that streaked across the sky leaving a trail of dust as it went, just as a swan sends forth a spray of water when it lands upon a lake." She moved her hand through the space in front of her as if recreating the magical streak.

Father Joseph looked skyward, shaking his head in disappointment. "Tsk, tsk. I am afraid I missed the celestial performance. The only strange thing I noticed tonight was the uncommon silence. No night birds came to serenade me during evening prayer as they most often do."

"Perhaps they were too stricken with awe and found no voice to match such majesty." Margaret spoke wistfully, grateful to have witnessed the show but yearning for a repeat performance.

Since the star's appearance, Celia's thoughts had immediately reverted back to her last conversation with Simon. Was he looking up at the night sky as well? Was this heavenly orb linking them together across the miles of sea and land that separated them? Did he wish upon it as she had just done? Would he—

She felt an urgent tap on her shoulder. "Sister Celia, Father Joseph is speaking to you. Did you hear what he said?" Goscelin's voice and touch brought her back to the cloister.

"Hmm? I am sorry. What did you say, Father?"

With fawning kindness, Father Joseph repeated himself again. "I said, the birds may not have spoken tonight, but these words did. This letter was brought to me—to us—a short time ago from Bishop William's messenger." He handed her the scrolled parchment, its seal already broken.

Margaret rose from her seat to stand beside Celia. "Who is it from?"

Despite the starlight, the evening was too dark for Celia to decipher the words. When her eyes narrowed further and still she had no luck, Father Joseph supplied Margaret with an answer. "It is from Duchess Matilda. She has summoned us home. We are to make our way to the southern coast to a town called Bexelei where we are to secure the services of Fristhan, a ship master. The Duchess has made the necessary arrangements for us to return to Normandy. Our work—eh, our study—here is done."

Celia's eyes opened wide with elation as she clutched the letter tightly to her chest, promising herself that she would read and commit to memory every word of it. Her work was done. The nightmare was over. Her smile widened at the thought of hugging Vivienne, of spending time with Rowena, and of beginning life all over again with Simon by her side.

"Oh, Celia, I am so happy for you!" Margaret locked her arms around Celia who was still seated on the bench incredulous over this sudden turn of events. "I know this has been your deepest wish—to return home—and I am overjoyed that your wish has come true!" Margaret turned to Goscelin. "Maybe there is something to that star after all!" She turned her head toward him, her eyes sparkling with hope.

"Ha, ha. Could be mere coincidence or could be a sign of good things ahead. I am certain in your case," he looked at Celia and Father Joseph, "you must both feel it to be the latter."

Goscelin stood and shook out his cassock so that its folds fell straight. "I must go write letters of introduction for you so that you can make your way southward. Judging from your excitement, I am assuming you will want to begin your journey at sunrise? There are abbeys along the way that will shelter you until you reach St. Stephen's Priory in Bexelei. From there, you should be able to find your vessel and sail for home."

As he turned to make his way back into the abbey, Margaret followed him out. "Wait, Father. Remember how they helped me and Cristina return to Westminster this past winter? May I do the same for them and see them off? Celia has been a dear, dear friend to me, and I could not bear to part from her without having an extended farewell such as this trip would offer."

Goscelin looked sternly at her. "It is not a very safe time to travel unnecessarily. How would you make your way back to us? A woman on the road without escort? No, it is simply not possible. You will have to say your goodbyes here at Wilton." Once again, he turned to go.

Margaret would not give up. "Wait! What if I stay in Bexelei and continue my studies there? Maybe it would be best for me to be farther away from the trouble that is brewing between King Harold and his brother Tostig who was once a close friend to my family. People know of our bond with him, and they may fear that my brother is helping Tostig regain his earldom in Northumbria. You could even write to Edgar and have him join me there. Then it will become clear to everyone that neither of us have any designs on the English crown or in stirring up a civil war on our own behalf."

For the slightest moment, Goscelin paused, infusing Margaret with hope. "Let me think on this, Margaret." He folded his arms into the sleeves of his cloak and rested them upon his chest. "Your safety is my utmost concern. Removing you from this region which is so close to all this dangerous political intrigue, well, that idea is not entirely unpalatable. Let me pray on this." He strode away, his shoulders hunched and head bowed as if already in deep contemplation.

Returning to Celia, Margaret bent down on one knee and kissed the hand that still clutched the letter. "And I shall pray for this too." Then she scurried away to the sanctity of the chapel where she could make her petition to the Lord.

"Well," said Father Joseph amusedly, "I suppose we shall see in the morning, whether there are three of us on this journey or two. I must go gather my things together. Are you coming inside?" He looked over his shoulder at her as he had already started to walk away.

"No, not yet." Celia wanted to express her joy outwardly, but she refused to share any of herself with this serpent whose mere presence had poisoned her life. Matilda was wrong. She herself was not the viper, Father Joseph was.

Without turning back, he mumbled, "As you wish."

Under the blue velvet sky speckled with tiny dots of light, Celia felt her own spirit resurrecting itself from beneath the smothering role she had been forced to play. Once she set foot upon that vessel, she would shed the pretense of these past years and be herself again. Like the heavenly body she observed just a few moments ago, she would launch herself toward a brilliant tomorrow, enveloping those she loved in her fire.

ST. STEPHEN'S PRIORY

SPRING 1066

It turned out to be a party of three.

With one horse among them, the trio moved at a slow but steady pace during the five day journey. Margaret and Celia walked contentedly side by side, while Father Joseph, his mount laden with their belongings and provisions, led the way. St. Stephen's lay just a short distance from the southern coast, nestled between Pevensey Bay and the village of Hastings. The Benedictine priory stood with quiet dignity upon the open meadow, sitting proudly atop the rolling hills of green. Its idyllic setting combined the sweetness of the earth with the beauty of the neighboring sea.

Adhering to their founder's philosophy, "Let all guests who arrive be received in Christ," the monks welcomed Father Joseph, and the nuns who lived in the adjoining convent readily accepted Celia and Margaret into their ever-growing population of novices. Like the clove pink blossoms that waved joyously and scented the air with cinnamon and nutmeg, the residents of Bexelei embraced the three travelers without reservation.

The priory itself was well endowed by both its patrons and nature herself. The rich soil of its land allowed for an enormous garden, replete with abundant vegetables and herbs. Its plentiful supply of goats and cattle provided a constant source of trade, and its proximity to the sea blessed them with food year-round, whether served fresh from spring through autumn, or smoked and stored away for winter.

Not long after their arrival, Father Joseph and Celia visited the wharf to locate Fristhan and arrange for their transport to Normandy. Now the day of their leave-taking had come; they were to report to the vessel just before midday when tide, wind, and current would be most favorable. With only a handful of hours remaining, Celia and Margaret busied themselves in the quaint wooden chapel where beams of sunlight bore through the triple arched glass window above the altar. Margaret was busy pulling off the used altar cloths and replacing them with new ones; Celia tended to the removal of the hardened tallow that had formed beneath the candle holders.

"I suppose it is a blessing to have something to occupy your thoughts while awaiting the hour of your departure, hmm?" Margaret, on her knees in front of the basket that contained the soiled cloths, looked over her shoulder at Celia for confirmation. The small space where they worked continued to warm and brighten with the deepening rays of sun.

"Yes, it all seems too good to be true. I am afraid to become too joyful." Celia continued to chisel away at the leftover gobs of tallow. "The smooth journey here, the ease of finding the ship master, the cooperation of the weather—and even beyond all of those things—the incredibly good fortune to be the last passengers Fristhan will be taking across the sea to the continent. He told us this would be the final trip he would be making for quite some time."

Margaret interrupted, "What is that you said? Why is this his last trip?"

"King Harold is no longer allowing trade vessels to barter with the enemy. All boats have been requisitioned to be on the lookout for an invasion by Duke William. Even the fishing boats have been restricted to a prescribed distance from shore. Within a fortnight, everything will be shut down and only spy work permitted. That is why I find it so hard to believe that I will soon be standing on the soil of my homeland. There is much that could go wrong between now and then."

Margaret paused what she was doing. "I once dreamed of that too —of going home, back home to Reyka." She shook her head as if to erase the thought. "I am so very glad that your dream is about to come true." She laid the clean linen upon the altar and began straightening out its edges. "And when you get back, what will you do? Will you go directly to the convent at Caen?" She returned the fabric that needed washing to the basket and knelt down again upon the ground.

Celia wished she could answer honestly and tell Margaret that she would be going to the palace and not the abbey. She wanted to tell her that she was going to reunite with her sister and Rowena and begin planning a fresh start for them all, together with Simon on his newly bestowed property. But this was not the time for true confessions, not yet. Perhaps someday she could send Margaret a letter explaining it all. She had come to appreciate and enjoy the company of this Saxon girl whom she had once thought pathetic and weak. But there would be a later time for that. Not now. She must maintain this pretense for just a few hours more. Nothing must get in the way of her departure.

"Well, yes. First, I will report to Duchess Matilda. I will share with her all that I have learned from Father Goscelin and from you too, Margaret. Then the Duchess will assign me to my next position."

Still on the ground, Margaret spun around to face Celia. She tucked her feet beneath her and sat upon her heels. "What could you have possibly learned from me? Most times, I am not even aware of what I am doing myself, so how could I ever teach anyone anything?"

Celia did not trust herself to turn around. It was safer to admit these truths without looking directly at Margaret. She could speak with honesty as long as she kept her face hidden. The false face she had been forced to wear throughout their time together would never deliver a message as sincere as the one she was about to say.

"You have taught me more than you will ever know, Margaret. You have shown me what true strength looks like. It does not need to hold a scepter. It does not need to brandish a sword. It can assume the vulnerable form of an innocent girl when that girl is anchored by faith. A foundation of iron is inside you, Margaret. A foundation that will never crumble or be destroyed. In spite of all that we have been through, Margaret, you are still pure of heart and genuine in spirit. You believe in virtue and always look for the goodness in everyone you meet. You see what is best in all of us, especially those of us who are flawed—like me. You have made me believe that I can one day match the image you have of me. And that gift I will carry with me forever—even if I never quite reach the level of virtue you think I am capable of reaching."

Celia's voice faltered a bit on her final words, but when she sensed Margaret moving toward her, she quickly changed the subject and began chiseling away more vigorously. "And what of you? What will you do after I am gone? Will you eventually return to Wilton and take final vows?"

When Margaret did not answer right away, Celia stopped what she was doing and listened to the quiet that enveloped them both. Slowly, she turned around and saw Margaret bathed in a shaft of light that made her seem otherworldly. Celia felt drawn to her angelic presence and moved closer to join her on the ground.

Margaret's words came out as a whisper at first. "I believe that is what God is calling me to do, but …. Sometimes my mind gets all jumbled up." She brought one of the cloths up toward her mouth. Celia could see Margaret's fingers pulsing beneath the fabric.

"What is it? Tell me. Your private thoughts are safe with me." Very gently, Celia tugged at the cloth to pull it away from Margaret's face.

"I have heard from King Malcolm again. He says there have been rumors of invasions from both the North and the South. Edgar may get swept up in the whirlwind of such rebellions. Some may look to my brother to be their figurehead, their leader of sorts. Malcolm has promised protection. Protection for Edgar, for me, for my mother and sister. His kingdom is far from here, but he offered to send emissaries to bring us safely to him. And he offered even more than that to me." Her hands twisted and kneaded the altar cloth; her eyes begged for Celia's counsel.

"Oh, Celia. What about that soldier boy of yours? How did you know? How did you know what was the right thing to do? You seem to have found peace in your decision to follow God and devote your life to Him. But how did you make that discernment? How can I silence this turmoil that rages in my heart?"

Dear Lord, thought Celia, *I cannot continue to lie to this girl. I cannot continue to pretend any longer. I may be sentenced to Hell for the treachery I have committed thus far, but let me not compound it with further deceit.*

Celia removed the cloth from Margaret's hand and placed it on the stone floor beneath them. "If there is unrest in your soul, then you have not yet reached a decision. This man, this King, he continues to create ripples in the serenity you believe you can find in the cloister. You have tried to ignore them, deny them, silence them, but still they remain. Right now, his love for you strikes like an agitating pulse on the surface of your daily life, and that disturbance will never entirely disappear. Instead, it will penetrate deeper, causing waves of discontent that will affect your very existence. You need to explore this feeling. Confront it. See if it seizes you with its power and sweeps you away in its current, or if it dissipates and fades away under the force of your conviction. You must go to him. Be in his presence. Only then can you put an end to your turmoil."

Celia inhaled deeply as she prepared to tell Margaret another truth. "As for me, I said that I would await Duchess Matilda's new assignment for me, but I should have added that it must be one I can accomplish wearing the simple clothes of a farmer's wife, not the habit of an abbess. I have made my choice and am content. Find your center of tranquility, Margaret. See him. Or at least write to him. You can serve God just as readily outside the convent as inside. Indeed, you will touch more souls and affect more lives as Queen than you could ever do as a prioress. The question you need to ask yourself is, how can you serve God most purely? What does your heart yearn for?"

With the halo of light still surrounding her, Margaret closed her eyes and nodded her head in agreement. But the conversation had an even greater impact on Celia who, for the first time in a long while, felt there was still some semblance of goodness inside herself. And this goodness she would carry with her on her voyage back home, tending to it, nurturing it, and cultivating it even further throughout the seasons of life to come.

*　*　*　*　*

Celia's eyebrows lifted with concern. Her voice quavered as she told Margaret what she had just discovered. "The Abbot said Father Joseph left already. Said he had some business to tend to before we departed."

"Well, then, let us make haste and get you down to the harbor as quickly as possible!" Margaret linked her arm in Celia's and began to usher her forward when Celia came to a halt.

"You do not think there is anything wrong with that, do you?"

425

"With what? With Father Joseph getting a head start? No, not at all. He probably just had to smooth out the details and arrange for the payment of your passage. Some paperwork, I am sure, that will later be turned over to your Duchess." The two girls walked the gravel path away from the priory until they came to the green meadow. One or two curious cows lifted their heads from the grass to watch them as they bounded over the hills. Most paid them no mind, lounging in the shade, shaking their hides to dislodge a pesky fly or two.

Celia felt her veil lifting off her shoulders from the tickling wind as she and Margaret ran down into the low lying valley that led to the coastline. *Soon I will be rid of this silly thing*, she thought, *and it can fly away completely for all I care.* She considered tossing it into the frothy waves as soon as they were far enough from shore and decided that was exactly what she would do. Then she would resume her normal identity and live freely once again without monitoring every word she spoke and every action she performed. No longer forced to be a false servant of God, she could return to being a true sister to one who was related to her by blood.

The cry of sea birds grew in volume with the ever-increasing speed of their footsteps. They sniffed in the tangy smell of ocean salt, and its taste rested upon their tongues. Margaret giggled to herself, remembering an earlier time when she had frolicked over the hills and bounded down to the seaport—the Flanders seaport—with Gerhard and Edgar when she first embarked upon this strange journey that had become her life. The carefree abandon she had once felt was now evident in Celia. It was pleasing to see her friend's spirits uplifted by the promise of love and happiness. Beneath their racing feet, the grass thinned, and the dark soil turned to pebble and then sand.

They slowed to a walk. "Do you have everything you need?"

"Ha, ha," Celia gestured dismissively to her small rucksack, "I came with little. But I am leaving with much more. I will never forget you, Margaret. Your bravery, your elegance, your purity. I hope someday you will be able to think fondly of me as well." Celia cast her eyes downward, ashamed of the lies she had told throughout their friendship.

"Someday?" She yanked Celia's hands as if to shake some sense into her. "I think fondly of you right now. If I am as pure and honest as you say I am, then I have a confession. I am not as joyful as I am pretending to be. Bidding you farewell is breaking my heart. I am going to miss you, Celia." She sniffled and tried to smile through her sadness. "Whatever will I do without you? My courage came from knowing you were by my side. Ugh. Look at me."

Margaret dropped her hands free from Celia's, wiping her face and chastising herself. "Let us take our shared secrets to the grave and bury the past forever. Let us think only of the future. Write to me when you have settled in. Tell me about your new life and your rekindled love, and I shall do the same—when I figure out those things for myself."

The sand shifted beneath their feet as they embraced, each willing only good things to the other through the intensity of their clasp. When they separated, Celia searched the horizon for the mast of Fristhan's vessel.

On the pier, sailors were tying and unfastening ropes, carrying crates of goods from arriving boats or placing them onto departing ones. Celia started to drift away, moving further down one part of the harbor then back again, growing desperate in her search for Fristhan or his crew. Margaret trailed behind her, following attentively.

"Out of the way, Sister," snarled a laborer when Celia had distractedly blocked his path toward the pier. She skirted off to the side just as another fellow, with fishing nets in hand, came storming up behind the first. Something about the man made Celia pull upon his sleeve.

"Wait. You work for Fristhan, do you not? On board *The Njord*? I saw you with him just a few days ago. Where is he?" Her voice betrayed her panic.

"Who? Fristhan? I will no' be sailing with him today. 'Tis greater wages to scout the seas now. Quick and easy work. Can get a bit of fishing in too whilst we are at it." He winked at her as he started to move away.

"Wait," she became more frantic. "Where *is* Fristhan?"

"He left. Set out early this morning."

He saw the shock and disbelief written upon her face. Sensitive to her anguish, he felt he should offer whatever information he had. "If ye're the nun who was supposed to cross with him, then ye must be the stuff of miracles. The priest told Fristhan ye had the fever and that ye were no' long for this world. But the good Lord must be preservin' ye for something greater since yer still among the livin'."

She continued to stare at him in disbelief.

Her dejection moved him. "I am sorry, Sister. I suppose God's ways are no' always our ways." Shifting his equipment from his hip to the front of his body, he moved down the dock and hoisted everything into the awaiting boat. He looked back once over his shoulder and felt sorry for the girl before he began rearranging the equipment on the vessel.

The pounding of his feet clanged upon her heart, tolling out a sentence of prolonged misery.

*   *   *   *   *

For two full days, Celia lay cocooned in her bedsheet, refusing food and speaking to no one. Being near enough to taste freedom and then to have it wrenched away crushed her spirit into tiny fragments, fragments that floated in disjointed pieces. She could not find a sense of wholeness. In her darkest moments, she even considered choosing a different kind of freedom, an eternal one, but she shied away because a tiny spark of hope still sputtered within the chambers of her heart. Maybe, just maybe, Simon had not forgotten her, and he would come back.

On bended knee before the cross, Margaret grieved for her friend. She prayed to the Lord for Celia's healing, and when that request went unanswered, she prayed to the Virgin Mary for some type of balm she could administer to mend the wounds that pierced Celia's heart. No answer came. The only message she received was to give it time. Be patient and let the hours pass as they will. When Celia was finally ready to heal, she would do so herself. Remain loyal. Be steadfast. Have faith. These directives became the code of conduct Margaret adhered to during the time that her friend was unreachable.

Wise words they were because two days proved to be enough for Celia to be disgusted with herself for wallowing in self-pity. What was to be accomplished by staring at a wall? Helpless like an infant unable to communicate its needs or change its circumstances? Thrusting aside the bed cover, Celia rose from the near dead to rejoin the living. She did not spring back to it with enthusiasm or vitality, but she decided she could certainly plod along and exist.

Unlike the busier schedule the nuns followed at Wilton, the daily chores at St. Stephen's were fewer and the rules more relaxed: morning prayer, tending to the church, breakfast, garden work, midday prayer, instruction for the children, stable work, supper, evening prayer, and bed. Aware of the convent's remoteness, the Prioress felt no fear of sanction or retaliation if her novices strayed somewhat from strict Benedictine rule. Mother Devona was a plump, easy going woman who looked upon her flock with tenderness and love. If they veered from the prescribed schedule every now and then, she did not fret—as long as they were punctual for prayer. And that latter requisite was only meant to protect them from censure by the Abbot who officiated the services and would surely take notice.

Celia took advantage of the gap between evening prayer and bed, treasuring the time as her own. Regardless of the weather, she spent these hours outdoors; the path from the convent to the sea was worn from her footsteps. Once there, she would sit down upon the rocky shore, remove her veil from her head, and stare at the horizon to imagine how her loved ones were faring on the opposite side. What mischief had Vivienne gotten herself into that day? Who were her companions now? Were she and Chloe still friends? Was Rowena still mourning Felix or had she met someone new? Celia created stories in her mind, populating them with those she knew, envisioning different scenarios and adventures they would undertake. At one point each night, she would include herself in their escapades, joining together with them in the fun.

Then her mind would come back to her surroundings—the rippling water kissing the shoreline, the slivered or full moon above, the soft breeze that lifted the loose strands of her hair to brush against her cheeks—and she would remember she was here, and they were there. Clenching the pebbles on either side of her sitting body, she would squeeze them in frustration, and then let them go, dropping them one by one until her hands, like her heart, were empty once more.

LOVE AMIDST THE PAIN

FALL 1066 – WINTER 1068

Spring had warmed to summer and summer had turned to autumn, but Celia took little notice of the changes. She moved from one activity to another, like a shell being shifted by the sea from one location to the next by a force outside itself. The only time of day that was of interest to her were the hours she spent teaching the children and those she spent in solitude by the seashore.

That night she welcomed the early sunset and relied on the sound of the crunching leaves beneath her feet in order to navigate the darkness on her way to the harbor. At the water's edge, she heard the lapping of the waves and sat down, tucking her knees tightly to her chest. Placing her veil on the ground next to her, she rested her chin on the bony points of her knees and gazed into the distant unknown. She knew their return to Wilton was upon them, although she much preferred staying in Bexelei. The truth was, Margaret's brother Edgar could be detained here no longer. He had arrived at St. Stephen's a few days ago, disgruntled and offended that he had been sent here to fetch two women instead of to York to join Harold and the English troops in battle against Tostig and the Norwegians. Edgar had begged to be included in the march north to defend a kingdom that he still viewed as his own. Even though it meant supporting the brother Edgar despised and going against the one he admired, Edgar would do it to preserve the realm he hoped to one day govern. But instead of being included in a critical confrontation with the future of the kingdom in the balance, he was sent on this lame mission. Certainly not the kind of engagement that would earn him memorable verses in a bard's song of heroic deeds.

So despite her wish to stay in this quaint coastal town, Celia knew she had to leave. Simon would associate her location with Margaret's; therefore, she must go wherever the Saxon girl went, follow her to whatever place she visited, for that was the only way Simon would be able to track her. Tilting her chin to the right, Celia continued to look westward out at the water. A small glimmer of starlight flashed at the edge of the horizon, almost as if it had dropped from the heavens to dance upon the liquid surface. An idea crossed her mind which she shut down immediately. *No more wishes, foolish girl,* she thought. But when a second star and then a third and a fourth fell from the sky and sparkled with possibility, she gave in and sent out her wish.

Upon the first, she envisioned herself on a boat. For the second, she held Vivienne's delicate hand in her own, feeling the girl's tiny fingernails prick against the space of her palm. Upon the third, she saw herself sipping wine with Rowena, laughing over stories involving the antics of the children. And on the last star, she felt her body lean in against Simon's chest as he wrapped his arms around her, and the two of them stared into the rippling flames of the hearth.

More stars dropped and illuminated the surface, but she had no further desires. With those four, all of her dreams were fulfilled. She blinked her eyes repeatedly, surprised to see hundreds of lights flashing at her from a distance, each almost equally spaced from the next. And then just as suddenly as they appeared, everything went dark, and once again she was left with the horizon and her loneliness.

Celia continued to sit there in silence, questioning what she had just witnessed. She doubted that those points of light were far-flung stars. They could mean nothing, but they could mean something. She decided she would tell Margaret and Edgar what she had seen, and if the flashing lights pointed to something more significant than falling stars, maybe Edgar would not be so disappointed at being stuck in Bexelei after all.

*   *   *   *   *

"I told you it was west of here. Come!"

Celia urged on Margaret and Edgar as they walked the path from the priory toward Pevensey Bay. They had all skipped breakfast, and the two girls had been excused from garden work, midday prayer, and teaching responsibilities under the guise of sharing the countryside with Edgar one last time before they departed for Wilton in the morning.

"We are not going to see stars in daylight, Celia. This journey is a foolish one." Edgar was irritated over the trail they were following, one that cut through a heavily forested area filled with brambles and overgrown bushes. Every few steps he had to detach a branch that clung to his tunic or tripped up his feet. His agitation grew when the pads of his fingers were pricked by thorns from his attempts at dislodging the stray limbs.

"Oh, stop your fussing, brother. There is no other way to Pevensey than this. The shoreline cuts away at certain points leaving only water. Even if we had a boat, we could not make use of it, for surely then we would be discovered." Margaret, the last of the three in the line, waited for Edgar to discard his most recent leafy assailant and resume his spot in between Celia and herself.

As usual, Celia was not as patient as her friend. The bumbling boy was just that—a useless child. The idea that he believed he should be king was laughable. But then again, most kings were self-centered and ill-tempered, so perhaps Edgar was worthy of the title.

"I told you already it has naught to do with stars any longer. It must be something greater. And you—of all people—should want to know what is happening on the southern coast of your country if one day you hope to protect the entirety of it!" After glaring at him for a moment, she turned her back and continued to create a path through the underbrush. Like the petulant child he still was, Edgar made faces and wiggled his fingers at Celia in silent complaint until he felt Margaret's hands push his back from behind.

In this formation, they walked another hour, Edgar limiting his frustration to exhalations of air rather than words. Then came the faint, far away sound of braying horses and some kind of pounding. All three stopped to listen.

"What do you make of that?" Margaret whispered above Edgar's head to Celia.

"I do not know. Let us go further. Keep the brush for coverage." Celia guided them forward, more toward the south, heading in the direction of the water's edge while still remaining immersed in the woodland. The noises grew louder. Celia motioned with her hand for the three of them to drop down onto their bellies and crawl forward very carefully. From this vantage point, Edgar pulled aside the twisted tendrils, this time with no hesitation or complaint. He had an odd feeling that what Celia had brought them to see would change the future forever.

Able to look out at the vista but still far enough away to remain safely hidden, they saw the shallow water overrun with hundreds of boats. The primary vessel flew multi-colored sails, each of them adorned with the picture of three lions, and on the highest point of the ship's masthead, a green banner with an enormous gold cross in its center rippled in the wind. The bow of the ship featured a figurehead of a young boy shooting an arrow which seemed just about ready to fly off its string.

"Oh, dear God. He has come." Edgar had barely enough saliva in his mouth to form the words.

Margaret panicked. "The Normans? We must go back! We must warn everybody. Hurry! We cannot risk being caught here!" She rose to her feet and started to pull on Celia's and Edgar's clothing.

"Sssh. Wait." Celia cautioned her. "Edgar will need as much information as possible. Let him observe a little while longer before he rushes back to London with this news. You and I can summon all the villagers to come to the priory. We will be safe there." She gently tugged on Margaret's arm to pull her back down to the ground next to her. "Just a little longer . . ."

The lead ship was obviously the Duke's. As it beached on dry land, he leaped from the boat in triumph but stumbled and fell face down. A circle of officers rushed to him with concern, but soon the echo of their laughter reverberated through the forest. Nimbly, William had risen to his feet with a fistful of sand in each hand, and said something to his noblemen that made them cheer. The archers in his army landed next, and then the coastline bustled with activity as soldiers, laborers, horses, and materials were transferred from sea to land. Huge amounts of timber were unloaded, piece by piece, providing visual evidence that these invaders planned on staying. And still the boats kept coming.

Celia turned to face Margaret and Edgar. "William will be sending out scouts to search the area. We must go."

With a nod of her head, she took the lead once more and crawled back into the thicket. After reaching a safe distance, all three ran, darting through the trees and bushes aware of the magnitude of their news. This time even Edgar was oblivious to the scrapes and scratches he picked up along the way, knowing that his next journey —to London and perhaps back here—would be one involving much greater consequences: life or death.

*   *   *   *   *

435

Before sunset, a trickle of villagers banged on the doors of the stone church, and by nightfall, it had become a steady stream. These were the hopeful ones, the ones who believed their stay at St. Stephen's would be temporary and a return to their cottages and farms and boats still possible. The more pessimistic ones bypassed the priory and headed further inland to other parts of the country where they would reunite with distant relatives or friends to start life anew. No hope had they that Bexelei would survive.

The families arrived in haste, their faces twisted with worry and fear. Mothers, hunched over from the heavy sacks resting on their shoulders, squeezed the hands of their nervous children. Some balanced helpless infants at their breasts. Fathers carried bags of essential belongings like fishing gear and farming tools. The more fortunate ones guided precious cattle, goats, or mules that would keep their families from starving in the days and weeks ahead.

Mother Devona quickly huddled the refugees into the pews of the church, offering them bowls of stew and hardened bread. To Margaret and Celia, she said, "After the children have eaten, bring them into the other room and provide them with some sense of normalcy." Her eyes, absent of their usual spark of joy, were rounded with concern. "Busy them with playful games. Take out the trunk. Give them the rag dolls, the wooden blocks, let them play with the seashell collection. Just keep their minds off what is going on beyond the safety of these walls." She lightly caressed their hands and nodded to them with appreciation.

After the simple meal had been shared, Margaret, Celia, and two other novices went from row to row explaining to the parents that they would now bring the children to the small space off to the side that served as their schoolroom. A few hesitant mothers were afraid to part with their young until they were shown the proximity of the room. Relieved that it was within sight and just a few paces away, they sent their little ones off with a light kiss and a pat on the head. The ones who were too frightened to be separated from their parents stayed with them until they heard the laughter and realized they were missing out on all the fun. Soon they too trotted away to join the others.

Each of the nuns went about the business of entertaining the children. Celia brought out the blocks, Mildred gathered together the dolls, and Margaret took out the shell collection. Gertrude, the practical one in the group, counted the number of children who had joined them as they sat so politely together in the center of the room. The youngsters ranged from three to twelve-years-old. Those beyond that age remained in the pews, considering themselves no longer in need of coddling or protection from the outside world. As Gertrude was counting, she said to her fellow teachers, "If we have our usual full complement of students, we can each supervise four children—" She stopped and shook her head when her number did not match up. She started again. Fourteen. Once more. Fourteen yet again.

Gertrude sidled over to the three others and tried to disguise her alarm. "We are missing two. I do not see Edmund or Adelaide. Perhaps they joined the group that left town?."

Sister Mildred, small and delicate as a sparrow, decided she would slip away. "Let me check the church to see if the grandmother is here or if someone knows the family's whereabouts."

Celia exchanged looks with Margaret. Both were aware that Edmund and Adelaide's parents were dead—their father lost at sea and their mother to subsequent heartbreak. Their paternal grandmother was all they had that kept them from forced servitude. To prevent this from happening, both Abbot Kenric and Mother Davona continually made it known to the grandmother that St. Stephen's would help them in the future should they ever need assistance. It was unlikely that either of the two children had a true calling. Edmund considered himself a future warrior and exceptional hunter—of rabbits, primarily—and Adelaide dreamed only of marrying into royalty, wearing a crown of laurel leaves and waving a stick for a scepter. Such visions made Margaret think that perhaps all children harbored similar dreams, remembering Will, Jack, and little Clainnis and the picnic back at Wilton.

Sister Mildred fluttered into the room, her eyes lit with panic. "No one has seen them. They did not leave with the other refugees nor have they made their way here." Before Celia could reach out and stop her, Margaret had run from the room.

Without grabbing a cloak, Margaret flew down the church aisle, carefully opening the door just wide enough to slink through. Alarmed, Mother Devona whipped her head over her shoulder toward the three nuns who were huddled together in the doorway of the schoolroom. She marched toward them to demand an explanation.

"Where in God's name is that girl going?" None of the three responded. Celia wondered even more deeply, how does one explain the foolhardy nature of courage?

*   *   *   *   *

As soon as she was outside the church, Margaret felt as if she had been thrust into a nightmare. The roads were deserted, but there was the constant sensation of being watched. She knew where Edmund and Adelaide lived. She had been there before to deliver leftover fabric from the convent that their grandmother could use for clothing for the children. It was a one room hut with a dirt floor and thatched roof, its wooden walls warped and leaning from the salty winds that battered against its faltering strength.

Before arriving at the cluster of shacks that constituted the village, she could smell them. She felt the vomit rise in her throat, a sour combination of disgust and grief. The Normans had torched them all.

Smoke was swirling in the air, dark and heavy closer to land and then white and thin as it rose higher. Her pace slowed as she drew closer to the smoldering embers of what was once a thriving hamlet. The breeze off the water must have spread the flames so swiftly that there was no chance anything could be saved. Her throat was singed, and her eyes teared from sorrow as well as smoke. If the family had not fled from their home, there was no doubt that their bodies must have burned inside of it. She crumpled to her knees, covering her face with her hands, angry at herself for having failed them. All around her came the slow snapping of timber and the whispered crackling of flames as the cottages gasped their last breaths. Treasured memories tumbled into the ashes of desolation, her sobs overpowered by the echoes of destruction.

Lost in her misery, Margaret did not hear the lone soldier approach. She was aware of nothing other than her own sadness.

Meanwhile he, noticing a maiden on her knees looking so vulnerable, took action. He sheathed his sword onto the side of his body and crept up on her from behind. He would need no weapon beyond his own hands in order to capture this young damsel. Sneaking up on her, he wrapped his thick arms around her waist and lifted her to her feet, pulling her tight up against the chainmail on his chest. She shrieked at the sudden assault. The cold, uneven metal pressed against the fabric of her clothing. She tried to spin her body around to face him. Limited to only the turn of her head, she saw the dreaded conical helmet of the enemy, the helmet's edge falling so low on the man's brow that his eyes remained hidden. The nose piece that extended from the helmet divided his face in half, making him appear doubly frightening. With each turn of his head, he filled her with even greater horror.

She kept screaming, but her cries were heard only by a few straggling woodland creatures who, already skittish from the initial devastation, now deserted the scene for good. With just the scorched trees for an audience, Margaret acknowledged the hopelessness of her situation yet refused to give up. Perhaps if she yelled loud enough, God would hear her plea and send a miracle on her behalf.

Someone did hear. Beneath the brambles and twigs that covered them were two children who recognized the voice of the victim. "Sister Margaret?" the tiny girl called out in fear. The young boy sprinted toward her, the spear pole in his hand bobbing up and down.

Still holding Margaret in his viselike grip, the soldier spun about to face the young intruder. Margaret screamed again but with a different entreaty. "Run! Run, Edmund! Take your sister and run to the church! Go!"

She scissored her legs back and forth as she dangled in the air, hoping to either make contact with the man's legs or the solid ground. She wanted to see if Edmund had heeded her demand. The sound of leaves crunching and branches shifting gave her the answer she hoped for.

Still pumping her legs vigorously, she struggled against the man's strength. With her feet still suspended, she writhed and twisted her arms, thrusting her elbow into his stomach, but it made no impact. It only served to amuse him further. "Aaah, a feisty one, you are. No doubt desperate to protect the only jewel in your dower. But you are ripe for the plucking you are. It will soon be time for you to bow down and meet your new lord."

Hoisting her up over his shoulder, he planned to make a delectable meal for himself once he got back to his tent.

*   *   *   *   *

Margaret exhausted herself, yelling for help that never came. Still, she kept alive her hope of escape. She must get him to drop her from his shoulder and put her on solid ground.—before he rejoined his fellow warriors. Then, she would need to elude only one man's grasp rather than many. As long as she could get down, she could use her knowledge of the terrain to her advantage. But first she must get him to release her.

She spoke directly to her captor. "Stop. Please. I am going to soil myself, and you too, if you do not put me down." He grunted and kept on moving. "Please. All this bumping up and down. I can not hold it any longer. It will take but a moment." He paused.

"Do it in front of me. There'll be no going into the woods." With a heave, he dropped her feet to the dirt. Margaret rubbed her stomach feeling the indentation where it had been crushed against his shoulder. She felt lightheaded after being suspended so long upside down. She shook aside the dizziness.

He grew impatient. "Get on with it. Come on." He stood with his hands on his hips, demanding her to perform for him. She turned around, but he yelled to her, "No! Face me."

In that tense moment with her back toward him, she reached into her pocket and grabbed the handful of seashells she was going to use back at the schoolroom. With her right hand full, she launched them directly at the man's face and darted immediately into the shadowy woods. His surprise and shock gave her the briefest head start in this race for her life. The cover of night also helped her, limiting him to the sounds she made. She twisted her way from one tree to the next, but still she heard his heavy footfall nearing. Her breath became shallow with panic, knowing he was closing the gap between them. Lifting her skirts to bound over the fallen log, she felt the tug on her veil and realized he was upon her. He seized her shoulder with one hand and yanked her head covering off with the other. Then he pulled on her single flaxen braid with such force that she immediately stopped running. She screamed with pain, raising both of her hands to anchor the braid to her scalp.

"Saxon slut. Just like all the rest of them. In spite of the garments you wear. Now you will pay for your deceit." He spun her body to face away from him and wrenched up her skirts until her marble skin was exposed. With one arm crooked about her neck, he shifted aside his tunic to let her feel his arousal upon the small of her back. In a grim dance of domination, he moved her to a nearby tree, not breaking their connection.

He let go of her neck and grabbed her waist. "Put your face up against the tree. Extend your arms."

Margaret whimpered. She could not bring herself to move.

"Do it, I say!" Very slowly, she lifted her trembling arms. Once they extended past the tree trunk, he reached around to grasp both of her wrists to pin them in place. Readying himself to enter her, he felt ripples of excitement pulsing in his blood.

Rushing footsteps came from behind them.

"Get off her, you bastard." Margaret felt her hands released and the weight against her body removed.

"Raping a nun! No better than the Englishmen we have come to despise!" Then came a loud thud, and the villain crumpled to the leafy ground.

Margaret heard the sound, felt her freedom, and asked no questions. Hurriedly, she fixed her clothing and started to run.

"Wait!" the man said. "This belongs to you."

She owed her savior at least a glance. He was a tall, muscular man whose dark brown hair was cut short above his ears. He stepped over the fallen scoundrel and tried to give her back the veil. His eyes were soft and apologetic, but she would not extend her hand toward him to receive the head piece.

"The region is dangerous. Let me escort you back to the convent. I will keep you out of harm's way."

Despite her shock over the encounter, Margaret had enough sense to realize she should accept his offer. Who knew what other villains were lurking in the shadows? She chose to place herself under his protection. Still trembling over what could have happened to her, she never looked up to make eye contact with him or speak. They walked together in silence.

She was aware enough of her surroundings to navigate their way through the forest, then past the decimated cottages, and ultimately onto the path that led to the priory. When they arrived at the door, he handed her the veil he had carried with him the whole way. She still had not looked up at him.

"You are safe now, Sister. I feel blessed and honored that God put me there to help you. And, Sister? May I be so bold as to ask you to help me before I take my leave?" He waited for her to acknowledge his request, but she did not react. When nothing seemed forthcoming, he went ahead anyway. "If you correspond from one abbey to another, would you be able to send a message from me to a novice at Wilton?"

Her eyes remained fixed upon the ground. She nodded but had no real sense of what he was saying.

"Would you … could you …? Would you tell Sister Celia that Simon asked for her. That I am here. In England. That I will seek her out, God willing, at the proper time?"

Again, Margaret only nodded.

"Can you do that for me?" Realizing his words were wasted and his request most likely ignored, he excused himself and began to leave. Who could blame her for being in shock after what had just happened? He would simply have to find another way to communicate with Celia.

But something broke through Margaret's shield. It may have been the reference to Wilton. It may have been his name. Most likely, though, it was the power of love that brought Margaret back to the world of the living.

"Simon?" He stopped moving away to look back at her.

A vague shadow of a memory crossed her mind. She was back in the Great Hall at Westminster. Celia was there, and this man as well. She remembered their closeness. She recalled her recent conversation with Celia about her plans for the future, and how those plans involved this man who stood before her. She studied the weathered face of the soldier who had saved her life and decided it was her turn to do something restorative for him. Margaret's thoughts began to flow more fluidly as she regained her sense of hope, her trust in faith.

"Wait. She is here. Sister Celia. She is here." Amidst destruction, suffering, and death, Margaret saw that one powerful thing remained —love. Through the tears that glistened on her lashes, Margaret announced proudly, "I will bring her to you." For just a second, she smiled. Then she tucked herself inside the church door to follow through on her promise.

*   *   *   *   *

They met in the cemetery under a sky stripped of all light. No stars, no moon, just vast emptiness, much like the stark side of humanity responsible for the recent destruction. The stone slabs emerged from the ground at odd angles. Some leaned sideways, some were stunted or chipped, some looked about to topple over onto the grave behind them. Many of the gray ones had turned to chalk, their engravings barely visible. A few etchings went as far back as the 700s and the time of King Offa. Here lay the bodies of those men who had lived and died for their right to call this patch of earth their own.

Simon leaned against one of the taller tombstones sturdy enough to bear his weight. He clasped Celia's hands in his own, raising them toward his heart. He gently kissed each of her fingertips. His tenderness moved her to speak.

"Take me with you. I will not be a burden to you. I can earn my keep. Viking raiders brought their women with them. Do we Normans not share their bloodline? I cannot bear to be apart from you any longer."

He gripped her hands tighter. "Celia. Celia. You know that is my deepest desire as well, but what lies ahead of us is more bloodshed and death. We will be building forts, constructing towers, seizing resources, all for the sole purpose of war. And until that moment of confrontation, the people in this region will be caught up in a gale of devastation set in motion by these two armies. The Duke will have us pillage their towns, scorch their land, and slaughter their families. Anything to bring Harold to this location. You know I will try to do everything I can to ensure the sanctity of the priory, but I can make no promises with regard to the surrounding villages and homes." Simon placed his finger beneath her chin to lift her face to him. "It would not be safe for you to be among us. I would never forgive myself if anything were to happen to you."

On a nearby tree, a lone nightingale took up residence on a branch that seemed to reach toward the couple with unspoken yearning. The bird's rippling whistle was marked by silent pauses. In the quiet, Simon embraced her tightly once again.

"And where is Margaret's brother? Edgar?"

Celia pushed against his chest to look at him suspiciously. "Why do you ask?"

He laughed at her skepticism. "Oh, Celia, I do not care about the boy in a political or military sense. I only asked to see if he could bring you both back north, to somewhere far removed from this eventual battleground." His smile melted away as he looked upon her with desire. Bending his face toward hers, he kissed her tenderly as the nightingale trilled with approval. A light breeze lifted a strand of her hair across her cheek. Delicately, he tucked it behind her neck and stroked her head with his hand. Intertwining his fingers in her hair, he kissed her again more passionately. Slowly, she drew her lips away from his, and with her finger, she gently traced the scar that ran from underneath his eye toward his chin.

Fascinated by the contrast between his ruggedness and his warmth, she answered his question. "Edgar was with us when we saw your army make landfall. He rode back to court with the news. I believe he will be returning here, but I am not sure in what capacity. I doubt he would be willing to be our escort. Knowing him as I do, I would imagine he is going to take part in this upcoming battle you speak of."

"Well, I pray the boy knows better than to join in. Harold's forces have no chance. They do not understand who they are dealing with. The Duke is a masterful planner and a valiant fighter. The excuse may have been the wind, but the real reason for our delay had nothing to do with weather. William knew a civil war was brewing in the North, so he took advantage. By holding off on our departure, he gave Harold a false sense of security that there would be no invasion, for who would sail in autumn with the winter coming on? But now we have come. And the coastline is unguarded, many of Harold's men are home harvesting their crops, and the ones who do make the trip will be exhausted from their prior battle. William has put us in a position to win."

"But what am I to do with myself while I await the outcome of this 'masterful' plan?" Her love for him made her impatient.

"I can tell you what I do not want you to do. I do not want you to think of any other man except for me the whole time I am gone." He kissed her again more aggressively. "And what you can do," he brushed up against her neck and caressed her, "is get back to Westminster. If we accomplish what we have set out to accomplish, at some point there will be a change of power and a coronation. I will come to you then."

She placed her hands upon his jaw to lift his face from her neck. Fastening her lips upon his, she drank deeply of him. With no memory of the vow she had made to herself after her mother's death, her body begged him for an even closer bond. "Come to me now," she whispered.

Between the crooked row of tombstones, he lay her down upon the soft ground. Balancing his weight on his arms, he swept his lips against her face and neck until he was at the rise of her bosom. Shifting onto one elbow, he very carefully untied the bindings across her chest and buried his face into her soft breasts. He felt her back arch with pleasure. When he was certain she had communicated to him that she longed for more, he gave in to her wishes, eager for the moment when they two could be one. She raised her hand against his chest to stop him from going further, but then decided against it. If there was one thing she had learned over these recent years, it was this: a chance to live was worth the price of death.

Slowly, she dropped her hand from his chest and wrapped it around his body to embrace him completely. Their hips moved together in rhythm until she surrendered to him completely. And despite the memory of the dead all around them, in that moment of acceptance, he filled her body with the promise of new life.

*   *   *   *   *

A week after the pillaging, the countryside went quiet. The church doors opened, and family by family, the villagers slowly ventured out from their holy sanctuary like little mice peeping out from their burrows to see if all was safe. And since there was no immediate danger because the entire Norman army had relocated eastward, there was also no reason for the villagers to stay any longer in their once peaceful hamlet. Everything was gone—every cottage, every boat, every animal—even the soil was left dead and lifeless. No one sought to rebuild. With their few belongings and their precious lives, they bid farewell to Mother Davona, Abbot Kenric, and Bexelei to join the others who had left at the first sign of invasion to start all over again elsewhere.

When it was safe to go out into the countryside, Edmund and Adelaide insisted on revisiting their hovel. From the ashes of their home, Celia sifted through the debris and found a few charred bones that could be put to rest in a proper Christian burial. On a dark, gray day in early October, the children and the residents of St. Stephen's prayed with Father Kenric as he commended their grandmother into the arms of the angels. Another stone was added to the priory's cemetery. As for the two children, they would remain with the order until they were old enough to decide their future.

After the assault, Margaret's visions had returned. They came upon her with an intensity she had never experienced before. All of her sights involved war. In one, she envisioned an impenetrable shield wall strategically placed at the crest of a hill, but like a tower of pebbles that topples over when the bottom one shifts, it crumbled into fragments when individual soldiers dropped their bucklers and ran. In another, she saw arrows flying, puncturing throats, ears, eyes. Then magically, they dislodged themselves from those body parts to drip huge amounts of blood that formed a red lake into which an entire cavalry unit drowned. Having no idea of the significance of these dreams, she told no one, concealing them beneath fervent prayers for peace.

With most of the priory's livestock stolen and its food storage ravaged, Margaret and Celia were scouring the woods for sorrel leaves whose lemony flavor would season their bland soup. Edmund had become quite the fisherman, walking through the tidal pools of Pevensey Bay and trapping them with the small net he had made. Adelaide sometimes joined him in the shallows, holding one end while they swept it back and forth across the water. In this way, the days passed uneventfully, even though Margaret could sense something significant was about to happen, thanks in part to the frequency and ominous nature of her visions.

To that end, the sound of a galloping horse startled the two women as they were filling their baskets with chestnuts and wild berries.

"Margaret! Margaret! Is that you? Come quickly. I have little time!" Seated proudly on horseback with his spear fastened to his back, Edgar sped to them, carrying a rounded shield and wearing a silver helmet that covered nearly his entire face. "They kept me from Stamford Bridge, but they will not keep me from this. I have been drilling and training with a select fyrd and am ready to bear arms against these Norman dogs." Holding his shield in front of his mouth so that the sound reverberated, he shouted his cry, "*Ut! Ut! Olicross!* That means 'Out! Out! By the Holy Cross!' This is how we kindle our courage and terrify our foes! We shall strike them down and laugh as they beg for mercy!"

Margaret saw more of the child in him than a fearless warrior. She must convince him not to go. "Edgar, do not risk your life like this. You are the future of this kingdom. Whether Harold lives or dies, you cannot dash the hopes of all those who pray for the line of Cerdic to be restored to the throne. If anything should happen to you, the House of Wessex shall be no more."

Remembering Simon's words, Celia chimed in. "Your sister is right. This is a war between William and Harold. It is a question of a broken oath. I can verify that as true. Their quarrel has nothing to do with you. Listen to Margaret. Keep yourself safe for the future."

Margaret moved closer to the horse to reach up and tap Edgar's leg. "Yes, brother. Bring us back to Westminster. Await the outcome and be there to pick up the pieces. If Harold defeats William, remember he is not a young man. And if Harold should die and William is the victor, you represent the only hope the English people have for the future."

Edgar had to keep tilting his head back so that his helmet did not cover his eyes. Other than that slight movement, he showed no signs that he had listened or cared about anything the two women had said to him. Faced with defeat, Margaret resorted to one final plea. She divulged a portion of her dream. "Brother, if the Saxon shield wall should break, this land will never be the same again. Everything will change. The people will come to speak a different language, their traditions will be replaced with new ones, and their knees will be forced to bend before a foreign king."

Celia came to stand beside Margaret. "Think carefully about what awaits you. Those who have escaped have passed through the priory and told us what they have seen of the Duke's encampment. Thousands of soldiers, expert bowmen and cavalry, palisades and embankments that extend for miles. Stay out of it. Protect yourself. Trust that your time will come."

Edgar moved his head back and forth between the two women, the helmet clicking as it shifted. "You make me laugh, Margaret. You too, Celia. What kind of people would ever want to follow someone who is not battle tested? Is that not one of the reasons why I was overlooked when King Edward died, and the Witan selected Harold instead of me? Complaints that I was too young, too inexperienced, too weak to rally an army behind me. Well, this is where that all ends.

This is where my reputation begins. Moments like these are when kings are made."

He began to turn his horse about. "I only stopped here to advise you to leave. Mother and Cristina are working to secure passage to return to Hungary. They will await news of the impending battle and then plan accordingly. I came to ensure that you follow their summons and leave here at dawn. Harold's troops are on a steady march from York and headed here. They are picking up men along the way, and we shall show these Normans how inferior they are to true Saxon warriors."

Margaret tried one last time to protect her brother. She ran in front of his horse in order to block his path. "Edgar, please. If you will not listen to me about having no part in the battle, then at least hear me out with regard to what you must do while you are in it. Do not believe their false moves. The Normans will resort to trickery and deceit to get what they want. Stay unified, stay strong, stay together. Do not be fooled by their pretense. It will only serve to bring about the downfall of this kingdom."

"Margaret, your words are too cryptic for me. God be with you as he shall be with me." Nodding to his sister and then to Celia, he stirred his horse into a gallop. The two women watched as he rode away, both of them fully convinced that he was headed straight into danger.

*   *   *   *   *

Margaret and Celia were already on the road heading toward Westminster when the two armies clashed. On the brink of victory, the Saxons surrendered their stronghold atop Senlac Ridge after being fooled into believing William's army had retreated. The field at Hastings was strewn with the bodies of soldiers from both sides, the most important of which being King Harold's.

Edgar was not part of the shield wall. In fact, he never even made it to the battlefield. After leaving St. Stephen's, he misjudged the depth of a gully between two sandbanks, and his horse's leg snapped when it was sucked into the silt. Forced to put the animal out of its misery, Edgar attempted to get there on foot. He did not make it very far when a group of wounded soldiers told him the news. William's banner now flew from the summit of the hill.

WESTMINSTER

WINTER 1066

Edgar's embarrassment and indignance over having missed the battle soon vanished due to the swift chain of events that ensued after the fight. With the corpses of all three Godwinson brothers left for the scavenging birds and dogs near Senlac Ridge, the Witan led by Archbishops Ealdred and Stigand put forth Edgar's name as King. Earls Edwin and Morcar supported the decision, especially after hearing rumors of the Duke's illness that kept him stalled in Canterbury for over a month. Even though Edgar did perform one act of state—confirming the appointment of a new abbot at Peterborough —William's recovery and the continued ravaging of the English countryside shook everyone's resolve. Confidence in their proclamation slowly diminished. And when the Duke's army marched toward London, setting fire to the houses on the south bank of the Thames and crossing to Wallingford to encircle the city, Stigand, Ealdred, Edwin, Morcar, and even Edgar too, submitted.

"I wonder if King Edward foresaw how busy his new abbey would be?" Margaret spoke in hushed tones to Celia, the two of them once again seated in the pews of Westminster. The church was filled to capacity with English and Norman noblemen placed on opposite sides of the aisle. Even the altar represented this split as the English archbishops and clergymen shared the space with Bishop Geoffrey of Coutances and his French priests.

"Your sarcasm is fitting," Celia agreed. "Three royal ceremonies in one calendar year. Just last Christmas we went about innocently decorating the hall with holly and ivy. Who would have imagined the upheaval that was about to come?"

"Well, there is certainly nothing innocent about this coronation, is there? Everything so carefully planned and monitored. The devil's hand must be in all this."

"Or God's justice. Depends on which half of the church you ask. Those on the Norman side would say Harold was the original usurper. He swore a sacred oath to support William's bid for the crown, and then he went ahead and accepted the title for himself." Celia stole a furtive glance around the people seated near them, then toward those on the other side, and later to the ones in the back. "You can feel the tension in the air, can you not? The panic beneath the surface. Why else would there be so many foreign guards planted along the inside walls of the church as well as outside?"

From the pew directly in front of them, one monk turned around to silence them with a glare. The ceremony was about to begin. A young acolyte with sunken cheeks and a faraway stare processed up the aisle, carrying against his thin body a cross whose width nearly matched him in thickness. The priests behind him—both Norman and English—chanted Lauds in unison with the other religious in the congregation who joined in. Next came the three bishops and then William himself. Celia felt a chill run down her spine when she looked upon the man who had forced her into this servitude by holding her sister hostage.

Cruel and ruthless was the spirit now clothed now in fancy robes and glamour. With his shoulders back and his body erect, William appeared stronger than ever, invigorated by his newly expanded realm. His black hair had receded a bit since the last time she saw him, but he showed no trace of the recent illness which had been reported by messengers from Canterbury. Although Celia despised him to the very core of her being, she felt liberated by the fact that his investiture sealed the end to her charade. He had achieved his goal. Now she could go home.

And as for Margaret, from time to time, she tried to steal a glance to see how Edgar was faring. Again, he sat between a set of brothers, only on this occasion it was the earls of Mercia and Northumbria, Edwin and Morcar, instead of the Godwinsons. Perhaps this was a family upon whom Edgar could depend. Margaret knew that such alliances were rather fickle when power was continually shifting. It was probably safer to trust no one.

William was seated upon a raised dais, elevating him above his subjects from both countries. The Bishop of Coutances opened the proceedings, asking the Norman nobles in French whether, by their own free will, they accepted the Duke to be their new King. When the group shouted back their affirmation, Bishop Ealdred asked the same of the Anglo Saxon nobles. Immediately after their positive response, there was great celebration which seemed to carry on outside onto the streets as well. But when smoke started trickling through the windows of the church, the congregation became confused. Outdoors, people were shrieking, soldiers were bellowing, and the air began to take on an acrid smell.

Celia reached for Margaret's sleeve. "Come, we must get out of here." Bodies were banging up against each other, the strong pushing aside the weak as people fought to get through the door. Margaret and Celia linked arms and managed to stay together as they let the stampede sweep them along toward the exit.

Just like Bexelei, Margaret recognized the smell of fire as the houses that lined the road next to the abbey were in flames. Englishmen howled and assaulted the Norman soldiers, telling them to stop. The foreign warriors had no familiarity with the language, so they listened only when weapons were pointed directly at their bodies. Only then did they drop their torches and realize their misinterpretation. The shouts inside the church were not ones of rebellion against King William but rather cheers of support. It was too late for any recourse or apology; the damage was already done.

Thus, William was crowned in front of a handful of clergy in an otherwise empty church. The unrest he initiated upon his arrival in England would continue. And that unrest was also reflected in Celia's heart as she would never know now if Simon had come for her as he had promised. She tightened her grip on Margaret, acknowledging that this attachment was her only link to him.

PALACE OF WESTMINSTER

WINTER 1067–1068

In the three months since the coronation, the defeat at Hastings was framed as God's judgement upon a sinful King. As such, William tried to win over the English nobility either by force or preferment. Those who fought against him lost the rights to their lands, but others, like Edwin and Morcar, retained portions of their earldoms. Edgar too was given a land grant in Northumbria, a location which would keep him and his family safe and removed from the Norman court. There was one problem, though. Before he could relocate north with his family there, William took Edgar and other English nobles with him on his triumphant return to Normandy. The new King wanted to reassure and thank his supporters who had not crossed the sea and reward them for their loyalty. But he also had to keep in mind the danger of being absent from England during this delicate time, so he traveled with Edgar, Edwin, Morcar, Stigand and others in order to guarantee the good behavior of their kinsmen. With rebellions brewing in the North, South, and West, William returned to England by Christmas.

"I see their approach!" Margaret was looking out from a window of the palace at the cavalcade of horsemen galloping toward the castle. Four men, armed with spears, swords, and shields, spanned the dirt path they rode upon. Behind them in single file came the King and his English hostages, and then followed a contingent of about twelve more warriors who served to protect the group from the rear. "I must go tell Mother and Cristina. Now we can finally head north!"

Margaret moved swiftly from the room, leaving Celia to gaze from the window. *Maybe one of the soldiers would have word of Simon,* she thought, as she continued to watch their progress. Before the portcullis, the King and his companions dismounted as stable hands came to relieve them of their horses. William removed his gloves, the first to march through the gate and into the courtyard.

When Celia saw Edgar, she marveled at the change in him. His body had filled out, his hair much longer than before. He seemed weary yet content, slapping the haunches of his steed before dismissing it to the servant. She saw him look about the countryside with a sense of pride, perhaps eager to secure the plot of land that would truly be his own. With that, Celia stopped observing and left the room. She headed down the hallway and to the stone staircase, not to detain Edgar but to question the soldiers.

As she neared the castle gate, one of them passed through, and she said, "Excuse me, sir. May I—"

The warrior lifted his helmet and sent her heart skyward. They both had to hide their excitement over such an unforeseen reunion. Simon maintained the illusion of calm better than she. "Yes, Sister. How may I be of service to you? I have only enough time for my horse and I to eat and restore our energy. Then I must be on my way north."

Celia's eyes lit up with possibility. "I had a question to ask of you, but it seems you may have already answered it." She wanted to draw closer, and she could feel the same wish coming from him, but they maintained the gap between them. He looked around at the workers who moved in and about the courtyard. The women carrying buckets of water, the farriers shoeing horses, the blacksmiths pounding metal.

None of them guessed at the desire that was raging between the woman and soldier who stood near the entrance way of the castle.

"May I inquire as to your next destination?"

His teeth shone bright against the smudges on his face from the miles he had ridden. "Northumbria. I have been assigned to serve the young man." Simon emphasized the word "serve" for its more cryptic meaning. "King William wants me to remain on his estate and ensure his safety, should there be further disturbances in that region."

"Well, that is a fine bit of luck, I should say, for us to be in the company of such a strong and courteous guide as yourself. I too shall be on that journey, and already you have allayed my fear of what we may encounter on the road." Celia enfolded her fingers together and squeezed her hands to stop herself from opening her arms and rushing toward him.

"Or what you all may encounter in the future as well. Rest assured, dear Sister, that I will be by your side to protect you—all of you—for as long as I live and breathe." He bowed his head slightly and winked at her with secret knowledge. With a smile that promised more excitement to come, he nodded her way and walked toward the stables. Before disappearing completely, he looked over his shoulder at her once more, sealing his promise with his eyes before disappearing through the arched doorway.

Once Edgar and his family were secure on the new estate, perhaps her journey with Simon could finally begin. She must confide in Margaret and tell her the good news. Over land to settle in a new home for them, then across the sea for a return home for her and Simon.

NORTHUMBRIA

WINTER 1068

Edgar paced about the room, walking in a circle around the long table that stood at the center. "We are no longer safe here. Our attempt to restore full power to Edwin and Morcar has failed. We must leave again."

Celia watched his agitated movements from the threshold, while Margaret and her mother sat next to one another on one side of the table, Cristina on the other. Still too young to be invested in the conversation, Cristina amused herself by tying and untying a string around her finger. "We have awakened the lion and have not enough strength here to subdue him. The brothers have surrendered at Warwick. William will be coming next for me." The finality of his words struck a chord of fear into the three women.

"Let us go home then." Agatha extended her prayer-formed hands in his direction as if begging her son to listen. The years had been hard for her, relegated to a position of helplessness and insignificance, never safe from worry over what those in power would do to her and her children.

"Home?" Edgar stopped pacing. He stared at Agatha.

"Yes, to Baranya. Let us be done with this hellish land." She dropped her face into her hands and shook her head from side to side, shuddering at the memory of what this kingdom had done to her husband, to all of them.

"Surrender now? Just give up everything? Leave my father's kingdom and mine in the hands of that Norman bastard? When we are so close to defeating him?" Edgar slapped his hand against the table for emphasis.

The room was a simple one with no other furnishings than the table and chairs. No tapestries hung on the walls, no sweet smelling rushes covered the floor, no decorations of any kind adorned it. It was a stark building they occupied and a meager existence they led, isolated in this remote, barbarous area where the people were as cold and unforgiving as the weather. Margaret knew her mother was comparing this austere lifestyle with the comfortable one they had enjoyed back in Hungary.

"And you fight for this?" Agatha gestured to the emptiness that surrounded them. After her husband's untimely death and Edgar's subsequent maturity, she deferred to her son as head of the family, letting him determine their fate. But in this situation, she was forcefully taking a stand.

"What am I supposed to do then? Be concerned only for my own welfare and not the welfare of the people of this land?"

"They are not your people and never were. Why should you care about them? Have they ever cared about you?" Agatha worked herself into a frenzy. Her motherly role of protector subsumed her.

Edgar was insulted by her implication that he had been used by the English and too dumb to see it. He would not stand for such a challenge to his authority, to his intelligence, to his manhood. "I am of my father's blood and that blood fed the hearts of many kings from Cerdic to Alfred to Edmund to father. I am of the House of Wessex, and although I may not have lived here my entire life, I am a Saxon through and through."

His voice surpassed Agatha's in volume. "William has robbed my people of their land, slaughtered them. Their men have raped our women. Am I to stand by and do nothing? Scurry away to the continent for safety? Resume life there and say goodbye and good luck to these people? Live in luxury and pretend I do not know that those I have been called to serve are being tortured and killed?" Edgar leaned forward, his eyes locked in upon his mother's. He lowered his voice and spoke through gritted teeth. "I cannot and will not give up on Father's dream. It is a dream I share, and I will live to see it through. Should God choose otherwise, then so be it. At least I can go to my grave knowing I sacrificed my life for his cause. For his honor."

Edgar slowly lifted his hands from the table and rose again to his full stature. "Gospatric has helped me make the necessary arrangements. We sail for Scotland in two days."

At the mention of Scotland, Margaret swallowed her breath. Her heart dropped. It had been over a year since she had heard from Malcolm—and no wonder, for she had never responded to his letter offering them sanctuary. She did not doubt that she, her mother, and Cristina would be protected there, but Edgar was not seeking protection or a place of refuge. No, somehow Malcolm was part of Edgar's plan, this plan to wrest the North away from King William. While she considered these things, Edgar marched out of the room.

"So this is what we have come to …" Agatha pushed her chair from the table. "A fractured family …" She extended her hand toward Cristina. "Come." As she walked away, she mumbled under her breath. "Perpetual vagabonds. That is what we are. Perpetual vagabonds."

Left alone to themselves, Margaret got up and moved closer to Celia who had shifted to the side of the door. She had tried to make herself small and unnoticed while each person exited the room.

"What will you do about Simon?"

"I must go now and tell him. If I could stay here with him, I would, but you and I know that is not possible. Soon he will be called upon to fight against the uprisings. He cannot leave, and I cannot stay. So we will continue to bide the time. I will tell him where we are headed and hope that he can come to me there."

Celia tried to be optimistic, fighting hard against the resentment she felt toward life and its cruel twists of fate. Everything seemed so unfair. But thinking in such selfish ways would do her no good, so she decided to look at the situation from Margaret's perspective. "But what may be troublesome for one person can be a source of joy for another." She smiled at her friend. "What will you do about Malcolm? Did your heart flutter at the idea of returning to this man? Or did your breath remain still and undisturbed, content with your plan to give yourself to God?"

Margaret shrugged her shoulders and gazed up at the ceiling. "I am unsettled. That is the truth of it. I can feel it in my soul." She looked at Celia for understanding. "I never did write back to him. And of course, I have not seen him in person for quite some time now. I guess I will not know my true desire until we are in each other's presence once again."

Margaret then extended her hand to lightly touch Celia's cheek. "But you, my friend, you do have the opportunity to be with your man. There are two nights between now and our departure. May your heart make good use of them."

Celia's face broke into a smile, both for her own good fortune and an appreciation of Margaret's kindness toward her. Margaret nodded her head and placed her hand on Celia's shoulder, gently guiding her toward the door. "Go to him, and savor these final hours until you meet again." It was Margaret's turn now to smile, and she did so with silent understanding.

*   *   *   *   *

It was dark and her footsteps were quiet. She made no sound upon the packed earth that served as the floor of Edgar's home. The timber building was a rather small one compared to the palace and convent she had occupied at one time or another. It did not take her long then to find her way to the rounded wooden door that led to the outside. The night was cold and rainy. She gathered up her hood and dropped it over her hair that she had purposely left free and unrestrained.

The path to the barn was full of puddles. In between the raindrops, she studied the ground to avoid slipping or soiling her feet. The stable was just a few yards beyond the house, but already the rawness of the wind seeped into her bones. Was she doing the right thing? She and Simon had limited themselves to snatches of conversations outdoors —at the well, by the firewood, near the stalls—their interaction never of an intimate kind. With the memory of their past tryst in their minds and their dream of the future burning brightly, they had the patience to wait, but now that dream was smoldering, and Celia needed to rekindle it before they were forced to separate from each other once again.

Simon was the only soldier who had remained with Edgar, the other three were summoned for duty elsewhere to places like Durham and York where tensions had escalated. King William commanded Simon to stay close to Edgar and watch over him, reporting back anything Simon could discover about possible rebellions. Celia and Simon shared more than just love between them. Both had been manipulated by William to spy for him, and neither had any liking for it.

The barn too was dark, and when she pushed lightly on the door, it creaked open with irritation at having been disturbed. The rain blew in sideways, and she had to lean her weight on the inside of the door just to shut out the weather. Simon heard the intrusion and yelled from his loft above, "Who's there?" He snatched the dagger from beneath the straw and held it in front of his body as he stepped cautiously down the ladder. The gleam from the blade was the only light in the room. From it, she could make out the contours of his body as he started to step down.

Smelling a sweetness upon the air, he called out, "Celia?"

"Yes." She lowered the hood from her hair and stood still in anticipation of his approach.

He wore only a long shirt whose fabric reached just above his knee. The neckline was open to his chest, and Celia yearned to touch the strength beneath it. He placed the dagger on one of the rungs of the ladder.

"We leave in two days." She said the words flatly, trying to hold back any emotion.

"I heard."

He did not know if he should approach and comfort her, or if he should remain at a distance. If he were honest with himself, he was afraid to draw nearer. Afraid that he would not be able to soothe her once he touched her. His grief over losing her again would be too great. He had no comfort to offer when he himself was dying inside over the prospect of having to say goodbye.

She moved first, dropping her cloak to the floor. She stood before him in a thin linen shift. The gap between them still remained. His hands longed to touch her skin, to feel the curves of her body. Trembling with desire, he took a step closer. She willed him to her, welcoming him as a roaring fire embraces a weary traveller. He dropped his knees to the ground and wrapped his arms around her legs. Burying his head against her, he cried softly into her body.

"Celia, Celia. My love. My life. How much more must we endure?"

She had no answer for his question. All she had to offer was herself. She reached down and placed her hands upon his head, letting her fingers run through his hair. She felt the shape of his head and caressed his scalp, trying to dislodge all thoughts of sorrow and doom. He looked up at her, his eyes wet with tears, and slowly began to stand. She felt small and delicate in his presence, his shoulders towering over hers. Placing his rough hands against her face, he bent toward her lips to kiss her. When they drew apart, he marveled at her beauty. "You taste sweeter to me than ever before. Every night I dream of you and never have my fill of wanting you."

Tenderly he reached for the bottom of her slip and slowly drew it up higher. She lifted her arms to liberate her body from it. His fingers traced the skin from her neck to her shoulders to her bosom. He burrowed into the softness he found there, letting his tongue wander over her body. Taking his face in her hands, she looked deep into his eyes and remained connected to him that way as they knelt together upon the ground. With his free hand, he spread out her cloak beneath them and guided her to lie down. And in that way, they came together in sorrow but departed from one another in hope. And that was enough to carry them through what was about to come.

*   *   *   *   *

There was no second night. Edgar had altered his plans. His mother's argument had some merit. She and his sisters were more of a hindrance to him than anything else. He would sail them back to Hungary and then return on his own to Scotland where he could fulfill his destiny. The vessel was going to leave at dawn.

When Celia crept back into the room and returned to their shared cot, Margaret turned toward her companion. With a heavy heart,

Margaret informed her of the change in plans. "Do you want to let Simon know?"

Still feeling his spirit inside her, Celia stared off into the distance. She wanted to preserve the beauty of their night together, hold fast to the ecstasy she felt in his arms, the heights she reached when he was inside her. Celia decided that the memory she wanted him to have of her was one of rapture not regret. That would be her farewell to him.

"He will find out soon enough." Celia closed her eyes and tried to return to the reverie of her last encounter with him, but the feeling had already drifted beyond her grasp.

STORM AND STONE

THE NORTH SEA – 1068

Nothing. It was all for nothing.

The boat tilted sideways. Celia bit her bottom lip as she fought against the pull, her hands clinging to the mast, fingernails leaving wedges in the wood. Unable to see clearly, she could neither discern nor anticipate, only react. At the mercy of the elements she was.

For hours, rain had poured down on the defenseless vessel, and now an even greater threat arose when the storm intensified. Oarsmen fought against futility, heeding the master's command.

"Bring her back out to sea. We will not make it to shore!"

Celia barely listened. Lost in her own thoughts, she refused to let go of the mast. Her breath quickened as the boat rose up on the crest of the next wave. Fast and shallow were the gulps she took as the vessel climbed higher and higher. On this night as black as doom, she could sense the moment they would begin to plummet. When the upper half of her body tilted slightly forward, the precise time had come. Recognition coincided with immediacy as the ship dropped rapidly into the trough. Unfastened items rushed past her, crashing up against the railing. A howl cut through the wind and rain. *An ill-fated passenger*, she supposed. Soon she too would be another. For the time being, however, she held fast.

Earlier that day there had been scant warning that severe weather was coming, and judging from the current frenzy of the men, they had underestimated its wrath. No longer mere nuisance, the storm struck them full force. The creaking and groaning of the boards signaled their buckling. The boat had taken on too much water despite the efforts of the passengers who—only a short time ago—had been schooled in the art of bailing. Celia heard the low rumble first, then the thunderous trumpeting of seawater as the wooden hull caved in to the mounting pressure.

She was frozen in place, her rage keeping pace with the ever-increasing water level on board the boat. *I never asked for this.* Her words alluded to something beyond the current tempest. *I have done what I have done. I accepted it then and I accept it now. Oh, what does it matter? I could not protect her. The end is still the same. I accomplished nothing and lost everything.* Driven by the wind, her hair lashed across her face like the whip of an overzealous executioner. In defiance, she shook aside the strands and stared directly into the gale, ready to face her final moments.

Just then, someone grabbed her wrist in an attempt to pry it from the post. She imagined it to be one of the worthless mariners who had put her into this predicament in the first place. "Get your hands off me, you louse. Leave me to my own ways!" Her eyes flashed as she narrowed her lips to spit upon the man trying to save her life, a life she had already bequeathed to the waters below.

But instead of the weather-beaten face of a sailor, Celia saw the flawless complexion of a young girl, her countenance the single glimmer of light amidst the darkness. The girl's eyes, green and luminous, reflected a beam of yellow at the center so radiant and so strong that it silenced the rain and wind and tumult. A thin line split the space between her eyebrows, marking her refusal to be ignored.

The girl tilted her head, and then her face softened as she heard the sound of the sea crashing upon the shore. Comforted by the idea that they were close to land, the spectral maiden tightened her grip on Celia's wrist. With urgency, she whispered the single word, "Come."

As much as Celia yearned to surrender her miserable existence to the depths of the sea, she—for some unknown reason—obeyed.

Perhaps she and Margaret were just meant to be together. In life and in death.

The sea surged about the vessel with swells that poured over the sides of the boat, dropping them deeper and deeper into the trenches and leaving them more vulnerable to the next onslaught. Celia and Margaret clung to one another, even as they lost their footing and crumbled beneath the frothy brine. The force of the sea snapped the mast in two, the top half swept overboard. It soon was sucked into the depths below.

"Keep 'er afloat, boys! Pull the tiller toward the bay! There is safety in the harbor!"

With each drenching, there were more shrieks. People calling out for one another, some were calling out for God, none able to move from one location to another unless propelled by the sea's wrath. For a brief moment, when her eyes cleared from the spray, Celia could discern tiny lights upon the rocky shore. But the next wave pummeled them both, throwing them forcefully down upon the deck. Their clasp was broken. Margaret slid away toward the sinking side of the vessel where the railing dipped dangerously below the water line. Caught up in the heaviness of her clothing, Celia fumbled from side to side to regain her footing. Still, she could not seem to get any closer to Margaret. When another wave hit, her head slammed against the remaining portion of the mast, and everything went dark. She did not see Margaret's body slip into the sea.

With the ever-changing current, the vessel shifted back and forth and up and down, launching people and objects from one side of the boat to the other. Like a lifeless doll, Celia was swept again across the deck, her clothes sloshed around her. A particularly abrupt and powerful shift sent her hip into the side of the boat, and she winced in pain. Her head throbbed when she shook herself awake. She dragged her body upward to look again for the lights on shore. Even more points of illumination had joined the others, and she felt comforted by their presence. But that sense of promise was wrenched away when she discovered Margaret was gone.

"Margaret?" Her voice was shrill with panic. "Margaret!"

She skated on sea water to the other side of the boat, slipping and sliding, losing her footing and regaining it, until she peered over the edge of the vessel into the roaring breakers. Waves crashed onto the back of her head as if compelling her to look more closely at the foamy surface. And when she focused with all of her concentration, she saw the marble skin of Margaret's face barely staying afloat. The hood of Margaret's cloak rested behind her head as if forming a pillow for her to float upon.

With a quick glance toward the lighted shoreline for reassurance, Celia dove into the frigid water, fighting against the current to get to her friend. Her face, not yet numb, felt each drop of water stab her skin. She gasped for breath from the sheer force of the water's power, but refused to give up. She was getting closer. And this was what drove her on.

She knew she could do this. She had done it before on a smaller scale with Clainnis. That sense of triumph inspired her now, and she found a strength deep within herself she had never experienced before. She had closed the gap. Sweeping her arm beneath Margaret's body, she pointed the girl's face up toward the sky.

"I am here, and I shall not let you go. We are going to make it, you and I. Lie back and ride with me upon the waves."

Celia kept a firm grip on Margaret's chest and, with the other arm, began stroking through the current toward the lights. As if by divine intervention, the water quieted. Serenity seeped into her soul despite the coldness of the sea and the heaviness in her arms. The body she carried did not move of its own volition. It made no sound, put up no struggle. Celia wondered if Margaret's spirit had already ascended to heaven. But that determination was not for Celia to make. Not now. There would be a time for that. Right now, she simply had to keep pumping her arms and legs to get them both to shore.

Tranquility was now growing inside her, expanding and warming her from within. From a far off place, she heard someone shouting. A skiff was coming toward them, but it was getting harder and harder to keep moving. Her chest seemed encased in ice, frozen and hard like the rocks that jutted out along the coastline. The boat drew near. She could not see any people on board. Was it an angelic vessel, coming to take them both to the world beyond? Salt stung her eyes. It felt better to keep them closed. The voices came at her again. *Surely, angels have no need to yell*. Perhaps it was some fisherman from the village. She was going to make it. Margaret was going to make it.

The boat was now close enough for the sailor to reach out his arms and lift Margaret's body from the water. Celia would think of her friend and be glad that she was able to serve her, save her. Perhaps in some way she was able to save Vivienne too. She would like to think so.

Our ways are not God's ways, Celia thought, as she pushed Margaret's body into the man's awaiting arms. She did not know she was handing over to this stranger his future wife and Queen.

Living is like that. There is sorrow and there is joy. And a person never knows how much she will get of either one. The important thing is to keep reaching out toward life, blissfully thankful for the ignorance. Celia had had her share of both. Glancing up at the heavens to find its brightest star, she thought of Simon. Then she gave herself permission to sink beneath the surface of the water, content at having helped her friend choose life.

HISTORICAL NOTES

PART ONE

CELIA

1) Cutting off hands after insult of hides - William's mutilation of people of Alençon - "... thirty-two of the individuals who mocked William at Alencon were mutilated on William's orders." - *William the Conqueror* - Bates - p. 28; "His mother was not the wife of Robert his father, but a poor peasant girl, the daughter of an humble tanner of Falaise." - *History of William the Conqueror* - Abbott - p. 23; "Finally, when they found that they could not make mere words sufficiently stinging, they went and procured skins and hides, and aprons of leather, and everything else that they could find that was connected with the trade of a tanner, and shook them at the troops of their assailants from the towers and walls ... These prisoners he cut to pieces, and then caused their bloody and mangled limbs and members to be thrown, by great slings, over the castle walls." - *History of William the Conqueror* - Abbott p. 48

2) Ride from Valonges to Falaise - "He arose and dressed himself hastily, and inasmuch as a monarch, in the first moments of the discovery of a treasonous plot, knows not whom to trust, William wisely concluded not to trust anybody." - *History of William the Conqueror* - Abbott - p. 41-44

MARGARET

1) Gerhard, the tutor - based on the aethelings' guardian, Walgar, who was alerted by one of the Danish barons that Canute was going to murder the two boys, Edmund and Edward. "He tipped off Earl Walgar, the aethelings' guardian and tutor in Denmark, urging him that 'if he held them dear at all, he should send them away' out of Canute's reach. Thus the

survival of the ancient Anglo-Saxon line hinged upon Walgar...there is a possibility that the confusion reigning in the near-contemporary accounts was, in part, due to Walgar's deliberate attempts to cover up his tracks and mislead everyone about the aethelings' escape route from Sweden.... In fact, the Continental odyssey of the princes has remained shrouded in mystery to this day..." *The Lost King of England* - Ronay - pp. 40-41

2) Margaret's virtue - "Whilst Margaret was yet in the flower of youth, she began to lead a very strict life, to love God above all things, to employ herself in the study of the Divine writings, and therein with joy to exercise her mind....When she spoke, her conversation was seasoned with the salt of wisdom; when she was silent, her silence was filled with good thoughts." *The Life of St. Margaret* - Turgot - p. 27-8, 32

3) Harold's trip to Hungary - "Although the Chronicles are muted, there is good reason to believe that Harold Godwinson was utilized on this second occasion [to find Edward the Exile]....It is entirely plausible therefore that Harold travelled with Baldwin to Cologne, and possibly then Regensburg, during which he carried out instructions to negotiate with Agnes and Andrew of Hungary, and with the exiled Edward to discuss the proposal for the exile to come back to England." - *The House of Godwin* - Key - p. 159

4) Edward the Exile's summons to England - "After having lived the life of an outcast of England for 38 years, Edward's exile was suddenly drawing to an end....In its hour of need England was reaching out for its long-forgotten son. Edward the Exile was once again Edward the Aetheling, the future king of England, and the wrongs and wounding neglects of the past were wiped away." - *The Lost King of England* - Ronay - p. 130-31.

5) Edward's arrival in August 1057 - "triumphant return" and "ecstatic welcome accorded by the English people" ; "but they only saw a foreign looking, middle aged man ... dressed in strange clothes and ... unable to speak a word of English" - *The Lost King of England* - Ronay - p. 136

6) The Exile's death - Edward was in fine health, so speculation continues about his death. Some, like Ronay, claim it was "not sudden illness but the poisoner's cup" and that "ruthlessness ran in the [Godwinson] family." Ronay continues, "I became absolutely convinced of Harold's guilt. Nothing has come to light to shake this conviction." - *The Lost King of*

England - Ronay - pp. 139-42. The Danish writer Saxo Grammaticus and other historians have suggested that the Exile was poisoned and that Harold "had the most to lose by the Exile's arrival and the most to gain by his removal." - *The House of Godwin* - Key - p. 161.

PART TWO

CELIA

1) Summer 1057 - King Henry & Geoffrey II Martel, Count of Anjou ravaged areas westward of Caen and Bayeaux as "revenge for the defeats of 1054" - *William the Conqueror* - Bates - p. 144

2) Battle of Varaville - "He held off until his opponents were crossing the marches near Varaville and then commanded his soldiers to pounce on the rearguard that was waiting their turn." - *William the Conqueror* - David Bates - p. 145

3) Robert de Grandmesnil, abbot of Saint-Evroult - expelled because of "his kinship with the Giroie family ... and the political support that he was giving them ... Robert was expelled without a trial or without the judgment of a synod ..." Robert went "to appeal to Pope Nicholas II, after which he returned to northern France seeking to regain his office with the support of papal legates. As they approached Lillebonne where William was staying, they heard stories of his fury and his declaration that, while he was very happy to receive representations from the pope on matters of faith, he would hang any monk from the duchy from a high oak tree who dared initiate a case before the pope against him" - *William the Conqueror* - Bates - pp. 175-6

4) Mallory's sickness - Ringworm "can also be passed on objects like combs, brushes, hats, towels, or clothing." - Yamini Durani, MD - "Ringworm" - www.kidshealth.org "Scalp Ringworm (tinea capitis): This causes scaly, red, itchy bald spots on your scalp. If left untreated, the bald spots can grow bigger and become permanent." "Ringworm" - *Cleveland Clinic* - www.myclevelandclinic.org

5) Val-es-Dunes - "The speed and disorganization of their retreat were such that many were drowned in the river Orne, which, depending on where they tried to cross, is between ten and fifteen kilometres west of Val-es-Dunes. Wace comments on the savagery of the pursuit and the numbers that were killed. No source mentions the taking of prisoners, therefore we can

probably assume that did not happen. In other words, the achievement of supremacy on the battlefield was followed by a massacre." - *William the Conqueror* - Bates - p. 84

MARGARET

1) King Edward's description - "tall, with milky-white hair and beard" - "the long fingers of his emaciate hands let light through the gaps between them" - *Edward the Confessor* - Licence - p. 206

2) Edward's guardianship over the family - "While Edgar was groomed for the throne, Margaret and Christina, his nephew's two little daughters, were given an education fit for royal princesses....the Benedictine monks in charge of religious life ... provided a sense of continuity for the children. They were taught to read the sacred manuscripts in Latin, introduced to the lives of the saints and the teachings of Gregory and Cassain and given a good grounding in the works of Augustine. They were taught French, because the king preferred to speak it in private, and instructed in deportment and courtly customs. The girls were also trained in needlework, while Edgar was introduced early to the martial arts." - *The Lost King of England* - Ronay - p. 143.

3) Malcolm's meeting with Margaret - "...she had read books to the devoted Malcolm, who could not read..." - *The Literature Network - A Short History of Scotland* - Lang - chapter 4

4) Margaret as pearl - "She was called Margaret, and in the sight of God she showed herself to be a pearl, precious in faith and works. She was indeed a pearl to you, to me, to all of us ..." - *Life of St. Margaret* - Turgot - p. 24

5) Malcolm's return to King Edward's court - "The English monk Orderic Vitalis, writing sixty or more years later in Normandy, has Maelcoluim 'assert that King Edward, when he gave me Margaret, his great-niece, in wedlock, gave to me the county of Lothian." Margaret and her brother came to England with their father [who promptly died] in 1057; it is not unlikely that in 1059 she was affianced to Maelcoluim in this way, and

that failure to send her north [and hence to guarantee Lothian] explains the ravaging of 1061." *The Kingship of the Scots* - Duncan - p. 43

6) Malcolm's invasion of Alba and campaign vs. Macbeth and Lulach - "...by 1061, Tostig and Malcolm had become blood-brothers" - *Edward the Confessor* - Licence - pp. 190-2

7) "*Quoniam Deus magnus Dominus. Et Rex magnus super omnes deos*" – "For Lord is a great God. And a great King over all gods."

"*Dominie labia mea aperies et as meum adnuntiabit laudem tuam*" – "O Lord, open thou my lips; and my mouth shall show forth thy praise"

8) Malcolm "invaded Lothian and attacked the isle of Lindisfarne" in 1061 - *Edward the Confessor* - Licence - p. 209

9) The Black Rood - "The Black Rood of St. Margaret was one of her most prized possessions. This rood, or cross, which was said to contain a fragment of the true Cross, was encased in ebony and heavily decorated." - "St. Margaret, Queen of Scotland" - Guild of St. Margaret - 2024 - www.guildofstmargaretinc.com

10) Malcolm's familiarity with King Edward's court - "The king, who was very merciful and mild, willingly extended his friendship unto him, and promised him help,—for Edward himself had lately been an exile as Malcolm now was. So Malcolm abode in England about fourteen years..." - *Chronicle of the Scottish Nation* - John of Fordun - p. 181

PART THREE

CELIA

1) Queen Matilda - "Matilda was a few years younger than William and, reportedly, beautiful. The marriage between Matilda and William proved to be a strong and trusting relationship; William is one of very few medieval kings believed to have been completely faithful to his wife." *Silk and the Sword* - Connolly - pp. 199-200; "She was one of the most beautiful and accomplished princesses in Europe....Matilda was seven years younger than William. She was brought up in her father's court, and famed far and wide for her beauty and accomplishments. The accomplishments in which ladies of high rank sought to distinguish themselves in those days were two, music and embroidery. The embroidery of tapestry was the great attainment, and in this art the young Matilda acquired great skill." *The History of William the Conqueror* - Abbott - p. 52

2) Walter of the Vexin (King Edward's nephew) occupied Maine. William besieged the capital Le Mans, "whereupon Walter capitulated. In August, he and his wife died in William's custody. Orderic, in this instance, may be right that William poisoned them" - *Edward the Confessor* - Licence - p. 217

3) William's illness - "...it is certain that William was extremely ill; so much so that he was prepared for death ... The narrative ... also tells us that a distraught Matilda, her hair disheveled, placed a token of her husband's gift on the church's [at Cherbourg] altar" - *William the Conqueror* - Bates - pp. 166-7

4) Harold's crossing of the Channel "about the beginning of August 1065, returning in October resulted in his capture by Count Guy of Ponthieu - *Edward the Confessor* - Licence - pp. 217-27; also in Abbott - pp. 77-82; also in Bates - pp. 194-200

5) Surrender of Le Mans - "The capitulation of Le Mans was performed ceremonially with the bishop, clergy, and monks of the city marching out

fully robed and carrying Gospel books and crosiers" - *William the Conqueror* - Bates - p. 185

6) William's rough wooing of Matilde - "...William's resentment at Matilda's treatment lost all bounds. He struck her or pushed her so violently as to throw her down upon the ground. It is said that he struck her repeatedly, and then, leaving her with her clothes all soiled and disheveled, rode off in a rage." *History of William the Conqueror* - Abbott - pp. 57-8

7) Harold swears an oath - upon the "chest containing the sacred relics of the Church, which William had secretly collected from the abbeys and monasteries of his dominions, and placed in this concealment" *History of William the Conqueror,* Abbott - p. 81; "Harold swears allegiance to William. Standing with this hands upon an altar, and a chest containing sacred relics ... , he utters a solemn vow that he will be William's 'man' and serve and obey him in everything. The gravity of the occasion is manifest in every detail of the scene. William sits on his ceremonial chair, sword in hand, extending one hand with a pointing finger as though to say, 'Swear!' ... his solemn moment is the turning-point of the story" - *The Bayeux Tapestry* - Norman Denny & Josephine Filmer-Sankey - pp. 22-3; also recounted in Bates - pp. 196-99; Key's *House of Godwin* p. 179; and Abbott's *William the Conqueror* - p. 80-81.

MARGARET

1) Edgar's rise - Edward decided "to declare Edgar 'aetheling' [throne-worthy], a title hitherto reserved for the sons of kings. Its assignation to Edgar, the grandson of a king, shows that he, like his father, was adopted into the reigning branch of the dynasty.... A series of names recorded in the Book of Life of New Minster, Winchester ... [includes] 'King Edward', 'Queen Edith', and 'Edgar Aetheling', as a group of three. The fact that a single scribe entered their three names together suggests they arrived and entered confraternity as a family unit....By calling Edgar 'aetheling', Edward created a kind of adoption since the title aetheling in the past had been borne only by the sons of kings....Decrees of the time placed aethelings on a specific legal footing, equivalent to that of an archbishop and second

only to the king....Edgar accompanied Edward and Edith on grand occasions; was adopted in a public ceremony; was granted lands and title, and the promise of a royal estate, and was sworn in as heir at the ceremony involving Harold [and other leading figures] which Hariulf implies took place. It might have occurred in 1062 or 1063, where the chronicles conspire in silence." - *Edward the Confessor* - Licence - p. 228-9; 231-2

2) Welsh campaign - "Gruffudd, who had probably fled from Rhuddlan to Ireland was killed there ... His severed head was then sent back across the Irish Sea to Harold, who in due course, presented it to Edward, an event that, according to John of Worcester, took place after 5 August 1064." - *William the Conqueror* - Bates - p. 192

3) King Edward's favoritism toward Tostig - "In the same eight years while Tostig contained the Scots, Harold had not contained the Welsh"; the main difference was the "unpredictable, belligerent" Gruffud" - *Edward the Confessor* - Licence - p. 210-12; "Harold was the needier of glory" (as opposed to Tostig); Harold had "stone pillars" erected - *Edward the Confessor* - Licence - p. 212

4) Edward's joy over the campaign - "His policy was in keeping with models of good kingship which advocated peacekeeping over war. As Hincmar preached, citing St. Augustine, 'it is beyond doubt a greater felicity to have concord with a good neighbour than to subdue a wicked neighbour by warfare'." *Edward the Confessor* - Licence - p. 213

5) Ealdgyth - "Of her personal attributes, we know very little, simply that Ealdgyth was described as 'beautiful' by William of Jumieges...Given that her husband was Gruffydd ap Llywelyn, it seems likely that her marriage was arranged at the time of one of her father's alliances with the Welsh king." - *Silk and the Sword* - Connolly - pp. 168-9; "No doubt her marriage to Gruffudd was a political match, designed to seal the alliance between the Welsh king and the earl of Mercia." - *Women of Power in Anglo-Saxon England* - Whitehead - p. 119

6) Convent at Wilton - "If Margaret and her sister Cristina were educated at Wilton, as some scholars have speculated, then their paths may have crossed with Goscelin of Saint-Bertin's." He may have "possibly

served as the chaplain or tutor of the nuns of Wilton" - correspondence from Katie Bugyis, author of *The Care of Nuns: The Ministries of Benedictine Women in England during the Central Middle Ages*

7) Presence of Eve at Convent at Wilton - "Eve was a child when Goscelin met her; he won her over by his words, she conquered him with acts of kindness. She was the ideal audience for Goscelin, emotionally intense and ardently receptive; though very eloquent herself, she silently drank in his words. For about fifteen years—until Goscelin fell foul of Herman's Norman successor and was banished from Wiltshire—he visited Eve frequently at Wilton, exchanging letters with her when he was prevented from seeing her....Some time after his banishment from Wiltshire, Goscelin learnt that Eve had left Wilton to become an anchorite at SaintLaurent du Tertre in Angers—without a word of farewell, without so much as informing him of her plans..." *Writing the Wilton Women, Goscelin's Legend of Edith and Liber confortatorius.* www.dokumen.pub

8) Saint Edith of Wilton - "One of the serving women had let drop a wax candle that had been put out carelessly, and was smouldering at the tip of its still-burning wick, into a chest full of the virgin's garments, and shut up the chest and went away....by the marvellous grace of the everlasting guardian, all the things were found to be as they had been before the fire, unharmed by all the burning..." *Writing the Wilton Women Goscelin's Legend of Edith and Liber confortatorius.* www.dokumen.pub

PART FOUR

CELIA and MARGARET

1) King Edward's wish for Margaret to marry Malcolm - "Edward took more steps to strengthen Edgar's position. As well as parading him in the filial role, he was building alliances which strengthened Edgar's hand. Orderic reports that Edward arranged a treaty in which Edgar's sister Margaret was betrothed to Malcolm of the Scots, with Lothian as her dowry." - *Edward the Confessor* - Licence - p. 230

2) King Edward's illness and subsequent death - "A neurolgical injury affected him, probably a stroke or the onset of a degenerative illness....Folcard's statement, that 'from that day until the day of his death he bore a sickness of the mind', implies the king was no longer in charge of his faculties. He could attend ceremonies and look like a king, but others governed for him....In that sense, the reign of Harold Godwinson began in November 1065. Edward remained but he was fading into darkness....Edith was sitting on the floor and warming his feet in her lap....Harold and Robert fitz Wimarc—the king's kinsman and steward of the palace—were also in attendance with Stigand and a few others whom the king had summoned. They probably included his physician Baldwin, Bury's new abbot. Members of the witan would have stayed near Westminster, involved in the manoeuverings." - *Edward the Confessor* - Licence - p. 238, 240

3) There is much dispute over what King Edward actually said - On January 5, 1066, in the room were Harold, Stigand, Queen Edith, Robert FitzWimark, - Ronay recounts the deathbed scene as told in *Vita Aedwardi Regis* - "I commend this woman and all the kingdom to your protection." "However," Roney states, "There is no word of Harold being called Edward's successor - *The Lost King of England* - Ronay - pp. 148-9

4) Harold's marriage to Ealdgyth – "He must have married her between August 1064 and his death in 1066" - *Edward the Confessor* - Licence - p. 212; "At some point, too, Harold further strengthened his personal position by marrying Ealdgyth, Edwin's sister, the widow of Gruffud ap Llewelyn,

for whose gory death he was directly responsible. Although it is possible that the marriage only took place in 1066, it too was part of a scheme to gain allies and remove enemies." - *William the Conqueror* - Bates - p. 192; "It is possible that Harold married Ealdgyth any time between Gruffydd's death in 1063 and the king's own death in October 1066. The wedding does not merit a mention in any of the chronicles of the time, and so the date of the event is open to speculation. However, once Harold was crowned king, he would have needed the support of Earls Edwin and Morcar...Given that Morcar was only confirmed as Earl of Northumberland in November 1065, it seems likely that a peace was brokered with the brothers sometime after this, with Harold's marriage to Ealdgyth sealing the agreement." - *Silk and the Sword* - Connolly - p. 172; "It is unlikely that Ealdgyth had any say in this arrangement. The exact sequence of events is not clear, for the precise date of the marriage to Harold Godwinson is not recorded....It is clear that Ealdgyth was a valuable commodity." - *Women of Power in Anglo-Saxon England* - Whitehead - p. 119

5) Edward's funeral and Harold's coronation – "Psalm 27: 'The Lord is my light and my salvation; whom shall I fear?'"

"Edward died on 5 January 1066, upon the eve of Epiphany. His body was wrapped in a shroud of Byzantine silk, with a circlet on his head and a reliquary of the Cross hung about his neck. The following morning, the funeral procession made its way through the cold from the palace to the abbey, accompanied by clerics chanting dirges and a ringing of the bells....once Edward was safely in his grave, Harold was enthroned to the shouts of his cheerleaders, crowned, anointed, and invested with the regalia. No king had been quicker to get the crown on his head." - *Edward the Confessor* - Licence - p. 241

6) Comet - "A strange star appears in the sky, a comet with a fiery tail, and the people gaze at it in terror. An astrologer tells Harold that this is an omen of misfortune" - *The Bayeux Tapestry* - Denny - p. 29

7) Matilda's vessel - William's flagship—the sails, the three lions, the effigy of William's "second son shooting with a bow" and "upon its mast head the consecrated banner which had been sent to him from Rome" - *The History of William the Conqueror* - Abbott - p. 102; "The *Mora's* stern bore

the head of a lion, while the figurehead on the prow was a statue of a small boy, whose right hand pointed to England and left hand held a horn to his lips. It also flew the pope's flag as a sign that the expedition had the blessing of God and the papacy." *Silk and the Sword* - Connolly - p. 204

8) William's fall - "In his eagerness to get to the shore, as he leaped from the boat, his foot slipped, and he fell. The officers and men around him would have considered this an evil omen' but he had presence of mind enough to extend his arms and grasp the ground ... saying ... 'Thus I seize this land; from this moment it is mine'" - *The History of William the Conqueror* - Abbott - p. 104

9) Pillaging of the region - "The inhabitants of the hamlets and villages ... fled in all directions. Some made their escape into the interior; others, taking with them helpless members of their households, and such valuables as they could carry, sought refuge in monasteries and churches" - *The History of William the Conqueror* - Abbott - p. 105

10) Harold's journey from Stamford to Hastings - "His journey from Yorkshire had been so remarkably fast that it could have been accomplished only by elite troops with horses. Many good foot soldiers must therefore have been left behind. All three of the early French written sources say that Harold tried to take Wiliam by surprise, a tactic that had worked for him at Stamford Bridge. However, later writers in England offer the opinion that, with hindsight, Harold's generalship was impulsive, with both John of Worcester and William of Malmesbury suggesting that he fought before much of his army had arrived, the former attributing it to bravery and the latter to rashness and folly." - *William the Conqueror* - Bates - p. 237

11) Battle of Hastings - "The Norman left wing ... had crumpled. If the English had stayed where they were and held their ground, they might have gained the day; but a part of Harold's undisciplined force ... broke out of the line against his orders and pursued the fleeing Normans. They were cut off and destroyed." *The Bayeux Tapestry* - Denny - p. 54

12) Harold's death - "... the Latin inscription immediately above him says, 'Harold the king is killed,' there can be no doubt as to who the falling figure is meant to be. Here there is a great question mark. Many history

books say that Harold was killed not by a blow with a sword but by an arrow that pierced his eye....Yet there are good grounds for supposing that the story is not true and was in fact based at a later date on a misreading of the Tapestry. Not until the 12th century, long after the event, do we hear any mention of the arrow. There are two Englishmen depicted in the group, one at either end of the horse. The one on the left is plucking an arrow from his eye, while the one on the right is falling beneath the sword.... It seems to have been assumed [and we would like to think it so] that both figures represent Harold who after plucking out the arrow continued his heroic but unavailing struggle until he was eventually struck down." *The Bayeux Tapestry* - Denny - p. 58; "Even if the tapestry is to be discounted as unreliable, the story starts to appear in sources c1080 that Harold had been killed by an arrow that penetrated his brain....Such a wound would have been instantly fatal. Malmesbury adds a story of a soldier who hacked at the king's fallen body and was punished by William for unchivalrous conduct." *William the Conqueror* - Bates - pp. 243-4

13) Edgar's brief reign - "It is true that the adherents of Harold, and also those of Edgar Atheling, made afterward various efforts to rally their forces and recover the kingdom, but in vain. William advanced to London, fortified himself there, and made excursions from that city as a centre until he reduced the island to his sway" - *The History of William the Conqueror* -Abbott - p. 120; "Following Harold's death at the Battle of Hastings, Edgar was proclaimed king by some of his supporters, including Archbishop Ealdred of York, but was hardly capable of mounting any real challenge to William the Conqueror and by December had come to terms with him at Berkhamsted." - *Silk and the Sword* - Connolly - p. 215

14) William's march toward London - "According to Poitiers, a detachment sent northwards towards London defeated some English who had sallied forth from the city across London Bridge, and set fire to houses situated on the south bank of the Thames....deliberate destruction was employed there to show William's disapproval and to undermine the morale of his opponents." - *William the Conqueror* - Bates p. 249

15) William's coronation - "According to Poitiers, after the English had acclaimed William as their king and after Bishop Geoffrey of Coutances had

addressed the French, who then did the same, the noise of the acclamation so alarmed the soldiers guarding Westminster Abbey that they set fire to some houses in the city." *William the Conqueror* - Bates - p. 256

16) Edgar's position after William's coronation - Edgar had "become a rallying point for those Englishmen who continued to resist the new regime after Hastings. Initially making peace with William, Edgar appears to have been caught up in the rebellion in the north in 1068, and he and his mother and sisters fled to Scotland, although this might not have been their original intended destination. Ailred of Rievaulx believed the family was trying to get back to Hungary." - *Women of Power in Anglo-Saxon England* - Whitehead - p. 123

17) Sailing for Hungary - "...they were heading for Hungary because they owned lands there, the children had been brought up there, and the king's friendship promised succour in their hour of need..." - *The Lost King of England* - Ronay - p. 112

18) Margaret and Malcolm - "Margaret was reluctant to agree to the marriage, she was more inclined to a religious life and had hoped to become a nun. Nonetheless, with pressure from Malcolm, her brother and, possibly, her own sense of obligation to the king who was sheltering her family, she eventually accepted his proposal. They were married at Dunfermline sometime in 1069 or 1070 and, by all accounts, it seems to have been a happy and successful marriage and partnership." - *Silk and the Sword* - Connolly - p. 216; "Walter Bower in his fifteenth-century *Scotichronicon (A History for Scots)*, wrote that Edgar and his sisters had attempted to return to the land where they were born but that God stirred up the sea and they were forced to land in Scotland, at a place which was thenceforth known as St. Margaret's Bay, because the people believed that she came to that place by providence. As soon as the king saw Margaret, said Bower, and learned that she was of royal and imperial descent, 'he sought to have her as his wife and succeeded, with Edgar the Aetheling her brother giving her away, more in accordance with the wishes of her people than her own desire, or rather God's command'." - *Women of Power in Anglo-Saxon England* - Whitehead - p. 123

BIBLIOGRAPHY

Abbott, Jacob. *History of William the Conqueror.* NY: Skyhorse Publishing, 2012.

Bates, David. *William the Conqueror.* New Haven: Yale University Press, 2016.

Bugyis, Katie Ann-Marie. *The Care of Nuns, the Ministries of Benedictine Women in England during the Central Middle Ages.* Oxford University Press, 2019.

Cole, Teresa. *The Norman Conquest.* Gloucestershire: Amberley Publishing, 2018.

Connolly, Sharon Bennett. *Silk and the Sword: The Women of the Norman Conquest.* Gloucestershire: Amberley Publishing, 2018.

Denny, Norman and Josephine Filmer-Sankey. *The Bayeux Tapestry, The Story of the Norman Conquest 1066.* NY: Atheneum, 1966.

Duncan. *The Kingship of the Scots 842-1292.* www.dokumen.PUB

Durani, M.D., Yamini. "Ringworm - Scalp Ringworm (tinea capitis)." www.kidshealth.org

Hollis, Stephanie, ed. *Writing the Wilton Women, Goscelin's Legend of Edith and Liber confortatorius.* Turnhout, Belgium: Brepols Publishers, 2004. www.dokumen.pub

John of Fordun. *Chronicle of the Scottish Nation.* Edinburgh: Edmonston and Douglas, 1872.

Key, Michael John. *The House of Godwin, The Rise and Fall of an Anglo-Saxon Dynasty.* Gloucestershire: Amberley, 2023.

Lang, Andrew. *A Short History of Scotland.* Transcribed from the 1911 William Blackwood and Sons edition by David Price. Released May 31, 2005; Updated: December 14, 2020. www.gutenberg.org

Licence, Tom. *Edward the Confessor, Last of the Royal Blood.* New Haven: Yale University Press, 2020.

"Ringworm." Cleveland Clinic. www.cleavelandclinic.org

Ronay, Gabriel. *The Lost King of England.* Rochester, NY: Boydell Press, 1989.

"St. Margaret, Queen of Scotland." *The Guild of St. Margaret.* 2024. www.guildofstmargaretinc.com

Turgot, Bishop of St. Andrews. *Life of St. Margaret, Queen of Scotland (1884).* Translated by William Forbes-Leith, S.J. Edinburgh: William Patterson, 1884.

Whitehead, Annie. *Women of Power in Anglo-Saxon England.* Yorkshire: Pen and Sword Books, 2021.

Writing the Wilton Women, Goscelin's Legend of Edith and Liber confortatorius. Stephanie Hollis, ed. Turnhout, Belgium: Brepols Publishers, 2004. www.dokumen.pub

ACKNOWLEDGEMENTS

A small Romanesque structure made of stone sits near the summit of Edinburgh Castle. Hundreds of tourists walk up the rocky path toward it everyday, checking off yet another box in the castle's brochure of sites to see. My visit to St. Margaret's Chapel, however, was so much more than that.

Seated on the wooden bench beneath a stained glass window, I felt something stir deep within me. Who was this woman, this "pearl of Scotland," this mother of eight whose piety and devotion altered the course of history itself? I simply had to find out more about her.

Thus, the seeds were planted for the book you hold in your hands. Forgive me for the liberties I have taken in portraying Margaret as she appears on these pages. This is, after all, a work of fiction. I do hope, however, that I was able to capture something of her iron resolve and undeniable goodness.

Celia, on the other hand, is not a historical figure. The resilient young girl from Normandy sent across the sea to spy upon Margaret is a character based solely on imagination. Together, their voices whisper across the chasm of time to give their account of the tumultuous years leading up to the Norman Conquest, weaving a narrative never told before in any other chronicle or source.

Thank you to my family for being patient with me when I have left their world to retreat into a Medieval one. Thank you to my mother who read every one of these chapters but passed way before she could witness the book's publication. Thank you to Dee Marley and to Historium Press for believing in this story about two women who--like pearls--endure great hardship but ultimately shine after overcoming such adversity. And lastly, thank you to my all-time favorite teacher, Sister Nora Doody, who fostered my deep and abiding love for the written word.

Margaret and Celia: two women on opposite sides of the English Channel who should be enemies. Experience teaches them otherwise.

https://www.catherinehughesauthor.com

Please visit my website if you would like to
learn more about my books.

ABOUT THE AUTHOR

From her earliest years, award-winning writer Catherine Hughes immersed herself in reading. Historical fiction is her genre of choice, and her bookshelves are stocked with selections from ancient, Medieval, and Renaissance Europe as well as those involving New England settlements and pioneer life in America. After double-majoring in English and business management on the undergraduate level, Catherine completed her Master's degree in British literature at Drew University and then entered the classroom where she has been teaching American, British, and World Literature at the high school level for the last thirty years.

Aside from teaching and reading, Catherine can often be found outdoors, drawing beauty and inspiration from the world of nature. Taking the words of Thoreau to heart, "It is the marriage of the soul with nature that makes the intellect fruitful," Catherine sets aside time every day to lace up her sneakers and run with her dog in pre-dawn or late afternoon hours on the beaches of Long Island. When her furry companion isn't busy chasing seagulls or digging up remnants of dead fish, she soaks in the tranquility of the ocean setting, freeing her mind to tap into its deepest recesses where creativity and imagination preside.

In Silence Cries the Heart, Hughes's first book, received the Gold Medal in Romance for the Feathered Quill 2024 Book of the Year contest, the Gold Medal for Fiction in the 2024 Literary Titan competition, and the 2024 International Impact Book Award for Historical Fiction. In addition, the Historical Fiction Company gave it a five star rating and a Silver Medal in the category of Historical

Fiction Romance. The book was also featured in the February 2024 Issue 31 of the Historical Times magazine and was listed as one of the Best Historical Fiction Books of 2024 by the History Bards Podcast. *Therein Lies the Pearl* is her second venture into the world of historical fiction.

www.historiumpress.com